if you could
see what I see

Books by Cathy Lamb

JULIA'S CHOCOLATES

THE LAST TIME I WAS ME

HENRY'S SISTERS

SUCH A PRETTY FACE

THE FIRST DAY OF THE REST OF MY LIFE

A DIFFERENT KIND OF NORMAL

IF YOU COULD SEE WHAT I SEE

Published by Kensington Publishing Corporation

if you could see what I see

CATHY LAMB

KENSINGTON BOOKS
www.kensingtonbooks.com

KENSINGTON BOOKS are published by

Kensington Publishing Corp.
119 West 40th Street
New York, NY 10018

All Kensington titles, imprints, and distributed lines are available at special quantity discounts for bulk purchases for sales promotion, premiums, fund-raising, and educational or institutional use.
Special book excerpts or customized printings can also be created to fit specific needs. For details, write or phone the office of the Kensington Special Sales Manager: Kensington Publishing Corp., 119 West 40th Street, New York, NY 10018. Attn. Special Sales Department. Phone: 1-800-221-2647.

Kensington and the K logo Reg. U.S. Pat. & TM Off.

ISBN-13: 978-0-7582-5940-0
ISBN-10: 0-7582-5940-9
First Kensington Trade Paperback Printing: August 2013

eISBN-13: 978-0-7582-8925-4
eISBN-10: 0-7582-8925-1
First Kensington Electronic Edition: August 2013

10 9 8 7 6 5 4 3 2 1
Printed in the United States of America

*For Dr. Karen Straight, Matt Farwell,
Dave Lamb, Trevor Lockwood,
Jimmy, Wendi, and Noah Straight,
and for Marcus and Nancy Sassaman,
with love*

1

Black.
That's what he was wearing when it happened.
I never wear black anymore.
He ended up wearing red, too.
That's what killed my soul.
The red.
He haunts me. He stalks me.
For over a year I have tried to outrun him.
It hasn't worked.
My name is Meggie.
I live in a tree house.

2

My family sells lingerie.
Negligees, bras, panties, thongs, bustiers, pajamas, nightgowns, and robes.

My grandma, who is in her eighties, started Lace, Satin, and Baubles when she was sixteen. She said she arrived from Ireland after sliding off the curve of a rainbow with a dancing leprechaun and flew to America on the back of an owl.

I thought that was a magical story when I was younger. When I was older I found out that she had crisscross scars from repeated whippings on her back, so the rainbow, dancing leprechaun, and flying owl part definitely dimmed.

Grandma refuses to talk about the whippings, her childhood, or her family in Ireland. "It's over. No use whining over it. Who likes a whiner? Not me. Everyone has the crap knocked out of them in life, why blab about it? Blah blah blah. Get me a cigar, will you? No, not that one. Get one from Cuba. Red box."

What I do know is that by the time Regan O'Rourke was sixteen she was out on her own. It was summer and she picked strawberries for money here in Oregon and unofficially started her company. The woman who owned the farm had an obsession with collecting fabrics but never sewed. In exchange for two nightgowns, she gave Grandma stacks of fabric, lace, satin, and huge jam bottles full of buttons. Grandma worked at night in her room in a weathered boarding house until the early hours and sold her nightgowns door to door so she would have money for rent and food.

Lace, Satin, and Baubles was born. Our symbol is the strawberry.

My grandma still works at the company. So do my sisters, Lacey and Tory. I am back at home in Portland after years away working as a documentary filmmaker and more than a year of wandering. You could ask me where I wandered. I would tell you, "I took a skip and a dance into hell." It would be appropriate to say I spent the time metaphorically screaming.

My car broke down on the way back home, which pissed me off. I had bought it in Seattle, the city I flew into from the Ukraine. It was an old clunker, but still. It couldn't go a hundred more miles? I put it in neutral and shoved it over a cliff.

I had to hitchhike. I know that hitchhiking is dangerous. What bothered me was that the dangerous part didn't bother me at all. I was not worried about being picked up and murdered. That's the state I'm in right now, unfortunately.

I rode with a trucker. At one point she took off her shirt and drove half-naked. She said it was a tribute to her late husband, who used to drive trucks with her. She would take off her shirt to keep him awake. I took my shirt off, too. I don't know why. She put in a CD and we sang Elton John's "Crocodile Rock" together six times. It was her husband's favorite song. We cried.

When I arrived at Lace, Satin, and Baubles, my sisters each grabbed one of my elbows and hauled me upstairs to the light pink conference room. There's a long antique table in the middle of it, a sparkling chandelier, an antique armoire, a pink fainting couch, a rolltop desk, a photo of a strawberry field, and a view of the city of Portland. Inside that room we run a company. It isn't always pretty.

My sisters did not have pretty news for me.

Tory raised a perfectly arched black eyebrow at me, swung her leopard print designer heel, and said, "You look awful,

Meggie. Ghostly, somewhat corpselike. You're not wearing makeup, are you? You need it."

"You don't look *awful*, Meggie. You look like you need... a...a...nap." Lacey was wearing one of our best-selling black lace negligees as a shirt. "Welcome home. I'm glad you're here."

"Yes, welcome home, Meggie," Tory said, her tone snappish. "Please don't go out in those clothes. It's bad for the company's image. Homeless is not a style, you do know that, right?"

I was not offended. I didn't care. I leaned back in an antique chair, stared at the ceiling, and linked my hands behind my blond, too long, frizzy curls. I needed a beer.

" 'Bout time you got here, though." Lacey put her leather knee-high boots flat on the ground and leaned on her elbows, her red curls tumbling forward. She has dark brown eyes, like coffee, like mine. "We're in serious trouble and we're going to need you to fix this immediately."

"Yep," Tory said, tossing her thick black hair back. "We're almost broke."

"*What?*" I said, shocked, my chair slamming back down. "Are you kidding?"

"No," Lacey said. "We are months from being out of business."

I looked from one sister to the other, back again, then uttered aloud the only thing that made sense at that moment: "Now I really need a beer."

I drummed my fingers against the table as my sisters launched themselves into a fiery and spear-throwing argument about why we were almost broke, which was their typical mode of communication. Verbal grenades were tossed. I interrupted the grenade tossing. "Why didn't you tell me that the company was in so much trouble?"

"Because Grandma told us to wait until you were back in the doors here," Lacey said. She is married with three teenagers. She says they are sucking the life out of her "through a straw and a strainer."

"She wanted you to enjoy your strange and bizarre year away

tramping around the world like a lost space alien," Tory said, "without the full knowledge of our impending disaster."

"She should have told me." Fear started tingling my back. This was not good.

"It isn't my fault the company's taken a dive, Meggie," Tory said. "It's the economy. The numbers aren't being crunched right." She glared at Lacey, who was the chief financial officer. "The designers are evilly moody, defiant, hormonally imbalanced, won't take direction, and won't be creative on their own. It's like working with temperamental one-eyed Cyclopses."

"You're the chief designer, Tory," Lacey snapped.

Tory humphed, examined her nails. They were painted purple. "I *manage* the designers."

"You hired them," Lacey said.

Tory rolled her eyes. Her eyes are golden, no kidding. They're stunning. Her full name is Victoria Martinez Stefanos O'Rourke. Hispanic-Greek-Irish. My mother adopted her when she was five. Her mother was Mexican American, her father Greek American. They were killed in a car accident on the way to the beach. Tory was in the car at the time but to this day doesn't remember anything. Her mother, Rosie, who was my mother's best friend, was the company's accountant.

When we were younger, before Tory's parents were killed, Tory, Lacey, and I called each other "cousin." I called Rosie and Dimitri Aunt Rosie and Uncle Dimitri. Tory called my mother Aunt Brianna. When she came to live with us, my mother told us we were now all sisters. I know Tory has struggled with feeling like a sister. Lacey and I have always been close, "like an Oreo cookie," Tory says, and it made her feel "like rotten milk."

Agewise, Tory is almost exactly in the middle of Lacey and me, with me being the youngest. She wears tight, high-end suits, dresses, skirts, and heels every day. We use her, and her style and flair for lingerie, for the media. She is currently separated from her husband, Scotty, and she is as miserable as a lost puppy.

"Working with the designers is like trying to lasso cats." Tory mimed lassoing cats.

I tamped down my anger. "You've fired three designers in the last year, right?"

"I had to. It was my given duty."

"Your *given* duty? Because?"

Tory glared at me. "One was a slut—"

"Why would we care if she's a slut?" I threw my hands in the air. "It's not our place to make judgments about our employees' sex lives, and if she's not boinking anyone's husband or boyfriend here at the company, or her boss—that would be you, Tory—or her subordinates, what's it to us?"

"She always told me about her boyfriends."

Lacey screeched a bit between clenched teeth. "You were jealous of her."

"If you told her she was fired for being a slut, the lawsuit against us will stretch to the North Pole," I said.

"I didn't *tell her* she's a slut."

"In a meeting," Lacey said, "Lorinda said you were the most monstrously difficult and snotty totty person she had ever met. I liked the words *snotty totty*, frankly. Monstrously difficult was well chosen, too."

"And what happened to the other designers?" I asked.

"Rebecca," Tory snorted. "She smelled like a chicken slaughter-house and she did not respect me or my position here—"

"She's a designer," I said. "She's an artist of clothes. Designers tell you what they think. Sometimes they say it nice, sometimes they don't."

"Rebecca had new ideas—" Lacey said, her face flushed.

"She wanted to add all sorts of bold colors and blurred designs, like paintings, and murals." Tory waved a hand dismissively in the air. "Who are we, Van Gogh? Ridiculous. Maybe I'll cut off my ear and send it to her."

"You brag so much about knowing designs, but you stifle and scare your employees," Lacey yelled, snapping a pencil in her hands.

"I don't stifle or scare anyone unless they're boomeranging idiots," Tory yelled back. "We sell tons of lingerie that I design—"

"Stop!" I shouted, slamming my hands on the table. "Stop fighting. I came home, I'm here, and I'm trying to figure out this mess. Back to the designers. Why did the third designer get fired?"

"I fired Chiara because she had a drinking problem," Tory said, tilting her chin up, her jaw tight.

"Chiara didn't have a drinking problem until about six months ago," Lacey ranted, hands up in the air, her silver bracelets clinking. "She said she started shooting back vodka to be able to handle you, Tory."

"Not true," Tory said. "She started drinking because . . ."

"Because?" I prodded.

"Because." Tory sat straight up. "She's a Gemini."

I fell back in my chair. Would I get a migraine from today? "Geminis drink more?"

"Where does it say that?" Lacey said, pushing her red curls back with both hands. "Have the stars formed a sign that says, 'Geminis are lushes'?"

"You lack the innate spirituality needed to understand star signs," Tory said.

"I don't *believe* in star signs," I said. "I believe in numbers, and what I understand is that this company is almost out of business and it has nothing to do with Geminis slamming vodka down."

"This financial screwup is no thanks to you, Queen Mommy," Tory railed at Lacey. "Who keeps leaving me here to run carpools for cheerleading and to go to football games?"

Lacey, her face flaming said, "Don't bring my kids into this. You never even come over to see them. You're a lousy aunt."

I saw Tory's face crumble, then she put her mask back on. "As chief financial officer, Lacey, why didn't you do something to fix this?"

"Ladies, can we refocus here?" I said, but it lacked gusto. All was lost with the "lousy aunt" comment.

"I can't get the numbers up unless you put together products that people with brains want." Lacey turned and grabbed a mannequin that was wearing a light blue bra and light blue panties. She charged Tory with the mannequin, as if it were a person starting a fight.

I put my hand to my forehead. Yep. Migraine.

"Look at this! Your design! The stuff you're turning out is boring. It means nothing. It's plain. It's normal. We might as well call it 'Stuff your bladder-challenged grandma will like!' " She took the bra off the mannequin and hurled it in Tory's direction.

Not to be outdone, Tory, her face rigid with outrage, grabbed another mannequin, dressed in a burgundy negligee with black lace and a snap crotch, and charged back at Lacey. "Some of our stuff is plain because that's what some of our customers want. This design, my design, is a work of lingerie art!"

I don't think she meant to, but Tory slammed the mannequin down so hard an arm broke off.

We had two mannequins facing off in battle, wobbling back and forth. I sighed.

"Why don't you go Botox your butt?" Lacey picked up the downed arm of Tory's mannequin and threw it against the wall. The arm shattered, and the bang echoed through the room. "I am sick of you blaming me."

"I'm sick of you, Lacey!" Tory detached the arm of Lacey's mannequin in revenge, and it went flying and hit the other wall. Another shatter and bang. "Say good-bye to your arm!"

The door opened and my assistant, Abigail Chen, who moved from Vietnam when she was a little girl, changed her first name, and "became American," said, "Ah, another fight. No blood then yet?"

I shook my head.

"Okay. Let me know. Blood stains, you know."

"Yes, I realize that," I said.

"But the dental plan will cover broken teeth." Abigail raised her voice above the ruckus, the insults, and a few swear words as Lacey and Tory roared, each ripping the other arm off the opposing mannequin. "It's good to have you home. I think the family needs you, Meggie." She is good at sarcasm.

"I think they need me to break up the fights. Remember, it's all fun and games until someone gets bashed in the head." As if on cue I ducked as the head of a mannequin was knocked off and went flying across the room, missing me by inches.

Abigail raised her eyebrows at me. "Welcome home, Meggie."

"Thank you, Abigail. Glad you haven't quit working at the animal house." I blocked a flying mannequin leg with my arm. "It can be dangerous here."

She called and left a message on my cell phone. She was calling the police. She would have me arrested. I would go to jail forever. I shivered, a graphic image paralyzing my mind, then deleted it.

I'm renting a tree house. It's circular in shape, five years old, and was built on a private acre lot off a quiet street up in the hills of Portland. There's a long, curving driveway, and it has a city view.

It's owned by a friend of my mother's. Zoe wants to sell it to me. She moved to Mexico because "The men are hotter."

The best way to describe the tree house: The house is built up on stilts and there is a maple tree growing up the middle. Another maple tree is growing up through the deck in front. There are three other maple trees next to the house, so their branches surround the house like a hug. Floor-to-ceiling windows let the sunlight dance through all day. I feel like I'm living in the trees like a bird. Or a sneaky raccoon.

I have to walk up fifteen steps, complete with a rope that acts as a handrail, to get to the front door. The door opens to a great room and a kitchen, with open rafters above. Bathroom to the left with a shower and bathtub, built for two, though I never use the bathtub as that would make me feel like I was drowning.

Yes, I have electricity and plumbing. No, it is not at all like the tree houses kids play in. The kitchen has granite counters, and the backsplash looks like a psychedelic rainbow that's been squished onto tiles. Zoe is an artist and she handpainted the design. The cabinets are blue, and an island with a butcher block counter divides the kitchen and the great room.

I have a wooden kitchen table and chairs and an oversized L-shaped leather couch in the great room. I have strung white lights through the rafters. Sometimes I turn off all the lights except for them. I like the twinkling.

I pull down a ladder to climb up to the sleeping loft where I have a king-size bed and a white dresser. I have to have a king bed. I need the space and the room so I will not feel like I'm suffocating under cotton and linen. If I could have found a bigger bed, I would have it. A skylight lets me watch the branches of the maple tree sway above me, the white stars, the glowing moon, and the weather.

The owner has six Adirondack chairs in purple, blue, green, yellow, orange, and red on the deck. I never sit in the red chair.

I can watch the sun come up as I'm on a rise. I watch the sun come up a lot. It's proof another day has arrived. Sometimes I sit out on my deck in blankets and think about whether I want to join the day or call it a day.

My tree house is cozy, a total of about eight hundred square feet, including the loft, but it's perfect.

A perfect spot for me to watch my own brain disintegrate.

That night I felt the black rat's claw ripping through my throat.

The claw stretched out my esophagus and then my intestines, the blood flowing, clogging up my scream as broken, black feathers rained down on my face.

The other rat's claw tore through my vagina. It broke through my uterus and popped my ovaries, then forced itself up, up, up, its goal to hold the other claw in its knifelike grasp, as two lovers might hold hands.

His face was on the rat's head, and he was laughing, giggling, his nose on mine, his lips an inch away, trying to tantalize me, to tease. At the moment that the two claws met, my organs shredded, awash in blood, he kissed me, soft and sweet, his tongue darting in and out. "I love you, my Meggie," he whispered, as the claws moved, wrapped themselves around my heart, and squeezed. I watched my heart burst.

I woke up not being able to breathe, my throat constricted. I opened up my mouth as wide as I could, my head thrown back, and I saw, in the labyrinth of sickness that was my mind, the rat claws retreat. When the claws were poised above me, they waved in farewell, mocking me, then disappeared, and I took my first shaky, ragged breath.

Sweat poured from my body and I stumbled naked down the ladder and onto my deck. It was raining. I tilted my head back to cool my face, the drops mixing with my hot tears. I dragged in one more breath, then another, until I could feel my own insanity ebbing.

Would he ever go away?

Could I live like this?

For how long?

I heard her heels before I saw her.

Everyone in our company, and I mean everyone, recognizes the sound of my grandma's heels. Regan O'Rourke does not walk. She strides. *Tap, tap, tap. Move out of my way.*

Think of a slim, limber fashion model in her eighties, that's our grandma. White hair, still thick, up in an adroitly rolled chignon. Makeup impeccable. An exquisite dress or tailored suit each day. Four-inch heels. She does not leave home without her baubles: pearls, amethysts, emeralds, etc.

"When I wear diamonds, I know I'm not wearing the scent of poverty anymore," she says. "People like me who have been in that wretched trench fear that the threat of a return visit is always around the corner for us. Sapphires help. So do rubies."

Hence, her love of her "baubles," as she calls them.

What Grandma has told me about life:

No one promised you a bucket of pansies, so don't be one.

Everyone thinks a great life is one filled with fun and fluff. No, that's a pointless life. A great life is filled with challenges and adversity. It's how you knock the hell out of it that shows what kind of person you are.

Keep a hand out to help someone up, but don't give them two hands or you'll enable them to be a weak and spineless jellyfish.

Always look your best. Not for a man, that's ridiculous, what do they know? Nothing. They know nothing. It's for *you*.

My grandma runs Lace, Satin, and Baubles with two iron fists wrapped in gold. She can't help but be intimidating. I think I am the only one who is not afraid of the golden iron fists. She and I are too alike for me to be afraid. Plus I know she loves Lacey, Tory, and me to distraction. We, and our mother, are her life. She has always made that clear.

When I left Lace, Satin, and Baubles to pursue my documentary film career, my grandma hugged me and said with her slight Irish brogue, "I'll probably forgive you before I die, but don't count on it."

She gave me two red bras, one for day, one for night. "Never forget your spirit. Now go shoot." She later added another zinger: "When this silliness is over, come back and run the company."

I felt guilty, but I had to follow my calling or wither; I didn't want to regret not doing it. Every few months Grandma would ask me to come back. It became a joke between us. In the last six months, however, I received calls once a week. The last call was unequivocal. "I need you home now. Stop this traveling gypsy nonsense immediately. You are giving me heartburn."

When I heard her heels outside my office, I hid my donut and an open jar of peanut butter and stood up to greet her. She didn't knock, she walked straight in. She was wearing a pink suit, tailored to her size 6 figure, and pink heels with a silver toe. Her baubles? Four strands of pearls.

"Hello, Grandma."

She eyed me, head to foot. "Did you fall out of bed, knock your head open, and forget to dress for work?"

She's charming. "No, Grandma. This is what I chose to wear."

"You're in old jeans, a baggy T-shirt, and tennis shoes." Her eyes, light green, emerald-like, absolutely stunning, glowered at me.

She's quite polite, too. "Comfortable."

"Completely unfashionable unless you are digging a ditch with your hands."

And she's considerate of people's feelings. "No digging today." I hugged her. She was stiff at first—she is not a naturally affectionate person—but I felt her soften up. I did not pull back to see her face when I knew she was wiping away tears. She would have been humiliated to know that I knew.

She cleared her throat, pulled away, then said to me, as if I hadn't been gone for years, "I've told everyone you're the chief executive officer now. I've set up meetings for you with all department heads to get you up to speed. Tory and Lacey are fighting, as usual, like drunken Tasmanian devils.

"You get Kalani. I cannot possibly handle her and her brother's wife's curses or her stomach ailments or her love life anymore. Our sales are down, our numbers are abysmal. Revamp the website. Do something to celebrate our anniversary. Don't forget to use the strawberry as a symbol. Rally the employees. There are four who need to be fired. Good at first, now they suck. Let's see how quick you can figure out who needs to go."

She turned on those four-inch pink heels.

"By the way, Meggie," she said, her voice quieter than usual. "I've decided to only work part-time now that you're here."

My jaw dropped. "Is this a joke?"

"No, it's not. I'm an old woman. I'm going to have some fun, which I will explain to you, Tory, and Lacey soon. You're going to be part of the fun if I have to grab you by the scruff of your neck and drag you to it." She paused. "Lace, Satin, and Baubles is yours now, Meggie."

"No, it's yours. I don't want—"

"It's yours, Meggie, your responsibility." She silenced me with those cool green eyes. "And it's Tory and Lacey's. And it's theirs." She tilted her head toward the other offices and the production floor. "They need jobs. This is their life and livelihood. In addition, you know how much money we give away to the community college for scholarships. I've had to lessen the amount because of this problem. You need to get that up again."

"Way to keep the pressure off me, Grandma."

"I am not here to keep the pressure off of you. Pressure is a part of life, part of this business. Buck up. You know every aspect of this company. You have an instinctive feel for what designs will sell and how to market our products. You grasp numbers almost as quick as Lacey. You understand how to work with people in the stores that carry our lines and with the employees and the factory. I know you can do this."

"I hope I can do this."

She *tap-tapped* back over to me and tilted up my chin with her well-manicured hand. She wore two pearl rings.

"Hope is not a vision. Hope is not determination and focus. Hope will not fix this. I *know* you can do this. You need to know that, too. Make a plan, take action."

She headed back toward the door, head high, shoulders back. "And I love you, Meggie."

She opened the door. "Your clothes I do not love. Total slop. Change them immediately."

She slammed the door.

Tap, tap, tap.

Who was that?

I slowed down as I turned out of my driveway to go to work the next morning, dawn barely breaking in violet and gold over the horizon. I hadn't been able to sleep, so thought I'd be productive at Lace, Satin, and Baubles. Or at least not indulging my "awake nightmares," as I refer to the nightmarish thoughts that traipse and tickle through my brain when I'm up. My breakfast was a sliced tomato, crumbled blue cheese in a Baggie, and a chocolate bar.

A very tall, blond man, in shorts and a gray T-shirt was running down the street. The gray T-shirt said ARMY.

My, he ran fast.

My, he was gorgeous.

My, he was all muscled up.

Sheesh.

He caught me ogling him like a freak, and I froze. He raised a hand and waved. I waved back.

I tried to smile, but it didn't work. My mouth stayed where it was. Flat. Straight across.

My breath caught in my throat.

Eye candy, as Grandma would say.

Do not touch the eye candy, I told myself.

You don't want an eye candy explosion like last time.

Lace, Satin, and Baubles takes up a corner of a city block in Portland that used to be full of factories and warehouses, which made rent cheap for the starving artists and writers who moved in. Now it's full of high-rent condos, high-rent shopping, and tiny dogs that are embarrassed to be seen in their Superman costumes.

Grandma saw the potential many years ago and bought the building. The building is painted pink with white trim, white shutters, and white doors. Our name, LACE, SATIN, AND BAUBLES, is in gold in front. There are two strawberries on either end.

The first floor of our building, what we call the production floor, is enormous. The room is filled with sewing machines and desks and workstations for people grouped by department. Everyone is together, from seamstresses to managers. We have many people who started in our company as seamstresses and worked their way up to managers.

There are lots of tables, shelving, and pink fainting couches. We have great air flow, and we keep the windows open as much as possible. It's bright, clean, cheerful, with light pink walls and pink lights in the shapes of tulips.

We have an enclosed patio with a fountain and garden that my Grandma and I planned years ago. The fountain is shaped like a strawberry and spurts water out the top. We have tables with pink umbrellas, three pink tulip trees, clematis, honeysuckle, trumpet vines, and planters filled with seasonal flowers.

We have an annual Christmas party at a fancy hotel. We have a Halloween party, where all families are invited for a barbeque and costume contests. We have a summer party and take all the employees and their families on a boat trip down the river for dinner. We close for four days at Thanksgiving, one week at

Christmas, and one week in the summer. We have potlucks once a month to celebrate everyone's birthday.

But we work, too, and we are home to many workaholics, including me when I was here. This is a business. We are not here to hang around and chat all day; we are here to build Lace, Satin, and Baubles, to employ people here and abroad, and to allow people the chance to have a career and support their families. We're here to sell some kick-ass lingerie to major department stores and boutiques. We maintain a website and mail out a catalogue four times a year.

I started working here when I was five. I ran errands. The employees told me what they needed—fabrics, more thread, clasps, etc.—and I went to get it. I worked here during high school and during all summers and vacations when I went away to college. After college I worked here full time, usually sixty to seventy hours a week, as Grandma continued to train me. I know this business.

Our offices are upstairs. Grandma's office, with a sweeping view of the city, is in the corner. Tory's is next to hers, and Lacey's is on the other side. We have offices for other employees, too. The office I moved into has a view of Mount Hood through a window that stretches across the entire light pink wall. It has white wood furniture, including a circular table, a huge white desk, a white dresser, and a pink fainting couch. Grandma likes the homey look.

The pink fainting couches were my grandma's idea. My grandma said that when she was young and starting the company, she was often hungry and sometimes felt faint. Hence, we have pink fainting couches all over, "to remind me that I know where my next meal is coming from and to always be grateful," she says.

Currently Sharon Latrouelle uses a fainting couch almost all day on the production floor because she gave her best friend a kidney and is still recovering. Roz Buterchof uses one, too, because she lost half a leg to cancer three months ago and needs to rest. Grandma paid her for the two months she was not in the office. Roz has worked for us for twenty-five years.

The company is wholly owned by my grandma. My mother, who is currently out on a book tour, as she is a nationally renowned sex therapist, doesn't want the company.

Therein lies a huge problem for my grandma.

Who will take over?

I swallowed hard at the thought of what I knew she wanted me to do.

I looked into a mirror with an ornate white frame hanging on the wall of my office.

I looked like pale, worn-out, skinny crap.

I looked around my pink office.

I did not want to work. I did not want to inherit this company.

I wanted to crawl into a dark cave and hide.

"Oh, Meeegie! There you are, Meeegie!"

I smiled back at Kalani Noe. We were on a Skype chat. Kalani calls me Meeegie. As in, Meee Gee. She cannot say "Meggie." She is the manager/owner of our Sri Lanka factory. I met her ten years ago; she's about five years older than me. At the time of our interview her face was all beaten up.

She applied for a job at the factory as a seamstress. Her husband did not want her to have a job. A job meant independence. A job meant money. Both threats to him. Her lip was split in half. One eye was swollen shut, and there was a purple bruise down her left cheek. During the interview, she kept dabbing at her ear, which her husband had partially *bitten* off.

"Hello. I Kalani. I want work here. Please. I work good. No blood tomorrow on face. Yes? I work here?"

That was about the extent of her English.

It was good enough.

She worked her way up, she learned English, and she got rid of the husband because she had a job, and money, and independence. Later she bought the factory, partially with a loan from my grandma.

"I glad to see you, Meeegie. I glad!"

"It's good to see you, too, Kalani. Wonderful, actually."

"Meeegie, you back?" She put her hands to her black hair. "You work for Grandma company now?"

"Yes, I'm back, Kalani."

"Oh me. Oh my. All these years. Now you back, Meeegie." She waved at me, both hands. "You come home. Finally. Good girl. You good lady. I glad. Family. Stick together. You grandma need you. She old woman now, I tell her that. She too old."

I pictured Kalani telling my grandma she was an old woman, *too* old. It wasn't pretty.

"Here at factory me, my momma, brother wife, other brother number two wife, niece, five here, no kid for me. Ya. That too bad, but I have the many niece and nephew, right?"

"Right, Kalani." Kalani had no children, she explained to Tory years ago, because her ex-husband hit her too many times "in the baby place, one time with bat, one time hammer," and she could not get pregnant now. "How are you?"

Kalani was good, she told me, except that her brother's number two wife had put a curse on her and now she had a rash because of the curse, so she cursed her brother's wife with a "fat butt. Now she have fat butt. That from me. But my brother like. He like her fat butt. Not so good curse." She sighed, crestfallen, then smiled. "Hey, Meeegie, I got boyfriend. Ya. He cute. Bang bang for me, but I no marry. He want marry, I say no way, Jose. That not his name. Name not Jose. I got that from Tory. You know, Tory?"

I assured her I knew Tory.

"You two no look like each other. That okay, that okay. She dark, eyes like gold cat, you pale, eyes like brown. Tory say she bad girl. She fun! She teach me okay be naughty."

"Oh, Lord," I muttered.

"She teach me women have pow—how you say—power. Women make decision. Not men. Men think with wiggly thing, balls knock together, you know? Women think with brain. Tory teach me men don't have no good brains. I think she right. They think sex—money. Nothing else. Women they think business. Tory taught me, I the boss of my life, not no stupid men. I like it. I like being boss. I good boss to myself. No bad more husband for me. Last husband, he boom-boom my face, nose in wrong place on my face, see?" She pointed to her nose. It was indeed off at an angle.

"You have a nice nose, Kalani, and I'm sorry about the husband. He was a pig."

"You no be sorry! He do it. I run away and he die in motorcycle accident, going fast, trying to hunt me. Like a hunter." She mimicked shooting someone with a gun. "God good to me. He kill my husband, thank you, God. I live and I work for you and you old grandma and that funny Tory and Laceeey!"

"And we're so happy you work for us, Kalani." I tried to get her to talk about the factory, the designs, a few issues we were having with products, the dye, the shipments, etc.

But first she wanted to talk about American TV. "These TV shows about New Jersey. They true, they true? What about everyone have gun in America? That true you think? Everyone skinny, have fast car? And you find husband on TV show? Everybody do it that way? That how you marry?"

The employees were good. They make "good bras for you, Meeegie, you American women, big boobs. I can't believe how big. Like rhinoceros. How you walk there, those big boobs?"

I told her it must be hard for some women, and I thanked her for all that she did for the company.

"Oh, thank you, Meeegie. I got house now, you know, years ago. Your grandma gave me extra money, I no know the word. Is it conus? No, not that word. Honus? No, not that word. Hmm. Oh ya. I know. *Bonus*. Start with b. Letter b. And I save, then buy house. My house. No bad men."

I do love Kalani, and I have to be sensitive to cultural rules and not being offensive, but this time I pushed. "About the last order of the athletic bras . . ."

I am well aware that outsourcing can tick people off. Truth is, if we didn't outsource some of our products, we could not survive. The labor is cheaper abroad, it's that simple, and our competitors use it.

Are Americans losing jobs here because of it? Yes.

And no.

We do employ about seventy-five people here, some of whom sew specialty items, but if we made everything here in the States, would we go bankrupt? Yes. We could not compete against other lingerie companies. We could not afford the people we need, and their benefits, and all the tax ramifications involved. If we go belly-up, *everyone* loses their jobs, here and abroad.

Lacey goes abroad and checks on the factory, Tory does, too, and when I worked here I also traveled to Asia. We do not tell them when we are coming, we simply arrive.

We've had several factories over the years. We have done our best to hire only the factories that have a safe and healthy environment. When there are violations, we give them a warning, and when they don't fix things, we move on. The problem with this, of course, is that when we move on, it's the workers who may suffer if they lose their jobs because of our leaving. However, we cannot work with factories where the bosses are not adhering to our rules and regulations regarding employees.

We insist on a forty-five-hour workweek only. We do not allow unpaid overtime. There is no child labor allowed at all, there must be clean ventilation, breaks are mandatory, no harassment is critical, and a fair and friendly atmosphere must prevail. We pay far more than their minimum wage. We turn down thousands of women a year who want to work for us.

We were naive once years ago. We hired a factory that had male managers. The workforce was mostly women. There was harassment, threats—some of the women had been hit, and who knows what else. It ended up being an unclean, unsafe, and unsanitary environment. My grandma warned them. Tory flew over there and raised hell. She yelled, she threw a chair in anger, she pounded a table. She was livid about the treatment of the women and insisted that several of the male managers be fired.

The managers nodded their heads, up and down, up and down. "You the boss, you the boss. Ya. We do. We do it."

They agreed to the changes we told them to make immediately.

Two weeks later, Tory and I headed back over for another surprise visit.

Same problems, same issues.

Tory and I gave money to all the women in the factory as a parting gift. We cut all our orders. The factory closed. In our defense, we could not possibly have continued our relationship with that factory. We could not support, morally or financially, a factory that disregarded the safety and health of the women.

However, we were friendly with a couple of the women who worked there. They spoke limited English, but they spoke enough to get across what happened when the factory closed: Many of the women ended up in prostitution.

Lacey came into my office semihysterical. Tory pounded in, raving. My grandma threw a pink lamp, then sank into an antique chair and cried. I have rarely seen her so upset.

It was heartbreaking. Absolutely devastating, although I hesitate to say it was "devastating" for us, when our employees ended up on their backs while we stayed safe and sound in America.

We were sickened.

That was one of the worst, if not *the* worst, time in our company's history. We questioned everything we did, everything we stood for.

We are more careful now. We stringently enforce all labor rules. We give bonuses. We insist that the workers, almost all women, are treated with respect. Ninety-five per cent of our managers are women. If we had this many women working for us here, and as few men as we have there, we would probably be sued for discrimination.

We like the factory we have now, and we like Kalani. Most importantly, when we fly over—and no, we don't warn Kalani—the factory is safe, the workers seem happy, and they all obviously love Kalani, who works hard but is truly a kind person. Plus, their numbers are fantastic.

That does not mean there are no problems.

Oh, how there are problems.

Small problems, gargantuan problems.
Often.

That night, after my dinner of popcorn and peaches, blended—
I have odd tastes in food—I stared at the door of the closet in
my tree house. Oh, what was hidden in there, behind Baggies,
detergent, and sponges, was worse than any long-toothed monster hiding in any closet.

No one else knew what was there. Only me. I could hardly
bear thinking about it.

3

He was trouble.

I knew it when I saw him standing in the doorway of his beige Craftsman-style home in a gray Army T-shirt and running shorts. He was barefoot. He was smiling. It was the smile that threw me and made me breathless.

"*You* live here?" The runner whom I had lusted over and called eye candy lived across the street from me? In this house with the white wraparound porch, the pillars, and the overhanging eaves that was so darn charming?

I could tell he was trying not to laugh. "I believe so, yes. Unless I'm a burglar."

What a dumb question. He opens the door to his own home, a little after dawn, and someone asks if he *lives there*?

He smiled down at me, and I mean *down at me*. He was about six feet six inches tall. I like tall men. Not heavy, but solid. Like a sequoia.

Yep. *Trouble.* "Damn."

"I'm sorry?"

"No, I don't mean damn, as in, I'm not glad that you're here, not at all. I am glad. I mean, I don't know you, but I am glad you live here in a house. I'm glad."

He kept on smiling.

I wanted to slam my fist into my head and knock myself unconscious.

"Yes, I'm glad I live in a house, too," he said.

He was wreaking manliness. Testosterone. Muscles. He looked like he'd been out in the sun a lot. Blondish hair. Thick, but short. He had a relaxed smile, and kind but sharp gray-blue eyes that look through you and in you and try to figure you out.

I had hit his truck with my car. With my boring, gray sedan that I bought two days after arriving. I hate the color gray.

I had pulled out of my driveway, gotten distracted by my breakfast, which was buttered noodles in a Baggie from last night that I was trying to eat, and I accidentally swerved too far across the street and hit it.

It was unfortunate. It was a black truck and looked pretty new.

I pulled away and did not enjoy hearing the screech of metal and bumpers clashing. I parked behind it and trudged up the driveway to the house. It was six thirty, but I saw a light on and thought I'd see if anyone was up and awake. If not, I'd leave my insurance card, my name and number, and an I-Am-Sorry note. The house was on a slight hill, with graceful maple and old, gnarled oak trees swaying around it and lots of green grass.

I was so embarrassed. "I hit your truck."

"You did?" He raised his eyebrows but did not look mad.

"Yes, I'm so sorry. I live across the street, I moved in a couple weeks ago—"

"I know."

"You know?"

"Yes."

He kept smiling and held out a big hand. "Blake Crighton."

"Meggie O'Rourke."

"Good to meet you, Meggie. I've been meaning to get over to say hi."

Oh yeah, he was trouble. Please be married. Please. Then I will endeavor to never think about you and I certainly will endeavor not to talk to you except to say hello and good-bye. I do not mess with other women's men. I wanted to grab his left hand and check.

"Do you want to walk down with me and see your truck and the damage I did to it?"

"I'll see it later. Do you always go to work at six thirty in the morning?"

His question was unexpected. He's a guy. I thought he would have charged right down the driveway to examine his precious possession like a ticked off bull. "Yes. I like to get there before the disasters of the day start."

"I understand."

In front of Blake, for that second, I wished I were the person I used to be. I was wearing no makeup except for a smidge of lipstick, as usual. I wore it only so my lips wouldn't feel chapped. My tight blond curls were back in a ponytail. My hair was too long and resembled a horse tail. I was wearing a white T-shirt and jeans that were too big, so I'd wrapped a leather belt around myself. I was wearing sloppy brown boots.

My hair used to have a braid woven here or there between the curls or, now and then, streaks of color, a blue streak, a purple streak, a feather. I used to wear dangly earrings and colorful or sparkly scarves, high heels or awesome boots, tight jeans, and this ethnic, natural jewelry.

I don't anymore.

"Do you deal with disasters also?" I asked.

"On a regular basis."

"They can make for a tiring day."

"Yes. No question."

He was a stud. An in-charge sort. Would he have to be in charge in bed? I got a graphic image in my mind—him on top of me—and felt myself get a bit sweaty. "Here's my cell number and my e-mail, and my work number, and my insurance card, and when you want to drop your car off to get it fixed, let me know and I'll get a rental car for you here, or a truck. Would you prefer a truck?"

"Neither. I have another car. I'll drive that."

"I'll let my insurance agent know what happened and that you'll be calling."

He grinned at me.

"You're taking this amazingly well," I said.

"It's a minor accident. No big deal. And I had a chance to meet the new neighbor."

"It's been an enormous thrill, I'm sure."

"Yep. It has. Do you want to come in for breakfast? Then I can prove to you in my own kitchen that I'm not a burglar."

"Breakfast?"

"Yes. I'm making eggs. I don't cook well, but this is one thing I can do."

Breakfast? With him? "Uh, no. I actually have to go to work. I like to be on time for my disasters."

"Can you go late?"

He smiled at me. I smiled back. Shoot.

"I . . . I can't." I took a deep breath. He scared me. Not scared me in a way that made me think he would leap out and swallow me whole or brandish a bazooka, but he was breathtaking in a ride 'em cowboy sort of way. "I have a meeting this morning, and people will probably end up angry and, if my sisters are in the same room together, they may start throwing things, like broken mannequins and bras, so I need to get in . . ."

"That sounds like a rather dicey situation."

"Yes. It is. They are." I was so embarrassed. I used to be able to talk to men, to flirt. I was confident. I was fun and sure of myself. I could even be witty and sexy. That was all, all gone. I wasn't fun. I wasn't sure of myself. I sure as hell wasn't witty. Sexy? Ha.

"I'm sorry again about the truck. I'll make sure I don't smash you again."

He grinned back. "No problem. And welcome to the neighborhood."

"Thank you." Please be married. Please. He put a hand up—his left hand—on the door jam. No ring.

"Shit," I muttered.

"Hey, don't worry about it." He shrugged his shoulders. "These things happen. Are you sure you don't want breakfast?"

He thought I was upset about hitting his truck.

It was almost funny.

What did he say his last name was?

* * *

I watched my mother on TV at work while answering e-mails, planning an agenda for a meeting with my sales staff, and making notes on what to say to calm down a currently pissed-off buyer for a major department store who got into it with the ferocious Tory.

My mother, Brianna O'Rourke, was on a popular talk show promoting her new book, *Couples and Coupling.* Her red curls were flowing down her shoulders. She was wearing a cheetah paw print dress and black heels. She's sixty-one and looks forty-five. She's the size of a ballerina with a size D chest.

She appears so sweet. Light green eyes like Grandma's, soft features, and one of those smiles that is twice the size of everyone else's. If you didn't know, you'd think she was a cross between a Southern belle beauty queen and an Irish elf.

Then she opens her mouth and words like *oral sex, stroking slowly, clitoris, orgasmic rhythm,* and *petting gently, petting hard* come out. She would sell thousands of books before the hour was over.

"Look here, Betts," she said to the host, a brown-haired funny gal. "Sex should be kinky."

I groaned.

The audience laughed.

"As kinky as two people want it to be. Think of it as a game. Not a board game, unless you're stacking checkers up on each other's buttocks. Not a tennis game, unless you're playing it naked. No, kinky sex is a fun game. Use your imagination. You can always use toys and costumes. What's wrong with dressing up as a Thong Princess? You don't know what a Thong Princess is? It's a woman wearing a thong, a tiara, a push-up bra with sparkles, and high heels. She carries a soft and furry wand so she can encircle the man's . . ." and then I heard one long *beeeeeppp* from the censors, which meant that my mother became too graphic.

The host was laughing, and blushing.

"You're blushing," my mother accused her.

"I am not."

"You are! Listen here, Betts. Sex is nothing to be embarrassed about. We've all grown up hearing about the bad in sex: unwanted pregnancy, diseases, open sores. Some of us were taught in church that sex was bad, for sinners. You sure as heck didn't talk about it, right? But what we've created in this country is a puritanical guilt and fear about sex. When you are in a committed relationship, when you're using effective birth control, when you've both been tested for diseases and come up healthy—let it fly." My mother flapped her arms like a bird.

"Let sex fly. We have to bring originality back to the bedroom. Do this one at home." She put her fingers up in quote marks in the air. "New Position Night."

"Wow," the host said, marveling. "I don't think I could do that for more than three Saturday nights. . . ."

"You can!" my mother announced, her sweet innocence shining through with that red lipsticked smile until she said, "Let's talk about the frog and the dog position. First off, the man must . . ." and *beeeeeppp* went the censors.

"Another position is the Rocket Ship. Now, some women, with their buttocks on such full display, might feel some embarrassment. If that's you, slip on some lace and silk. This is how you do it," and *beeeeeppp*.

I groaned. "Oh, egads, Mother—"

The hostess said, "I'm learning a lot today." She fanned herself with her hand.

"Good. You can take it home with you tonight. If I can add one more thing . . . rip out your old bathtub and put in a nice long tub for two. In a bath together you can use oil to full effect. Get up on your knees and have your partner take some warmed-up oil and . . ." *beeeeeppp*.

I wasn't even embarrassed, not that I would take a bath again in my whole life because of the drowning nightmares.

When I was in middle school, my mother started to make a name for herself as a nationally renowned sex therapist. Unfortunately, she didn't talk only about communication, date nights, giving each other a compliment a day, making time for romance, all the boring stuff "experts" drone on about.

Oh no. She had to delve in deep and graphically. She used plastic, anatomically correct models. She used bananas and donuts. She used an occasional whip and whipped cream. She talked about vibrators, how to use them, when to use them together. Again and again she harped about "happy in the bedroom, happy in the home."

Tory, Lacey, and I heard kids gossiping about us, laughing. We were called The Kids Of The Sex Mom.

It was humiliating.

In our defense, and to make up for our mother, Lacey and I wore prim, proper clothes. Crew neck sweaters. Jeans that were not tight. Tennis shoes. No makeup. Tory dressed, however, in her words, "high fashion, elegantly slutty." We all played sports, hard, and we played to win.

Then our mother would arrive at Back to School night. Black leather skirt and jacket, cleavage out, and that toothy smile and innocent Southern belle/Irish elf look.

She was mobbed by other parents.

We wanted to hide.

I blew my mother a kiss as the show ended.

We are as different as a whip and whipped cream.

I love her with my whole heart.

My grandma said that being around all the lingerie was what turned my mother on to romance and sex.

My mother said that was quite possible. The deciding factor, though, for a career outside the business, is that my mother and Grandma cannot work together.

My mother said she could not work with Grandma in the business because "I would kill her."

My grandma said she could not work with my mother, "or I would have to visit the insane asylum on a weekly basis and take up serious drinking."

They love each other; they cannot work together.

It's like watching two bulls charging at each other at full speed in high heels and exquisite jewelry. Bulls can't charge well in high heels, but you get the idea.

My mother went to college and took a class in psychology because a man she was interested in was taking it. She was hooked. Not on the boy, although she said there was a romance. She was hooked on psychology. She became a licensed therapist and started working with people, quickly finding the dynamics of marriage, a union she would have no part of, fascinating. She combined her practice, which was soon incredibly successful, with a column on love and sex.

From there she started writing books, all of them honest, frank, and often funny, all of them best sellers. The goal: better, hotter sex. Although she promotes wild and creative sex, she always, always harps that the best sex is had with a person you love and are committed to. She actively preaches that no teenager should be having sex.

She loves her job, but way beyond that she loves Lacey, Tory, and me. She loves her mother, too, although she refers to her as "The whiskey-drinking, cigar-smoking devil's assistant." My grandma refers to my mother as the "dildo-promoting, craft-obsessed sex queen."

When my sisters and I were children, I don't remember my mother having any boyfriends. When we were teenagers there were a few men, though they didn't last long, and she never introduced us. There have been a few other men since, but not for a while. She is extremely private about that part of her life, and we know we don't know the half of it.

Her legions of fans would be shocked to know how utterly domesticated my mother is. I believe this is in direct response to my grandma being a hard-core career woman, when most women did not have careers. My mother bakes, sews, embroiders, knits, quilts, and loves doing crafts.

In fact, her way of rebelling in high school was to have a knitting club, a quilting club, and a cooking club. The girls would meet at Grandma's house once a week to chat, knit, quilt, and cook. Sometimes they even went to quilting and craft conventions.

As my mother tells it, this enflamed my grandma. She wanted her daughter out there protesting this or that, rebelling, finding herself, writing editorials in the paper, filleting the establishment, or, her most ardent hope, working with her at Lace, Satin, and Baubles to promote the company.

She wanted a hard-core businesswoman daughter who had loud opinions and a flaming mouth to share them. But no.

Knit, quilt, cook.

The funny thing is, my mother is still meeting with these women whenever she's in town. The women have the following jobs: federal judge, owner of a cosmetics company, social worker, teacher, biologist, medical researcher, car wash owner, and then there's Judy who owns a strip joint.

She loves being home in her Snow White cottage-style house, with her chintz, stripes, and flowers. You can almost see the dwarves, evil witch, and friendly animals around the corners. She loves cooking and listening to country music with the three of us, and Grandma, if she can "behave like a woman instead of a battle-ax-throwing, temperamental bra goddess."

She has a practice in Portland and writes her columns and books from an upstairs office in her home, which is about ten minutes from mine, Grandma's, Lacey's, and currently Tory's downtown condo.

Although she dresses drop-dead seductive, even inflammatory, when she's on tour, at home she often wears pink crew neck sweaters and beige slacks. Another favorite? A white cable-knit sweater and blue slacks. She wears flats instead of four-inch heels. She pulls her hair back in a bun and wears her glasses and no makeup.

She meets her girlfriends, and they sew and craft and embroider all day long.

It's blunt, kittenish sex therapist and Betty Crocker mixed.

Drives my grandma straight up the wall.

"Hello, darling," my mother said when she called that night. "I'm so upset that you're home and I'm out on this darn tour! My mothering instincts have gone over a cliff! I feel anxious. Tell me how you are."

I told her about being back at the company. I danced around

talking about the past, she noticed. She gently pried. I deflected. She respected the deflection.

"I'm concerned that you're working too much," she said.

I had worked fifteen hours that day. "Don't be."

"Do you still have your poor eating habits?"

I was eating bacon and a vanilla milkshake. "No. I'm eating healthy."

"Are you getting enough sleep . . ."

Three hours last night. Insomnia. "Sleeping like a baby on a cloud."

"I'm sewing you an apron. I saw a pattern for one the other day. The picture on the pattern package was bright purple with ruffles, and I said to myself, 'That's Meggie!' I hope you like it. I thought we could make a blueberry cobbler while you wear it. Wouldn't that be fun?"

I hate cooking and baking. "It would be delightful."

"We could do some oil painting after that."

I hate painting. "Lovely."

"Then we'll watch a cooking show."

Must we? "I'd like that."

"Can't wait, honey!"

I love her.

Lacey poured me some healthy green concoction with berries, spinach, and vitamins and set it on my desk. I noticed she looked pale. "What is this yuck?"

"Drink it, Meggie, it'll clean you out. Help your bowels."

"Sure it will. Looking at it and thinking about it going down my throat is enough to clean me out. No. I'm not drinking it." I stood up, opened my small refrigerator and pulled out a beer, then grabbed licorice out of my drawer. I don't know why I like a beer for breakfast. Maybe it calms my nerves. I rarely drink alcohol at any other time.

"Fine. I'll drink it," Lacey said. "So let's talk business. I've tried to keep us afloat. I'm about to kill Tory. I can't blame her, though, for all our problems. The company's sinking and I feel like hell about it."

"Don't blame yourself. The economy tanked. People do not need fifty-dollar bras at any point in their lives, and they especially don't need them when they don't have a job and their home is in foreclosure. How much longer do we have?"

"Six months. Tops."

I was good at numbers, but Lacey was genius. She could look at any balance sheet and sum it up in seconds. She has a bizarre adoration for numbers.

"We're selling, Meggie, we're selling quality lingerie, but it's not enough. We have to be selling huge. The competition out there is killer. We need to do something drastic, immediately."

"I know. I'm thinking."

"Think hard."

"What's our debt level?"

She sighed. "High." She told me the number.

I choked on my beer, and it splattered across my desk. "That's a disaster."

"No question."

I swore. "Why? Why did Grandma, why did *you,* let it get that high?"

"We went through our savings after the economy collapsed. The debt racked up only this year. I warned her. I showed her the numbers. She gets them, Meggie, but Grandma believes in the company. She believes we'll turn it around. She didn't want to lay anyone off, which is what I told her we needed to do. It's a scary time, and she knew she'd be throwing our people to the wolves."

I hate debt. Hate it. When times are tough, the debt is a dead weight against success.

I stood up and looked through the window overlooking the floor below, where our employees worked at desks and at sewing machines, some with both, and gnawed on red licorice. A few of our employees have been with us since before I was born.

Take the Petrelli sisters, Edith, Edna, and Estelle. They're all in their seventies, but they come to work every day, where they run the sales department, even though they have generous retirement programs.

"We need money to travel during the summers and meet men," Edna Petrelli told me.

"Yes. On cruises. That's where we meet 'em and that's where we leave 'em," Edith said.

"Who wants a man for more than the length of a cruise?" Estelle asked. "Especially when they're old? All those farts, the horrible breath, like they ate a possum for lunch."

"And they're babies. All men are babies. Whining about their hemorrhoids, their gas, their bones creaking. Who wants to listen to that?"

"Do I look like I want to be a caretaker to an old man? Do I look like I want to spend my golden years waiting hand and foot on an old coot, hearing about his bladder and weak prostate? No, I don't!"

"We want amusement for a while and then we send 'em home."

The ladies took several cruises a year, but not to normal places like the Bahamas. No, they went to Alaska to see the glaciers. They went to Antarctica. They went to Vietnam, China, and Hong Kong. They were adventurous and fun.

Maritza, Juanita, and Valeria are also sisters, from Mexico. We have two women, a mother-daughter team from Ethiopia; their names are Lele and Tinsu, and they wear head scarves and bring dessert every other Friday. No one is absent on Dessert Friday.

We have five African American women, all sisters, maiden name Latrouelle: Delia, Gloria, Sharon, Toni, and Beatrice. When there's a family reunion, wedding, or anniversary, we lose all five at once.

We also have six women working here who were, tragically, former prostitutes. I know who they are, and so does my grandma, but no one else. You would *never* guess which ones they are. Never. One leads our toy drive at Christmas, the other is head of her church's women's ministry program.

I watched our employees, most working so hard, except for

an ex-employee, Mrs. Wolff, who was wandering around with a pink hat, smiling vacantly. She is a friend of Grandma's and she has early onset Alzheimer's. Her daughter brings her in now and then and stays with her while she visits with people she can no longer remember. It's safe. She likes being here. When Mrs. Wolff ran out of money, Grandma started paying for her care.

I watched Lance Turner. He had worked for us as a manager, one of our only male managers, before his unit was called up and he went to hang out in the hell of Afghanistan. He came back with part of his head dented in from an IED. He only works two-thirds time. When he first came back he was a mess, physically, mentally and emotionally, but month by month we see improvement. We pay him for full-time work.

Lance, Tory, Lacey, and I went to high school together. He is a kind and gentle soul. He was homeless for part of high school because his father was in and out of jail and his mother was nonexistent. He lived with Grandma for a long time.

He has the kindest wife, Marina, and four kids. The oldest is seven. As Grandma said, "I will not abandon that man ever. Meggie, you are to see to this. See to it that Lance is taken care of." Like all of her longtime employees whom she loves, Lance gets money from her personal estate when she dies, enough to pay off his house, although he doesn't know it.

The employees fifty and older were the ones I worried most about if we closed. I'm sure that was my grandma's worry, too. They know the business inside and out. They're loyal. They're of a generation that believes in production and working hard. But ageism discrimination is alive and well in America, and if we went out of business, they would be in a world of hurt quick.

"I have one more thing to tell you, and you are not going to believe this, Meggie." Lacey finished off the green yuck.

"What is it?" I returned to my desk and drank my beer.

"I'm knocked up."

Dang, but I choked again. "You're *pregnant?*"

"Yes. That's what knocked up means, doesn't it? Hello?" She threw her hands up. "One time, one time! Matt and I went for dual massages at a spa, then we hung out in the hot tub and he got all frisky. He drove us to our favorite place overlooking the city, the place we always went to mess around when we were in college—"

"On the hill with the view."

"Yep. And he invited me to crawl in the back of our minivan! Our minivan! What was I thinking? And I said yes. It was like we were twenty again." She rocked back and forth, hands to her red curls. "So I did it! I'm too old to mess around without birth control! I have three kids already, one is a hellion, one likes pink too much, and the third isn't too bright. My stomach pooches and my butt hangs and my boobs aren't in the place they should be, but Matt is smiling at me and there I am, bouncing on him in the dark in the back of our minivan, which I use to haul our kids' asses around to play rehearsals and football and cheer-leading and crap like that."

"So, amidst the cleats and pom-poms, you indulged?"

"Duh. That's how a baby is made, isn't it?" She patted her red cheeks.

"Usually. Not always. In the future, we'll probably be able to swallow a pill and women who don't want to get pregnant the normal way won't. It'll be the sperm-and-egg pill and it'll attach to the side of your uterus and—"

"Oh, stop, did you not hear me, Meggie? I am knocked up!" She threw herself back in her chair like an octopus, arms and legs out. "What am I going to do?"

"Looks like you're going to have a baby. Congratulations." I laughed. This was excellent news. "Do your kids know about the baby?"

"They will by tonight. They think I'm getting fat. They'll be absolutely disgusted."

"This is proof that you and their father engage in inter-course."

"I'll leave the part about parking with their father in the minivan out. They'd never get in the van again."

"What did Matt say?" Matt's a popular college math profes-sor. They met during college. He's two years older, she graduated early, and they got married. She had Cassidy when she was twenty-one.

"What did that horny toad say?" She opened up her dark brown eyes wide, feigning fury. "He laughed. Laughed! He said, 'That's great, honey, good job!' I can't believe it, Meggie. Four kids! And I have morning sickness like the devil."

"Oh, Lacey, I'm sorry." Her morning sickness was legendary. It was not limited to morning.

As if the word set her off, she rolled her eyes, then went pale, put a hand to her mouth, and flew out of the room.

I took another sip of beer, had another licorice.

I felt tears burn my eyes, as if they were on fire.

I remembered.

At two in the morning, unable to sleep because my flashbacks to a time of broken black feathers were keeping me awake, I headed down the steps of my tree house in my ratty pink robe, the maple leaves rustling above, whispering a soft message.

I sat on an iron bench in the garden under a willow tree and watched the city lights twinkle in the distance.

I closed my eyes, trying to unwind in the wind.

I jumped when I heard his voice, when he called my name. I knew it couldn't be him, *I knew it,* he wasn't here, but I still whipped around, scanning the grass, the maple trees, and the pine trees before moving to the tree house, my hands out and up, as if I could defend myself. My heart pounded, a dull thud echoing throughout my tense body.

There was no one. I was still all alone. I put my hand to my constricted throat.

The maple trees rustled, they whispered.

I sank back onto the bench and tried to listen to them, to the wind, not him.

"I want to have some adventures before I die, become a stiff corpse, and rot in a steel coffin."

"Lovely vision." I nodded at my grandma. It was Saturday

noon, and we were at her white Queen Anne home. She was dressed in a dark green silky dress with a square neckline and bone-colored heels. The baubles: emeralds. "I'll come with you on the adventure."

"Me too," Tory said, winding all that black hair into a ponytail. "Let's start in Vegas. High-stakes poker. Give me a date and I'll check all of our horoscopes to see if we'll have good luck. Leo for Meggie. Scorpio for Lacey. Virgo for Grandma."

"I'm in," Lacey said. "Only don't ask me to do anything that causes me to feel dizzy. I hate morning sickness." She swayed, put her hand over her mouth.

"You're having a girl," Grandma said.

"How do you know?" Lacey asked through her fingers.

Grandma waved her hand. "Because I know."

Grandma's formal table was polished, the china laid, the crystal glasses sparkling. Her home is exquisitely decorated and refined. While Lacey tried to battle down morning sickness, the rest of us nibbled on tiny, crustless sandwiches that Grandma had ordered in: tomato, cheddar, and watercress or ham, brie, and apple. Cream puffs, miniature cakes, chocolate fudge, tarts, and pink meringue cookies sat on doilies on a three-layered silver tray. I ate dessert first, as per my usual. If I died by a freak accident before the meal ended, I didn't want to miss out.

"What do you want to do, Grandma?" I asked her, sipping my beer. It went well with the tarts.

"I want to do something dangerous." She tapped her manicured fingernails, her hair up in a chignon. "I want to dance on a bar. I want to bungee jump. I want to go on a trip with you girls and your mother, if she doesn't make a complete fool out of herself on her book tour."

Lacey, Tory, and I laughed. On another talk show our mother had given graphic directions on how to give a blow job using an ice-cream cone. It made headlines because that part of the show had to be blacked out.

"I've worked all my life and now I want to have some fun. You three are going to have fun with me. We'll call it the Bust Out and Shake It Adventure Club."

"You want to bust out and shake it?" Lacey asked.

"Yes. We are going to take off and live life dangerously together." She poured tea out of a silver teapot, passing each fragile, flowered teacup and saucer to us. "You three are going to bond and become friends if I have to knock your knotted brains together."

Her expression suddenly changed to one of pain. She put the teapot down, reached back, and rubbed her shoulders. I had asked her about these sudden spasms when I was a little girl. "Does your back hurt, Grandma?"

And she would say, her Irish brogue soft, "I'm patting the fairies."

When I was in my teens she would say, "I'm squishing all my brilliance up to my brain."

And when I was in my twenties she would say, "Quit asking. I don't want to talk about it."

I know the pain is because the whippings somehow caused back problems.

"Are you okay, Grandma?" Lacey asked, soft as butter.

"Must you treat me like I'm a weak old bat? Of course I'm okay. Had a twinge." She impatiently rolled her shoulders. "Girls, I don't have a minute to waste. I might even get laid. I know exactly who I want."

"Who do you have picked out for this night of heaven?" Tory asked.

"It's that tall man on TV. Tells everyone how to run their lives. Rah rah rah, blah blah blah."

I didn't know who she was talking about.

"He stands up onstage, paces back and forth, big teeth, he's like a counselor and a male cheerleader and a black-haired lion mixed up altogether, only I can't concentrate on what he's saying because he's so sexy. It doesn't matter what sexy men say." Grandma waved her hand. "You have only to watch the body. He's a tall drink of water, and that's who I want in my bed."

"We'll try to get him for you, Grandma," I told her, loving the chocolate fudge.

"I'm going to be like you, Grandma," Tory said. She hiked up a bra strap. Her bra was watermelon pink, another best seller of ours because of the padding. "I'm never giving up sex, not even when I'm old."

"No reason to, young lady." Grandma took a sip of tea, pinky up. "But there's someone in this room who has given up sex, and that's a poor trajectory. Very poor."

"It's Meggie," Lacey said, pointing, as if my grandma and Tory would have a hard time locating me. I sighed. "She's in the desperate desert zone."

"Meggie, you need to find someone right away," Grandma said, "It'll put some color in your cheeks."

"No, I don't." *No, oh no.*

"Yes, you do." Tory wagged her finger at me, those gold eyes sharp. "Use it or lose it, and my guess is that yours is already half gone."

"Funny, Tory, thank you," I said. *No, oh no.*

"You don't have the look of a woman who wants to get laid, and that will put men off," Tory said. "Look at me. Look at my body and how I dress. My image says that I'm interested and I'm a making-love hummingbird. Your image says that you have a dried prune for a vagina."

"You always make me feel warm and fuzzy about myself, Tory." I knew about my dried prune image. I didn't need to be told. "I will never be able to look at prunes the same way." I ate a cream puff with no prunes.

"And you have the look," Lacey said to Tory, her face tight, "of a woman who wants to get laid every hour, on the hour, in the back of a pickup truck, guns hanging in the back window."

"Good. And I bet Scotty, that half-brained, camel-nosed jerk, misses me!" Tory's eyes misted, and she wiped them on a white linen napkin. "I hate that guy." Scotty is six four, with glasses, slacks, and button-down shirts. So, so bright, he invents things for a huge computer company, makes tons of money, and doesn't care about the money. He is sweet and protective of Tory. She's furious that he's not chasing her down for the umpteenth time after her last unnecessary temper tantrum. Every day he doesn't beg her to come back, she gets more entrenched in her anger.

"You need new bras and panties, Meggie," my grandma said. "I can tell. This is a disgrace. Hold your shirt tight so I can see what size you are now."

"They've shrunk," I said. I held my shirt tight against my chest.

"Like deflated balloons," Grandma said. "Thirty-four C."

Tory and Lacey nodded.

"Down a cup. Size small panties. You should be at least a medium. Curves are better than bone, remember that," Grandma said.

Not wanting to have a discussion about my shrinking bust, I grabbed a pink meringue cookie and said, "Let's talk business."

And that was it for our frolicking conversation about my prune, the hated Scotty, and Lacey's baby girl. Grandma pulled out pink folders, so did I, so did Lacey and Tory, and we had ourselves a serious, detailed business meeting about Lace, Satin, and Baubles.

It took three hours. Numbers were bandied about, our factory in Sri Lanka was discussed, our employees in Portland were discussed, designs and manufacturing and sales were heatedly debated. One lemon tart was thrown, a glass was dropped too hard on the table, and Tory stalked out twice, but we got through it.

"Get crackin' on the company, girls," Grandma said, shutting her final pink notebook. She does not mess around with the business and neither do we. We take it very seriously. Too many people depend on it. "You need to reinvent. You need to refigure out this market. The economy has slashed us to the bone. You need to modernize and be unique, but you need to stick with what Lace, Satin, and Baubles is all about: a family company that makes a seductive, sexy, high-quality product with soul. Know your customer. Invite them to know us."

"We'll get on it, Grandma," I said, exhausted.

"I love you three. You're difficult, opinionated, fiery. Like we raised you to be. Good job." She poured herself and Tory generous shots of whiskey. I don't like whiskey.

It was high praise. Grandma rarely compliments.

We headed out the door after we kissed Grandma good-bye.

"Tony Robbins!" she declared as we headed down her winding drive, the birch trees forming a canopy overhead, two fountains trickling, the grass a green swath of soft earth-carpet. "That's who I want in my bed, Tony Robbins! Call him, girls! Call him right away for Bust Out and Shake It Adventure Club. I'm sure he'd love to join."

She lit a cigar and settled on her front porch with her whiskey as we waved.

"I know who he is," I said. "Excellent teeth."

"Me too," Lacey said. "Nice choice."

"Think he'd do a threesome?" Tory asked.

Not with me and my prune. *Oh no.*

At two in the morning that night, with the white lights looping through the rafters, I grabbed a pad of paper and colored pastel pencils and started drawing lingerie.

I remembered drawing and designing lingerie with my grandma, starting when I was twelve.

"Lingerie has to speak to you," she told me. "It's not all about sex. It's about the woman. It's about who she is, who she wants to be. It's about her intimate self. We have to be the place women go to to buy lingerie, not only because we create lacy, slinky, seductive tidbits, but because our lingerie says something to their souls. We have to speak to their souls and know them, and they have to know us, our brand, our image."

I drew and sketched and colored for hours.

Speak to their souls.

Know them.

Know us.

Know Grandma.

Grandma. She had a life story. Her childhood was a secret tucked away across a vast ocean, on a craggy island. Would she die before we understood what happened to her?

I closed my eyes. I let my mind wander into a daydream. It started in the rolling hills of Ireland. I saw a young, red-haired girl, her back arching in agony as she was whipped, blood streaking her white skin. As she screamed, my dream sent me over the curve of a rainbow, past a dancing leprechaun, and onto the wings of an owl flying across the Atlantic. I saw my grandma at sixteen years old picking strawberries under a burning sky, then sewing nightgowns by a dim light at night, all alone. It spun past silk, satin, lace, baubles, The Irishman, and into our pink building downtown. It swooped past by my grandma's cigars and her whiskey and twirled around her elaborate chandeliers, the fainting couches, and tulip lights.

I saw myself, how I'd always wanted to film her, know her story, understand her history, and how she'd refused, that brogue adamant.

Maybe she would say yes now?

Did I have a right to know the story? No. Did I *want* to know? Yes. It was part of her. I loved her. She was my grandma. She was Lace, Satin, and Baubles.

Know Grandma.

The next day Abigail Chen brought in a box full of lacy, satiny, gorgeous 34 C bras, panties, thongs, negligees, and nightgowns. "Your grandma said she picked these out herself. She said to tell you if you wear the same blah blah blah bra and grandma panties here again, she's going to, and I quote, spit nails."

Abigail opened up the box and took out handfuls of exquisite fluff. "I do love what we make here, Meggie."

"So do I." I don't wear that fluff anymore.

No, I do not.

I would not.

I am being true to me, the beige me.

4

$\backsim$

"They're restless."

"What do you mean?" I took a sip of beer. It was ten in the morning. Time for breakfast. I pulled out beef jerky and ate that, too.

"I mean that the employees know the orders have slowed further," Lacey said. "They know we're not hiring, even when Duluse left for Africa to find himself and Caterina left for California to go to yoga camp, and Elga died."

"Elga was seventy-six. Did they expect us to replace her? Her knowledge about the company was endless." I still missed Elga. She was a major smart aleck and said things like, "Roger's head is up his ass and he can't see past his intestines, so don't listen to him today" and "Murta's hormones are driving all of us crazy, so I locked her in the closet." I thought she was kidding until I found out that Murta was, indeed, locked in the closet, and happy about it because, as she told me, "Menopause is a nightmare and I need some time alone. Shut the door, Meggie."

"They understand that we're struggling and that is gross that you drink beer this early." Lacey put her heels up on my desk, I put my boots up.

"It's not gross. I like it, so I do it." I would also like to have a roll in bed with Blake. Can't have all ya want. That body was something else. I would like to forget the cacophony in my head while straddling myself across him.

"But beer?"

"I'm sorry, Lacey." I set the can down on my desk with a bit too much force. "I have beer in the morning now and then." It started years ago in the middle of the swamp. "Maybe we should go over your odd habits. Let's start with how you can eat only an even number of Oreos, not one, not three, it must be an even number."

"Oreos are organized. There's the black cookie, then the cream center, so I like to keep it organized. Two, four, six, or twelve at a time."

"What about how you will never get up on the right side of your bed, right foot down first, because you think it will bring bad luck?"

"It will. Three times in my life I got up on the right side, right foot down, and bad things happened."

"And bad things have never happened when you got up on the left side?"

"No, they happen, but if I'm up on the right side, *for sure* they'll happen."

"Ah, well, that makes sense. What about how you watch horror movies to de-stress and how you imitate Tina Turner when the kids aren't home and prance about your house in those silver high heels and short silver dress and shake your butt?"

"What's wrong with that?"

"Nothing. Zero. It's fun. But don't bug me about my morning beer." I dropped my boots down and looked out my window. There was Mount Hood. I used to ski there. Loved it. Hadn't skied in years. He didn't ski, so I gave it up. If I didn't, I paid for it later. Looking at Mount Hood almost made me hurt. "Okay, so the employees are asking questions."

"Yes. They want to know what's going on."

"I'll tell them soon."

"What?" She was alarmed.

"I'll tell them."

"You're going to tell them what's going on with the company? Our nosedive?"

"Yes. We have to. It's not fair to them. I'm going to try to turn things around. You're trying, too. Tory's on board. It's not enough. The three of us are not enough. We tell them, then they know and can help, too."

"It'll scare them. Cause stress. Panic. Frenzies. Revolts."

"I'm scared. I'm stressed. I will not be revolting." I did not want to fail here, too, but if I did, I would do it ethically. "They have a right to know. We have a number of single parents here. If they want out, they need to start applying for other jobs while they're still employed here and will look more attractive to new employers. They need to start saving money to prepare at home. Some of them might be looking to buy a house, which would not be a good idea at this point. Some might be looking to buy a new car. Do you want them to have that car repossessed if things collapse here? We have months, Lacey. That's it."

She took a deep breath. "Okay, Madam Daredevil. You're right."

"We'll talk to Tory and then present to everyone."

"She'll throw a fit."

"She always throws fits. Do you think that bothers me?"

Lacey shook her head. I drank my beer.

Four huge bags of clothes arrived in my office, all from an up-scale boutique.

Dresses, skirts, slacks, sweaters, cool jeans, boxes of high heels. Knee-high boots. A new red coat, which I quickly wrapped back up.

No red.

The card said, "Stop looking like a slob. You're going to be mistaken for a woman who has lost her marbles. Grandma."

She was pretty close to the truth there. Good thing I like marbles.

That night I took my film equipment out of my bedroom closet. I had dumped it in there when I first rented the tree house.

My mother gave me a camera when I was fifteen. I asked her for one because I wanted to take pictures of my beloved granddad, Cecil O'Rourke, because he was dying of congestive heart failure.

I told her exactly what I wanted to do. She put both of her hands on my cheeks, kissed me, and said, "You are a precious child." She bought the camera that day, and I started taking photos of The Irishman, which is what Grandma, my mother, Lacey, Tory, and I often called him.

I took photos of him bending over a chess game we were playing. I took photos of him with Lacey baking cinnamon rolls. I took photos of him admiring Tory's new pink boots.

I took photos of him painting fields of flowers next to my mother. He played the fiddle and the flute, and I took photos of him concentrating.

I took many photos of him hugging my grandma. My granddad was the only person to whom my grandma catered. It was almost as if she changed personalities. She was gentle, kind, and romantic around him. My granddad, at six feet three inches tall, with a much more pronounced brogue than my grandma, was tough and blunt. He was the owner of a construction business, but when he came home, the tough and blunt left, and the love came in.

Theirs was a love match like no other. Both of them told me privately what they thought of the other.

Grandma said, "Cecil is my heart. That's why I make sure he's happy."

Granddad said, "Regan is my life. I love her even more than I love Ireland."

Grandma said, "Without The Irishman, I would be dead, literally. He saved me."

Granddad said, "My life would have no meaning without her. I would be lost, might as well be dead."

In the last weeks of his life I caught him looking joyful, peaceful, sad, thoughtful, in pain, uncomfortable, exhausted, and in love when he and Grandma sat and held hands. I took photos up until his last day, at his encouragement. "Take the photos, Meggie. Not all of them will be happy, but life isn't always happy, is it? It takes guts to live right, and it takes guts to die right. You girls need to remember one thing, and only one: I love you with all my heart."

He died in bed with my grandma late one night, Irish music playing in their bedroom. She has never been in love again.

Granddad was my father, and he was Lacey and Tory's father, too. He called us "his gifts," but he was our gift.

My mother printed my photographs and we put them in a scrapbook together. We all cried and cried over those photos. The Irishman was right. They weren't all pretty, but they showed *him*, his strength and courage, his dignity and honesty.

Photography became a healing element in my life, then it became my hobby, then my calling. As I clicked away with my camera, the whole world opened up to me, but I could still hide behind the lens, as if a black shroud made me invisible.

I took photos of people slumped against walls downtown, the homeless pushing carts, teenagers smoking, people standing alone, or businesspeople with stricken looks on their faces. I took photos of people in groups, I took photos of children with their parents, and people crying.

My mother soon gave me a video camera, too, and I started making short films about people in high school, how they liked school, or hated it, what irritated them, what made them mad or happy. It was surprising how honest people became when there was a camera pointed at their face. As I was an intense, somewhat socially awkward, driven and Type A person even then, it opened up conversations with people for me.

I double majored in finance and business in college, then earned an MBA. However, I took film classes in college, too, classes after college, and joined an amateur filmmaking group. I made several films on weekends, editing until the early hours of the morning after I'd worked at Lace, Satin, and Baubles.

I had some success, even won some minor awards.

Eventually I could no longer ignore the voice in my head yelling at me to leave Lace, Satin, and Baubles and become a documentary filmmaker full time. I couldn't *not* do it. It was me, I was it, even though it meant leaving the company. I struggled with the decision night after night after night, because I felt

I owed it to Grandma, to my family, to stay. I finally decided I owed it to myself to take time off, especially since Grandma ran the company.

I had loved my career as a filmmaker, though I hadn't made much money at all.

I wrapped both hands around a camera on the floor of my bedroom and thought about my grandma, the business, our looming financial problems, pink negligees, zebra-striped bras, garters and bustiers, lace thongs that were barely there, buttons and baubles, and our employees.

Know them.

Know us.

Know Grandma.

"Hello, everyone." I stood on top of a chair to address all of the employees of Lace, Satin, and Baubles.

"Hello, Meggie . . . hi, Megs . . . hi, honey."

"First." I smiled. "I want to tell you all again that I'm so glad to be back at Lace, Satin, and Baubles."

They cheered. They clapped and hollered.

I choked back a rock, which seemed to have lodged itself in my throat. I could not even speak for a minute. Beside me, Lacey clapped, while Tory stood still and uptight on my other side. I could feel her withering anger. As she told me when I worked here before, "They love you, hate me. You're the angel, I'm the devil. Angels are so dull, though. Devils go out and play."

"Thank you for working here. Thank you for your creativity and your dedication, your loyalty to my grandma and to the company. Thank you for building a company we can all be proud of. We don't simply sell lingerie. We sell beauty. We sell dreams to women. We sell products that make them feel better, prettier, stronger, more powerful. We sell lingerie so women can get out there and write the stories of their lives and look awesome doing it and, at night, or during the day"—I grinned—"they can feel happy and confident when they're with whomever they wish to be with in their negligees and thongs."

They laughed.

"On another note, and unfortunately, after looking over our books, our numbers, and our projected numbers, I don't have good news for you. I want to be honest and up-front. You've been loyal to us, I want to be loyal to you and to your families." Fear, I could feel it. It rolled at me in electric waves. What I said wasn't a surprise to them, but once the truth is out in the open, their fears become their reality. "As you know, the economy has about collapsed. People don't have money for much of anything, and our higher-end lingerie has taken a hit."

I did not say that the company had made mistakes, too, because I did not want to place blame on Grandma, Tory, or Lacey. But we had. Mistakes in advertising and marketing and sales. Mistakes on our website. Mistakes in our catalog. Mistakes in how money was spent, and not spent. Mistakes in products that shouldn't have been out there at all. Mistakes in employee costs.

I was working to fix all of the mistakes, but it was easier to blame the economy at the moment.

"I'm sorry for what I have to tell you next, I truly am. As you probably know, we're struggling. We've been struggling for some time. We will have to shut down within the year if we don't get our sales numbers up." Okay, that was a little lie. I didn't see how we could stay open for six months without a few miracles.

I heard the collective gasp. I saw people's hands flying to their faces. I saw them slump and lose color.

Lance with the dented head from Afghanistan studied the ceiling, grim.

The Petrelli sisters looked grave, too. I knew, without a doubt, that they were concerned about all the other employees, the business itself and Grandma, and not themselves.

Maritza, Juanita, and Valeria exchanged worried glasses, and they wrung their hands. They were thinking of their children. Lele and Tinsu's eyes became wider, as if they couldn't believe what I was saying. Lele said, "But I like working here!" as if that would change anything. That thought was echoed by many people.

"We don't want to close. As you know, my grandma started this company sewing nightgowns in her room in a boarding house after she picked strawberries all day when she was sixteen. We love the company. It will break my grandma's heart if we close. It is not the goal." I bent my head for a second, gathered my thoughts. "However, if some of you want to apply immediately for other jobs, I understand. Please do. We will give you the highest recommendations. I understand if you leave. You have your families to think of first. We have always been a family-centered company and we always will be, but family centered means that we know your family comes first."

When I finished, it was quiet. Absolutely silent. No one even seemed to breathe. You could not hear a pin drop, and there were many pins at Lace, Satin, and Baubles.

"I'm staying," Maritza said. Her sisters said they were staying, too.

Abigail Chen raised her hand. "I'm staying, Meggie."

"I'm staying, too, Meggie. I'll see it through," Delia Latrouelle said. Her sisters—Gloria, Sharon, Toni, and Beatrice—nodded beside her.

"Me too, Meggie. I've been here for decades," Edith Petrelli said. "I don't want to be anywhere else."

"Your grandma hired me. I will stay with her until the end," Tinsu said. She is one of our top seamstresses. "I am loyal to her and to you ladies."

Lele said, "Me too." I hoped Dessert Friday was this Friday. We needed it.

"When Bryson was born ten weeks early and I stayed with him for weeks at the hospital, you all came to visit and you kept paying me," our custodian/handyman/gardener/electrician Eric Luduvic said. "I'm in, Meggie."

"When my partner died, your whole family came to the funeral. Your grandma wouldn't let me work for a month so I could get my head on straight," Tom Zillnerson, our marketing manager, said. "I'm not going anywhere. I'll help."

I saw Lacey sway beside me. She looked pale. I saw Tory watching Lacey.

I didn't cry. But I felt like crying. "Thank you." I ignored the waver in my voice. "Thank you."

"How do we fix this, Meggie?" Beatrice asked.

I took a deep breath. "That's where you come in."

I told them I wanted their ideas. To come and talk to me, to write me an e-mail, to draw me a picture of a new product. "Think creatively, go out on a limb in terms of design, production, manufacturing. Think critically. What can we cut? What can we do different? Where is the waste? Talk about it among yourselves and tell me. Tell Tory, tell Lacey. People, this isn't going to be pretty. We're all going to take salary cuts, including Tory, Lacey, and me. In fact, percentage wise the three of us have agreed to take the highest cuts, as we feel responsible, but I promise that if we do survive, I'll make it up to you."

They nodded at me.

I felt the fear, but I felt the strength, too.

Tory's voice broke through. "Here we go! Quick, everybody, clear your butts out of the way. Lacey's gonna toss her cookies again and she needs a line to the bathroom or it's gonna get gross."

Lacey waved, hand over mouth, then darted out. They cleared a line quick, quick, quick.

We needed to turn this company around quick, quick, quick, too.

"Grandma, I want to talk to you about something."

"Then speak."

We were out on her front porch that evening, each in a rocking chair. She was in a classic turquoise-colored dress. The baubles: blue aquamarines. She and I had finished dinner: chicken cordon bleu, salad with walnuts and cranberries, and hot bread. I ate the pumpkin cheesecake before dinner, then a beer, then dinner.

"Meggie, quit drumming your fingers." She put her cigar down and picked up her whiskey shot glass. "You're irritating me."

I stopped drumming my fingers. "I don't want to irritate you,

Grandma. With that fiery temper of yours, no telling what you'll do."

"Your clothes are irritating me, too. I can hardly think through your decrepit fashion sense."

I was in a white T-shirt and jeans. The jeans had holes in the knees.

"I sent you new clothes." She sipped her whiskey. "Yet you persist in looking like a hobo."

I leaned forward and told her, so gently, my idea.

She said, "Hell, no, what the hell are you thinking, you hellish granddaughter?"

"Your story is important, your history is important. You're inspiring, Grandma, you've overcome so much."

"I've overcome far more than you could ever guess at." She blinked, and I could tell she was surprised she'd said that. I was surprised, too.

We sat in silence as she puffed on her cigar, took another sip of whiskey. She never throws it back, says it's a waste of whiskey.

"I can't speak of it." Her luminescent eyes filled with tears. "And I won't."

"Why?"

We sat in silence again. It thrummed with her agitation, the cigar smoke floating off into the wind.

"You remember the story I told you about Ireland, sliding down the curve of the rainbow with the dancing leprechaun and then coming to America on the back of an owl?"

"Yes."

She dropped her shot glass down with too much force, then pierced me with those green eyes of hers, so sharp, so tough. "The rainbow was a slide into despair and death. The leprechaun was a dangerous and evil man who left scars on me for life, and the owl represents how I wanted to fly away from the cataclysmic disaster that came next."

I nodded and tried to control my shock.

"Do you want me to tell that story, Meggie? What about the

fire, should I include that, too?" She leaned forward, her brogue so thick. "Do you think you could handle that part?"

I thought of all she'd accomplished. I thought of where she'd come from. I thought of what she'd hidden, how she'd made a life for herself here through grit, determination, and sheer will. She built a company from nothing. She built it out of desperation and fear. She was an inspiration. Her past would inspire others to overcome their own rainbows, leprechauns, and owls.

"Yes, Grandma, I do."

She slammed her whiskey shot glass down and actually threw her cigar, from Cuba no less, over the railing.

She glared at me. "Hellish granddaughter."

My mother calls Lacey's father "Sperm Donor Number One."

She calls my father "Sperm Donor Number Two."

She decided in her early twenties she wanted children but no husband. "Why have a man hanging around your whole life? What if you want a new one? What if you get sick of him? What if he tries to tell you what to do? What if he's mean? What if you make a mistake but can't divorce because of the kids? You're stuck. All problems.

"I like a man who acts like a man. Strong. Chivalrous. Protective. I like the testosterone and the machismo. But basically I like them for entertainment and amusement only. I do not like them to be involved in my real life. That, I can handle on my own and I do not need, or want, their input."

We have never met our fathers.

They don't even know they have daughters. They were one-night stands, carefully calculated to match my mother's ovulation cycle. She says she knows nothing about them beyond that. All she will say about them is that they were chosen for their handsomeness, their kindness, their intellect, and humor. How she figured all that out in one night is beyond me.

Did I miss having a dad, off and on? Yes. But I had The Irishman. He was my dad. So there were Sperm Donors Number One and Two out there somewhere in the world. So what?

I had a dad. I had The Irishman.

I still missed him.

I didn't need to know more, did I?

Did I?

"I'm glad you're back, Meggie."

"Me too, Lacey."

Lacey and I sat on her porch swing on Thursday evening. I'd had dinner with her and her husband, Matt, my niece, Cassidy, who is seventeen, and my nephews Hayden, who is sixteen, and Regan, who is fifteen. They hugged me hard when I came in.

I brought Cassidy a coffee table book on knitting, which she squealed about in delight and hugged close to her. She brought it to dinner and barely looked up.

I brought Hayden a book on the history and clothes of Coco Chanel. He loved it.

And I brought Regan a sob story book about the animals in Africa and their endangered habitats. He cried, but he loved it, too.

Matt and the kids were cleaning up inside. I could hear them laughing and fighting with one another. Lacey's house was blue on the outside and sky blue, light green, and lemon yellow on the inside. She loved color. She had lots of durable, soft furniture; framed art that her kids had done; a huge kitchen with a table in the middle of it; and a bunch of pets wandering all over. It was a happy home.

"How are you doing, Meggie?"

"Fine."

"No, be honest. How are you doing?"

"I'm fine, Lacey. I don't want to talk about it."

"Okay. I'm here."

"How are you feeling, pregnant momma?"

"Exhausted. All the time. And mad. I caught Cassidy naked with her boyfriend, Cody, in the back of our camper trailer. I found them because the whole thing was rocking in the driveway, like a ship on a stormy sea. Damn that wild thing."

Cassidy Brianna is, in Lacey's words, "the daughter from

Hades. Her father is Lucifer. Her mother is Cruella De Ville. She landed on my doorstep. I couldn't have given birth to her."

Cassidy is my middle name. Brianna is my mother's name.

Cassidy has a boyfriend named Cody, who is also seventeen. She is having sex with that boyfriend. When Lacey found out, she yelled, she raged, then she grounded her "for forever, you reckless, nonthinking hormonal gnat!"

Matt about passed out when he found out, and wasn't much help. Lacey said he literally clutched his chest when she told him. Cassidy's still a tiny, helpless baby girl with ribbons in her hair in his mind, and he hardly knew what to do when he found out his baby was cavorting around naked with a male.

The grounding and yelling didn't help. Cassidy snuck out in the middle of the night. They put a lock on her door so she couldn't get out. She climbed out her window and scrambled down the oak tree. She and Cody had a naked tumble in Cody's car in the parking lot at school. Lacey found out because a friend of hers told her. The police picked up Cassidy and Cody and gave them a ticket for indecent exposure/curfew violations when they were naked in a park at three in the morning playing Adam and Eve.

Cassidy occasionally smokes pot and drinks screwdrivers. My sister found this out when she took a sip out of Cassidy's water bottle by accident. She thought the kid was drinking orange juice.

Cassidy's tall with long red hair, a crooked but huge smile and dark brown, happy eyes. She is Lacey's mini-me. She is kind and funny and loves her family. She brings my sister breakfast in bed on Saturday mornings, complete with a flower. She loves to cook elaborate dinners, and sew, quilt, and knit, which she had to learn from my mother, as my sister and I know nothing about that stuff.

She recently made me an embroidered pillow with flowers that said, "I love you, Aunt Meggie."

Cassidy's on birth control. As Lacey said, "She's going to do it. I don't want to be a grandma. I am facing the doom of my reality."

Cassidy is exactly like the other women in our family: hell on high heels.

Only I don't wear high heels anymore.

I wear tennis shoes.

Not the fashionable sort, either.

"These teen years are killing me." Lacey grabbed my hand as we swung. "Sometimes I feel like problems are simply not solvable. You have to wait them out. Or maybe accept that things aren't going to change. Or that it's completely out of your hands."

"So, so true."

"Not that I'm giving up on trying to control Cassidy! She is turning my hair white." We heard Cassidy laugh. "She needs a chastity belt. She needs to be a nun."

"She reminds me of Tory at the same age."

"Arghhh. You are so right. She's a Tory, all over again."

"Does Tory see the kids often?"

"No. She doesn't like kids." I could tell that hurt Lacey like a sword to her heart.

"Do you invite her over? Does she feel welcome?"

Her lips tightened. "I have, and then we get in a fight and she doesn't come. The kids see her when Mom and Grandma are here, too."

What a dynamic. What a mess.

"I love you, Meggie."

"Love you, too, Lacey." Cassidy laughed again in the kitchen. "Good luck finding that chastity belt."

I love to walk at night when it's inky dark and completely quiet.

On Wednesday, I returned home from work after ten. I was jittery and stressed, the fear of failure wrapped around me like a straitjacket. I headed out wearing my ripped University of Oregon sweatshirt and my blue baggy sweats. It was a clear, cool night, the moon a white and gray beacon. I heard a car approaching but didn't think anything of it until it slowed.

I happened to be on a stretch where the houses were far

apart, but I didn't walk faster. I did nothing different. I didn't reach for my cell phone. I didn't try to run. I think that's what depression does to you. It makes you inactive within your own life. Your brain works as if it has sadness flowing like a stream through it. You become eerily unafraid. Probably because you're not sure you care about your future. Not a good place to be.

The car stopped beside me. I imagined a creepy person, a hatchet murderer. I turned to face my soon-to-be torturer.

"Hello, Meggie."

Man's voice. Low . . . rumbly . . . and there was the man who was so much trouble.

"Hi, Blake." I noticed he was in an SUV, not his truck.

"How about if you get in my car with me?"

I told myself to speak. He looked delicious. Blond and smiling. "Thank you, no. I'm fine." *I might not be able to control my hands around you.* "I'm taking a night walk."

"I can see that, night walker, but it's not safe, so I'm going to drive you home."

I would like you to be the driver in my bed. I'm glad I did not say that out loud. "It's not that far."

"It's too far for this time of night. Come on in."

I would like you to come on in me.

He got out of his SUV, walked around, and opened the door. He was wearing a gray suit and tie, so civilized, but behind the civilization was that tough look. I love when men look like men. Not primped and pretty, but harder edged and manly. The kind of man who oozes protective masculinity, ready to fight for you if he has to.

"Climb aboard."

I would like to climb aboard you. "I need to walk."

"There is always tomorrow for walking."

What would it be like to wake up to him tomorrow? He was so huggable. "I need to walk tonight."

"And I need a beer. The sooner you're in the car, the sooner you're home and I'm having a beer."

I thought of him drinking a beer naked. I liked his body, liked that thick hair, liked those sharp gray-blue eyes that did not miss a thing.

"Here. I'll escort you." He held out a hand.

I smiled, couldn't help it. I put my hand in his and there it was: fire and electricity, all blended up together. He blinked. I saw his eyes change. They were friendly at first, now there was something more.

Mutual lust. *Hello, mutual lust.*

I kept smiling at him, couldn't help it. Sparks were careening off him, to me, back to him. Whizzing, dizzying sparks.

I climbed in the car when I could gather myself together.

He closed the door, walked around to his side, and climbed in. For a moment, I didn't move. I could feel him, feel all of him, so close to me.

I turned my head away and did not look at the man who was trouble. He would be warm in bed. I bet I could forget a whole lot with his arms around me, my legs around him, mouth to mouth. Yep, I could forget for a few minutes.

And then I'd be where I am now.

Was it worth it?

Maybe. Maybe not. Would it be worth it to him?

Probably not. "Dang it."

"Dang what?" He had not restarted the car.

"I mean, dang...uh, I forgot to do something at work. It came to me that second..."

"Ah." He asked it first. "Meggie, are you married?"

That hurt. I winced. I tried not to show it. "No." I waited in that thick silence. "Are you?"

"No. I was once, when I was twenty three. Lasted two years. I was in the army, and we hardly saw each other. It would be me to blame for that. She found someone else who was home."

"I'm sorry."

"She was a great lady, no I am not still pining for her, and we were way too young."

"Do you still talk to her?"

"No. We divorced, and that was it."

I knew that he was noting that I had offered no explanation of my own marital status.

We were quiet for a while. He was waiting for me to speak. I could tell he was comfortable in the silence.

"What do you like to do, Blake?"

"I like to kayak."

That sounded fun.

"I like to fly-fish. I like to camp. I like to be outside. I like to ski."

Ah, skiing.

"What do you like to do?" he asked.

"I don't like to do anything at this particular moment, but I'll try to think of something and tell you another time so I can make myself sound interesting."

"You don't like to do anything?"

I shook my head. "Not much. I work."

"That's not a good sign."

"It's a poor sign. People should like to do things." I did not tell him that I think I would like to hophop into bed with him.

"Why don't you like to do things?"

I used to like to do things. I liked to film, travel, meet new people, shop for ethnic food and ethnic clothes in whatever country I was in for my work. I liked to explore. I liked hanging out with my family, skiing the fast runs, and walking through the woods. That stopped after him.

"Have you ever felt like you're wrapped in black?" I asked.

"What do you mean?"

"I mean, that your life is wrapped in black. It's heavy, it's dark. You're trying to find the one pinprick of bright light, but you can't. That's about where I am." I stuck my hands in my sweatshirt pockets. I had no idea why I'd even said that to him. Why on earth had I told him, the giant, the neighbor, a man whose car I'd bashed, *that?* Why?

"Okay, you can drive now," I told him. "Please do. Or I might yet again regale you about black and tiny lights." I rested my head on my hands, then brought it back up. No need to look totally pathetic.

"Yes," he said. "I do know what it's like to have a life wrapped in black."

"You do?"

He nodded. "And I know what it's like to be searching for light in there, too."

"Did you find it?"

"I did. Eventually."

"I'm glad to hear it."

He wasn't smiling now. His face was serious, contemplative. "I think it's a good question. I can relate to people better when I know that at some point, or at many points, their life was wrapped in black. The black brings depth."

"Yes, it does. Only I didn't want quite this much depth."

"Why are you wrapped in black now?"

"I think I'll save that splendid story for another time."

"I have time now."

"No, not now." No, never will I tell it. From you I want only a short and brief affair and then I'll move on. No need to add a whole bunch of emotional entanglements that I can't handle and you shouldn't have to attempt to handle.

"Later?"

"Actually, no."

"Why?"

"Because I don't want to talk about it."

We were silent together. The night wrapped all around the truck, soft and secretive, as the moon glowed.

"Maybe you'll want to someday."

"Nope. I won't. Thanks for the ride."

He took the hint. He drove to my tree house.

I opened the car door when we arrived, wanting to charge up the steps and hide inside by the trunk of my maple tree. He grabbed my hand, gently. I turned back.

I could tell he was going to say something, then changed his mind. "Don't walk so late at night anymore, Meggie. It's not safe."

"I'll remember that."

"Thank you. See you soon."

See you soon?

I sucked in a breath, then turned and, none too gracefully, dumped myself out of the car.

I did not look back because I didn't think I could handle staring at that handsome, tough and square-jawed, high-cheekboned face anymore.

I could crawl on that man's lap and enjoy him for hours, but I could not handle any more problems in my life. I could certainly not handle a relationship. It wasn't even fair to him to inflict myself on him. I was a mini tornado of emotions, out of control of my own self.

The moon lit the way to my tree house.

He found me hiding in the bathtub. I was under the boiling red water, hoping he wouldn't discover me. He yanked me out, studied my wet nakedness, then lifted me up and wrapped my legs around his body. He kissed my neck, then moved lower to my nipples and back up again, biting me here and there.

When his lips reached my lips, a rat climbed out of his mouth and into mine and bit my throat. The blood flowed, and I tasted its hot violence. He laughed.

"I won't let you go, Meggie," he whispered, his mouth on my ear, caught between his teeth as he tried to bite through. "I can't."

I struggled to get away, but he held me tight, until I was inside of his body, trapped, invisible, even to myself. His body filled with smoke and blood, choking me, then a black feather floated down and that's how I knew I was dead in the blood.

My own piercing scream woke me up. I struggled and fought, the comforter wrapped around me like a cocoon. I tried to run, couldn't, tripped, and fell straight down. When I realized I had endured another ragged nightmare, that the black feather wasn't there, I stumbled back to bed, panting, sweat dripping off my forehead.

I tasted blood and wiped my lip where I'd bitten down too hard. I used a Kleenex to stop the flow, then put one hand on my heart to slow its racing beat. I ran a hand down my body to make sure I was in one piece. I was losing it. Totally losing it.

Through the skylight I could see the moon, full, almost orange, the maple tree leaves floating in the shadows. I tried to still my breathing.

I sleep naked.

I didn't used to, but I do now. I don't even have pajamas anymore. They feel too tight, too restrictive. My nightmares squeeze me enough.

And I sleep alone, too.

Always alone.

I heard the knock on my door at six o'clock on Sunday night. I was wearing my ripped University of Oregon sweatshirt and blue sweatpants. I had on one pink sock and one red. I couldn't find a matching pair. My horse-tail hair was wrapped in a messy bun on top of my head.

I peeped through the peephole and smiled. It was my fifteen-year-old nephew, Regan Donnelly. Regan, named, obviously, after Grandma, and Donnelly for his dad's mother's maiden name.

Regan is fifteen, six feet tall, and a total jock. He is an outstanding athlete. His green eyes are exactly the same shade as my mother's and my grandma's. It's absolutely uncanny.

Regan's a mess. His blond hair's a mess, his clothes are a mess, and he usually wears mismatched socks. He's disorganized and often seems confused. Lacey has said many times, with worry, that Regan is "not too smart. He has a light, but it doesn't shine too bright."

Yet somehow Regan can pull it together on the field. He's always the starting quarterback. He always plays most of every basketball game. He hits home runs in baseball. It's effortless. He loves sports, he loves his family, and he loves animals. Not in that order.

"Hi, Aunt Meggie. I want you to meet my lizard. His name is Mrs. Friendly." Regan held up a lizard. I was nose to nose with it. It stuck out his tongue.

"His name is Mrs. Friendly? He's a boy?" I opened the door, and he and the lizard came on in.

"Yes. I renamed him Mrs. Friendly." He pushed his hair off his forehead. He was sweating, probably ran here from his house. He runs even when he doesn't need to run.

"So why the Mrs.?"

His brow furrowed. "I don't know. It's confusing to me, too. A friend of mine is moving to Alaska and his parents say no lizard, so I took him. You'll like him. I think you'll be friends."

I looked at the lizard. I didn't think we'd be friends. "Want some cookies?"

"Yeah. That'd be good. I need to be fed. Today I've only had three bowls of cereal, four eggs, half a pizza, three oranges, and lasagna. I'm starving." Regan settled down at my kitchen table, still holding the lizard. "Aunt Meggie, I'm glad you live here again."

"Me too."

"I missed you in my heart." He pointed at the lower right side of his chest.

"I missed you, too, Regan."

He got up and hugged me, Mrs. Friendly hanging in one of his hands. I tried not to touch Mrs. Friendly. Regan sniffled, then wiped his nose and tears on his sleeve.

"These are good cookies for my belly, Aunt Meggie." His voice wobbled. He is so dear. "Did you make them?"

"Uh, no. You know I'm a terrible cook. Cassidy made them for me."

"Yeah, you are." He stopped, caught himself, eyes wide in alarm. "No, no. No. I'm sorry. You're a *good* cook, and I have a problem."

"What's the problem?"

He sniffled, one more tear slipping out of his green eye. "Mom says no more pets since I already have . . . uh . . . I already have a couple."

"Four cats, three dogs, two mice—except I heard that one escaped and you can't find it—two hamsters, one hamster is missing, too—your mom told me that maybe it's with the mouse—and a rabbit."

"Uh, two rabbits, a gang of frogs, and also we have a bunch of tropical fish, too, but they don't count because you can't hug them."

He said this in all seriousness. I did not laugh. "Only animals who are huggable count, then?"

"All animals count, but fish aren't furry and can't give love, so they're different." He straightened his shoulders and looked hopeful. "How about it, Aunt Meggie?"

"How about what?"

"I mean, I think Mrs. Friendly wants to live with you." He held the lizard up so we were face-to-face again. "I think you'd like his company. He's shy and kind and loving and friendly, and I think the tree house is the perfect home. There are a lot of leaves here he can look at, and I think he'll like those white lights you have hanging from the ceiling. He'll think they're moons."

Moons? Why would a lizard care about moons? I shook my head. "Hang on, you want me to have Mrs. Friendly?"

"Yes. It's a gift. From me to you, Aunt Meggie." He rolled his lips in. I could tell he was about to cry again. "A patient and smart lizard for you. Mom and I think you'll like having Mrs. Friendly."

"Does your mom even know you're here?"

He squirmed. "I'll tell her tonight, but I know that she thinks that you'll uh, like, uh, like having Mrs. Friendly." He choked out, "Please Aunt Meggie, I don't want to give Mrs. Friendly up. He needs a home and I can't have more pets and you'll be a good mom to him. See, you can hug him and stroke him. He likes the attention."

I stared at Mrs. Friendly's nose. Or his snout. Or his pokey thing, whatever you call a nose on a lizard.

"See? He smiled at you! He smiled!" Regan declared, peering

down at me through his messy blond hair, those mom-grandma eyes so devastated at the thought of giving up the lizard.

I sighed. I have a hard time saying no to my sister's kids. "Okay, Regan. I'll take Mrs. Friendly."

"You will? Oh, great!" He practically tossed Mrs. Friendly at me. I caught him in semi-midair. "See? You're already best friends! Thanks, Aunt Meggie! I'll go get the cage. I left it on the ground." His floppy feet thundered out before I could change my mind.

"You're welcome," I said to Mrs. Friendly, nose to nose.

He stuck his tongue out at me.

He didn't seem that friendly.

5

Over the years, I made many different documentary films. One of the films that seared my heart the most was about homeless kids in Portland. They told me why they left home, almost all bone-shaking stories that will make the hair on the back of your neck not only stand up but actually want to walk off your skin.

They told me what life on the street was like: cold. Hungry. Lonely. Dangerous. Preyed upon by criminals, pimps, addicts. Many were addicts themselves or seemed to be struggling with a mental illness. So many were able to articulate, pinpointing to the finest detail, their struggle. One girl compared it to being a whisper. "A bad whisper. No one wants to hear us. We're invisible. We go away after the whisper is over."

She had stringy hair and was smoking a cigarette. "I think that life is supposed to be more than me wondering if I should jump off the Marquam or the Fremont Bridge, and seriously debating with myself which one would be better."

In the following years I filmed what life was like in a Haiti orphanage after the quake, profiling the kids but also the staff members, their hope and hopelessness, their despair and joy, their unrelenting struggles and their cherished goals for the children.

I filmed nuns in San Francisco helping the poor. Praying with the dying. Teaching school. Serving meals to the homeless. I interviewed them when the Vatican was critical of their work. The pope and the bishops told them, via a letter, that they needed to be inside more, praying, and should spend more time speaking out against gays and gay marriage.

I juxtaposed the nuns' work against the extraordinary wealth of the Catholic Church, the opulence of the Vatican, the priceless art within it, the white pointy hats and red shoes.

"Jesus would be with the poor," one nun said. "We're to stay inside and pray more? Can we not pray as we're counseling women in shelters? Can we not pray as we hold the hands of the sick? Can we not pray as we tend to the children from broken homes?"

Another nun said, "I have worked all my life for Jesus, to follow him and his teachings, am I now to stand up and rail against homosexuals and gay marriage? Jesus loved everyone. He says nothing about gays. I want to follow Jesus's love. I want to stand for what he stands for: love, not hate, patience, and forgiveness. Where does the Bible say it is my place to judge?"

Another nun was blunt. "Are the pope and the bishops, with their pedophile priest scandal, in any position to moralize to nuns out in the trenches and tell them to rail against gays?"

Filming was my life. I took people's journeys and lives and gave them a voice. My goal was always the same: connect people. Share what life is like for others. Inspire, encourage, emotionally move someone, change their way of thinking, their perceptions, maybe their prejudice.

And, most important, bring invisible people forward, invisible issues forward, to be visible.

If you could see what I see, I would often think when I was filming.

If you could see what I see.

I heard my grandma's heels—*tap, tap, tap*—before she strode into my office the next day.

She was in a sleek black dress, her white hair pulled back. The baubles for the day? Blue topazes. Striking against the black.

"I'll do it, Meggie. Part of me thinks it's the stupidest thing you've ever thought of and the stupidest thing I'll ever do, but the other part of me, probably the part that's swimming in the dementia I don't yet know I have, says that it's time I talk about the rainbow, the leprechaun, and the owl."

I stood up and hugged her. "Okay. I'll bring my cameras in."

"Good. Can't give those up, though I still haven't forgiven you for deserting me for that *other* career, and don't you ever forget it."

"I think the story of your life is important, Grandma."

"Don't give me that pseudo–psycho–ego-stroking crap. My story is no more important than anyone else's. You're going to film the other employees then, too?"

I nodded. "Yes. The ones who have been here the longest. I'm going to ask them about the bra they were wearing during an important moment in their life. I'll put the stories up on the website. I think it will make our company more personal to our customers. They'll feel like they know us, as we always try to know them."

She fingered the blue topazes on her necklace. "People want pretty, people want the gloss and shine when one tells a story, but there's none of that in my earlier years. It's more like broken glass and splintered wood."

I stood quietly as she dabbed at her eyes.

"I don't need the gloss and shine. I'll take the raw truth." I put my arm around her shoulders, so sad that I'd made her sad. Maybe we shouldn't do it. "It'll be okay, Grandma."

"Oh, shut up, Meggie." She threw her hands up in frustration. "I know it'll be okay. I was crying because you're wearing a sloppy beige shirt and large, manly jeans and floppy tennis shoes. Tennis shoes! Strike me down now with a sledgehammer. How come you're not wearing the clothes I bought you? Perfection—all of them." She strode toward the door—*tap, tap, tap*. "The day you don't look like a skinny garbage hauler will be a glorious day indeed."

I laughed.

She doubled back and kissed both my cheeks. "I love you, Meggie."

"You too, Grandma."

Our tears mixed.

I had a feeling that she had a lot more to cry about than I did.

"By the way, I'm planning our first Bust Out and Shake It Adventure Club event. I'll let you know about it soon."

Ohhhh boy.

Her heels tapped on out.

Tap, tap, tap.

"Hello, Meeegie!" Kalani grinned at me through my computer.

"Hello, Kalani, how are you?" It's so automatic to ask "How are you?" in America. The automatic response, especially in a business transaction, is "fine."

With Kalani, she took it literally. She always told me how she was down to the last detail.

"Oh me me me? I fine, I fine. No, not fine!" All of the sudden, her happy expression changed to anger. "My brother number two wife, she did another curse on me. I got gas now. I curse her, too. Nothing bad happen her. I think I need work on my curses. I need more, what you call? Black Magic. Ya. I need that. But I okay. I like my house! Every day I say, thank you God, I got my own house. I work for you, Meeegie. And your grandma, that good, old woman, that why I have house.

"You good woman, too, Meeegie. Okay, so I have women's bleeding today, tummy hurt here. That a curse, too. So I say how I am. How you, Meeegie?"

"I'm fine, Kalani. I need to talk to you about the bras I received from you yesterday. The padding is . . ."

"Oh ya! The padding good." She grabbed her boobs. I bent my head and rolled my eyes. "See! Even me small Asian woman, with that bra, I got the boobies! Big ones!"

"Kalani, I didn't want that much padding. We talked about how much padding there should be—"

"Ya. I changed my mind, though." Her smile reached ear to ear.

She changed *her* mind? "Kalani, I need you to change your mind back to what we discussed."

Her face fell. "You no like bra I sent?"

I could be gentle, but I was stressed and under fire about our catalogue, Web site, products, and going right the heck out of business. "No, Kalani, I don't. The padding is way too much. It's like having another full boob over your boob. It looks completely unnatural. It doesn't look good under a T-shirt. You might as well tell women to stick balled-up socks in their bras. No, I don't like it. Why did you make it different when I specifically told you, down to the millimeter, what we needed? We talked about it, I e-mailed you, we discussed it."

Kalani's eyes started to swim in tears.

"Oh, damn," I whispered. "Kalani, this isn't personal. I don't mean to hurt your feelings."

"I know. I know. I sorry, Meeegie. I thought my idea a good one. More booby, more sales, you know?"

"Kalani, I always like your input." No, I really didn't. "I like your ideas." No, I really didn't. "You know a lot about designing bras." Not enough, but okay. "But I already told people here about the bra that you and the women in your factory are making for us, using all your skills and talents, all your knowledge about lingerie..." Her expression lifted. "And they're so excited."

"They excite?" She wiped her tears.

"Yes." Heaven help the teeny, tiny white lies I tell sometimes to save someone's feelings. "People are excited about this new bra."

"Excite good, that good." She smiled.

"You're right. Excite good. If you could stick to the measurements that you and I, Kalani, did together, then that would be perfect."

She sighed. "You know, you right, Meeegie. I stick to measure. I do again."

I felt my shoulders slump with relief. "Thank you, Kalani."

"No, I thank you, Meeegie!" Up came the smile. "I do right

this time. I don't think I do the sexy thing with my boyfriend this weekend. I think next weekend. This weekend I got the cramps, no fun, you know what I mean, Meeegie? Sexy thing better when you don't have the women's curses in the ya ya place."

"You're right, Kalani. You're right about the ya ya place."

"I do the pads good now! Bye-bye, Meeegie. I love you, seeester!"

"Love you, too."

"Hayden says he's a girl." Lacey ran her hands through her red curls, then briefly put her head down on my desk. She had shadows under her coffee-colored eyes.

Hayden says he's a girl? "What?" I dropped the cracker in my hand. Lacey and I were spreading guacamole on crackers, then dipping them in salsa. I was chasing it down with my morning beer. Breakfast.

"He says he's a girl."

"I don't understand. Is he joking?"

Lacey's hands shook and her voice plunged down to a whisper. "Remember how Hayden always wanted to wear fancy dresses and skirts when he was a little boy, starting before he was two?"

"Yes."

"And remember that pink bike that he wanted with the white flowered basket?"

"Yes."

"And remember how he loved playing dolls and thought Cassidy's dollhouse was the coolest thing ever? How he's always liked makeup and nail polish?"

"Yes."

"And remember how he kept trying to sit on the toilet as a little boy, even though Matt told him that men pee standing up and how he cried and refused to do it?"

I nodded.

"He says that he's not a boy"—her voice cracked—"he's a girl."

I thought of Hayden, sweet Hayden. I loved that kid. Funny, witty, gently effeminate. Loves clothes and style. Artsy. An actor in school plays. "I thought he was gay," I said.

"Me too," my sister said, the tears falling. "You and I have always thought that. Remember when he was three and he came out all dressed up in pink with Cassidy's pink parasol and that hat with red roses? You looked at me and said, 'I hope you like his partner.' And I agreed. But Hayden says he's a girl in his head and in his heart. He does like guys. Does that make him gay if he thinks he's a girl?"

I leaned back in my chair. "I don't know if it makes him gay. Maybe it makes him straight. He believes he's a girl and he likes guys. I'm so confused. This is too much. How is he doing?"

"He says he's known for years." She put a protective hand on her stomach. "I remember him telling me when he was so young that he wanted to be a girl many times. He just sobbed when he was in boy clothes. He told me when he was three that he didn't like his penis, that it was 'wrong.' That was his word for it, 'wrong.' He hit it, like he wanted it off. One time I caught him with scissors. He was going to cut it off." Lacey and I both shuddered.

"I remember fighting with him in first grade when I told him he wasn't allowed to wear dresses anymore. I let him in kindergarten, because the kids all dress strange then, but I didn't want the kids at school to tease him. He insisted on pink socks. The kids teased him, but he kept wearing his pink socks."

I remembered how brutal that teasing was on Hayden. He refused to change, though. He was true to himself. "When did he tell you this?"

She bent her head, and I held her shaking hand. "On Monday. The reason he told me is because he says he keeps thinking about . . . thinking about . . ." She started gasping. "He says he's desperate and thinking of kill-kill-killing himself."

"Oh, my God." My entire body felt like it was filling with sharp chards of ice.

"He says he's so depressed and it's been like this for years. He said, 'Mom, can you at least try to understand this? I feel like a freak. I've got a penis and I know I'm a girl. I don't have boobs, but I have balls. I am so screwed up. Please, Mom, you have to help me. Please help me. I don't want to die, but I can't live like this.' Then he said . . ." Lacey tried to get a deep, ragged breath in and couldn't. "He said, 'Mom I can't be a boy anymore. I have to be me. A girl.' "

"And you said?" My hands were shaking. Oh, Hayden, don't even think about it.

"I had to get over the shock first. I felt like I'd been hit in the face, but I was looking at my son, my son crying, and I said I would help him, of course I would. He said he's transgender. *Transgender.* I've been blind, Meggie. I thought he was gay. I didn't want to see the truth, didn't want to deal with it. He knew it, too. He knew his mother didn't want to deal with it, that's why he didn't talk about the transgender part with me. What kind of mother am I? By being deliberately blind I've let my kid hang himself out there all alone. If I'd opened my eyes to the obvious, been a better mother, I could have talked to him about it, been there for him, supported him."

"Lacey, you've been a great mom . . ."

"I've never been a great mom," she wailed. "I'm exhausted all the time. I yell at the kids. I work too much. I'm a blind, in-denial mother whose son can't talk with her about being transgender, so he's completely alone and wanting to die!"

I got up, sat down next to Lacey, and hugged her as she cried.

"We need to do everything we can to tell him and show him we love him and accept him, because this is going to be a hard, hard road," I said, even as my mind was trying hard to grasp this one. "We cannot have a suicide. We cannot."

"I know, I know. I love Hayden. I love him so much." Lacey put a tissue to her face. "And he is a she. My son will be my daughter. I can hardly get my mind around it. I can hardly get it. It's not what I wanted, but what else do I do? Punish him? Deny what he's saying? Try to invalidate his feelings? Yell? Tell him he's wrong? Take him to a shrink so a shrink can tell him he's wrong? Make him feel more freaky and lost than he already feels? I saw this. I saw this when he was two. I heard him ask to have ribbons in his hair, pink ones. I saw him reach for his sister's Mary Jane shoes. I saw his fascination with dolls and glitter and magic wands and princesses. He refused to wear swimming trunks, he insisted on a bikini. He was born like this. He was born a girl, and a penis and balls dropped down."

She burst into another round of tears, her shoulders shaking.

"Daughter. Son. Niece. Nephew. We love him. We love her," I said, utterly shaken. "She's a part of our family, and we're not going to get lost in all the details."

"Right. No details." She blew into her cupped hands, in and out, her face red. "I have to accept it, I know this, that my son wants to be *my daughter*."

"I love you, Lacey." I brushed the tears off her cheeks. "And Hayden will look pretty in dresses and high heels. Grandma will probably pick them out for him."

"Or Tory. She'll have him in a leopard-print bra in no time."

"Hopefully Hayden won't dress slutty."

Lacey paused in her semihysteria and shook her head, a mixture of disbelief and humor. "Right. I don't need a *slutty* daughter."

"Heavens, no."

"I already have Cassidy, who doesn't want to keep her skirt down or her jeans up. Can't have another kid like that."

"No, never. Long skirts for Hayden. No cleavage. No tight jeans."

"Modest ladies clothing only."

"Churchlike."

For some strange, strange reason we found ourselves hilarious. When we were done laughing, we cried some more.

I checked on Mrs. Friendly the Lizard that night, and he was quite quiet in his cage. Perhaps he was enjoying all the moons he saw in the rafters.

I headed to the deck and sat in a yellow Adirondack chair with a jacket on. The maple trees swayed and swished and whispered. I was so glad I had found this house. Being wrapped in a hug by trees is helpful to my precarious and somewhat demented mental state.

I thought of all the pain Hayden had been through, knowing he was a girl in the body of a boy. It didn't take much to understand. There are millions of things that have to go right in utero for babies to turn into healthy people, complete with eyelashes, elbows, a heart, Grandma's eyes, Daddy's chin, Mother's nose. Estrogen, progesterone, the circulatory and respiratory systems, a liver, and intestines that curve the right way down.

Reproductive systems, too.

It is absolutely understandable that gender would flip now and then. That the body would not turn out like the mind. A girl body, a boy in his head. A boy body, a girl in her head.

I thought of how Hayden said he wanted to die, and my heart clenched tight. How can you even move forward in life, be happy, when a basic, fundamental part of personhood—your gender—is not correct in your own body? How do you get through that psychologically?

I thought of the film I made on the homeless kids. I remembered what the girl told me about being invisible, a bad whisper, and wondering which bridge to jump off so she, too, could die and escape the pain.

In the last year I have been trying to be invisible.

I have been a bad whisper.

I have often wondered if I should jump off a bridge, too.

It's amazing what we have in common with our fellow humans.

Sometimes it's euphoria, sometimes it's tragic.

The most important thing is to see that it's there.

"We're going to have a fashion show."

"A fashion show?" Lacey said, aghast. "Those are expensive."

"Yes they are." I pushed aside fabrics for nightgowns, a design book, and two pink folders that Lacey, Tory, and I had been working on in our pink conference room. The chandelier above us twinkled, catching the sunlight streaking in the windows. "We'll strip the costs down as much as we can."

"Having a fashion show is like planning an invasion, Meggie," Tory protested. "A fashion invasion. Location. Stage. Models. Clothes. I feel my ovaries shrinking in stress already."

"We all know they're a ton of work, stress, trouble. That's why you and I and Lacey are going to organize it along with a whole gang of our employees."

"What do you mean that you, Lacey, and I are going to organize it? Not me." Tory leaned forward. She was wearing a red wrap dress. One of our red, pure lace negligees showed through. She was dressing more seductively ever since she threw her temper tantrum and left Scotty because she didn't think he paid her enough attention. I understood. She wanted other men to show her they thought she was attractive, since Scotty wouldn't. "I'm busy."

I stared right at her. "I am, too. So is Lacey."

"I have three teenagers, all strange," Lacey said, her voice pitching. She shoved her red curls back off her face with both hands. "I'm knocked up again. Matt told me he wants the gender of the baby to be a surprise, which will drive me crazy because I like to obsessively plan ahead. Cassidy snuck out again last night and I was up until three making sure she came back in safe so I could scream at her, Regan is crying because he wants me to save all the dogs at the pound, and Hayden's wearing panties. You think I'm not busy?"

Tory glared at us, fidgeted.

"You want to help save this company or not, Tory?" I asked.

She kept the glare but blinked. She wanted to save it, I knew that. "I suppose I can help some."

"Not some. We're all going to have to work till our heads spin. We'll show off the lines, invite a bunch of people. We have to do something different, though. We have to be fabulous and colorful, but we need depth, human interest, something more than models strutting, which we've all seen a thousand times.

We need a show that will bring us media attention and increase sales. We have to stay true to our brand, the history of this company, to Grandma and our traditions, yet we have to haul this company up to a higher place. We have to relaunch."

"We have to sell what's behind the product," Tory said. "Steaming hot sex."

"Seduction," Lacey said. "Romance."

"Yes. But more," I said. "That's what all lingerie companies sell. Lingerie is a promise. It's a hope. It's fun and frilly. But we have to have more than that. We must be more than that."

"But what?" Tory asked. "What are you talking about?"

"I don't know." I put my feet up on the chair next to me and studied them. My shoes were brown and scuffed. Years ago I would not have worn them if I was running through a mud field. They depressed me. "I don't know, but I know that that's what we have to do."

Lacey climbed on the conference table and lay down, her pregnant belly sticking up.

Tory stared out the window, arms crossed, face set. I was well aware of how difficult my coming back had been for Tory. I felt bad about it.

I climbed up on the conference table with Lacey and lay down beside her.

Tory looked at us and turned away.

I saw stark, harsh hurt in her eyes.

"Tory, come and lay on top of the table," I said.

"I'm fine."

"Come on, Tory," I said.

"No." She fixed her gaze out the window. My years away had given me a totally new perspective on Tory. Her own family disappeared in one horrific crash. She went to a new family with two sisters. She'd felt left out forever, as if she didn't belong. It about knocked me over to think about it.

"Please, Tory?" I said. "Be a threesome. The three O'Rourke Musketeers. Or the three O'Rourke Fashioneers."

"I don't do threesomes," Tory quipped.

Lacey reached for my hand and held it.

"We have to have a fashion show that's more than a fashion show," I said. "And we need the results to be spectacular, or we can roll this whole place up and call it a day."

Lacey whimpered.

I saw Tory's back tighten up.

I thought of Grandma.

Losing the business would kill her.

I brought my video camera into work.

Grandma sat behind her desk and I put the camera on a tripod. Her desk was white with gold trim. Her corner office was elegant, with light pink walls, white shelving, the expected pink fainting couch, and pink curtains.

She wore a red suit, red heels, and her signature four strands of pearls.

"Okay, Grandma," I said quietly. "We're ready. Talk to me. I want you to start off in Ireland. Tell me about your life there. Your family. Where you lived."

"This is ridiculous." She threw a hand in the air. "I'd rather walk naked through the production floor."

"Please don't, Grandma. If you did, then all the employees would be clamoring to prance about naked, too, and it would be distracting. I'm ready when you are."

Her eyes raked me, head to foot. "What are you wearing? Is that a beige T-shirt? You didn't even iron it, did you? Is it clean?"

"Yes, it's clean. I haven't sunk that far into a fashion abyss—"

"You have. And your pants? They're so big you could have someone else climb in there with you. Maybe a baboon. Are you trying to attract a baboon? I know I taught you about fashion. You neglected my lessons." She sighed.

I waited.

She turned to the camera. I turned it on.

She opened her mouth to talk, then shut it. "Turn off the camera, Meggie."

I turned it off. She focused on her chandelier, and I saw her chin tremble, her eyes fill.

"Grandma—" I heard the breathy sound of my voice, my pain for her.

"Stop it, Meggie."

I didn't move as I watched her struggle to get control of her emotions.

"Turn it back on. Let's get this regrettable episode of my life over with."

I turned it back on.

She said, "I was born in County Cork, Ireland . . ." She closed her mouth. Her lips tightened. She brought a shaky hand to her pearls, as if for comfort. "Turn off that damn camera."

I turned it off. I waited. I wanted to hug her, I knew I had upset her, that this had upset her, but she would detest the pity.

I visibly saw her square her shoulders, and her emerald eyes became steely, almost frosty. "Turn it on."

I turned it on.

This time she talked, straight through. When the tears fell, she brusquely, impatiently, swiped them away and kept talking. When she was done, she said, "That's it, Meggie. Turn it off."

I turned it off and clutched my hands together to keep them still. I felt ill. I tried to hide my tears.

"If I wanted your tears, Meggie, I would have asked for them. I'm not telling you about the rainbow, leprechaun, and owl so you can blubber on. I surely haven't blubbered on."

"I'm so sorry, Grandma," I whispered, broken. I shouldn't have asked her to do this. I'd had no idea about the depths of her misery, her tragedy. Had I known I never would have broached it.

"I never asked for your apology, young woman, or your pity, so get rid of it. This is my life. You wanted to hear it, and there it is." She tilted her chin up, always proud. "Buck up, Meggie. Bad things happen to everyone. It's life. No one gets out un-scathed. The strong ones deal with it. The weak ones crumble. Don't you ever be weak."

I nodded.

She turned to leave, her heels tapping. "And put on some lip-stick, for God's sakes."

When she left, I crumbled.

I offered to take Lacey's kids all weekend because she looked ripped.

I tried to keep them busy. We went to the movies and pizza on Friday. They all slept in until eleven on Saturday, then we had omelets. They all visited with Mrs. Friendly. I took them to the beach and we decided to spend the night, swim in the hotel's pool, and jump in the freezing cold Oregon waves. I brought them home on Sunday at six in the evening.

Lacey was so grateful, she cried on my shoulder. She smelled like morning sickness, and milk and chocolate chip cookies—two more things that keep the morning sickness away, she thinks.

The kids thought she was crying because she missed them.

Ah, no.

There was no missing of the teenagers.

Poor Lacey. Three teenagers and a surprise pregnancy.

I spent part of Sunday night on the telephone with Tory, who was crying and, alternately, hitting her punching bag as hard as she could, which brought on panting.

"I called Scotty and told him I had a date on Saturday night and he said I'm sorry to hear that and I said why are you sorry and he said because you're probably going to sleep with him and that's a bad idea and I said why is it a bad idea you don't want me anyhow and I can do what I like I'm not living with you anymore and he said that's right, you're not, you left me, as if he wasn't responsible for my leaving and I said are you dating and he said he didn't have to tell me if he was or wasn't and I screamed at him and called him a cheating, skinny, too smart, anteater, emotionless bastard and he hung up on me, that ass-hole. . . . Now I'm *really* glad I didn't take his last name when I got married!"

"I'm sorry, Tory."

"And I even looked at my star sign, the fish, Pisces, and it said that a former problem with a lover would be solved. It was wrong! That makes me even more mad! What's wrong with these star sign readers!"

She kept punching and panting.

6

My name is Abigail Chen. I work here at Lace, Satin, and Baubles as Meggie O'Rourke's assistant.

My real name is Lan, which means orchid in Vietnamese. Hardly anyone knows that, only a few people left in my family. I don't know why I'm saying it now, Meggie. Maybe it's because you're filming me and then there's a record that I existed as Lan, a long time ago, when I was a young girl in Vietnam.

I took the name Abigail when I came to America. Lan, in almost every sense, was gone. I arrived with my mother and only one brother. Only one.

You want to hear my story and then about a favorite bra? Okay, I can do that. My mother, two brothers, and I escaped from Vietnam in the middle of the night on a boat. We had to. Saigon had fallen. That's where I lived. We tried to get out earlier. My father worked at the embassy, and he tried to get us out on a helicopter, but that didn't work. He couldn't get us seats. He tried to get us out in a car, but that didn't work, either. He tried so hard, he was frantic. I didn't have a word to describe it as a child, but as an adult, the word frantic is correct. We were being bombed. We were being invaded. It was absolute chaos.

My father was sent to a reeducation camp. They do not reeducate you in a reeducation camp. They starve, beat, and torture you. That's your new education. Later we learned that he lived ten years there. He was an educated man, so the North Viet-

namese wanted him dead. They got their wish. We were told by my uncle, who was there in the camp with him, that my father ... my father ... I'm sorry. So many years have passed, and I still cry over this. Still cry.

My father was regularly beaten because he had worked for the government. He had even attended college, UC Berkeley, in America. He spoke English. He taught us English.

My uncle said he became sick and weakened and died working outside. Dropped one day in the field. They beat him, wanting to force him to get up or be beaten again, but he was dying. I loved my father, a kind and gentle man, and whenever I think of this ... oh ... oh ...

My mother and brothers and I had done what my father told us to do if he was ever arrested: Get out. Get out of Vietnam. My mother sold all we had, and we snuck onto a boat with a whole bunch of other frantic people. We were on it for weeks. This rickety boat, all crammed together, bopping around in the ocean. No toilets, no privacy. Crying and sickness and diarrhea. There was hardly enough food and little water. The Thai pirates came. They raped my mother. I saw it. I tried to stop it. The pirate kicked me in the head. That's why I have this scar. See? It's huge. My hair covers it so one sees it.

My older brother has scars, too, from getting in fights in the resettlement camps. We ended up in a camp in Thailand. Pirates from Thailand, a camp from Thailand. Both dangerous.

One of my brothers died there. He was seven. He became sick, so weak. He died in my arms, his eyes wide open. He was there one second and I kissed him on his cheek, and he smiled and said, "I love you, Lan," then the next he was gone. My mother was out in the fields working.

When my brother died my mother cried all day for weeks. She didn't speak for a month. We all slept together on a mat on the floor.

Eventually we were sponsored by a church in America. When we arrived in Portland we were met by my aunt, my mother's sister, who arrived about two months before us on a different boat. They were both so young, I realize now. My mother and father had me when they were 18.

Your grandma, Meggie, hired my mother and my aunt. They had nothing. Two dresses each. They barely spoke English. They were scared and traumatized. My mother had lost her husband, her young son, her country, my aunt had lost her husband and a daughter. Your grandma hired them as seamstresses. Amazing. Whenever I think about it, I want to cry. Okay, see? I am crying.

Your grandma gave them new bras and underwear, and she took them shopping for more dresses. They never forgot it. My mother said, "I arrived in rags, and Regan O'Rourke had me in lace and satin by the end of the week."

They still live together, as you know. They bought that yellow house where my brother and I grew up, and they're so proud of it. They like working here. I like seeing them here. We're a family and we work for your family. We consider your family our family, and we are loyal to you.

You asked me to talk about my favorite bra, too, for this video. I will tell you that it was a bra my mother brought home for me when I was thirteen. It was light pink, made by our company.

"This is for you, Lan," my mother said to me. "Beautiful. Like you, my orchid, like you." I put it on and it fit perfect, and my aunt said to me, "You are a woman now. An American woman.

"Yes, an American woman," my mother said, her eyes all teary, and I knew she was thinking of my father and brother. "You, Lan, me, your aunt, your brother. We are Americans now."

We had lost so much because of violent men. But we were here. There were no bombs, no guns, no women raped on boats, no invading armies, no threat of starvation. They had jobs, and we had food. I remember my mother and my aunt both adjusted the straps to make my pink bra perfect for me as I stared at myself in the mirror. They kissed my cheeks. They were proud of me, their American girl.

That pink bra is my favorite bra, Meggie. It was when, in my head, I became an American. My father died so I could be American, and I honor him every day in this country by working hard and loving my mother, aunt, and brother, my husband and my children. Please stop crying, Meggie, it's okay . . . it's okay . . .

7

⌇

"Thank you, ladies, for joining me on this sunny afternoon for our first Bust Out and Shake It Adventure Club event," Grandma said. "The three of you look like wrecks."

Lacey, Tory, and I stood in the circular driveway of Grandma's home, her fountain flowing high in the middle. She had told us to wear jeans and boots—not fancy boots. It was Saturday, and I was so tired from working that it felt like peanut butter had invaded my bloodstream. I could hardly move.

Lacey was battling morning sickness and was the color of white sheets with light green stains. Cassidy had been caught by the PE teacher, a friend of Lacey's, having sex with Cody in the locker room. Cassidy's excuse was, "I earned an A on my AP Chemistry test and I wanted to celebrate, Mom!" Regan had brought home yet another mouse that was now loose in the house, and Hayden had been crying.

Tory was wiped out, as she can't sleep without Scotty, that "freakoid, nerdy, computer obsessed weirdo robot and I hate him."

"Your outfit, Grandma," Lacey said, grinning, though bent over from nausea.

"You are flippin' rockin' it, Grandma," Tory said, thumbs up.

"Love it, Grandma, I love it," I said.

Grandma was dressed in leathers. She opened up the trunk of her red Porsche, pulled out a helmet, and put it on over her perfectly coiffed hair. "Guess what we're doing today for our first event?"

"What?"

"The four of us are going to be daring and dangerous."

"Daring and dangerous?" Lacey said, swaying a little, hand to stomach. "I am not daring or dangerous. I am having a surprise child and he is making me sick." She suddenly turned and threw up on Grandma's hydrangea plant.

"Did you have to pick the purple one?" Grandma asked, taking her helmet off. "And it's not a boy, it's a girl."

"How do you know?" I asked.

"Because I'm magic," she snapped.

I patted Lacey's back. "Want some crackers?"

"No, I'm good."

"Gross, Lacey, gross," Tory said, examining her nails, which were painted bright red with tiny pink flower on the pinkies.

Grandma picked up her cell phone, dialed a number, and said, "We're ready, gentlemen!"

We heard the growling blasts seconds later.

Three Harleys appeared at the bottom of the hill and roared on up.

The men on top of the Harleys were dressed in full leather. They were definitely hard-core biker dudes. Dark glasses, tattoos, bandanas. Scars. Grandma told us later that two of them were ex–Hell's Angels. The other one was a family doctor, the brother of one of the Hell's Angels.

"What's going on?" Lacey said.

"We're going on a motorcycle ride to a biker bar," Grandma said. "Get on, ladies."

Grandma opened a box and pulled out leathers for Tory and me.

"Oh, this is spectacular," Tory breathed. She pulled on her leather jacket and pants and yanked on a helmet. She pointed toward the roughest-looking guy, one of the Hell's Angels. The Hell's Angel guy gave her the thumbs-up. His name, we later learned, was Harold Jr. "I'm taking that guy right there. He's enough to get my mind off Scotty."

Grandma climbed on the back of the other motorcycle, the doctor driving.

The third biker waved. His name was Monster Mouth.

I looked at Grandma, whose hands were up in the air as if she was going to ride the bike that way, then to Tory, whose arms were already around the waist of her Hell's Angel, and finally to my Monster Mouth.

"Might as well do it," I muttered. I pulled on my leather pants, jacket, and helmet.

"What about me?" Lacey yelled.

Grandma dug in her pocket. "You, my dear, being pregnant yet again—do you not know what a condom is, can you not use a diaphragm—are going to drive the Porsche."

Lacey's face said it all. Grandma doesn't let anyone drive her red Porsche. No one.

"Really? Really, Grandma?" Lacey said, bopping, the pale look leaving as joy spread like a song across her face. "I can drive it?"

"Did you think I would put you on the back of a motorcycle? Hello? Has pregnancy taken your brain synapses along with your uterus? No pregnant people on motorcycles. Now get in there, and let 'er rip!"

"Oh, thanks, Grandma!" Lacey tipped up on her toes and wriggled about, clapping her hands, before her face paled and she leaned back over the hydrangea bush.

"Don't do that in my Porsche, Lacey!" Grandma called.

Lacey wiggled her bottom in reply.

It was sunny.

It was warm.

We rode fast.

Monster Mouth was an excellent driver.

We danced with the biker dudes in the bar.

We drank beer (except for Lacey) and had terrible nachos. Tory and Grandma had martinis.

We laughed and talked.

One of the Hell's Angels recited a poem, all dramatic, about a pirate who lost his love when he sailed the seas. She wasn't waiting when he came back; her soul had gone to heaven without him. The doctor motorcyclist regaled us with a raunchy song about three truckers, which we learned and sang with gusto.

Monster Mouth showed us how he could break small pieces of wood against his forehead.

When we walked out, back to the bikes and the Porsche, Lacey and Tory had their arms wrapped around each other and were singing the raunchy song, their foreheads marked where they'd tried to break wood.

Grandma looked at me, nodded at Lacey and Tory, and whispered, "That's what I wanted. Right there. Those two happy together and not spitting or hitting or flinging things."

"You have your wish, Grandma."

"You *three* are sisters, Meggie. Tory's never felt included. You need to fix that. Promise me."

"I promise, Grandma."

"Sisterhood is not always by birth, it's by love."

She kissed my cheek, and I climbed on behind Monster Mouth. His forehead was red and sore.

He winked at me.

I winked back.

I could feel him crawling inside me.

The rat was back, black and insidious.

He stroked my insides with his sharp claws, my heart, my lungs, my arteries. He bit me, here and there, his rat body lumbering around, squishing me, puncturing my organs, until he bit through a hole in my stomach and crawled out.

The rat giggled and Aaron's face appeared, then his body. He whispered, "I will live in you. I will breathe in you. I will bite you. Bleed for me, my Meggie. Wherever you are, wherever you wander, bleed. I bled, now it's your turn."

He opened up his rat's mouth and bit my face off.

I woke up and tried to scream, but my breath caught, my voice caught, my life caught.

I ripped off all the sheets, looking for the rat between the folds, under the bed, behind the dresser, but I couldn't find him. He was inside of me, invisible, giggling.

I lay naked on the couch the rest of the night, with all the lights on, and watched the sun come up.

It was the only way to keep the rat outside and a fingerhold on my sanity.

I fired four employees within the first few weeks of being at Lace, Satin, and Baubles.

"You're a firing machine," Lacey said to me.

"You betcha."

"I was going to do it . . ." Tory said.

"No, you weren't," Lacey interrupted.

"Yes, I was."

"You should have done it earlier, both of you," I snapped. "They weren't working. They didn't appreciate the job or the product."

"When I talked to Agnes about being more productive, she said I was trying to fire her because of her age and threatened to sue because of ageism," Lacey said. "She's only sixty-one."

"And you should have said that sixty-one is young," I said, "and the Petrelli sisters are all in their seventies, their jobs far more complex and difficult, and they are more competent and work more efficiently than she does. You should have told her she needs to do her job, to do it without complaint, and if she can't she can find employment elsewhere."

"I didn't want the lawsuit, Meggie." Lacey rubbed her forehead. "I was afraid of that threat."

"I'm aware of that. That's why I had a camera pointed at her since the third day I arrived."

Lacey's and Tory's mouths dropped. "You did?"

"Yes. I also had a camera on Willy because he threatened to sue because he said we weren't accommodating his medical issues well enough."

"He says his joints hurt, his knees hurt, hips hurt..." Tory said. "Always in pain."

"He doesn't have a medical issue," I said. "He's obese. He doesn't like to move. Being obese and hurting because you're carrying two hundred extra pounds is not a medical issue, and I was sick of him asking people to do things for him. We have Kara'a here who's battling a kidney disease, and I understand she's hardly missed a day of work in marketing. Sharoq has only one hand and she always does her work and does it quick. I had a camera on Tamish and Monique, too."

"You are a tough bird, sister," Lacey said.

"Yep. But I don't want to be sued, either. Yesterday when Agnes's attorney called, I sent him a copy of the tape showing how Agnes takes naps repeatedly, comes in late, wanders around the production floor, and does nothing except read her celebrity magazines and pick at her pointy teeth.

"When Willy's attorney called, I sent him a copy of the tape showing Willy smoking out back and looking at porn for hours on his computer. I gave him the phone records of Willy's calls to Vegas to some phone sex place. If Tamish and Monique hire an attorney, I will produce evidence from Tamish's computer about her continual chats with a psychic on company time. Monique liked the psychic, too."

"How do you know?" Lacey asked.

"Because I'm psychic."

"Super. What am I thinking right now?" Lacey asked.

"You're thinking that you feel enormously pregnant."

"No, I'm thinking that I'm glad you're back."

"Thank you." I felt my irritation lower.

"Me too," Tory said.

I eyed her. "Is this a trick?"

"No, not a trick at all." She crossed her arms. "I'm glad you fired them. I'd been wanting to get rid of them, but the lawsuits scared me."

"You're not scared of anything."

Tory sat back in her chair. "I am of lawsuits. I'm not stupid. I understand the financial morass we're in, and I envisioned the costs of those lawsuits sinking us to the bottom of the ocean. They could have gone on and on, and attorneys, those demented sharks, are so expensive. What if we lost the lawsuits? I did the math and thought it was easier to pay 'em. I didn't even think about filming them."

"It's not easier to pay them." My voice sounded sharp, ticked off. "They're lazy and spineless. Plus, I hate when people try to take advantage of me."

He'd done it. He'd pushed and pushed, believing I wouldn't take that final step.

"I hate when people take and take and don't give back." I kicked my chair, then stood and glared out the window at that stupid Mount Hood, mocking me for not skiing anymore.

"I hate when people try to cheat." *He had cheated me out of a choice. He had sucked me dry. I had let him because I felt I had to.*

I inhaled, my breath sounding like scraped sandpaper.

"I hate when people manipulate other people." *I hadn't even known I was being manipulated for a long time. I was so over my head with his emotional issues, his fury, I couldn't even see truth. That was the way he wanted it.*

"I hate when people use threats to get what they want." I picked up a mug on my desk. *He had threatened again and again.*

I threw the mug. It shattered against the wall. I liked the sound.

I was his crutch, his toy. He broke the toy.

I threw another mug. It broke, too.

I hate myself.

I bent over, my hands on my knees, one debilitating flashback after another churning through my mind.

I do hate myself.

When I could breathe again, the fury simmering back down, I noticed that Lacey and Tory were staring at me, mouths open. "I'm sorry. Sometimes my anger gets away from me."

"No problem," Lacey said.

"Looks like your anger not only got away from you, it went

flying up and around, smashed some ceramic mugs, then settled back in," Tory said.

Lacey waddled over and gave me a hug. "Give me a hug, baby."

Tory said, "Might as well give you a hug, too, since you're so deranged and crazy. Who knows what you'll do next, like a rabid animal."

I hugged them for a second, my past making me sickly dizzy, then said, "Okay, that's enough. I'm not totally whacked out."

"Yes, you are, my sweets," Lacey said.

"You are a whacked-out woman," Tory said. "Teetering. Edgy. You're like a cannon and you just shot off a ball, but it's partly your star sign, so don't blame yourself." She patted my shoulder. "That's why I don't blame myself for checking up on Scotty, the Viking slug-face algae."

I laughed. I would not further contemplate a Viking slug-face algae. I looked at the broken pieces. I hadn't liked those mugs anyhow. "Where do we keep the broom?"

If I were to say that being the CEO of Lace, Satin, and Baubles was a challenging position, it would be putting it mildly. It would be like saying Mount St. Helens blowing its peak off was a wee blast.

I will not get into the full details of running a company like this, but there are many people and many moving parts. The people and the moving parts explode on a regular basis.

Tory's the design director, Lacey's chief financial officer. We also have a creative director beneath Tory who is in charge of seasonal ideas and direction, whose job it is to figure out what the consumer wants to wear. Plus about a hundred other things. We have sales and distribution people. This involves all of our orders, retailer relationships, shipping and warehouse management. Also, another hundred things.

We have a brand director, who mostly does our advertising and works with our marketing director.

We have an operations manager. I'll simply say she operates.

We have a product director. She works with the designers and the developer. The designers and the developers often scream at each other. What the designer wants to do and what is economically feasible may be at extreme odds. Sort of like two fencers going at it, their swords clanking, only the designer and developer battle with their mouths and an occasional thrown catalogue.

We design products, we develop prototypes, we edit the prototypes, we do fit testing, we try out new colors and materials that we hope our consumers will adore, and we endlessly try to figure out how to advertise and package our lingerie so it's, in my grandma's words, "a delightful process . . . makes a woman feel her inner sensuality or her temper tantrum, whichever is closer to the surface."

We also work with the stores that sell our products. There are many relationships there, too, that have to be managed and— I'll say it—soothed. We have Web site people, catalogue people, and people that handle the models and photographers for both.

There is Kalani's factory abroad, the supplies, product development, the supply chain, her employees, and our employees here. Most of our employees like each other, some don't, a few hate each other. There are personnel issues that come up. Accounting/financial/payroll issues take up boatloads of time.

We try to solve problems we know are upcoming, we solve problems we didn't know were upcoming, and we solve problems that are tiny and easily remedied. We also work through gargantuan and mind-numbing problems that sometimes don't have any clear answer. We do our best based on our analysis of that situation, at that time.

All of our employees report to Lacey, Tory, me, or Grandma. I am involved with all pieces. I don't micromanage, but I manage pretty tightly.

Then there's my grandma's expectations of me and the company. "All of our lingerie, all of our products must be perfect, don't ever lower that standard, Meggie. Never. *Everything must be perfect.*"

The thing is, I agree with Grandma. Everything we make must be perfect, down to the tiniest bow on panties or lace-trimmed garter. Perfection must prevail.

I am not real worried about hurting people's feelings while I turn this place over and revamp. We either get it together or all of us, including the women in the factory in Sri Lanka, who may or may not be able to line up something else, who may sink into poverty as soon as you can say the word *brassieres,* will lose their jobs.

I am fighting for the life of this company. I am fighting for my grandma's legacy, her employees, and her massive scholarship fund at the community college.

I am fighting. I am trying not to fail. Failure would not be acceptable to my grandma.

It really isn't that pleasant.

Falling in love with Aaron Torelli was like having my breath taken away, my heart lassoed, and my mind hijacked.

It was a rush. It was a thrill. It was like nothing I had experienced before.

We met in India. I was making a film about orphans living on the streets, and he was there with a crew making a film about Bollywood and the impact it had on the youth there. Amidst the cacophony, color, spices, cows, temples, squalor, rickshaws, and music, we met, smiled, and were in bed together in three days.

Aaron was magic. Heat, sensuality, intensity, and finely honed intellect all wrapped up in a tall, muscled package with longish black curls. He had a black feather tied into one of the curls and smoldering brown eyes that said, "I want you, you want me, it's all a matter of time." He was independent, free thinking, and had a smile that stopped my heart in its tracks.

He had been in the independent film business longer than I had, and he had made several films that had done well at indie film competitions. I had worked with another filmmaker recently in Watts on a film about kids trying to get out of Watts via education. I had also worked on a film in the Appalachian Mountains about the ingrained poverty there and had been involved in another film following veterans of the Vietnam War and how their lives had turned out.

I loved it. I lived for filmmaking. Filmmaking was part of my soul, as it was Aaron's.

We talked for hours. He was specific in his compliments of me and my work. "You understand how you have to dig deep, sometimes get dirty, get imbedded with your subjects to make a film . . . you know that your film can have a huge impact, for years, on other people . . . that your films can show our failure as a country, a society, a materialistic and selfish culture, the sickness of the world . . . did you know, Meggie, that you're the smartest woman I've ever met? It's like our brains are one, even though we just met. We're one, we're like a cosmic gift to each other."

I can honestly say I have never been as physically attracted to any man as I was Aaron. Chemical reactions? Brain waves? Zen goes sexy? Whatever you want to call it, it was there and sizzling. He started calling me My Meggie.

Our relationship wasn't even a whirlwind romance. It was as if I were picked up by a tornado of love and lust and flung through the eye of the storm and the only one there to catch me was him, with that endearing smile.

I was unprepared for his personality.

I was unprepared for the force of it, the charisma, the romantic aggression, the sweet words.

I fell hard.

I had never fallen like that before. I doubt I ever will again.

For that, I am grateful.

I saw Blake at his house as I drove home that night. He was on his wraparound deck, talking on the phone. I liked his house. I liked the classic, Oregon style to it. I liked all the lawn. I knew he had a view west, as his house was up on a hill, so he would be able to enjoy spectacular sunsets through towering pine trees.

I wondered what he did, where he worked.

It didn't matter much, though. What I wanted to do was to get lost in that body. I didn't want an intellectual connection, I didn't want an emotional connection, I didn't want the mess that comes with being involved with a man.

I never wanted to be involved with a man again in my life.

But I did want *him*.

Physically, that is.

I wanted relief. I wanted some time out. I wanted him to be for me alone, a time for fun and release, a sunny vacation, so to speak, in the midst of a life covered and flattened in stress.

I sizzled and simmered for that man.

I wanted the sizzling and simmering to help me forget.

She called and left a message on my cell phone. She was in contact with her attorneys. They would be calling me soon. She was suing me. I would be ripped down to nothing.

I sucked in air as waves of dizziness roared through, twirling me around and upside down. When my head cleared, I deleted the message.

"We need to do something to the Web site to make it more alluring," I said. "More fun, more intriguing, more depth, make the customer stay longer, buy more."

Lacey and Tory leaned over my shoulders at the table in my office. Lacey smelled vaguely like morning sickness. Tory had a musky, fruity perfume on. I would have to say I preferred Tory's scent.

"Our Web site doesn't need to be a sadistic bondage circus act," Tory protested, flicking her black hair back. "Or a bordello."

"No one said it did. It's not oomfy," Lacey said.

"What does oomfy mean?" Tory said. She was wearing a red dress with a ruffle. I tried not to dwell on the red or I'd start feeling sick.

"It means it's not catchy enough," I said. "We have to liven it up. Make it edgy but seductive, sexy but not slutty . . . a new setting behind the models, a new layout, new colors, maybe a theme." I kept studying the Web site, page after page. "Something radically, splendidly different...and we need to get our strawberry in there more."

"What do you think we should do?" Lacey asked.

"We have to sell our image, ourselves. We need to stand out against all these other lingerie companies who have so much more money than we do. The photos here of the models are what all our competitors use. Tall, way too-skinny, anorexic-looking young women with bouncy chests and frowns modeling our stuff. They're frowning because they're hungry, probably."

"But we sell lingerie," Tory said. "We need the tall, skinny girls with bouncy chests. That way our customers buy into it. They want to *be* those girls. If they buy our stuff, they can trick themselves into thinking they'll look like our models."

"No one can look like a model. The models don't even look like models," I said. "You two know that because of all the shoots we've been on. They have good bones in their faces and they're thin. An army of stylists, perfect lighting, excellent photographers, and Photoshopping take care of the rest. It's false. It's a false image. False advertising, when you think about it."

"We aren't false advertising," Tory huffed.

"Sure we are. Women do not look like this in real life."

"Help me see inside your tricky brain, Meggie," Tory said. "No one wants to look at heavy or obese women or women with no chests, flabby stomachs, and cottage cheese thighs in lingerie. Brutal, but true."

I flicked to the last page of the Web site. "No, they don't. But we have to give this a makeover. It's not working."

Lacey darted for the bathroom, red curls flying behind her.

Tory was quiet for a second, but I could feel her anger careening around the room, prickly and hard. "You come in here and want to change the whole company, strip it down and re-build it, Meggie."

"I wouldn't rebuild if things were working."

"And you're the lingerie genius, Miss Brilliant Panties, Thong Woman. Hail to Meggie, even though you've been gone for years." She threw her arms up. "You're an arrogant know-it-all.

You don't even wear nice clothes. You don't even wear our newest lingerie. Your underwear is probably stained beige!"

She had me there. Except it was white. Old, white, unraveling. Yesterday I noticed my white underwear had a hole in it.

"Have you ever taken the time to appreciate what I did, Meggie? How hard I've worked? All I get from you is criticism and what I've done is wrong and you can do better and you're taking over and it's your way or the highway. Gee. Maybe I should have left the company for years to make a bunch of films and tramp around the world. Think you would have liked getting stuck here dealing with Grandma? With the factory? With all the employees? With a tanking economy?"

"I didn't say you did everything wrong, Tory. You've done a lot right. You're a talented designer, but the company is sinking—"

"And that's my fault." Tory's hands went to the waist of her red dress. Gall. Red still makes me so sick.

"No, a lot of it's the economy, but we need to rebuild Lace, Satin, and Baubles. We have to get excitement going again, reach a broad, younger customer base—"

"So you think I sucked at the excitement part." Those gold eyes shot bullets at me. "Scotty the slug-faced rectum idiot probably thought the same thing."

I paused on that colorful sentence for a sec as Lacey walked back in, listing slightly. "This isn't personal, Tory. It's not against you. I don't have time to sit around, have tea and crumpets, and say things gently about what needs to change here. We need to move fast. I'm being honest and blunt—"

"I'll be honest and blunt then, too. You're a steamroller. You're plowing me over. You have no sense of fashion, you're stick skinny and look like you're made of bones, your hair is a mess, and you act like a cold, controlling, premenopausal zombie."

"A zombie?"

"Here's the truth, since you're always criticizing me." Tory crossed her arms. "I don't know if you're mentally and emotionally healthy enough to run this business."

"Mentally and emotionally healthy enough?" Whew. Now my latent fury was awakened. "Well, you may have me there."

She flipped her black hair back. I wanted to pull it out of her head. I stood up and faced off with her. "Okay, Tory, let me give you a rundown of where the company is exactly, then you can decide if I'm mentally and emotionally healthy enough to handle the responsibilities here."

Analytically, like a living computer, I evaluated our designs and products; which ones were selling and which weren't; where marketing, sales, and PR were falling down; and where we were too heavy as a company and not streamlined enough. I discussed our catalogue and Web site, then I talked about how we should have had a larger share of the market by now, been in more major department stores, and how that could have been accomplished.

I dove headfirst into the financial predicament that Lace, Satin, and Baubles had sunk into, detailing all the numbers in our financial reports, the assets we had, our mind-blowing debt, and how much salaries and benefits were costing us. I talked about the stability and problems of our factory overseas, those costs, and our own restricted cash flow. I told her our net worth, to the penny, and predicted exactly what day we'd shut our doors.

When I was done, Tory looked stunned. Anytime she'd tried to interject, I'd shot her down and annihilated her arguments.

Lacey was grinning. That was not nice, and I'm sure it only made Tory feel more isolated, two sisters against one. I glared at Lacey. "Tory, we can reinfuse this company or we can kiss it good-bye. You are making over $200,000 a year. Do you want to lose that salary?"

"I won't lose it."

I leaned forward. "You will. You are going to lose that money. We have months to turn this company around, and if you don't get on board, if you put up roadblocks, if you do anything to stand in my way, we will close this place, lock the doors, and sell off the inventory. There will be nothing left."

She went pale.

"The thought of losing $200,000 bugs you, doesn't it? Those heels cost $350, don't they? That dress is another $500. It's all going to go, Tory. All of it. Now my head is messed up and I have been wandering the world. I am the first to admit that I am not a paragon of emotional or mental health. I am still semi-crazed. So what? There are brilliant people all over this country who have mental health issues and they are still highly functioning.

"I can get back out there and wander some more, if you want. I can walk out and leave you with this disaster. Frankly it appeals. I liked Montana. Mexico, too. But I don't want to walk out, because I care about our employees. I care about Grandma, her time in a strawberry field, and saving the company for her so she knows her legacy, to her family, to her employees, to this community, and to her scholarship fund, will outlast her. It's what she wants. I care about this company because I think one day Hayden will run it. We will then have a company that is run by four generations, and that's something our family can be proud of."

Tory fidgeted in her ruffled red dress. She ran a hand through her hair. She had lost some of her fight. I tried to shut out that red.

"So, say the word, Tory. Tell me that I'm not mentally or emotionally stable enough to run this show and I'll get up and leave."

"I'm trying to express," she said, her voice weaker but still snobby, "that I know this business and you don't. Things have changed since you left—"

"You clearly don't know it well enough," I snapped. "If you did, this place would be making a profit instead of losing money like diarrhea. You know the design end of it. That's your forte. It's your talent and your gift. I know the whole business better than I know my own face. There is not a department I haven't been in, and run, and you know it. Are you in or out?"

"I can't let you come in here and push me around."

I eyed her carefully. I decided to call her bluff. I was tired anyhow. The rats came and got me every night, crawling inside my body and making me bleed with their sharp teeth. Last night I thought I heard Aaron calling me from my bedroom closet and

I actually got up and opened the doors to check, one hand up to protect myself.

I stood, grabbed my brown, saggy purse, and headed out. Quick as she could sprint on four-inch red heels, Tory was up and leaning against the door.

"Okay, Meggie," she said. "Go for it. It's on your head."

"Thanks for that image. I will go for it, but I want you out of my way."

"You can't fire me."

"You're not fired." I took a deep breath. "Honestly, Tory, there is no one better to represent our lingerie to the public. You're a rebel. You're cool. And I have loved the vast majority of your designs, but we have to do something different here and you have to be open to it. There's a good saying out there: 'Lead, follow, or get out of the way.' The employees in your design department are not following you. They don't like you. They quit and throw fits. You must be more respectful to them. You must lead as you allow them to create. And if you won't follow me, I will leave. Your choice."

She glared at me.

She knew I'd won.

I do not like red.

I didn't move for a full five minutes after Lacey and Tory left, then cracked open my morning beer and opened a bag of dried apricots and a box of chocolates for breakfast. I did not get any pleasure in "winning" against Tory.

I could see how she would think I was being an arrogant know-it-all. Grandma asked me to come home, so did Lacey. Tory didn't. I came in, Grandma crowned me CEO, I insisted on changing things, I fired employees, I addressed the employees, I initiated planning for a fashion show, I was rebuilding from the ground up and questioning and criticizing everything that had been done previously.

I took over. I had to, but I sure hadn't done it with much tact and I'd done it with zero appreciation for Tory and her hard work.

Zero.

She's a talented designer, there's no question of that. Most of her designs had been enormous moneymakers.

I ran a hand through my hair. It became stuck in a ball of tangles. I needed to get my hair cut.

I needed to apologize to Tory, first. She has a mouth that won't stop. She can be rude and argumentative. She can be arrogant and showy.

Underneath it, that woman is quivering and sad, and it's not only because of losing Scotty and how that chips away at her heart each day.

I know what happened to her, and I know she has never felt like she belonged.

Feeling like you don't belong will turn you into someone you're not proud of.

I wondered how long it had been since I told Tory that I loved her.

I brushed my fingers through my curls before I left for his house. It was still a mess. I had no makeup on. I looked at my T-shirt. It was saggy blue. My jeans were too big. I was in pink flip-flops. I should get something else on that was nicer.

I paused. I didn't have anything else nicer. This was it. I had left the clothes Grandma gave me at the office in my closet.

I put my chin up.

I was not going to get all gussied up for one short visit to Blake's house. I had already changed once for a man. I changed my appearance, my personality, my goals, my life. I would not change one ounce of myself again until I damn well felt like it.

This is how I dress. This is me now. I'm not happy with it, but I am not going to do stuff to my face and clothes so I can appeal to some man, even a cowboy-rancher type I wanted to sleep with. It's against who I believe I should be—which is a woman who is finally in charge of her own screwed-up life.

I turned and stomped out of my tree house, down the steps, and headed to Blake's, my chin still up, my heart tripping and thudding like a crazy thing.

*   *   *

"Hello, Blake."

He grinned at me and seemed so pleased. Surprised, but pleased. It was almost nine o'clock at night.

"Hello, Meggie. Come on in."

"No, thank you."

"Please. I'm having dinner. Chinese takeout."

He opened the door wide and held out his arm. I took a quick peek but didn't move off the porch. His home was manly inside. It was an older Craftsman but had obviously been fairly recently remodeled. The kitchen cabinets were white, the wood floors shone, the lighting was soft. There were tons of windows and wide trim, white walls, clean. Not too clean and neat—that would be weird—but nice.

He had the leather furniture and reclining leather chair one would expect of a man, and of course the big-screen TV, which was playing some sort of sports game.

"I ordered too much," he said. "Help me eat it."

He was a sexy sequoia. A broad-shouldered oak tree. A mysterious banyan tree. I had no idea why I was thinking in terms of trees looking at him.

"Thank you, but no. The reason I came over is that I see you haven't had your truck fixed that I bashed, and I called my insurance agent and he said you hadn't made a claim, so I wanted to make sure that you hadn't lost my insurance card, or if you didn't know of an auto body shop to send it to, I know of a good one."

And, by the way, I would like to take your clothes off with my teeth. I am so glad I didn't say that out loud.

"I'm getting to it."

"You're getting to it?"

"Yes, haven't had time yet. Been a bit busy at work."

"Can I . . . can I help you? I can drive the truck anywhere you want to get it fixed, then I can drive it back here when they're done. Oh, ugh. You probably don't trust my driving. I understand. I can arrange to have it picked up."

He kept smiling at me. "I trust your driving and I want you to come in for Chinese food."

"And I . . . can't."

"Can't?"

"Right. That's the word for it."

"Why not?"

I decided to be honest. "You are too gorgeous to eat Chinese food with."

He raised his eyebrows and laughed. "Thank you. Nice to hear. You can't eat Chinese food with men you think are gorgeous?"

"I can't eat Chinese food with you. You remind me of a fortune cookie."

"I like fortune cookies. Why do I remind you of one?"

"Because you're very edible." No, I wasn't embarrassed about this. I should have been. I am too miserable to be embarrassed.

He laughed again, and those eyes glinted as eyes will when two people know they're attracted to each other. "I think that's all the more reason for you to come in and eat fortune cookies with me. There's two."

"I'm going to skip it because I'd rather not make a fool of myself tonight."

"Why would you make a fool of yourself?"

"Because I like you and Tuesdays are my night to make a fool of myself."

"I'm glad you like me. Too bad Tuesdays are a problem. Come on in anyhow."

"Nope. Nope to you and your deliciousness and to the fortune cookies. If you need help getting your truck to wherever you need it to go, let me know. Happy to help." I turned to go. "I feel guilty whenever I see that thing with its dent."

"Does guilt come easy to you?" He asked it jokingly. I didn't take it as a joke.

"Guilt lives with me," I said. "Good night, Blake."

"I'll let you have all the shrimp if you eat with me."

This time I laughed, my laugh rising into the leaves of his oak trees. "Wouldn't want to take that from you, sex god. See ya."

I was burning up for that man. But I was getting an idea of what kind of man he was. I don't think he wanted what I wanted.

That was gonna be a problem.

"I'm sorry, Tory."

I stood in Tory's office. Her walls are light pink, like mine, except for one, which she painted gold and hung a collection of gold-framed mirrors on. She, too, has a spectacular view and a pink fainting couch. She also has two long tables, together, that are piled high with fabrics—silks, satin, cotton, lace, etc.—and design plans, folders, colored and charcoal pencils, and pads of paper.

One pink wall is almost completely filled with designs for lingerie that she's drawn. She has three wire mannequins, a sewing machine, and a white desk like mine. She has white shelving crammed with more fabrics and framed pictures of models wearing her designs.

"What are you sorry for?" Tory snapped. She wasn't in a pleasant mood.

"I'm sorry for taking over like a steamroller. I'm sorry for acting like I'm Miss Brilliant Panties. I'm sorry for my attitude since I arrived, how I haven't been friendly enough, and I'm sorry for leaving you and Lacey here."

"Alone with Grandma, General Battle-Ax." She leaned a hip against her desk.

"Yes, alone with Grandma, Mrs. Warm and Friendly."

"Who doesn't think I do anything right."

"She does, Tory. She told me so when I was gone, and I told you what she said." I had. Grandma had complimented both Tory and Lacey. "Have you not heard how she talks to me? Yesterday she told me I was having an 'efficiency problem' and was a poor role model for style, which was not surprising, and that I was acting like a general in the army with a stick up her butt, which is almost hilarious because she's the one who said it."

"I feel like . . ." Tory bit her lip. "I felt like she only wanted you home, that I wasn't as good as you, as smart, as creative, not enough like her."

"Grandma wanted me home to be with you and Lacey. She wants us together. She's made no secret of that, ever."

"She wants you to run the business. You, Miss Brilliant Panties."

"You have never wanted to run it, Tory, you've told me that many times. You've wanted to be on the creative side, the designing. You wanted to represent Lace, Satin, and Baubles, you didn't want to run this place. That's the ugly part, the numbers part, the personnel, the manufacturing and distribution, the details."

She shrugged. "You're right, I didn't. But I didn't need to hear it subtly and not so subtly that you're the buzzing queen bee in her mind for running this place."

"But you made it clear you didn't want the job to her, too. One time you told her, 'Grandma, I would rather walk naked through Siberia than be CEO.' "

"I did. I'd do it, too."

"And you also told her that running the company could be compared only to having your toenails ripped off by a knife-wielding gargoyle. You said that being president would ruin your hair and your nails, and your vagina would dry up."

She smiled, faintly. "I did. I can't have my vagina drying up."

"She wanted me home to do the job because you and Lacey don't want it. Lacey has three kids. Now she's pregnant. You think Grandma's easy on me? She's not. During my year of wandering I heard from her often about how I wasn't meeting my responsibilities, what was I, a weak woman, she and Mom hadn't raised me to be weak, I'd had time off, now I needed to get my bra fastened, my panties untwisted, my thong out of my crack— her words—and come home. She can be a beast. But I am sorry, Tory, for how I've been."

"Thank you. I deserve that apology. You've been incredibly difficult, and it's been hard to put up with you." She sounded haughty and superior and did not apologize for how she'd been. I didn't expect her to. She knew I didn't expect it, so we let it go.

"I love you, Tory."

The tears poured from her eyes, her shoulders shook, and I had to hug her until she was done. It was her way of apologizing.

"On another subject," she said, shoulders back now, tough girl expression firmly in place as she mopped up with a tissue. "I know how to take revenge on Scotty."

"Revenge on Scotty? Why are you taking revenge?"

"Because," she said, pacing her office, hands on her hips. "Because"—her voice choked up—"he . . ." She punched the air, and I knew she was thinking of her punching bag at her condo. "He had a . . ." She took another swing, her face miserable and superticked. "He had a date last Saturday night and that pissed me off!" She swung a fist through the air again. "It pissed me off!"

"But you left him. You walked out of your house. You've dated several men."

She reeled on me and pointed her finger. "I only went to dinner with them so I could tell Scotty and make him jealous and come get me. That doesn't mean that *he* can do it, Meggie! So I'm taking revenge. Are you in or out?"

"I think I'll be in."

"Splendid." She high-fived me. "I love the vengeful side of myself."

"The boat sank."

"What?"

"The boat sank with our order on it," Lacey said, her red curls bopping, face flushed. "The crew was rescued by an American tanker going by, but all of the merchandise is gone. Sunk. Drowned. Bottom of the sea. The bras may end up on the coast of New Zealand or China or Greenland one day, or a shark may be caught with our push-up bra wrapped around its chest. Does a shark have a chest? An octopus may be able to poke his tendril things into our thongs, but women will never wear that shipment."

I stood up and leaned my head against the cool window of my office. Mount Hood was invisible in the distance. It was raining. It was getting colder. Soon it would be ski season. I would not be skiing. I wish Mount Hood would quit reminding me of that.

Lacey leaned back, her hands above her hips. "Shoot, shoot, shoot."

"I can't believe this."

"Me either. It wasn't the whole order, though. We'll have more come in, not a complete disaster."

I was trying to save Lace, Satin, and Baubles.

I had a sunken ship. We were literally a sinking lingerie ship. I did not miss the sad irony.

I went to the mini fridge in my office. "I wish you could share this beer with me, Lacey."

"Hayden!" I stood up to hug Lacey's second-oldest child when he ambled into my office. "Now my day is wonderful."

"Hey, Aunt Meggie!" He gave me a huge hug.

"It's good to see you." Hayden was wearing sky blue pants, white tennis shoes, and a white shirt. His brown hair was back in its usual ponytail, highlighting his delicate features. I felt myself getting all choked up. *This was the kid who said he felt like killing himself.* "How ya doin'?"

"I'm doing okay." He looked me in the eye, then down. I felt bad. There was no reason for him to look down when he looked at me, or anyone else. "Mom told you about me, right?"

"Yes. I love you as a boy or girl, Hayden. Always have, always will."

He sniffled, wiped his cheeks. He has the prettiest blue eyes. "Thanks, Aunt Meggie, I figured you would understand."

"I do." I did. A little bit I didn't. I was struggling. You can't accept that your nephew is your niece overnight. These things take time. It's not the easiest thing. I stopped for a minute. If it was hard for me to fully understand, how had it been for poor Hayden?

"I'm sorry I didn't tell you when you first came home, Aunt Meggie, that I've waited all this time, but you know I love you."

"Hayden, it's for you to tell me, or anyone else, for that matter, when *you* want to. This is your business. Come and sit down, sweets."

After some prodding, and a few more tears from those blue eyes, he opened up. "I've always been a girl in my head, you know, Aunt Meggie. I didn't want to be a boy. I remember I cried looking at my penis when I was three and I realized Cassidy didn't have one. I didn't want that there. I wanted to look like a girl. It was like this thing hanging between my legs, it felt weird, like it was in the wrong place, wrong body. . . . I've always felt in my head, like, I'm a lie."

"You're not a lie, Hayden. You are who you are. You were born a boy physically, but you are a girl. I'm sorry, honey, for everything you've been through, all this pain, the confusion, the stress . . ." *And please don't kill yourself, honey. Please. Oh, please.*

"I haven't worked out what I'm going to do. I've been thinking about switching schools and going to the new school as a girl, but I don't know. With Facebook and Twitter the kids at the new school would probably find out anyhow. And I like my friends here, even though everybody thinks I'm gay." His voice cracked. "I feel like I can't hide myself any longer and myself is a girl, you know? I have to act like a boy and I'm not a boy. I hate the secret. I hate that I have to hide my own self every day just because other people can't handle who I am. Does that make sense?"

"Yes. You're an exceptionally brave person, Hayden."

"Thanks. I don't feel brave. Mostly I feel scared to death. I have two and a half more years of high school, and I don't want to get beaten up all the time."

I put my arm around his shoulders. "Take karate."

He laughed, as I knew he would. "Yeah, karate. I can be a girl who karate chops anyone in her way."

"Not a bad way to be, is it?"

He laughed. "Nope. It's not."

"I love you, Hayden." *Please. Not another thought about killing yourself. Never, please.*

"Thanks, Aunt Meggie. I love you, too."

"Tell me what you're working on right now for the company."

His eyes lit up. "I've got the best idea for this frilly nightgown. You wanna see it? I sketched it out in drama class. It'll be fabulous, conforms to curves but lets a woman move to her own beat, too."

Hayden is a gifted, rockin' designer. He has an instinctive knowledge of what women want to wear when they go to bed. And no, it's not all sexy. Most of it is comfortable, fun, and in Hayden's words "snazzy and adorable."

I saw the designs. I laughed. They were perfect.

Hayden thinks like a woman. I hugged him.

Honey, please don't kill yourself. Nothing on earth is worth that. I could not live through it.

We love you. With everything we have, we love you.

Tory can be torrentially vengeful, and the revenge she planned against Scotty because he had the temerity to take a woman out on a date was, in her words, "phallically mind altering."

"I'm not going to tell you what I'm doing, Meggie. It's a secret. My horoscope said I would surprise even myself, and I have. You and Lacey will get a front-row seat to my deliciously medieval and evil plan." Tory sat on top of the conference table and shifted pink silk from one hand to the other. Lacey lay back on the pink fainting couch, looking ill. Her stomach grew by the day. I put my ratty tennis shoes up and leaned back in my chair.

"How is it deliciously medieval?" I asked.

"Let's say it's a long lick and it sucks and leave it at that."

"No one, like Scotty, is going to die, are they?" Lacey asked, an ice pack on her head, but she didn't seem that worried.

"Nope. I promise. If he died, I wouldn't be able to be deliciously medieval again and that would ruin my future revenges. You'll both come?"

I liked Scotty. Tory would be hell to live with. She's temperamental, difficult, and constantly needs Scotty to prove he loves her, adores her, and will never leave. She has deep-seated abandonment issues, which anyone who knows her story understands. Even Scotty understands.

She has a happy family one day, living with parents who adore her, and the next day, at five years old, she has no family, lost in a bloody, mangled car wreck, in which she's a passenger. Her parents are dead and she's an orphan. In her young mind, she's been abandoned.

I remember when Tory came to live with us in my mother's Snow White house. She slept in my bed, or Lacey's bed, or our mother's bed, each night for a year and cried. She clutched a purple dinosaur from her father and a yellow lion from her mother. She still has them.

My guess is that Scotty is utterly exhausted by Tory continually slamming out of their house and having to beg her to come back. He probably wants to see if she does love him and if she's mature enough to work things out. I don't blame him.

But Tory's my sister, so I'll stand by her. Besides, I was most definitely curious about the deliciously medieval and evil plan. "I'll go with you," I said.

"Wouldn't miss it," Lacey said, putting an ice pack over her face. "I bore my own self to death and this will add excitement to my life."

I hoped the medieval and evil plan did not end in any arrests.

8

∽

"Lance, can I talk to you?"

"Sure, Meggie. Hey, how you doin'? Are you all still coming to Sarah's birthday party on Saturday?"

I assured him that all of us, including Grandma, but not my mother, as she was still on her book tour, would be there.

"Great! Can't wait! Your mom already called me. She sent Sarah a five-foot-tall dollhouse. Sarah loves it. I'm barbequing. Some of my army pals are coming, too. Bart recently was released from the hospital, lost his left leg, below the knee, from a bomb outside of Kandahar, but he's up and at 'em, his wife says. You remember Bart from high school?"

I sure did. "Lance, I have a delicate and difficult question to ask you. . . ."

Hey. My name is Lance Turner.

Meggie asked me to be on this video for Lace, Satin, and Baubles, so I'm gonna do it because Meggie and I go way back, but man. Talking about bras? I'm a man. I don't wear bras. I'm a real man. Hunting. Fishing. Football. Army. I'm an army man. A veteran.

But my wife wears pretty bras. Like pink. Blue. I don't let her wear no white bras, though. Never. NO white bras. Not in my house, not on her. She does what I tell her on that. She knows why I don't like it.

I like when she doesn't wear a bra at all. She's got the best rack. Yeah, you should show Marina this video. Hey, Marina, no bras, wife, okay? I mean, when the wife's at home, why does she wear one? Probably the kids. She wants to look proper.

She's the best wife, and it's not easy being married to me with all my Afghanistan problems and flashbacks. I've suffered from depression, anger, anxiety, panic attacks. Shit, all of it.

But Marina, man, she knows what to do with me. I start getting uptight, my thoughts go crazy fast, I'm restless, I'm angry, she wraps her arms around me and gives me a hug, and a lot of times I get way more than a hug. She's way friggin' better than the counseling I was getting. That guy, he didn't get it. He'd never even served. Made me feel like I was a specimen to study, not a man.

Marina knows I need some lovin', her lasagna, the kids running around, that's what's getting me better. And the job here. No kidding. Your grandma she . . . okay, this is embarrassing. I shouldn't start crying over your grandma, Meggie. She saved my life when she let me live with her during high school. You know she did. Give me a minute off camera. Shut it off for a sec. Embarrassing to be crying. I'm a man. . . .

Okay, I'm back. So you want a bra story for your video? I got a story about a bra. And it makes me angry. Pisses me off. It's about a woman I saw in Afghanistan. We had a mission. It was late, dark, we were in a village. We'd heard that the enemy was convening at a house. So we've got all our gear on, guns are ready, and we blast into this house. Two of the men stand up and start shooting, so we shoot back.

When the dust clears, those men are full of holes, one of our guys is down and bleeding, and there are two kids and two women dead. The other women and kids are screaming and holding each other. One of the women who died, her burqa was ripped open and I could see her bra. It was pretty. Had all this lace. Bright white. Totally clean, you know? Except for the blood. The blood on that white bra. I'll never forget it. Bright red blood, some black in there, too. One of her kids crawled up on her, crying, getting blood all over herself. The kid was probably three.

So we killed a mother. A mother. Damn. Sorry. Trying not to cry here. I regret so friggin' much. The guys who shot back, yeah, they were terrorists. Early twenties. But they don't know better there. There's no education. All they do is read the Koran in school and shout, "Down with America." That hatred is programmed. Girls are smothered. They follow some violent leader.

I try to shut off what happened over there, but I can't. All the stuff happening in front of my eyes, the bombs and gunfire, all that I took part in because I was told it had to be done. I still hear it, still smell it, still feel it. But this is what I know: War kills whatever is in its path. It's a killing of the body and a killing of the mind. See what happened to my head? See that dent?

We can't force another country to change. We can't force Iraq and Afghanistan to be us. They don't want to be us. They hate us. We can't force them to be modern and normal. They don't want to be modern. They don't know what normal is.

What we need to do is get out of there so other men aren't haunted by a dead mother's white bra stained with blood and her kid climbing on top of her screaming. That's what we need to do. And that's why my wife is not allowed to wear a white bra. Any other color, okay. Or, no bra. I think I said I like it when she wears no bra a minute ago, but I can't remember. She can't wear white.

That's what I know about bras, Meggie. I feel like I'm gonna have another panic attack thinking about that mother. That's war for you. She wasn't a threat to us, but we were to her, and a bunch of kids have no mom now in Afghanistan. My kids have a mom who makes lasagna. Did I say that Marina bakes lasagna? But that mom won't cook anymore for her kids. How fair is that?

Yeah, I'm crying again, so we gotta end this video now, Meggie. Right now. Tell your grandma I love her when you see her. I told her yesterday, but you tell her today. Are you coming to Sarah's party on Saturday?

9

Lacey, Tory, and I met at my tree house on Sunday evening. It was a clear night, the moon gold and orange, the leaves hugging my house starting to turn butter yellow and scarlet red.

We drove out to Tory's ex-home. I took my dull gray car and Tory took her car, a Porsche like Grandma's, in case Lacey became tired and needed to leave. Tory's home is on an acre plot in the country with white flowering cherry trees lining a long drive to the front door. Her ex, Scotty, was not home, but he would be in a few hours. He was on a business trip and his plane was arriving late.

Tory's yellow home with white gingerbread trim all over, the one she'd slammed out of months ago, was true country style, down to the white picket fence. A white deck surrounded the front of the house, with five rocking chairs and a porch swing. She had a polygonal tower, a red front door with a glass oval cut out in the middle, and three dormer windows.

We squished into Tory's Porsche in the driveway as she declared, "I hate Scotty."

I held her hand.

"It was Scotty who wanted to live in the country. He loves the smell of his lavender and his tomatoes and carrots and lettuce and corn and stupid cucumbers. He loves that vegetable garden. We could have fed half of Asia. I married a farmer. Farmer Scotty, I called him. Mean man. And look at my house! I don't get to live in my house anymore!"

"You left him and the house," Lacey said.

"Are you sure you want to take revenge on him?" I said. "Maybe you should take him to dinner."

"He's already dating some other slut girl. Of course I'm sure!"

"By the way, Tory," Lacey said. "How did you even know he had a date?"

"Because." Tory had that stubborn expression on her face.

"Because . . ." I prompted.

"Because I know these things."

"Someone told you?" Lacey said.

"I know these things, spiritually. I'm a Pisces. We're intuitive. Almost prophetic. We feel things in the air, in others' auras."

"Ah." It clicked. "You knew he was going out on a date because you're a spiritual Pisces. That explains it perfectly."

"You're still stalking him, aren't you?" Lacey said.

"I'm not *stalking* him." She slammed a hand on the steering wheel. "I drive by the house sometimes to make sure it's okay and to make sure no other woman is cooking in my kitchen. *My kitchen,* my copper pans. I designed it and I don't want her in there."

"I think he asked you to stop stalking him, didn't he?" I said, but I knew the answer.

"He said if you're going to stalk me, come home. He should be begging me. And what? He's the boss of me? My revenge will make him think twice before he goes out on another date with a bimbo slut doctor."

"How do you know she's a doctor?" I asked.

Tory glanced away. "I already said. I know because I'm a Pisces and smart with auras."

"And the truth is?" Lacey said.

Tory tried to appear self-righteous, then gave in grumpily. "I introduced myself to his date at the French restaurant."

"You what?" Lacey asked.

I sucked in my breath and pictured that pretty little scene. Scotty and the woman sitting down in some fancy candlelit place. Tory appearing, like a squawking bat out of hell. "You must be joking. No, of course you're not. You stalked him. You waited for him to leave his house, you followed him to the restaurant, you watched him meet another woman, and you went and sat down at their table and said hello."

"I'm friendly," Tory said, chin out.

"Ah, yes. That's the word we would all use to describe you," Lacey said. "Along with demure and shy. Did you do anything else at the table?"

"I ordered shrimp. I like shrimp."

"You sat at their table, with them, and ordered shrimp," I confirmed. "Did Scotty ask you to leave?"

"Yes, he did." Her brows drew together.

"And you didn't," Lacey said.

"No. His eyes were sad and I didn't want to leave him sad. Plus, I wanted to tell the bimbo slut doctor what I thought of her."

"Oh. You. Didn't." Lacey slapped a hand to her forehead.

"And you told her . . ." I said.

"I told her that Scotty was still married, and the stethoscope Barbie nodded and said she knew that we were separated. I told her that I thought her boobs were fake, that mine were much better, that her nose went off at a slant, she seemed uptight, and I didn't like the color she was wearing."

"What color was she wearing?" I asked.

"Red. It wasn't her color. She looked like a blood clot."

"You didn't tell her that."

Tory nodded. "I did."

Lacey and I sat in silence for a sec, absorbing that tidbit.

"What did Scotty do?"

"He was angry," Tory mused. "I liked seeing the anger. Some passion is still there. He hauled me out of the restaurant and I didn't even get to eat my shrimp. So now he's getting this"—she spread out her manicured nails—"gift. I had it specially made for him."

At that moment, our friend Lola D'Andreau drove up in her roaring blue truck. We went to high school with her. She's a renowned wood carver. Coming up behind her was her friend

Keeter in his cement truck. He brought a couple of muscly friends with him. One was named Trucker, the other was named William.

We all stood around, chatting under the gold and orange moon, until Keeter said, "Let's get this baby up."

Tory took them to a spot in the front yard and pointed. While the men went back to the trucks for their equipment, Lacey, Tory, and I went around to the back of Lola's truck to see the "gift." Lola threw her arms out, as if presenting a work of priceless art. In fact, she even singsonged, "Ta da! Ta da!"

"It's not . . ." I asked, almost breathless.

"It couldn't be . . ." Lacey said, then covered her mouth and laughed.

"*It is.*" I laughed, oh, how I laughed. It was mean and naughty, and Scotty didn't deserve it, but I bent over double I laughed so hard.

"I think that Scotty will understand the symbolism," Tory said. "He's a Sagittarius. They're quick, decisive, literate. Scotty likes literature. He'll link the two. Good job, Lola."

"Thank you." She put a hand to her chest. "I'm proud of it."

First, Lola, Keeter, and company set up lights outside so they could see. Then they dug a hole in the front yard. Next they poured in quick-dry cement. Finally Lola, Keeter, Trucker, William, Tory, and I carried the wood carving to the cement. It was very, very heavy. We put the "stub" of the wood carving, about two and a half feet of wood, in first. The stub would hold the "art" steady in the ground into the next millennium.

When we were done, the gold and orange moon had moved, the stars were bright, and Tory spread her arms out wide and shouted, "We now have an artistic masterpiece! A modern art symbol of my relationship with Scotty, the overgrown, bubble-butted squid!"

Lola glowed with pride, her hands together as if in grateful prayer. She bowed slightly. "Thank you, Tory. I worked so carefully on it, every inch, every curve and groove, to make it realistic."

"It's impressive, Lola," I said. "It's good to take pride in your work."

"You should win an award," Lacey said, in all seriousness, then she laughed.

Keeter said, hands on his hips, "I feel inadequate. Small."

Lacey said, "That's what got me knocked up."

William said, "The moon shines upon it, glowing, ethereal, soft and gentle, illuminating its inner core of natural tree beauty and the secrets of the ages within."

Lacey raised her eyebrows.

"William's a poet," Lola said helpfully. "In touch with his manhood."

Trucker said, "We're gonna be famous. Ain't nothing done like this before."

Tory danced around it, arms out. "No one would have the balls to do this except for me."

I stroked Lola's masterpiece.

The wood carving was seven feet tall.

The wood carving was *a penis.*

Lola had carved on the penis, "My name is Scotty. I am a dick."

Yes, a dick. Lola had carved a dick, commissioned by Tory.

It was now cemented into the middle of Tory and Scotty's front lawn, glowing under the lights, as William, the poet, had noted.

"Moonlight, starlight, blue jays call, majesty, royalty, it has no balls," William intoned.

We heard sirens in the distance.

We didn't think they had anything to do with us.

We were wrong.

A neighbor had called the police. Her name is—this is not a joke—Gladys. Gladys is eighty-two years old. Tory is friends with her. Tory kept an eye on her when she lived here and continues to check on her. Gladys has no children and a small home she's lived in all her life. This whole area was once owned by her family, who were farmers, before she sold part of it to a developer. I don't know what she's done with the cash, because her house isn't it great shape, but she's a multimillionaire.

Her vision isn't good without her glasses, so that night when she peered across the street to Tory's house, seeing the lights off inside but people outside, she thought she was seeing, as she put it to the 911 operator, "burglars standing around in a circle on the front lawn, having a séance and building a rocket ship."

The police came to stop, I'm sure, the séance.

Gladys said to us later, "Dears, I'm so sorry. Had I known you were installing impressionistic body art in your yard I would have come to help. You know I'm an artist myself. Oh, by the way, I love your new bra, the Squish and Squeeze. It really does squish and squeeze, doesn't it? Look here. Tory brought me the magenta one." She pulled up her shirt. Lacey and I admired how our Squish and Squeeze bra squished and squeezed.

Gladys showed two of the police officers her Squish and Squeeze, too, after introducing herself as the woman who reported that the rocket ship had landed in front of the burglars. We think there may be a tiny slice of dementia moving into Gladys's brain. She called the police officers "dears," too. They were surprised at being flashed, but they were gentlemen.

"They made the Squish and Squeeze!" She pointed at Lacey, Tory, and me.

Not only did the police come, the police chief of Portland came, too. As I understood it, the chief likes to go out on calls with his officers to keep himself up to date on what's going on in this fine city of Portland.

Eventually there were six police cars on Tory's property. Six. Word spread.

I later learned the words from headquarters were: Giant penis on the loose.

And "Man's yard attacked by penis."

And "Penis Invasion. All cars report."

And "Approach with caution. Penis response: unpredictable. Be ready to take down penis."

One more: "Consider the penis to be armed and dangerous. Taser first, no live shots."

The police, between laughing, were quite kind, once they found out that Tory was the owner of the house. They took photos with their cell phones. Tory posed in front of the penis at their request, her arms wrapped around it, one high heel kicked in the air, smile bright, black hair blown by the wind.

Tory said things like, "Husbands shouldn't be dicks," and "I'm a Pisces and we don't take any fish crap," and "I adore modern art."

The cops laughed again.

I put a hand to my head. I felt a headache speeding on, like in one of Gladys's rocket ships.

I like to learn new things. It's the academic nerd that lives within me. I like learning about new cultures, new insects found in jungles, new information about space and infinity, the history of the universe, etc.

I learned something new that night.

I learned Blake's occupation.

What is his occupation? What does the blond giant with the muscled arms and friendly smile do for a living? Blake Crighton is the police chief of Portland.

Yes, the chief.

Getting to work after only three hours of sleep was a torture. I didn't get in until nine.

Lacey wasn't there, and neither was Tory or Grandma. The production floor was humming louder than normal. I heard people laughing, the chatting loud. I skittered up the stairs because I did not want to talk, and poured myself a cup of coffee. I ate peanut butter and pecans for breakfast. My head was banging.

Abigail knocked and entered my office. "Heard you had an interesting evening."

"How did you know?" I dipped a pecan in the peanut butter.

"Word flies around town." She mimicked a bird flying, then burst into laughter, which she tried to suppress with no success.

"You make for a poor bird." I rolled my shoulders under my sweatshirt. Grandma would hate that I was wearing a sweatshirt to work. I hoped she would not come in today.

"It's on YouTube, you know."

My head whipped up, my hand jerking my coffee cup over. "You must be joking."

"Nope. It's getting more and more popular." Abigail stood on her toes, she was so excited. She bopped up and down.

"It's also online in different newspapers. Lace, Satin, and Baubles is mentioned many times, as in, 'Tory O'Rourke stands next to a seven-foot-tall wood penis'—is it actually seven feet tall, Meggie?—'that she planted in her estranged husband's front yard.' You have to read the rest, it's the best fun. Fantastic fun! Says she was mad at her husband for going on a date with a doctor who did not wear the color red well. There are people who can't wear red?" Abigail seemed baffled by this. "Should I not wear red?"

"You look good in red."

"I'll ask Tory," she said, my opinion clearly not counting. "She knows about fashion."

I groaned and placed my banging head on my desk.

"On a money note, it's great publicity, Meggie. The phones are ringing off the hook, people are calling, reporters, bloggers, even two talk shows here, and one in San Francisco, Los Angeles. . . . You have to call all these people right away. It'll help our sales."

"No. I will not be calling them. Say I am unavailable."

"Meggie, you can't. You have to take advantage of this."

"No, I don't. I'm leaving the press to Tory. She had a penis made, do you get that? This is now exclusively hers. I suppose everyone here knows? Obviously by your maniacal grin that's a dumb question, isn't it?" I needed my morning beer for my nerves. Perhaps I would pour my morning beer over my head.

"Impressively dumb, but yes! In fact we're constructing a penis in the middle of the production floor using Styrofoam to celebrate the uptick in sales. Get it, uptick? I made a joke. We're rising. Get that joke, too? Didn't you see our art?" She clapped her hands. "In honor of our reuse and recycling policy, we're wrapping bras we messed up around it. It's a brassiere penis."

"You've made a penis?"

"Sure have. With bras around it. The Petrelli sisters were extremely innovative." She tapped her temple. "They knew exactly what to do to make it look realistic. Eric carved the Styrofoam. We like it. Makes us laugh. Maybe we should take a photo of the Styrofoam penis and send it to the news outlets?"

"No. Oh, please. No."

I limped to the windows overlooking the production floor and pressed my forehead to the glass. Yep. There it was.

Ho ho ho.

The Petrelli sisters, Lance, Eric, Maritza, the Latrouelle sisters, and a bunch of the other rebels waved at me. Ho ho ho. Aren't they funny? I pushed my hair off my forehead, with both hands, the pain pinging around my cranium.

"Kalani's calling in a few minutes via Skype, Meggie, so turn on your computer and look at her smiling face and hear about her gas problems and black magic."

"No, nope." I grabbed my beer out of the mini refrigerator. "Not her. Not now. No way."

"You should talk to her. They're having problems with the Valentine line."

"Again?"

"Yes. Again."

"I think I'll get Cupid to shoot me."

"She's calling in now, I can hear Skype."

Lacey burst into my office, her red curls boinging about. No matter what she does, that red hair saves her. She always looks stylish and cute.

"Oh, save me! Save me! Have you seen YouTube?" She then went pale, leaned over, and rushed down the hall to the bathroom.

What would Grandma say?

It would be head banging, that was for sure.

"Hello, Kalani."

She beamed, waved both hands. "Ah, there you are, Meeegie! Good to see you!"

"You too. How are you?" As soon as the words "how are

you" were out of my mouth I wanted to pound my head on my desk, split it open, and, with blood dripping down my face, excuse myself. I was in for a long report.

"Oh, I good and I bad."

"What's wrong?" I wanted her to tell me about the Valentine line. I wanted to talk about the output, the materials, shipping . . . But first I had to be nice so I didn't hurt her feelings. One time she thought I was abrupt with her. She shut down Skype, didn't talk to me for two weeks, and told Tory I was a "mean blond mermaid."

"What wrong, what wrong?" Kalani wrung her hands. "You know I still cursed. That woman witch married to brother. First she give me rash, now I smell bad smells in the air. She do it to me."

"Your brother's wife made you smell bad smells in the air?"

"Ya. She do something to my nose. At my mother house last weekend, she touch my nose and now I smell bad smells. Yuck. I curse her. She curse me. My curse work. Her noodles too wet at dinner. I tell her. Your noodles too wet."

"I bet she didn't like that. Can we talk about the Valentine—"

"She so mad I say noodles too wet, she say bad words and leave kitchen. I do whole dinner myself." She threw up her arms in frustration.

"I'm sorry, so—"

"And also that man my boyfriend he tell me I marry him, I say no and we have the big fight. I say you bang bang me, you know that word, Meeegie, bang bang?"

"Yes." Oh, I sure knew that word today.

"But I no want other husband. I had husband. He bad, you know, move my nose wrong place on face—"

"Yes, I know and—"

"But boyfriend he bring ring. And he bring the flower. And he beg and cry but I say no. Tory say, you know Tory?"

"Yes, I believe I know who Tory is." A tall, wood penis soaring into the sky floated to mind.

"She say you be the boss of your life, Kalani. I stay free

woman. New word: freedom!" Kalani put her fists in the air in victory. "I say liberty. You know that word, liberty?"

"Yes I do." I gave in. "Would you be happier married to your boyfriend?"

"Ah, no. Then he try boss me around, tell me I his maid, I learn that from Tory, too. I no work all day then come home and be maid to husband. He tell me I no maid to him, he cook dinner, he shop food, but I say no. Hurt my heart, though, Meeegie, I tell you."

"I'm sorry, Kalani."

"Yeah. Me too." She brushed a tear off her cheek. "How you? You got boyfriend now?"

I thought of last night. "No. Definitely no boyfriend."

"Good thing. You have boyfriend, they beg you marry you say no and then you hurt heart."

We chatted more, and I heard about her sister's neighbor who has warts on her "left butt," and her mother who is battling with burps. I was finally able to angle her over to the problems she was having with the Valentine line.

Bras are tricky to make. You'd think we'd have it all down to a science, but things go wrong all the time. For example, bras have about twenty-five to thirty different pieces to them. Cup, wire, the wire channel to cover the wire, the pad, the fastenings, the rings and slides that have to be attached correctly on the straps, the back panel, etc. Also, bras are sewn within millimeters and there is no room for error. Colors can run, colors can bleed, colors may not match where they should, it's endless. All for a bra.

"Tell me, Kalani, what's going wrong?"

"Going wrong in factory? Oh yes. That. That. Okay, Meeegie. I tell you." She smiled brighter. "You see. We have small problem. Two small problem. See this pad?"

She held up a pad that would be in a bra. "Too small. Not right. We start over."

I groaned.

"Oh, Meeegie. No worry! Also one more problem. See, when

we put mold on for cup, color slides. Different colors each cup.
You see?" She smiled even brighter and held up two bra cups.
They were different shades of red. She bopped up and down as
if in celebration.

"That won't work, Kalani."

"Ya! I know, I know! Teeny one more problem. See this bra
lining that too thin?" She pulled her shirt off and her bra off—
one of ours, of course—and put the lining over her small boob.
"I put bra lining over my boobie and my nipple poke out still.
That not good. See nipple?"

"Yes, I see your nipple. No, that isn't good. You have to fix
that." The lining is important, especially if there's not padding.
You have to have enough lining in the bra so women's nipples
aren't coming first through the door, to put it crudely.

I put my fingers to my temples. *Bang, bang, bang.* I grabbed
my beer.

"That all. Small problems, Meeegie. Oh yeah. One more
problem." She poked one finger down toward her crotch. "I got
itchies in the ya ya place today. I think too hot here. I put ice on
me at lunch break."

"Sorry, Kalani." I was going to die. "Sorry about the itchies."

"Ya, but hey! Good news, too! I see that Tory on YouTube
this morning. You know that Tory?" I assured her, yet again,
that I knew Tory.

"That tall, you know, *doo de doo de da da,* what funny. La la
funny. You American women. You take that revenge. You get
back at the bad men. I like it. Tory, she say you take revenge
when man bad. And she did, she did! I proud of you, Meeegie! I
show all the ladies here! That our Meeegie and Tory and
Laceeey, I say! They like women on the Jersey show!" She put
her fists back in the air. "Liberty!"

I groaned.

"Freedom!"

"We have to milk this one," Tory said, her zebra-striped heels
tapping into my office, Lacey following her, clutching her stom-

ach. "I've already invited the media here. Want to talk to the media with me, Meggie, Lacey?"

"No," I said. I brushed a hand through my hair. Had hardly brushed it this morning. Note to self: Stay out of sight until all media are gone.

Lacey's face lit up. "Can I?"

"Yep. Get in there with me. There is nothing we could have done to raise sales like this, and I wasn't even thinking of that when I hired Lola. My horoscope was correct: I got a surprise."

Tory held a press conference at twelve o'clock on the production floor, Lacey standing next to her, all our employees behind her, next to their Styrofoam artwork covered in colorful bras, negligees, and panties.

Tory said, "My husband and I are estranged, but I thought we were working things out. When he went to a French restaurant with that . . . slu . . . stup . . . wh . . . that *woman* who should not be wearing red as it's not her color, and she had a boob job, I'm just saying, on a date, it hurt. All women know that hurt, don't they?"

Our employees dutifully shouted, "Yes!"

"I wanted him to know how I felt, and I said it in a way that he won't forget."

Laughter.

"It's still my house, and if I want modern phallic artwork in my front yard, I'll put it there."

Our employees cheered.

At the end of the questions, Tory held up several see-through, pink and black lacy negligees with ribbons. "Want to be a woman who stands up to life? Who plays hard and lives hard and loves hard? Do it in our negligees!" She wiggled her hips.

We sold out of those three almost immediately.

The press loved it, the online newspapers ran with it, the talk shows called for interviews, and the YouTube video continued to be quite popular.

And our sales.

Way, way up. As Tory predicted.

Tory had bought us some time.

I laughed out loud, then grabbed my head with both hands.

Abigail Chen thrust open the door to my office an hour after the press conference. "Incoming torpedo, ladies," she panted, eyes wide in fear. "And she's not happy. Up and at 'em!"

Tory, Lacey, and I jumped up.

I heard the *tap tap tap* of Grandma's heels.

I heard her swearing.

"Hello, Mrs. O'Rourke," Abigail said. "Nice to see you..."

"There is nothing nice about today," she said. "No calls, no interruptions."

Grandma swept in, resplendent in a shiny lavender dress. The baubles: diamonds. Hair: a perfect chignon.

She slammed the door so hard, I think the whole building shook.

"What *the hell* is going on?"

I didn't speak.

Lacey didn't speak.

Tory didn't speak.

We knew not to. Let her rant, *then* speak, unless she has invoked her scorched earth policy of shredding us, then leaving the room in a flurry of fury.

"I am trying to have one, *one,* relaxing day, and I hear laughing in the employee room of Midah's Spa and Salon. Midah had completed my hot rock massage and I am lying with cucumbers over my damn eyes, and there's *laughing,* then I hear your name, Tory"—she stabbed her manicured fingernail at Tory—"and I hear the name of our company, and I ask Midah what's going on."

Grandma, now and then, would take a day off to get her hair and nails done and get a massage. She did not like vacationing—"too boring"—and she didn't like relaxing. "What on God's green earth am I supposed to do while I'm relaxing? Relaxing makes me irritated." But she did like the occasional spa trip. I think it helped with the painful fairies plaguing her back.

"And Midah says, 'It's nothing, Mrs. O'Rourke. How about

a mimosa?'" Grandma mimicked Midah's high-pitched voice. "And I say, 'Do not lie to me, young woman. What is it?' She brings me a computer and I see a wood penis in Tory's front yard."

"Yes, Grandma, I—" Tory started, then shut her mouth. In the face of Grandma's fury, everyone stands down.

"You what? What were you thinking?"

"I didn't know it would end up on YouTube. How could I know that? It was only for that weasel, cross-eyed, dusty old Scotty!"

"Blah, blah, blah! You should have predicted it would wind up on YouTube," Grandma said, those green Irish eyes snapping, her brogue thickening. "Especially when they were filming you. Did you lose your mind?"

"It's been amazing advertising," I said.

"We're all over the Internet," Lacey said. "It's already increasing sales, raising our profile. The press was here—"

"This is not what I wanted for this company!"

"But Tory's brash act adds to our mystique, our brand, who we are," I said. "We're not only bras and lingerie, we're fighting women, fun and daring, we don't take any crap from men—"

"Oh, hush up," Grandma said.

Tory wrung her hands. Grandma's the only one who can make her nervous. "I didn't know—"

"You don't know a lot, Tory," Grandma said. I saw Tory's face start to crumple.

"That was too harsh, Grandma," Lacey said.

"I agree," I said. "Tory does know a lot. She's an excellent designer, she knows a zillion people in the business, she has hundreds of contacts—"

"Hell's bells, close your mouths!" Grandma said. "Tory, you know nothing about *love*. Nothing."

That stilled all of our mouths as quickly as if they'd been crammed with hell's bells.

Grandma stalked over to Tory. "Will this increase sales? Yes. Is it the image I want for my company? No, it's not. I feel like my hair is on fire I'm so mad, but that is beside the point, you ridiculous, wood-carving she-devil. What you need to think about is Scotty."

"Scotty?" Tory peeped out.

"Yes, Scotty. I'm sure all those computer geek nerds at his work know, so you've humiliated him professionally and personally. You are in love with Scotty—"

Tory whimpered.

"And you do this?"

Tory's manicured hands flew to her face.

"How will this help you in your ultimate goal?" Grandma spread her hands out, diamond bracelets flashing.

"What ultimate goal?" Tory cried.

"Getting Scotty back."

Tory moaned and bent her head. "Oh, Grandma! I was so mad that he took another woman to dinner, that it wasn't me, that he's moving on, that he hasn't tried to get me back. My horoscope said that revenge would be mine. I saw it as a sign."

"No, you didn't. You don't believe that horoscope crapola any more than I do." Grandma stabbed the air with her finger. "Maybe you and your temper tantrums are too much for him anymore, Tory. Have you thought about that?"

"Yes, yes, I have. When he came home last night I saw his face. He was shocked to see all the police cars, the cameras, the reporters. He saw me and I waved and smiled. He was so relieved to see me, I saw it, and he sort of sagged. Maybe he thought I was hurt, that's why the police were there. But then he saw the wood carving and his mouth dropped open and he looked at me, then at all the people around me, who were noticing him and advancing with their cameras and notebooks, and he turned and left. I tried to call him, but he's not taking my calls . . ."

"You are a bull, Tory," Grandma said. "It works in business, but it doesn't in a marriage. Bulls don't belong in the marriage bed. Scotty is a kind, smart, gentle soul, and you are a raving, difficult, temperamental woman. You are constantly testing him, constantly testing his love for you, throwing obscene fits to get his attention. Grow up, Tory. Coming home and being a loving wife is not setting aside your ambition, your womanhood, or your equality. It's recognizing that Scotty, the man you love, needs attention and affection. He shouldn't have to spend his entire evening calming you down about whatever imaginary conflict you've dreamed up."

"I should move back into my house," Tory said. "That's what I should do. I should move back in and walk around naked, bake cakes naked . . ."

"You don't cook," Grandma said.

"I'll learn. I'll clean when I'm naked."

"You don't clean. You have a cleaning lady," I said.

"I'll pretend I'm cleaning."

Grandma shook her finger at Tory. "You need to think love."

"Think love?"

"Yes. The only other man who loves a woman as much as I see Scotty loving you is Matt. But Lacey knows he's a gift and treats him like that."

Lacey raised her eyebrows at me. Ah, praise!

"Stifle it, Lacey." Grandma whipped around. "I could come after you for any number of things, including that maternity dress. It looks like a tent. And you, Meggie." For a second she was at a loss for words. "I hate that outfit." She turned back to Tory. "Seduce him. Date him. Woo him, you idiot. Sometimes you girls are so stupid I hardly know what to do. If I could buy you new brains, I would."

Grandma turned and stomped out of the room. "You three," she turned back, "and I didn't think I would have to say this again, but you three stay out of trouble! I want no more penises on YouTube!"

She slammed the door. I swear that building shook again. She yelled down to the floor, "Get rid of that penis!"

Tory looked bereft. "Do you think I could turn the penis into a fountain?" I held her as the bravado and daring collapsed and she was left with what she had before the buzz saw even hit the wood: a broken heart.

* * *

Blake had been very cheery when he saw me standing on Tory and Scotty's lawn.

"Good to see you, Meggie." He was all dressed up in his police chief's uniform.

"Ah. Yes. Hello. Good to see you, too."

"I must say I'm surprised to find you here."

"I feel the same, Blake."

"But it's made my night, how shall I put it?" He rocked back on his heels and smiled at me. "Special."

"I'm glad I could be part of your special night."

Two police officers came up to talk to him, and I quickly snuck away, trying to catch my breath. *Blake was the police chief?*

He walked back over to me in two minutes, standing right in front of me so I couldn't weasel away.

"I see that you're Portland's police chief."

"Yes. That I am. And you're Meggie O'Rourke, CEO at Lace, Satin, and Baubles, a company owned by your grandmother, Regan O'Rourke. Your mother is the renowned ... uh ... therapist, Brianna O'Rourke, your sister, Lacey Rockaford, is the chief financial officer, and your sister, Tory O'Rourke, apparently the mastermind here of the artwork, is the design director."

"Yes. Should I ask how you know?"

"You should. You told me your name and I looked you up."

"It's so simple these days, isn't it?"

"But you didn't look me up. My heart is crushed."

"Aren't you funny? No, I didn't look you up. To be honest I forgot your last name." He has such a friendly grin. It softens up what is otherwise a hard, square-jawed face.

"Meggie O'Rourke, this is an odd way to get to know each other better, but it's been a fun evening."

"Delightful. Pure delight."

We both turned to the penis.

"It's a fine wood carving," he said, mock-impressed.

"Lola has mastered the chain saw and chisel, that's clear. Will you be making any arrests?"

"Nope. As I understand it, it's Tory's house. It'll probably be a code violation because you can't have something like this . . . this . . ."—he waved an arm—"in front of your home, as it's offensive to the neighbors. Although"—he studied Gladys, who was now posing on the other side of the penis with Tory and waving—"she doesn't seem to mind, now that she knows there are no rocket-ship-building burglars. Anyhow, it looks like your sister and her husband have a few things to work out."

"They do. Many things. Large and small. I hope they will."

"Do you like the husband?"

"Yes. I do. Scotty's a kind man. Definitely not a dick. I feel guilty for being here."

"He's home soon?"

"Yes. I don't think tonight will be his best."

"Probably not."

He smiled at me.

I smiled back.

Other police officers came up to talk to him, his phone rang, and I moved away, but studied him surreptitiously. Like a spy, I suppose.

He was in charge. He was liked and respected by his officers. He spoke well, and he handled the situation.

I tried hard not to like him.

I talked to my mother that night from her hotel room. I could hear her knitting needles clicking. *Click, click, click.* I was eating chocolate ice cream and a banana. She'd visited the host of a well-known talk show today in New York. She talked about whispering. As in, whispering to your partner what you want him to do to you. She regaled the audience with her Seven Tips for Whispering Success.

"Tory is hurting so much, honey," she said. "I'm going to call Scotty tomorrow."

"And say what?"

"That I love him, that he is as sweet as a cinnamon roll. I'm almost finished with his hat. I want to keep things snug as a bug in a rug between Scotty and me so when he gets back together with Tory, all will be peachy between us." She sighed. She regularly agonized over their separation. "Oh, my dear Tory, still hurting."

We talked about Tory, then I asked, "What color is my hat this year?"

"I'm not telling you, as usual. You know it's a surprise and I finish your hat, Tory's and Lacey's at the same time so you girls don't get hurt feelings about who receives the first hat."

My mother knits us a new hat and scarf each year. They're unique, colorful, comfortable.

"How are you doing, my love?"

"I'm fine." I scooped ice cream up with the banana.

"No, sweets. Tell me." *Click, click, click.*

"Nightmares, flashbacks, odd sightings of him. Yesterday I thought I saw him running past the business and I ran outside to check on my hallucination. Rats and blood. Red. The usual."

My mother is one of the only people I can be totally honest with. She questioned me further, kind, confidential. Whenever I talk to her, I feel better.

"I love you, sweetheart," she told me before we hung up. "I can't wait until this book tour ends. It is killing me to be away from you and your sisters. I want to be in my kitchen kneading breads with you girls."

"I love you, too."

"I hope you like the hat and scarf I made for you this year. It took me three trips to find the exact color of yarn I wanted to use for you. Both will complement those yummy chocolate brown eyes of yours and your golden hair."

Click, click, click.

10

~

By the time we left India, Aaron and I were engaged. He bought me a ring with a red stone at a bazaar. I bought him a plain gold band.

We started working on another film together in Los Angeles about life as an illegal teenage immigrant, specifically about kids who were brought here from Mexico when they were three or four, how they felt American, went to American schools, and listened to American music but had no legal standing and their lives were left in absolute limbo.

I had been in and out of Portland, but Aaron didn't want to live in Oregon, so we settled in L.A. Later I realized he simply didn't want me near my family. Isolation was best.

I had brought him home for five days between films. The visit had not gone well.

My mother insisted that I make Christmas cookies with her, four different types: sugar, pinwheels, fudge mint, and divinity. Then we made decorative wreaths using pine cones and branches from outside.

She told me, "The domestic arts and crafts should be a part of every woman's life. It brings serenity. In the depth of the serenity and peace we create today, your brain will accept that Aaron is a monstrous mistake."

My grandma said, Irish brogue sharp, "Aaron's head is filled with nuts because he is one. He's too passionate about himself.

Narcissistic. He has delusions of grandeur. This will end as poorly as an untreated bladder infection. You'll wind up screaming."

Lacey said, "I know you think that Matt is boring, but here's what a 'boring' man like Matt gets you: constant and loyal love. Friendship. Compassion. Someone to listen to all your phobias and oddities. Help with the kids. Laughter. Stability. A man to hug grandchildren with. I love Matt with all that I am. Aaron will never be around to hug grandchildren with you."

Tory said, "There are two types of men: the type you screw and the type you marry. Aaron is the type of man you screw, not marry. Why are you hesitating here?"

Aaron did not contact his mother about our engagement because she was "dead to me. Dead by the time I was eight, spiritually, but her body wouldn't leave the planet."

I wouldn't listen to my family. I was so in love with Aaron I could barely breathe. Now I know I was in lust with him. Overwhelming lust. Aaron was sex with feet. He was hot. He was wildly passionate and romantic with me. It is hard for a woman to think under that kind of onslaught. We were both film people: We wanted to show the world what was going on with people who were invisible to others, we wanted to show the injustices and unfairness, we wanted to give a voice to people who needed someone to hear them. We understood each other.

We eloped to Kalispell, Montana. I know, makes no sense. But he wanted to see Montana—"it calls to my manhood and my inner soul"—even though he'd never been there.

I bought a white wedding dress with spaghetti straps, a brocaded bodice, and a full skirt at Goodwill for sixty dollars. The hemline was a little stained, but I ignored it.

Aaron bought a black T-shirt with a rat on it and stood in front of the hired minister in that. It became his favorite T-shirt. After the "ceremony," Aaron went off to get beer and I wandered out to a dock jutting into a lake by myself, in a wedding dress, and stuck my feet in the water. I remember looking at my reflection, stunned that I was now a wife.

I don't know what I was thinking.

Clearly, I wasn't thinking at all.

My body was doing the thinking.

In Montana Aaron got in touch with his manhood and his inner soul, and we returned home to Los Angeles and kept working. I would show my family they were wrong about him. The bait and switch behavior started immediately after the honeymoon. Aaron became controlling and angry, frustrated, irritated. Morning, noon, and night I had to handle some new emotion, fear, or problem he was having. He raved and raged, his emotions pitching and diving.

I told myself that he was artistic, free spirited, that I loved his openness. I told myself that he did things for me, too, even though I soon couldn't think of anything. In fact, I did it all, the house cleaning, the cooking, the cars and maintenance, the leg-work behind our next film project . . .

I told myself it was okay. That we would get through it.

It is amazing what we women tell ourselves is okay when it absolutely isn't.

The next night Blake walked up the stairs of my tree house and knocked on the door. My heart jumped and I sternly re-minded myself that I was my grandma's granddaughter and she had faced far worse than an impossibly sexy police chief.

"Hello, Blake." I felt rather faint. He was devilish and deli-cious.

"Meggie. May I come in?" He was smiling. He was in jeans and a light blue shirt. He handed me a huge bouquet of pink tulips and yellow roses.

"Yes, of course. And thank you. They're beautiful." I stepped back so he could enter, and I told myself to breathe. Something rather strange happened and I didn't get it as quick as I should have, because I was bedazzled and dumbfounded by how that man filled my tree house and how close to my bedroom he was standing. Why, we would only have to climb that ladder lickety-split and we could be bouncing on my bouncy mattress under the skylight in seconds. . . .

I snapped my mind back.

Blake's gray-blue eyes were on mine, then they dropped

briefly to my chest. They stayed there for a millisecond, then he looked away, toward my maple tree, and took a long breath. I saw that huge chest go up and down.

I wanted to run my fingers through that blondish hair.

His eyes came back to mine for a second.

Oh, those eyes. I wanted to see them half closed with passion.

I am not nervous around men.

But I was around Blake. Nervous, skittish, awkward.

He tilted his head back and stared at the ceiling.

I stared at his neck. I have this thing about men's necks. I like when they're muscled and tight and look kissable.

"Uh, Meggie."

And that voice. Deep and controlled.

He was setting me on fire, and I told myself, sternly again, to cool it.

"Yes?"

"Uh, I would like to talk to you, but I am having some trouble concentrating."

"You are?"

"Yes." He glanced away again, then back at me, then down to my chest again.

I looked down.

Oh, shoot!

Shoot!

I crossed my arms with the roses and tulips in front of my chest. "Whoa. I'm sorry."

"Don't be sorry," he said, his voice strained. He transferred his attention to the rafters of my tree house and my hanging white lights. "It's a great . . . white . . . tank top." He ran a hand through his hair, then over his face.

"Hang on." I dropped the bouquet on the counter, then scooted on up my ladder to my sleeping loft. I hadn't even thought when I opened the door. I was in faded, tight jeans, which were not a problem. I was wearing thick white socks. Also, not a problem.

And I was wearing a tightish white tank top, rather thin from too many washings.

And no bra.

None.

The tank top outlined the curvy parts.

And, good golly, it was see-through.

I about died.

Then I laughed. Might as well show that chief what lurks beneath my sweatshirts.

"Okay. Dressed appropriately now." I had put on a bra, a white T-shirt, and a blue sweatshirt. Blake was standing near my maple tree, and smiled when I came back down. "I wasn't trying to be . . ." I swallowed hard. What was I not trying to be? I was not trying to be provocative. But I couldn't say the word *provocative* to the man towering over me. It would be easier to say *bottom* but not as hard as saying *nipple*.

Stop, I told myself. *Stop now.*

He raised his eyebrows at me, those lips turned up at the corners. "You weren't trying to be what, Meggie?"

"I wasn't deliberately trying to open the door to you like that. You knocked, I opened up, I didn't think about whether I should open up, you were there and I wanted you in . . ." *Oh, dear God.* It would have been better if I'd said the word *nipple* fifty times.

"Well, Meggie, maybe one day you'll be dressed like that deliberately when I come over."

"Gee. Maybe. You're pretty cute, but you're trouble." I felt myself blushing. I am too old to blush. I escaped into the kitchen. I saw the lemon meringue cookies that Cassidy had made me. "Do you want to drink a cookie?"

"I don't think I want to drink a cookie," Blake said, following me into the kitchen. "But I'll eat one."

"Yes. Eat one. Here." I handed him the whole platter. There were at least twenty cookies on it.

"Thank you."

He sat down in front of the platter of twenty cookies at my table. I put my head in my hands, then joined him, hoping my brain would show up soon.

"Good cookies. Did you make them?"

"No. My niece did. She's a naughty girl but she bakes like a dream. I'm totally undomesticated. Cooking, baking, zero interest in it."

"You grew up with your mother and your grandmother. I would not have expected you to be queen of homemaking."

"Actually, my mother loves to cook, quilt, embroider, sew, and garden. She's Betty Crocker reincarnated with red hair and knitting needles."

"I saw her on a late-night talk show once. After I met you, I listened to her again."

What was my mother talking about when he listened to her? I wiped my forehead. Oh, the topic could be anything. *Anything.* I skipped past that one.

"I'm more like my grandma. She hired a cook as soon as she could afford it. She taught me about all aspects of the business. For Show and Share in kindergarten I brought in spread sheets of Lace, Satin, and Baubles."

He laughed. "I bet your kindergarten friends appreciated that."

"They thought I was strange. I got used to it."

"I don't think you're strange."

"I don't think you're strange, either. I think you're yummy." I dropped my head in my hands yet again, that red flush back and blooming. "Why do I speak out loud?"

He chuckled. "Thank you. And you, Meggie, are beautiful."

I don't feel beautiful. I feel like a sponge mixed with detergent and Baggies. I quickly ducked and swerved and asked about what his job as police chief entailed. He winked at me, and I could tell he was choosing to let me duck and swerve.

He worked with his police officers, all levels of the chain of command, neighborhood groups, other state and national agencies, and the union. There were endless meetings. Speeches. Gang violence and domestic violence to address. Crimes to solve. Decisions on who to arrest and when. Training on how to handle the mentally ill. Lots of "building relationships" types of things. Conferences. Speaking at conferences. Hiring. Firing. Undercover operations. Drug busts.

Blake asked about my day. He wanted to know the details. I'd rarely met a man who wanted the details. Basically, for them, "how is your day" is a perfunctory question to pretend that they care, when what they really want to do is tell you about their day, their problems, and their physical aches and pains. They want a hot dinner and then they want you to hop eagerly into bed and serve them like a brainless robot.

Blake was different. He asked how I liked being at the company again, what I found interesting, what I found hard, what I did each day, who I worked with, etc.

We chatted so easily, the words flowing like a crystal clear river through a field of pink tulips and yellow roses. It was as if we met over lemon meringue cookies each night.

"Okay, Meggie, I'm off. I've stayed way too long and I know you have to get up early for work."

"Don't you?"

"Yes."

He walked to the door, then pulled me close into a hug. I stiffened up at first, but he held me closer, not tight, but closer.

I took a scary dare and put my arms around his neck. I inhaled the scent of him, resting against his chest for a second, relaxing into his strength. I closed my eyes, wanting to remember what it felt like to be hugged by him, how his arms felt around me, how safe it felt, how friendly, how smokin' hot . . .

I pulled back and wrapped my arms around my waist. I bent my head.

The last man I had hugged . . . but no, I would stay away from that and the black rats.

He wrapped one of my curls around his fingers. "One day you're going to tell me why you feel like you're wrapped in black, right?"

"Probably not." No way.

"I don't know what's wrong, but when you want to talk, I want to listen."

I didn't even nod. I couldn't even move.

He took a step closer, kissed my cheek, then left.

I wanted to leap on his strong back, spin him around, and head for my bedroom with my legs wrapped around his hips.

I didn't have the right amount of guts to do that yet.

I told myself to gather the guts and go for it.

That night I looked at my bathtub, fit for two, for Blake and me.

I used to love taking baths.

I used to have bubble baths in all sorts of scents: vanilla, orange musk, lemon, cinnamon apple, even chocolate.

I could not take a bath now to save my life.

I sat in several meetings the next day.

I always insist that all meetings be quick.

I look at the agenda before it starts, if I don't write it myself. I have only the people who must attend come to the meeting. All electronics are off. Everyone must pay attention. We move quickly. I listen. We discuss, and sometimes the discussions get heated.

My style of leadership is to lead. I want people to feel that they have a voice and that I'll listen. I want to be approachable.

On the other hand . . .

Decisions have to be made, and I make them. If they go well, we all take the credit. If they go poorly, it's on my head. Sometimes I think we get bogged down in discussions and "hearing everybody's opinions," and these squishy feel-good attitudes at work, where there are meetings for the meetings, consensus building, and other time-wasting junk.

I don't operate like that.

I don't have the time or the patience, and right now the company absolutely doesn't have it, either. I expect people here to eventually settle down, even if they don't agree with my decision or Grandma's, be professional, and back me and the company.

I've known many of these people for years, some for decades. I think they're talented and hardworking. The ones who weren't hardworking I've fired since I've been here. I'm considering firing another person because she gossips, something I try to smash down. I'm cutting payroll by cutting out people who aren't cutting it.

To me, this is a business, not a charity. If people are lazy or negative or incompetent or too difficult, they're out. Someone else would love the job.

Yes, I have been told that I'm demanding and exacting. So what? I'm not Santa.

That said, meetings—with all the noise, hoopla, emotions, people not staying on track—can drive me absolutely out of my head.

Especially ones with Tory and Lacey.

"We need to talk about the fashion show," I told Tory and Lacey. I had already made a list of what we needed to do. My intimidating list included, but was certainly not limited to, finding a place, building a runway, advertising, invitations, the decor, lighting, choosing the lingerie the models would wear, finding models, organizing the show itself, getting the music, affording it . . .

"We're absolutely going to do this?" Lacey asked. She was wearing a lime green maternity dress, snug and stylish.

I sat back in my chair at the table in my office, my boring white tennis shoes crossed in front of me. I noticed they had dirt on them. I tried to care about that. Nope. Couldn't do it. "Yes, we are."

"Tell me again why?" Tory asked. She had on pink stilettos, a black midthigh skirt, a low-cut pink satin blouse, and one of our burgundy negligees from the Delicate Devil line. It reminded me again of how outstanding our products are. We simply needed to get ourselves, our brand, and our message out there more.

"We need to use this as a marketing tool," I said. "It has to be different from anyone else's fashion show. It's our anniversary celebration."

"I feel nauseated," Lacey said, already off topic. "Why do we have to be sick when pregnant? We're supposed to procreate, right, so why does our body rebel?"

"You sure procreate a lot," Tory drawled.

"I like kids."

"Kids are noisy."

"The fashion show?" I interjected.

"How would you know if my kids are noisy or not? You hardly come over and visit us—"

"That's because I'm hardly ever invited except if it's a holiday or birthday and Mom and Grandma are there, too." I saw Tory's eyes mist, but she stuck her chin out farther. "It's not like I get a special invitation. Just me."

"I invited you for years to come by yourself and you hardly ever did." Lacey slapped the table with her hands, her face flushed. "The kids don't even know you that well—"

"That's because you say bad things about me to them, so I know they don't like me—"

"I do not say bad things about you, Tory, to my kids." She stabbed a finger at her. "Never have I done that."

"I've never heard Lacey say anything bad about you to her kids, Tory," I said. "We need to talk about the location and lighting. I think that—"

"You haven't made me a part of your family, Lacey. I'm like the ogre aunt. The mean one. Sharp teeth. Eats children."

And there was the crux of the problem. Tory was hurt because she didn't feel a part of Lacey's family, and Lacey was hurt because Tory didn't make more of an effort. I leaned back and muttered, "Here we go."

"You're not a part of my family because you don't want to be. I feel like you don't love my kids!" Lacey said, her voice wobbling. "How do you think that makes me feel? And that skirt barely covers your butt!"

Tory's temper flew up ten notches. "Maybe you should have covered your butt so you wouldn't be pregnant for a fourth time."

"I like to ride my husband like a damn horse. Maybe if you rode your husband like a damn horse more often he would have wanted you to stick around."

Bad call.

Tory's face lost color instantly.

Lacey put both hands up and said, "I'm sorry, Tory. That was mean, uncalled for, awful. I'm a wicked pregnant witch. I'm sorry."

"Okay, that's enough," I said. They were about ready to cry. "You are both being way too mean—"

"You don't know a thing about my marriage, Lacey!" Tory stood up and hit the table with her fists. "Nothing. Not a thing. You're a mother to an army of brats—"

Another bad call. "This is gonna get nasty," I muttered to myself.

"They are not brats!" Lacey was on her feet, too, Mother Bear roaring. "They're just strange and troublesome. Cassidy can't keep her pants on and Hayden believes he's a girl and Regan collects animals like they're stamps, but they are not brats." My sister shook that same finger at Tory and charged at her around the table. "Take it back!"

"You take it back that I don't ride Scotty like a horse, because I do!"

It went from there. Like a bonfire.

I lost another mannequin.

"Any chance we could talk about the fashion show?"

No. Clearly not. I started answering e-mails.

Regan arrived at my house about ten o'clock the next night, awash in tears, a gray, scruffy-looking cat in his arms.

"Honey, what are you doing here? It's late."

"What a relief. You're up. This is a bad day. I snuck out of the house to see you. There's been a disaster! You have to rescue this poor cat for me, Aunt Meggie. It's a stray. Our neighbor was going to take it to the pound, but the pound will kill it." The waterworks flowed. "I don't want him to die."

"Come on in." The cat made a hissing sound at me. "Whoa. That's a hissy sort of cat."

"Jeepers does that because he's unhappy. I named him Jeepers because when I heard he was going to the pound I said, 'Oh, jeepers! He's lonely. He doesn't have a family to love him.'"

"He has your family."

"No," Regan moaned, his whole animal world shattering. "He doesn't. Mom said no more cats. I think she's being mean. Cats are friendly. Smart thinkers. They don't make a mess, and you have a cat door here, too. He can go in and out when you're at work."

"Honey, I don't want a cat. I'm hardly here."

He plopped down in the middle of my floor and stroked the hissing cat, hugging him close in his huge arms. "Please, Aunt Meggie. Please. All houses need a friendly cat to be a home."

"Who told you that?"

"No one. It's what I feel inside." He tapped his aching heart. "Right here in my gut."

I sat down beside him. "I'll think about it. Want something to eat?"

His face showed his gratitude. "Yes, thank you. Mom doesn't feed and water me enough." He said this in all seriousness. "Tonight there was only spaghetti, salad, peaches, garlic bread, and apple pie."

"How about a club sandwich and milk?"

"That'd be great. My stomach is all rumbly from starving."

I made him a sandwich. Good thing I had the meat. I like my club sandwiches with crackers and pickles, but I left those out for Regan.

"How's school, Regan?"

His brow furrowed. "I don't get math. It's sooo hard. And science is hard and English Lit is hard and history has all these dates and the dates get scrambled up in my head like a bad puzzle. I have to study a lot and the other kids seem to understand everything. Cassidy and Hayden are so smart. They have to help me all the time and quiz me, and it doesn't"—he pointed at the back of his head—"it doesn't stick in my brain good. But this cat, I think if he lived here you would wake up with a smile on your face."

"You think so, Regan?"

"Yes. I know it."

It hissed.

"He doesn't like me."

"He does. I can tell by the way his ears are moving. He's loyal and has a loving personality. Please, Aunt Meggie," he whispered. He held the cat up so we were nose to nose. "Please?"

He hissed at me.

His name is Jeepers.

I am still waiting to see the loving personality.

The next day I saw a black Corvette. I knew it wasn't Aaron's, I knew he wasn't in it, but I followed it anyhow, all the while acknowledging that this part of my brain was filled with mucky holes and pits of delusions.

I pulled up beside the Corvette and peered in. There was an Asian man driving. He looked at me and smiled.

I smiled back, shaky, sick, weak.

I knew that the Corvette was what triggered my nightmare that night.

Aaron wrapped a huge, human-sized Baggie around me. He filled it with detergent so I couldn't breathe, then stuffed sponges down my throat. He dragged me to the closet by my hair, climbed to the top shelf, and threw that thing I was hiding from myself down at me. It turned into a knife and landed in my cheek.

I woke up in bed with my face covered in something wet. In the darkness, I thought it was blood.

In a semi panic I slipped down the ladder, landed hard, and ran to the bathroom, tripping once, sure my cheek was bleeding.

There was no blood on my face, only tears.

Only tears.

I have acknowledged that I am not completely mentally well.

By the end of the first year I was having serious doubts about my marriage, which I worked hard to smother. Aaron and I tried to work together on another film. It was on young prostitutes in Las Vegas. It did not go well. I could not do anything right, at least in Aaron's eyes.

"Why did you shoot that scene at that angle? . . . Too close,

Meggie . . . let me do it . . . you are not in charge of this production . . . your sound is off . . . bad choice of cameraman . . . I know far more about the art and the science of filmmaking . . . follow me, and learn what I teach you, so I don't have to reteach you . . . damn it . . . this looks fake, ridiculous, boring."

Halfway through the film he crashed and refused to get out of bed. He wore that black rat T-shirt for a week, straight through.

I finished the film. I worked all day, came home at night, and listened to him rant.

He said I was, "Taking over the production . . . let me see what you did today, that's shitty footage . . . you can't think that's going to win awards . . . I'll fix it in editing. Damn, that's bad . . . there's no honesty in your work . . . it looks like it's been Photoshopped. It needs more grit, what is this, Sleeping Beauty meets Jack the Pimp?"

I would make dinner, and listen to him rave, as he pushed his long black curls out of his face. I used to think the curls and black feather were so avant-garde, so stylish; now I saw them as his desperate attempt to look avant-garde and stylish. He even bought new black feathers now and then, to "uphold the image."

We argued endlessly, and after a while I gave up. There was no resolution. I was always wrong. He ended the arguments by shouting me down.

We went back to Los Angeles.

I hated it.

I craved Oregon like I craved air.

We lived in a dark, cheap apartment in an unsafe neighborhood. Aaron's moods were unpredictable, like flash floods and tornadoes that came out of nowhere. Aaron alternately freaked out, fell into depression, or ran on optimum speed on a highway of energy and electricity. He would be fine one week, working and egomaniacal, and crying his heart out the next. He would self-medicate with alcohol, and then prescription pills, for a "back injury."

"It's either prescription pills for all my pain or pot. Take your pick, Meggie." He flicked his black feather back over his shoulder. I grew to hate his black feather.

I was livid about the drinking and the pills. Aaron drank now and then when we dated. I never saw a pill.

He slammed his fist into walls one night after his mother, Rochelle, paid us a surprise visit.

She was drunk and obnoxious, a monster of a woman, shaped like a short pear. She had huge, pendulous boobs that stuck out to the side and jiggled. Her brown hair was cut like a dead beaver on her head. They launched into a screaming argument, and she threw three plates and called him a "bad, neglectful son who lies about things that never happened, you never told me anyhow, it was your sick imagination." Aaron said, "You're a lousy, drunken bitch. You sacrificed me for him. You put me on a platter and handed me over with a knife and fork . . ."

Their relationship was a cauldron of resentment, secrets, and rage. He did not want to talk about it, but I began to understand.

After her visit he became even more irrational. He was arrested for driving under the influence. He crashed his car in another incident. I insisted he go to a doctor, a psychiatrist. He refused. I started thinking about leaving him, but I couldn't do it. Divorce was a failure. I could not fail.

I felt like I was living with my hands over my head. I worked as much as I could. When I arrived home, it was like entering a damp cave where black rats launched themselves at me, their claws scraping, an iron door locking me inside.

11

Hola, my name is Maritza Lopez. I work for Lace, Satin, and Baubles. I have worked for Mrs. O'Rourke for sixteen years. This is my favorite bra that we make. You see, it is white. Pure white. I like the color, no lace, no padding. That's it. I have five of these. You want me to explain why I like this bra, Meggie? Tell my story first? Okay.

I came to America seventeen years ago. I came with my sisters, Juanita and Valeria, and my mother, Nola. My family saved for years to come to America. We wanted to work and go to school. We were so poor in Mexico, and it was dangerous where we lived with the drug wars. People disappeared, or they were shot. Men, women, little children, too. They killed so they could ship drugs that killed other people. Makes no sense.

My father went first, with his brother, to work in America and send money. We hadn't heard from them in two months, but he had sent enough to pay a coyote to take us over. A coyote is a man, or men, you pay to sneak you over the border from Mexico. So the coyote, he packs us into a semi truck. You know those big metal trucks for hauling food? I still get scared when I see them. There are so many people squished in there with us. It is hot, it's dark, and they lock the doors.

I'm sorry, Meggie, I cry when I think about it. Give me a momento. Un momento. I'll start again. We travel and travel, it gets hotter and hotter, Mexico is so hot, then Texas. People start to cry, they pound on the walls, they yell and scream. Some of the people faint, we run out of water and food, they don't stop to let us go to the bathroom, it is a terrible mess.

My mother, something is wrong with her, my sisters and I can see that. She has no water in her, and we keep driving in that heat. Almost everyone is screaming now, and crying, and there's some people who are not moving, their families try to wake them but they don't wake up.

I hold my mother in my arms and rock her back and forth as people keep pounding on the walls of the truck. It's like a coffin. A long, metal, hot coffin and we are all in it and we are dying together.

Finally, the coyotes stop the truck and we all fall out except for ten people. They're dead . . . I'm sorry, Meggie, for crying again. This part is hard to say. I try not to think about this. Our mother is oh . . . she is dead, too. So close, so close we are to being in America. She worked so hard to get us there, Daddy worked so hard, but she doesn't make it.

The coyotes make us get out of the truck, so we carry Mother, too. We're in the desert. There are a lot of men with guns, men from Mexico. We are crying over our mother and they pull us away. My sisters and I . . . I cry hardest here, Meggie, I'm sorry. We are raped. On our backs in the sand, by a cactus. I'm screaming. I'm a virgin. My sisters are virgins, too. He hits me with his fist. It hurts so bad, oh, it hurts. I remember that I had on a pink bra, with lace.

When they are done, we snap our bras back on and we crawl over to our momma. We hug her. The truck pulls away with the coyotes, they shoot off their guns, they laugh, it is a funny joke to them, and we're stuck in the desert.

We don't know what to do. The border patrol comes and finds us. First, my sisters and I try to run, we feel so bad about leaving our momma in the sand, but we are afraid . . . oh, we are afraid the Americans will do to us what the Mexican men did. But they catch us, we hurt, we are crying, Juanita faints, I hold her. But they give us water and food. There is blood on our *skirts from the rapes. So much blood. They put our momma in a bag, but we kiss her and hold her first. We say, "We love you, Momma, we love you."*

We take her wedding ring, her earrings, her necklace for us, memories of our momma. She had a pink bra on that day, too. My sisters, too. We all had pink bras. Bought cheap in Mexico, only new thing we ever bought.

Border Patrol feeds us again, and gives us more water, and because I am the oldest, at seventeen, we get special permission to come to America. They try to find our dad and police tell us our dad is dead, too, and his brother, too. Someone shot them. They don't know who or why. So we go to Oregon because we met a woman who says she'll take us. We come here and ask for jobs and your grandma, she is the best person in the world, she hires all of us. We finish high school, she makes us, and we work here.

We're happy. First we were seamstresses, but now we work in marketing, operations, and the supply chain.

But, me, I never wear the lacy bras. Never a pink bra. Reminds me of too much. I like to be plain. Safe and plain.

White. That's why I wear white bras only.

Yes? Is that what you wanted, Meggie? Me, my life, and my favorite bra? Did I do okay? I'm sorry I cried. Still, those bad memories make me cry. I'm sorry I made you cry, too. Oh, Meggie. You're a good friend to my sisters and I.

Te quiero.

12

⤾

On my way back upstairs from the production floor, I ran into Hayden.

"Aunt Meggie!"

"Hayden. So good to see you. You've made my day." He gave me a hug, then we walked back to my office, chatting, and sat down. He was wearing red pants, high-tops, and a striped shirt with flowers on the cuffs. His dark hair was back in a ponytail.

"How are you, Hayden?" *Don't kill yourself, honey, don't.* I knew that Lacey and Matt were sending him to a counselor. I hoped the counselor knew what she was doing.

"Good. I've decided that I'm going to go public."

"Public?" I froze.

"Yes. You know how I'm the features editor for the school newspaper? I write articles on students and teachers doing cool things, and fashion, what all the kids are wearing, events that are coming up, like the plays and musicals and concerts. So, I'm going to write about myself."

My first thought was that Hayden was going to get the crap beat out of him. "What are you going to say?"

"I'm going to say the truth."

"And that is . . ."

"That I'm transgender. I'm a girl in my head, that I want to be a girl, that I was born a girl, and I'm going to start dressing like a girl and be my own girl self and start wearing makeup and take my hair out of the ponytail and I'll be wearing skirts and heels."

I leaned back, stunned. He would be teased mercilessly. Harassed. Isolated. Whispered about. I tried to clear the fuzz of buzzing stress out of my head. "You're going to write about this?"

"When I get the nerve, and I think my nerve is almost here. I'm going to post photos of myself now, and then what I'm going to wear the first day that I come to school as a girl."

"Did you talk to your parents about this?"

"Not yet. I'm talking to you first because you're cool. So. What do you think?"

What did I think? I thought he was going to be chop suey. "I think, Hayden, that you need to think about this."

"You mean, like, because of the teasing and stuff? They already tease me sometimes, but I have my friends."

He did have friends. Hayden was actually pretty popular. The kids thought he was gay, but he was nice to everyone, and the girls talked to him all the time about their problems and clothing. Still. A boy turning into a girl, from one day to the next? He would be a sitting target. Like a rose in the street soon to be trampled by stampeding rhinos.

"Hayden, I think this will raise the level of teasing to a frighteningly intense and ugly level." *And I don't want this to push you over the edge, honey.*

He dug a toe into the floor. "I know. But what's worse, Aunt Meggie? I can take the teasing for being gay or I can take the teasing for being who I really am. You know what I mean? I'd rather be teased for dressing like a girl when I am a girl. Does that make sense?"

"Yes, it makes sense." I reached for his hand across the table. Hayden is one of the kindest people I've ever met. He's had to do so much work on himself, he's been so confused and lost, that it's made him into a perceptive, resilient, introspective person. Many people never get near this stage of personal development and depth. They never hit the black, and they skim and they skate and remain shallow.

"It makes sense, Hayden, and I am behind you one hundred and ten per cent." I kissed his forehead. I actually felt my hands tremble, and my stomach was jelly. "On to work ... I need you to help me with the fashion show. You saw my e-mail from two days ago?"

"Yes, I have it. I do have a few suggestions for the show, the lighting, the invitations, the décor for the tables. I wrote the e-mail to you last night, but I wanted to edit it and think about things tonight, so I'll send it to you tomorrow, boss." He grinned at me. "I gotta show you the new robe I designed. The material is soft and velvety. It's like polar bear fur and a rainbow combined. You'll adore it."

I adore you. We all do. Don't take a step that will ruin all of us, forever.

Who am I to judge anyone for anything?

I have made serious, enormous mistakes in my life. I fought with Aaron often. I yelled back. I avoided him and left to travel for my work whenever I could. I nagged. I was depressed living with him, so I wasn't much fun to live with myself. I was often cold and unresponsive because I was overwhelmed and so unhappy. I was impatient and visibly frustrated. I shut down on Aaron, then did something terrible. I probably handled very little correctly.

Worst of all, I'm so relieved, to the base of my soul, that I'm not married to him anymore, and that makes me feel more horrible than ever.

As for Hayden? What is there to judge? He was born a girl in his head with a boy body. He is brave enough to address it. He is brave enough to change. He is brave enough to face an unfriendly, hostile world with who he truly is.

Hayden is far braver than I am.

On Wednesday, as I returned to my office after meeting with the Petrellis, Abigail told me that Kalani had Skyped me and would be Skyping me again in ten minutes.

Tory said, "She's your problem. I'm going to look up my

horoscope, then I'm going to whip my design team into shape. They're scared of me, you know."

"I know."

Lacey tried to skitter into her office, muttering something about "pregnancy-related hormone surges," but I grabbed her elbow and wouldn't let go. We sat at my table and turned the computer on.

When we connected, Kalani beamed at us. We heard about her foot problems—"flaky foot," her witch sister-in-law who cursed her with black magic and caused the "flaky foot"—and her "sad and blue mood" on Saturday.

She told Lacey, "You getting even bigger, Laceeey. Ya. That baby must be size of, what you call—a monster! You face. Face much bigger now." Kalani held her hands outside her own face about six inches, as if Lacey's face had exploded.

"Thank you very fucking much," Lacey muttered, and smiled sweetly, "you skinny crow."

I kicked her underneath the table. Kalani is blunt, not mean.

"Ya! You not skinny!" Kalani laughed. She had not caught the whole sentence. Sometimes English is mangled between us, fortunately.

"So, Kalani," I said, "I hear you have a problem at the factory?"

Kalani laughed. "Yes. Teeny problem. Teeny as a bird. The color bleed, ya, Meeegie, the color bleed. Blech. Bad. Pink and dark pink now a swirl. We got bad material. Bad. I talk to Jayanadani at suppliers and she said it our fault. It not our fault. I call her again. Tell her she lie."

"I'll call her." Jayanadani was who we worked with to get our materials and supplies over to Kalani.

"Hey, but lookie!" Kalani said, always positive. She pulled her shirt off and pointed to her bra.

"What in the world is that?" Lacey groaned.

"Lookie! This like, how you say, Hippie Bleeding Bra. Remember you have hippie in America? I know, I watch show on TV about hippies. It say Woodstock. I know you do Woodstock,

Meeegie and Laceeey. Woodstock and hair long and messy and no shirts and colors that bleed. Bleeding colors and hippie. Now we have new line, right? New line we call Hippie Bleeding Bras!"

I forced a smile. "I'll take care of the problem, Kalani."

"Ya. No problem. I likie Hippie Bra. I wear for my man tonight. Don't let him stay with me, though. He go home. I no want his socks my floor. I pick up my husband sock once, I never do again. See my eye scar? Bad husband. And see this? That scar on my arm? Him, too. Knife."

We listened to Kalani's story about her bad husband and then got back to business.

"Bye, Kalani, Lacey and I have to go." I waved. "I saw your numbers for yesterday. You all did well."

"Ya. We do well. We women. I don't like to hire no men. Too slow. Complain. Lazy. Don't like working for me, I a woman. Women better employees. I no like to hire much men."

"I didn't hear that, Kalani."

"What?" She looked confused. "I say again—I don't like hire men. Sometimes they try to touch women here, that bad, I no let that happen ever. I saw man do that long time ago, he rip my employee's shirt, she scream, and I pick up piece of steel, I hit him. Hit hard on his head. He on ground. Lots of blood. I hit again, then I fire him. I see it again, I hit other man in chest with—how you say—shovel. Bam bam! He out, too. And men, they pee pee on toilet, no clean up. They think they boss. Not them. Me. I the boss." She pointed at herself in her Hippie Bleeding Bra. "Men likey take over even though they not smart or quick. They too dumb to know they not smart or quick. They like to boss women around and then—how Tory say, you know Tory?"

"Yes, we still know Tory."

"She say men shoot back tequila and play with their balls. I don't need no shooting back tequila in my factory and I no want to see men play with balls. So—women only!" She smiled again, so innocent.

Other countries do not, obviously, worry about political correctness, and Kalani does not see the need to hide the fact that she discriminates against men.

"Men, they act like they smart, try make me think I not smart, but I smart because lookee me. This my factory and I make bleeding bras. For Woodstock!"

"I'll get back to you, Kalani, but stop all production. We don't want Hippie Bleeding Bras."

Her face fell. "No bleeding bras for hippie women at Woodstock?"

"No. I'll get back to you. Thanks, Kalani."

She smiled again and cupped her boobs. "Okay-dokay. Byebye, Meeegie! Bye-bye, Laceeey! You big lady now, Laceeey! You getting bigger all over! How you butt? Big, too?"

"Fuck you very much," Lacey said, smiling. "You skinny centipede."

I flinched. So glad Kalani did not understand the f word.

"Okay, thank you much! Bye-bye, seeesters! I love you."

Lacey waved, both hands, her middle fingers slightly up.

"Love you, too, Kalani," I said, grabbing Lacey's hands.

I shut off Skype.

"A Hippie Bleeding Bra line, now that's a fab idea," Lacey said. "You're going to call Jayanadani?"

"Yes. I'll get this materials problem fixed, insist they change it out or we don't pay, then I'll have the other factory near to Kalani ship over more materials and we'll start over. You're meeting with Delia and Beatrice today, right . . . have you heard from David at Tieman's . . . I'll call Joy Ridge's boutique, they're opening more stores . . . you soothe Jay's feathers up in Seattle, I'll soothe Marty's in Arizona . . ."

Our conversation went on at length. We grabbed pads of paper and scribbled; we shared jobs and tasks. Lacey and I work together well.

It's a sister thing.

*   *   *

Grandma *tap-tapped* in an hour later. Blue silk dress, bone-colored heels. Baubles: sapphires. Definitely adequate to keep the stench of poverty away, as she would say.

"Heard about the bleeding bras. Have that under control? Good. I talked to Adele and Zonya. They're getting that last shipment out to Chicago. I heard from Monique's, she said coast to coast they sold out of the lingerie that Tory advertised on YouTube, same with a whole bunch of other stores, you're on that, right? Good." She reached back and "patted the fairies" on her back to relieve the pain of the whippings. She was doing that more lately, I'd noticed.

"Ride Kalani's butt, we want to catch this. I want to see the latest numbers, how's that storm affecting New York and our deliveries, have you talked to Gildy's Accessories in Georgia and Louisiana, good, stay on that. New markets are . . ."

When she was done, she said, "Please start dressing better when you're here, Meggie. What are you, a plumber today? A meat grinder? A corpse? Get that hair done." She kissed my cheek and walked out. "Lipstick. Again. Wear lipstick."

Grandma and I work together well, too.

About ten that night, still working, I stared at my reflection in the window. I knew Mount Hood was out there. Waiting for me.

I ran my hands over my face.

I was too skinny.

My hair was ragged.

Jeans too big.

Tennis shoes, beaten up.

I didn't care.

I wish I did.

I thought of the chief. Hmm. Maybe I could start caring a mini-bit.

Lacey called me about ten o'clock at night.

Cassidy had been suspended from school. She had been

caught smoking a joint in the *boys'* locker room. Not the girls', the boys'. Lacey was having a meltdown.

Cassidy called me from her bedroom, where her mother had banned her to, about an hour later.

"Aunt Meggie," she whispered. I knew she was trying not to let the melting-down Lacey know she was on the phone. "I was thinking of you. Unfortunately, I'm out of school for a week— there was a slight misunderstanding—so I was thinking that you and I could go to a dessert class together. I've already looked it up online and there's one in downtown Portland. Five nights, once a week, and we'll learn how to make pastries and cakes! Want to go?"

I tried not to laugh. I explained to her that, one, I knew she was grounded, and two, I didn't think she should be able to go to cooking class, as she'd been expelled for smoking pot.

"I had a calculus test," she whispered. "I'd studied for it, I knew what to do, but I was nervous."

"And you thought smoking a joint was the answer?"

"Yes, I did."

"In the boys' locker room?"

"Sure, why not? No one was in there except for us."

Us? "You and Cody, the boyfriend?"

"Oh, my gosh!" I heard Cassidy suck in her breath before she hissed again, "It says here on the website that they'll teach us how to make lemon mousse cake, orange petit tarts, Baked Alaska, strawberry cheesecake, and a chocolate mint mousse. I would love to learn how to do that. Wouldn't you?"

"It does sound yummy. You know I don't cook." I hate cooking.

"You will here. This will be so much fun. Grandma Brianna taught me. I love to cook and bake with her. She understands how the tiniest bit of spice or vanilla can change the entire taste of the dish."

"Yes, the tiniest bit." I had no idea what she was talking about.

"Did you like the bouquet I left at your door yesterday?"

"Oh, honey, I loved it. It was exactly what I needed. You are so thoughtful, Cassidy."

"I wrapped a purple ribbon around it because you look good in purple."

I used to look good in purple.

"I'm into organic fruits and vegetables now, too, when I cook. I won't use anything but organic. It brings out the flavor naturally, without the dilution of the pesticides and herbicides and all the other junk."

"And how is pot smoking healthy, you organic-food-loving twerp?"

"Pot is an herb."

"No, it isn't. It turns your mind to lazy mush. It alters your reality. It's toxic for your physical health and it's a gateway drug—"

"Oh, my gosh again, Aunt Meggie!" Cassidy's voice pitched in excitement, then hushed back down to a whisper. "I clicked on another page on this website and they have cooking classes for hors d'oeuvres. We have to do that class, too. I'm going to ask Grandma Brianna to come when she's not on her sex book tour. It would be so much fun if we all did it together. Do you think Grandma Regan would do it with us, too?"

"Grandma Brianna, yes. Grandma Regan, no. She says that domesticity makes her feel dizzy. I'll make you a deal, Cassidy. No pot at all, no drinking for three weeks"—I thought it best to start small and have realistic goals—"and we'll sign up together for the next round of dessert classes. What do you say?"

She paused, she thought, she made a *hmmmm* sound. "Okay, Aunt Meggie, I'll do it."

"I'm delighted."

"What about the hors d'oeuvres class? If I don't drink or smoke pot for six weeks after that, can we do that one, too?"

"Yes. Hors d'oeuvres class it is."

What other answer would a good aunt give?

I watched Blake on television later that week while I was eating popcorn dipped in peanut butter and strawberries dipped in melted chocolate chips. I was in plaid pajama bottoms, one pink and one green sock, and a gray, fifteen-year-old University of Oregon sweatshirt. Hard to be this glamorous.

There had been a shooting, gang related.

He spoke well. Tight, crisp, factual, calm.

He was a man you could trust. A man who was courageous and strong and had the whole thing under control. Your neighborhood was safe again, and the bad guy was behind bars. His gun was back in his holster, and he would be riding away on his white horse into the sunset. He was The Cowboy In Charge.

"I want you to come home and get naked in my bed," I said out loud to the Blake on TV. "Come stark-naked. For a few hours."

I watched Blake answer more questions, those gray-blue eyes drifting to the camera briefly, insightful, hard, but personable, too, as if he had a relationship with all the people of Portland. If my skin could catch on fire from staring at him, it would. I imagined myself prancing around in flames in front of him. Tantalizing.

"Afterward, before breakfast, you will go home, Mr. Sex on Wheels. You will give me a kiss on the cheek. You will not ask me on a date, I will not tell you I like you, we will not develop any sort of emotional bond or commitment where either you or I could get hurt. You will leave."

I tossed a strawberry up in the air and caught it with my teeth, the melted chocolate splattering on my cheek. I wiped it off with my sweatshirt sleeve.

"I will go on creeping through my life and I will handle my flashbacks and day nightmares and night nightmares as best I can with the blood and the rats so I don't cartwheel straight out of my mind and I will work until I can't think straight and then you will come over at night and we'll strip down naked and start our hoo-ha all over again. How does that sound, Blakey?"

I tossed another chocolate-covered strawberry up, same result.

When they flipped to another story, I turned off the TV and all the lights except for my strand of white lights looped through the rafters. Jeepers climbed up and hissed, then went to sleep on my chest.

I watched what happened over a year ago in my head like I was watching a scary movie that I knew would end badly.

This probably sounds self-destructive. It is. But I have found it more destructive if I don't let the memories in. If I shut them out, I become more mentally screwed. They stalk me, trail me, taunt me continually, but if I run through them and feel the terror, the utter shock, the shearing pain, it will leave me in semi-ruins, but that particular memory will retreat for a while. I closed my eyes and gave in, letting the past I'd buried smash through. I rocked myself back and forth, back and forth.

I saw Blake's headlights come down the street about two hours later.

I went to sleep about one in the morning.

I felt better knowing he was there.

I did not have a regular sex life during my marriage.

Why?

Aaron often withheld sex.

He used sex as a weapon. If I was late getting home one night from filming, we wouldn't have sex for a week.

If we had a fight, no sex for two weeks. If I was out of town for work, it could be three weeks. This was combined with the oh-so-emotionally-debilitating silent treatment, as if I were a child who needed to be punished.

I would ask him to talk to me, to work out the problem, to tell me how he was feeling, and he would sigh and act pained, as if I was too stupid to talk to. Or he would say, "There's nothing wrong," I would say that of course there was something wrong, because he wasn't speaking to me, and he would deny it again. He would look at me with fury, reproach, or condescension.

Although our sex life was uncontrollably passionate when we were dating, it started to change after we married. About six months into our marriage, Aaron started to criticize my love-making. Try that one on for size. He stripped me of confidence in the bedroom faster than he could have flipped the sheets off.

"You're uncreative, rigid . . . too slow to orgasm . . . don't try hard enough . . . show some enthusiasm . . . your foreplay is like being scratched by a raccoon . . . you're loose inside, squeeze, damn it, squeeze . . . I wish you had bigger boobs . . . have you lost weight, I don't like it . . . seems like your rhythm is off . . . you're a prude, that's what you are . . . cold . . . you make weird sounds, I almost laugh listening to you . . . you groaned like a bear . . . What? Am I boring you? . . . maybe you're gay, that's why you're not turned on . . . arch. Come on, arch . . ."

The truth was, I wasn't good in bed with Aaron past the first year. I was probably quite poor. It is extremely hard to be good in bed when you don't love or at least care deeply about the person you're with. You have to feel safe. Wanted. Welcome.

It eventually became hard for me to kiss Aaron on the lips. Kissing is so much more personal than sex. He liked French kissing. I used to, but as our relationship tanked, I became repulsed by French kissing him. I felt like I was being invaded by a wet, flicking sponge. I sure didn't want to give him a blow job, and I didn't want to spend any time in foreplay, because I didn't love him. I didn't like him. I wanted out of his arms.

The tragic thing about sex is how horribly it can mess you up in the head and how utterly alone it can make you feel. If you are with the wrong person, if it's not a healthy relationship, if you feel hurt or threatened or demeaned, it's like you're having lonely, shattering, even dangerous sex with yourself, only there is someone bucking on top of you. You don't look in each other's eyes, you don't kiss, you don't move with love and thoughtfulness, with giving, there's zero heart connection.

You roll out of bed, and a piece of you—dignity, self-respect, esteem—is still left in that bed. The best part of yourself—your soul—has been left between the sheets.

That's how I felt with Aaron.

Like every time I rolled out of bed, I was less than when I'd crawled into it.

But I wanted to have sex with Blake. I wanted that physical bliss. I wanted to forget. It would be lusty and safe. He's a good man. He's stable. I could kiss him on the lips. I betcha I could even French kiss him. When he left, I could go back to fighting the clawing, black feathered rats in my head all by myself.

That's the way I wanted it.

"We're going bungee jumping?" I pictured myself springing up and down in midair, held by a harness my face turning to white cream. "Hell no. And I mean heeeell no."

"Do not say no to your grandma," Grandma said. She rapped her knuckles on my desk. She was in her rubies today with a purple dress. "Better manners, Meggie. Be classy, not a weak chicken."

"I am not going to bungee jump," Tory said. "My boobs would hit me in the face and knock me out. I am not risking damage to this fantabulous surgery I've had done."

"Your boobs will be safe," Grandma said. "Wear two bras. Let's go, girls."

"I can't bungee jump, Grandma," Lacey said, as she adjusted the vogue, black maternity dress my mother had bought her.

"Of course you can't. I would never let my great-granddaughter bungee jump when she is but a tiny, curled-up butterfly in your stomach, but you're coming with us."

"Great." Lacey laughed and clapped. "I will love this. Love bungee jumping."

"Grandma," I said, "I appreciate the invitation, but I have to stay here. I have about two hundred e-mails to answer, calls to return, we've got a shipment problem in Georgia, packing issues in Seattle, I've got calls in to places for the fashion show—"

"I can't go, either," Tory said. "I've got a meeting with that creepy man from Wanda's Closet. He gives me the creeps."

"I can go," Lacey said, so smug. "Meggie, Tory, quit whining."

"Cancel all of it." Grandma cut her hands through the air. "All work and no play makes a woman's estrogen dry up. I worked too hard my whole life and now I'm making up for it because I'm old. You girls follow me out this door right now or I will announce to all of our employees that I'm going to double their salaries and give them free teeth whitening."

"Teeth whitening?" Lacey said.

"Yes, it's not covered by the dental plan, but it should be."

"I could use a teeth whitening," Tory said.

"Teeth are not supposed to glow in the dark like yours, Tory," Lacey said. "You know that, don't you? Your teeth are so white, they're almost blue."

"And you have teeth like a hamster, Lacey."

"That's enough, ladies!" Grandma said. "Out you go."

"I think I'm going to barf," Tory said. "I don't like heights."

"I feel sick," I said. "I don't want to be attached to ropes and thrown off a bridge. I am not going to bungee jump. I'll probably wet my pants. Too scary."

Grandma leveled her gaze at me. "You've become too scared to live, Meggie, and I will push that fear out of you if it's the last thing I do. And the other last thing I'm going to do is get rid of the fighting between you girls. It's nauseating. Move your butts."

Bungee jumping is not for the faint of heart.

Grandma was strapped in first because "clearly I'm the one with courage. De-wimp yourselves, girls."

I would go next, then Tory.

Lacey said to us, as we trudged onto a bridge, above a rushing river, frozen in fear, "I am so glad I'm pregnant. So glad." She then turned and tossed her cookies.

Grandma said to the employees of Bungee Boogles, "I have no fear. Strap me in and let me rip."

I said to them, "I think I peed my pants a bit already."

Tory said, "If my heart pounds any harder it will come out of my mouth. Be ready to catch it."

The employees were thrilled with Grandma, telling her she was "awesome, ma'am, you are wicked awesome!"

Grandma threw her arms straight out, smiled, tipped her head to the heavens, and said, "I am living my life, yes, I am." She then walked to the edge; listened for their count of three, two, one; and did a swan dive, elegantly, gracefully, with utter strength and courage.

Her jump was like her personality.

I tiptoed to the edge, my body wiggling like a slug on a hook, and declared, "I am going to die. The lines will snap. I will unravel. I will be in the river within seconds. Tory, make sure you take care of the pets that Regan brought me."

"I'm not taking care of the pets. I don't like animals," she snapped. "They bite, they poop, they slobber."

"This is the last thing I ask of you before I die." My knees were knocking. I peed a tiny squirt in my pants, I know I did.

"Ask Lacey to do it." Tory gave me a frustrated look. "I am not taking care of any animals even if this is your last request. Grandma is a certifiably batty old woman. She's not only lost her marbles, she has eaten them. This is what we'll be like when we're old. Doing crazy-ass things and dragging our innocent granddaughters along to do it. What is wrong with her?"

"You ready, lady?" one of the employees asked me.

"No. I'm not."

"Okay. Uh. Yeah. Your grandma did it."

"Okay. Uh. Yeah," I said back to him. "I'll do it. Better to get it over with. Good-bye family."

I hemmed, I hawed, I wasted time. The employee gave me a tiny push, and I was off, flying freely, straight down, through the air. I wriggled, I screamed, I think I fully peed my pants, I swore, I flapped my arms.

And then I bounced. Bounced and bounced, up and down, the river not up my nose, the lines intact, my neck not snapped in half.

I stared back up at the bridge as I bounced, bounced, bounced. Grandma was cheering. Tory flapped a hand at me as in, "Meggie ruined this! She didn't die, now I have to do it." Lacey shouted, "Hallelujah! You're still with us!"

I bounced some more.

My underwear was wet. I was still shaking. I bounced again. I felt a lot better.

Tory's jump was like her personality, too.

She swore like a drunken demon. She complained about her

boobs getting squished. In fact, that's what she yelled up to us on the bridge when she was still bouncing: "My boobs did get squished. I knew that would happen!"

She argued with us when she was still hanging from the rope. She swore again and said, "My crotch was not prepared for this shit!"

At the end, the four of us hugged. We laughed. Grandma took us out to an old-fashioned ice-cream parlor and we had sundaes with chocolate mint ice cream, a load of hot fudge sauce, and whipped cream. I took off my underwear in the bathroom and tossed it out.

We clinked our sundaes together.

"Cheers to family," Grandma said. "And cheers to life. Cheers to pushing the fear out of yourself and to taking dares. May the three of you always have adventures together."

We laughed and clinked our sundaes together again. I saw Grandma smile, then she dipped her head and had another bite of hot fudge sauce. This was what she wanted. Tory and Lacey not fighting, her "girls" all together, no one feeling left out, me living again without fear.

We dropped her off at home.

We knew she'd head straight outside for a celebration cigar and her shot of whiskey.

The expensive type, of course.

That night I thought about the fashion show as I sat on my deck under the whispering maple trees in the orange Adirondack chair. *Know them, know us* kept running through my mind. I thought about Grandma and her story. Ireland. The dancing leprechaun. The rainbow. The owl. Lace. Satin. Baubles. Lingerie. Nightgowns. Bras.

I thought about our employees, how creative and interesting they were, the hobbies they had, the challenges and problems they'd endured. Their life histories.

I had a spark of an idea.

Would my idea work?

Know them.

Know us.

Know Grandma.

I grabbed Lacey in her office and yanked her down with me to Tory's.

We sat down at Tory's table, crowded with fabrics, lace, paper . . .

"I have an idea," I said. "For the fashion show."

"What is it?"

I told them.

Lacey's eyes just about bugged out of her head. "Cover me in oil and bake me over a fire pit."

Tory said, "People will think they're at a comedy show."

"What will Grandma say?" Lacey asked, hand to throat.

"I'll take care of Grandma," I said.

"Better you than me," Tory said. "I don't need that temper hacking me in half."

"We're going to rename it," I said. "It's going to be called Lace, Satin, and Baubles: A Fashion *Story*."

It was such an out-of-this-solar system sort of idea it would work. I knew it.

My doorbell rang on Sunday night about seven.

Jeepers was lying on my chest making a hissing sound, which I finally realized did not mean he hated me. I had already fed Mrs. Friendly, the lizard. He stuck his tongue out at me. I was still wearing my jeans from work and a pink T-shirt with the name of our company on it.

"Hello, Meggie."

"Blake." I didn't know what else to say, so I said his name again. "Blake."

"I have steaks."

"You do?"

"Yes. Come on over."

Tempting.

"I promise I won't burn yours, Meggie. Trust me."

"Ha, trust you?"

He took my question seriously. I hadn't meant to say it aloud.

"Yes, trust me, Meggie."

I studied him. I thought. "I'll trust your steaks. Only your steaks."

Ah, that smile melted my cold and untrusting heart.

"I can't imagine being police chief, Blake. I think about bras and lingerie all day long. You think about creepy and demented people, guns, officers, the public's safety, crimes. It can't be pleasant." I had been in charge of the salad, with tomatoes, carrots, red onions, and croutons, and setting the table. He had been in charge of the steaks and corn.

"It's not always pleasant, but I like it. I like making the city safer. I like working with my officers and the community. It's a challenge, I like challenges. There are a lot of different facets to the job."

"And you like to be in charge." He handed me steak seasoning across his kitchen table. The steak was excellent.

"Yes, I do. I have a lot of experience, I'm trained, I know what I'm doing, but—"

"But?"

"But there are days . . ."

"And today was one of those days?"

"Yes." He seemed weary. His gaze shifted, and I knew he was thinking about the latest problem.

"Will I see it on the news?" My salad was pretty tasty, too.

"Yes."

"Do you want to talk about it?" I tried to keep the sympathetic tone out of my voice, because I am not getting emotionally involved here—heck, no, I'm not—but it snuck in, and I saw his eyes gentling as he looked at me.

"I'd rather talk about something else."

"Are you sure? I'd like to listen." I wanted to help. No, I didn't. Yes, I did. I cared about him. No, I didn't. . . . Yes, you do, dive in. . . . I shook my head. Oh, how confused and muddled I am. . . .

"Yes, I'm sure. I've been talking about it all day. I need some time away from it."

I wanted to run my fingers through that thick blond hair. "Maybe you should have become a painter instead."

He smiled, his face relaxing. "Maybe."

"Or a ceramicist. You could have worked with clay." The corn crunched. Delicious.

"I could use my artistic talents."

"Do you have a hidden artist behind the tough guy demeanor?"

"Not at all. Could not draw a stick figure to save my life."

"Ah. Well, perhaps it's not too late for you to become a dolphin trainer."

"Sounds relaxing. I could be in the water."

"Or, you could come and work for our company and sell bras. How do you feel about bras?"

"I feel . . ." He looked at me, those gray-blue eyes searing me, but laughing, too. "I feel good about bras. Why don't you show me yours?"

"Ha." I cringed, thinking of my old beige bra. I would dig a hole with my teeth through his floor before showing him my beige bra. "Maybe another day."

"I live in hope, Meggie. Let's talk about you."

"No. Too boring. Let's move on."

"I don't think I want to move on."

"Let's do anyhow."

"Okay, not you. Let's talk about your company. Last time you told me some things you were worried about. How is it now?"

"We're struggling." I knew I could trust him to keep what I told him to himself. He was a trustworthy man. "It's a mess."

"Tell me about it."

I talked about the Fashion Story and my concerns. I talked in generalities about the financial situation. It was a relief to talk to someone outside the company. He was insightful, and he cut through the crap. I started to see some of our problems more clearly, simply by listening to Blake.

"I don't know much about bra and negligee selling, or I would try to offer better help and advice," he said later.

"You've actually been a huge help. Thank you."

"I only know what I like," he drawled.

"Not surprising. Being a man, you would have an opinion on that."

"Haven't seen any negligees in a long, long time, though."

"You must be kidding."

"No." He seemed serious.

"Why not?"

"Haven't met anyone I wanted to see in a negligee."

"I haven't met anyone I wanted to see in a negligee, either."

He laughed. I do try to have a sense of humor now and then.

"Bring a bunch of negligees over here one night, Meggie, and I'll tell you which ones I like."

"Gee whiz. Thanks. What a guy."

"Can I ask you a question, Meggie? Why aren't you married? I'm surprised that you're single."

I felt my whole body clench up, like ice had been poured down my mouth and then someone had shaken it through my body. "I was married, and I will not do that again."

"Never?"

"No."

"That bad?"

"Worse."

"What happened?"

"That, I don't want to talk about."

"Why?"

"Because it's too personal, and I don't want it between us." And I am still trying to get sane.

He was silent for a while. "But it is between us."

"No, it's not."

"Sure it is. It's something you don't want to talk about because it was painful. It's something about your life and your past."

"Right. It's in the past. No need to dig it up."

"Well, when you're ready to talk about it, I want to hear it."

"Why?"

"Because I like you. Because I'm interested in you. Because I want to know what was so hurtful about your marriage."

"It's not relevant to you and me, though."

"I could not disagree with you more, Meggie." He leaned toward me. Those shoulders were massive and huggable.

"You're an interesting guy, Blake."

"Why?"

"Because you're curious. Because you like to have a full conversation. Because you like to listen."

"Why is that particularly interesting?"

"Most men aren't like that. They like to talk *at* women. They like to lecture. They like to pontificate. They don't listen well. They don't want to know that much about the woman they're with. They want to know surface stuff: what they look like in jeans. What they look like naked. Are they good in bed? Will they listen endlessly to all their problems and whining? Will they cook well? Will they smile a lot? That's about it. That's what they want. Food and sex."

"Pretty insulting, Meggie." That jaw of his tightened up.

"But true."

"No, it's not."

"I think it is."

"Then you have a sad and erroneous opinion about men. I know plenty of men who love their girlfriends and wives and it's not because they smile pleasantly, cook well, or like rolling around in bed. My best friend is so in love with his wife, when she goes out of town a few times a year to visit her mother and sister, he cries. He calls me and I can hear him sucking it up. He's a captain with the fire department—tough, disciplined, focused—but he doesn't like to be without her.

"My uncle Brody has been married for forty-five years to my aunt Roslyn. I've watched him watching her. She needs something, he's up and getting it. She opens her mouth to speak and his head about swivels off his neck to hear it. They still take"—

he put his fingers up in air quotes—" 'naps' in the middle of the afternoon, and he's constantly kissing her. My stepfather, Shep, loves my mother and has repeatedly said when she dies, he'll die. I think he's right. My father cannot live without my mother."

"That's sweet."

"You don't sound like you believe it."

"It hasn't been my experience."

"Tell me about your experience."

Now he was ticking me off. "I already said no. What are you not understanding about that word?"

Our eyes clashed. Our personalities clashed. We are two strong-willed, opinionated people, and those types usually butt heads.

"Maybe one day you'll say yes."

"I doubt it." No I would not. I thrummed the table, so agitated, lots of black and red and rats swimming my way now.

We sat in silence, each waiting for the other to break it.

"What's your favorite type of food, Meggie?"

"Italian. But I love steaks, too. Good job, by the way." I wanted to run. This was getting too deep for me. Too involved.

He smiled at me, but I wasn't fooled. Those eyes were sharp and assessing. He was a brilliant man. Capable. Commanding. Military trained. Special forces. Police chief. No one should ever underestimate him. It would be a stupid, stupid thing to do.

I would not underestimate him. I had met my match.

And I could tell that my "match" wasn't happy with me and how tight I held my past to my chest.

If he knew the truth, he wouldn't want to talk to me. He wouldn't want to spend time with me. He wouldn't like me.

I don't like me.

How could he?

Best to keep him out in the future. Keep him out, shut him out. Shut Meggie in.

My fears are not limited to my nightmares.

I have what I call daymares, too.

Different things will trigger my daymares and haul me back

in time to places I don't want to be: black feathers on a bird, a picture of India, Los Angeles, small apartments, the color red, angry men, feeling overloaded at work, any sort of mind manipulations people try to play on me, rats, Japanese cherry trees, the hint of the scent of pot, hospitals, doctors' white coats, and video games—all will send me spinning.

I am, for example, still scared of my bathtub.

13

〜

"Mom's on TV again." Lacey walked into my office the next morning and turned on the TV in the corner. I was having breakfast: bacon and a Baggie full of peanuts. I had not slept well because of Aaron's rat claws squeezing my neck.

"Hello, Mom," I said to the TV. I grabbed a beer.

"Please don't embarrass us too badly, Mother," Lacey said, her prim side showing. "Please."

Our mother, appearing Southern belle-ish, with those sweet cheeks and lovely smile, her red curls flowy, said to the host, "Let's talk about your marriage, Shenolyn."

"Oh, no, Brianna," Shenolyn said. "Let's not."

"All right then, we'll talk about marriage in general. I discuss it in my book *Couples and Coupling*. You see, marriage is a complicated relationship. I personally opted out of marriage."

She patted her chest. Our sign. It was her way of saying, I love you, Lacey, Tory, and Meggie. "I could not imagine sleeping with only one man for decades. I could not imagine the domesticity of it. I wanted, and needed, more freedom, but I do understand that some people feel that desire to marry. So let me tell you how to keep your marriage fresh and ooh la la . . ."

"Oh, please, Mom, don't," Lacey said, her puritanical streak showing again.

"Let's hear it, Mom," I said. "Fresh and ooh la la."

Tory walked in. "What's she saying today about ooh la la?"

And there went our mother. Words like "testicle massage . . . you must twist on top, like this . . . smear the chocolate . . . a spank should not hurt, if you're into that, many people aren't, so ask your partner first . . . equality in the bedroom, unless you want to role play the powerful position . . . fake swords add a competitive and dominating element . . . never leave anyone alone in the house in a cage, there could be a fire. . . ."

Lacey stood and paced, her hands on her arched back. "I will never, ever let my children see this."

"But I do not," our mother said, "and I will stress this, I do not believe in the swinger lifestyle."

"You don't?" the host asked. "Please explain what the swinger lifestyle is and then tell us why it doesn't work."

Our mother described the swinger lifestyle and how couples swapped partners for a night or weekend. "The swinging lifestyle is beneath all of us. It's dangerous. It's dirty. It's slutty. It definitely veers off into a beastly area. Same with bed hopping. This"—she made quotes in the air with her fingers—" 'hooking up' mentality with no emotional attachment, no love and friendship, is a sexual mistake. Don't do it. It will only shred your confidence and self-respect. Sex is special, it's not a drive-by shooting, it's not a 'wham, bam, thank you, ma'am.' It's the gift of yourself, it's a relationship."

She smiled, leaned slightly forward. Her purple lace negligee showed. She hiked it up for the cameras.

"Thank you, Mom," I said. "Nice advertising."

"She looks so innocent," Lacey said. "Like a red-haired lollipop."

"She's a ball breaker if I've ever met one," Tory drawled, then said, "On TV."

We all laughed.

Our mother's last words were, "Don't you be afraid of lubrication creams!"

We knew the truth about Brianna O'Rourke. She was Betty Crocker meets Knitting Queen. Glasses and flat shoes. Snow White house, and cooking club with her girlfriends.

"Who wants me to read their horoscope?" Tory asked. "Good. You first, Meggie. Today is your day to reach out to a Pisces in need. That would be me. . . ."

Aaron knew how to start fights, lie his way through, shut me down, twist things to blame me, minimize his transgressions, not take responsibility for his behavior or attitude, and attack.

A day later he'd turn on the charm and romance me. He'd be emotionally available, my best friend, and all over me with praise and compliments.

For a while.

It was his way of keeping me constantly in emotional flux, confusion, and mental mayhem. I couldn't see my own way out. He was so clever, the way he manipulated me.

He wanted compliments on his lovemaking. He wanted compliments if he made dinner. He wanted compliments on his looks. He wanted compliments on everything. It's exhausting to constantly compliment someone. It's exhausting to be constantly asked, in one way or another, to compliment. "My people loved my idea today. . . . did you notice that I rewrote the beginning of my film? It's much better now, isn't it. . . . Don't you love my hair? . . . I am sick of doing all the work around here without getting thanked. . . ."

My own health was deteriorating rapidly. I lost weight. I couldn't eat. I started having problems swallowing. I had constant, freewheeling anxiety.

I did, however, find the strength to refuse to work with Aaron on my next film, as I could not endure working with him again. I also knew I would be gone a lot, and that would save me. He threw fits each night for weeks.

When I received excellent reviews for the film, I hid them from him. When he found out, he raged. "You hid them because you didn't think I could take it, right? Honestly, I can't believe, my friends can't believe, that you had even one accolade. I mean, the film, if you can call it that, was *okay*, Meggie, but it wasn't great. The film we made together was much better. What did you do, sleep with the reviewers?"

After that fight, I left for Oregon. I didn't even tell him. He called me ten times a day, begging me to come back. I didn't return the calls. I ate and slept like a normal person.

When I arrived, Lacey said to me, crying on my shoulder, "What happened to you?" She picked up my hair like it was a dead animal. "Have you decided not to brush your hair?"

Tory said, "I am nauseated. What are you wearing? Those jeans are way too big. You've lost too much weight. Is that a shirt from twenty years ago? Is this a joke? Is this a fashion joke? It's not funny, Meggie."

My mother said, after I cried on her dining room table, "Let's bake a cake. The serenity will allow you to think rationally about leaving Aaron. No. Let's bake three cakes. Here we go, dear."

My grandma said, "You are more unhappy than a rabbit with his neck caught in a noose. Don't be a pansy-wimp. Divorce is the only answer sometimes, so grasp it and go. I need you back up here with me anyhow."

Marriage, to me, was a lifetime commitment, through thick and thin. I didn't *want* a divorce. I had spent my whole life trying to be excellent—at Lace, Satin, and Baubles, in school, and in filmmaking. To admit that I had *failed,* chosen poorly, made a mistake, I could hardly wrap my mind around that one. Plus, I had vowed to stay *"till death do us part."* Aaron wasn't dead, and neither was I.

I returned to Los Angeles, but after three months I once again felt like I was living under a black cape of doom and destruction, constantly attacked and bone weary. I told Aaron I was leaving him.

He had a breakdown and dropped into semihysteria. He promised things would change. They didn't.

I left.

He was committed when he stood on top of a building in downtown Los Angeles after threatening to jump. One of the police officers almost lost his life trying to save him.

I learned then what I should have known before I married him.

He should have told me.

I had a right to know.

I would clarify by saying that this was "personal fraud." Had I known about it, I would not have married him. That makes me sound like a terrible person. However, it is the truth.

There are many questions I have about marriage, not that I will get married again.

When we take vows "until death do us part," the implication is that the marriage will last until someone is residing in a coffin. But is the death of a marriage, through affairs, abuse, neglect, addictions, personality disorders, or continual misery and loneliness, also death?

What if there were secrets you didn't know before you married that you had a right to know? Isn't your spouse breaking the vows before the vows are said? If so, does that mean we can walk out free and clear? When we make a commitment, is that forever, regardless of new circumstances?

Is it immoral to leave a mean or neglectful spouse if he comes down with a disease because you can't tolerate the thought of being both caretaker and punching bag?

Is it immoral to leave a mentally ill spouse who won't agree to treatment? Even if the person agrees to get treatment, is it okay to leave? What if by staying your health fails because you're married to someone who will never be able to function as a spouse, who will always take and take and suck the life out of you? Is it fair to expect someone to give up their entire life to stay with a mentally ill spouse?

But isn't staying when things get tough part of marriage? The good and the bad? The lucky times and the bad surprises? Rich and poor? What about the love you had for that person on your wedding day, the commitment you made? Wouldn't you want that person to care for you, to love you, if your life fell apart? How can you justify leaving a spouse who has an illness in his head that he did not bring on himself?

What role do children play in a divorce? If there's no abuse, and the spouse is a good-enough parent but a lousy mate, should we stay married, and suck it up, until the kids are grown?

What do we owe our children? How much sacrifice is too much? Will a divorce simply cause a whole new set of problems, particularly for the children, and not solve anything?

What do we deserve in life, in marriage? Is it spoiled and entitled to even talk about "deserving more?" Is a good-enough marriage good enough? Do we expect too much?

I struggled with these questions years ago.

The end result was staggeringly poor.

"Did you tell Cassidy no sex, too?"

I put my cell phone on speaker as I walked to my dull, pesky, gray car from work. Ten o'clock at night. Way too late. "Hi, Lacey. What are you talking about?"

"When you told her no smoking pot or drinking for three weeks and then you'd take her to dessert class, did you tell her no sex, either?"

"Uh. No."

She let out a screech through clenched teeth.

"Problems?"

"Of course there are problems. I have three teenagers. There are always problems. It's a matter of which problem is setting me on fire." Lacey's voice went into shrieking mode. "The police brought her home. She and Cody were having sex in the middle of the football field on the fifty-yard line this afternoon."

"The fifty-yard line?" Sometimes I am glad I don't have children. "Well. Perhaps they were talking about sports, naked? Any chance of that?"

"Zero chance. I asked that kid what she said to the officers, and she said, 'We didn't even know they were there until they were, like, three feet from us! It was a surprise!' Honestly, Meggie, I think she was impressed by how quietly the police snuck up on them."

I shut the door of my car and leaned back in the seat. "Then what happened?"

"I guess that stupid boyfriend, Cody, rolled off and they dressed! I am not going to live through these teenage years. I can feel my hair graying."

"The police brought her home."

"Yes. My daughter was brought home in the back of a squad car. This is something to write about in the Christmas card along with Hayden turning into a girl and Regan's growing collection of animals."

"She's a daring one, isn't she?"

"She's a horny one, that's what she is. I was so furious my hair felt like it was tingling, and Matt was so upset he had to lie down on the couch while the police were talking to us. He said he felt faint. Cassidy boinged up and brought out her cinnamon rolls, plates, napkins, and darned if we're not all sitting around eating cinnamon rolls with the police officers.

"They said they weren't supposed to eat on duty, but they saw the cinnamon rolls and couldn't resist. When the police were leaving, Cassidy thanked them for the ride, and they said you're welcome, and she said it was nice to meet you, and they said it was nice to meet you, too, and she said she was sorry for the trouble, and they said that's okay, young lady, all polite. I could tell they thought she was a nice girl except for the fifty-yard line madness.

"I shut the door and started yelling at her, and then, right in the middle of my yelling, as if she's not even listening, she says"—Lacey mimicked Cassidy's voice—"'I am so glad that I didn't promise Aunt Meggie I wouldn't have sex because then I wouldn't get to go to dessert class.'" Lacey made a screeching sound through her teeth again.

"Lacey, you need to calm down. You're pregnant. Please. For the baby—" My words fell on deaf ears.

"So I railed at her, but I could tell she was only thinking about baking pastries. Matt was still lying on the couch, white as a dove. When I was done she wrapped her arms around me and said, 'Mom, I'm so sorry for upsetting you.' Notice that she didn't apologize for the fifty-yard line fiasco. She said, 'I'm going to make you dinner. I know you're tired. Sit down, please.' So that horny girl made my favorite spinach salad with the bacon crumbles."

"Oh, I love that salad."

"She brought it to Matt, the traumatized husband, and me. She had Hayden and Regan in there helping, and they're all laughing and talking. She made those crispy bread things with the basil and tomatoes and cheese for appetizers."

"One of her best."

"Then she made crab cakes. They were delicious, and she made that white sauce with the chives for dipping, too."

"I love her crab cakes. Are there extra?"

"No. Are you kidding? Finally, she melted chocolate over vanilla ice cream. Delicious." Lacey's voice was calmer.

"She's a horny chef."

"She's so naughty." Lacey sighed. "I love that child, but she cannot keep her pants on or her skirt down to save her life."

I didn't know what else to say except, "I'm looking forward to dessert class."

"You . . . you're here." I stood up, wobbly with surprise, and gaped at Blake. He was in faded denim jeans that fit him smooth and perfecto, and a dark blue shirt. He was tall and filled up my pink office like a friendly, thick chocolate bar.

As Lacey, Tory, and I were going over the incessant, exhaustive details for The Fashion Story, Abigail had knocked, opened the door, and introduced Blake with a flourish. "Meggie, Tory, Lacey, oh fabulous, you're not fighting or decapitating mannequins or throwing arms. May I present Portland Police Chief Blake Crighton?"

"Hello, Meggie." He smiled.

I felt my jaw drop, like I was trying to catch something with my mouth.

Tory said, "Holy moly."

Holy moly?

"I remember him from Wood Carving Night," Tory said, standing. "He is desire on wheels, isn't he?"

Lacey said, and I'm not sure she realized she'd spoken aloud, "Now, that's a wowza man for you."

A wowza man? I shushed them, blushed. Why must I blush around Blake?

"Hello, Lacey, Tory." Blake extended his hand, smiling, shaking Lacey's and Tory's. "It's a pleasure to see you both again."

"This is a bad day," Tory said. "I wish I had met you first. Do you like martinis? You are yada yada yada."

"Thank you, and no, I'm not a martini sort of man."

"Hello, Blake," I managed to squeak out.

"Sorry to drop in on you without warning, Meggie, but I knew if I called you'd say no."

I'd say yes to you, handsome.

"I'll say yes," Tory said. "Let's go."

"No to what?" I said.

"An early dinner. You said you liked Italian, and I just heard about an excellent Italian restaurant."

Lacey said, "I am so glad you've come to take Meggie to dinner. She needs to eat. I mean, she does eat. She eats some, but not much. She might eat you."

I groaned.

"That's not what I meant," Lacey said, waving a hand in the air, her red curls on top of her head. "I'm pregnant. I can't think anymore. My husband knocked me up for the fourth time. I think I told you about that when I saw you last. What? He thinks we don't have enough kids as it is? Is he trying to make me insane? I already am, clearly."

"You seem sane to me," Blake said, looking like he was about to laugh.

"Thank you. I fake it a lot." Lacey waved her hand in the air again. "Not in that way, I don't. I mean, I do now and then. We all do, right? I'm tired, I need sleep. Okay, I'm going to stop talking. Meggie can go and eat you—"

I had never seen Lacey so flustered.

"Not that she's going to eat *you*," Lacey went stumbling on. "That's presumptuous at this point. I mean, eat lasagna or spaghetti on you. Something like that. Bread."

Blake turned me upside down, too. I had sympathy for her.

"Oh, Lord God Jesus Mary the Apostle Paul, shut my mouth." Lacey groaned. "It's the pregnancy hormones."

"I would eat you for dessert," Tory said, her eyes moving up and down Blake's body. "You look like you're full of nutritional value. My husband, Scotty, is full of crap. He has no nutritional value at all. He won't even take my calls. Hey, chief, it's not stalking to call him now and then if he doesn't say, 'Don't call me anymore, Tory,' is it?"

"No. He should tell you to stop calling. However, perhaps you shouldn't call him repeatedly."

"I call him now and then." She coughed. "Every day. Not on the hour, though. Once in the morning, once in the afternoon, once at night. Sometimes at teatime, to tell him what I think."

I groaned. Tory doesn't take teatime.

"What is your opinion, chief? Do you think I should move back into my home and cook dinner naked? I think that if I seduce him back into my bed I can fix things from there—"

"Okay, I think we've had enough conversation with Blake—" I interrupted.

"Why are you trying to embarrass Meggie?" Lacey turned to Tory.

It was hypocritical, we both knew it. But why point it out to a pregnant lady?

"I'm not trying to embarrass her. You're the one who started talking about Meggie eating Blake." Tory pushed her black hair back with her hand.

"You're the one who said you would eat him for dessert. Can you pretend you have some manners when we have the police chief standing here?"

Blake seemed perfectly calm, amused even. The man is so not thrown by anything. This is nothin' for him.

"Blake, I don't think I can go to dinner. . . ." I could see that he was disappointed, it was a flash, but I caught it.

"Yes you can!" both Lacey and Tory semi-shouted.

"Go!" Lacey said.

"Brush your hair, then go! Here, I'll get you fixed." Tory darted to her bag and grabbed a brush and two bulging handfuls of makeup.

"No, Tory, my hair is fine."

"It is not. Look at it." She stabbed her finger at my hair. *"Look at it!"* She was clearly appalled.

I ignored that one, but I felt so self-conscious, I wanted to cover my head with my hands. "Blake, I'm sorry, I'll be working late—"

He rocked back on his heels, waiting this one out with a smile.

"No, you're not," Lacey said. "We're done. Good-bye."

"I will pull you out to his car by your messy hair if I have to," Tory said, slamming the makeup down. "You are not saying no to this piece of meat. He's better than my own husband, that piece of slimy meat. I would like to grill my husband on a barbeque—"

"He's not a piece of meat," Lacey said. "That's rude."

It was dinner or stand there and be humiliated. "I changed my mind. Let's go to dinner."

I grabbed my saggy brown purse from my desk, then his elbow, and turned him toward the door.

Lacey whispered, "Have a good time and call me no matter how late it is!"

Tory stood in front of me briefly, leaned in, and whispered, "Tell me your bra is not beige. If it is, call me from the restaurant and I'll bring you a purple one."

Abigail Chen clapped when I said good night. "Niiiiicce!" she said. "Nice!"

The production floor became treacherous territory because the employees stood and gawked, as if I'd grown three heads and a fluffy yellow tail. A bunch of them came up to meet Blake.

Shake his hand.

Chat.

Tell him how wonderful I was, as in, "Meggie is the best boss ever. You know her mom's a sex therapist, right?"

And, "Meggie's awesome. I'm glad you're taking her out to dinner. Don't piss her off, though. She's inherited the same temper as her grandma. You know Mount Vesuvius? Or St. Helens? You remember that explosion? She's like that."

The Petrelli sisters said hello, then to each other, as if Blake and I weren't standing there, "She needs a cruise . . . definitely . . . she and the chief . . . Alaska, I think . . . he looks outdoorsy . . . she's still pale, maybe a place where they could get some sun? . . . We did like the Greek isles . . ."

Finally, finally, we were through the production floor.

I knew my hair was a mess. I didn't have any makeup on. I was wearing jeans and a dark blue T-shirt. The T-shirt was a smidgen too tight from too many washings. I had on boots.

I exhaled too loudly when we finally escaped. "I need a beer," I said.

"I'll get you one."

"Thank you." He put his hand on my back and it tingled. I imagined a whole bunch of employees peering out the window at us. I heard a cheer going up. I didn't look back.

So embarrassing.

Blake drove us to an Italian restaurant about thirty minutes away in the country. I could not help but think about sexual tension as we chatted.

Physical attraction is an electric mystery.

How do you describe it?

Why is it that a base, fiery attraction will zing between two people and not between two others? You can look at a man and think he's good looking, kind, smart, and . . . nada. Nothing. But with some other man, it sizzles like steaks on a barbeque. He may not even be as good looking as the first one. What is that? Why? Is it hormonal? Chemical? Met in a past life? Star signs, as Tory would say?

Blake and I have that zingy attraction. It's constantly there when I'm with him. I watch him, he watches me. I take great care not to touch him because I know it would only take one look from him and I'd be divesting myself of all of my clothes and straddling his hips. He feels it, I feel it, we don't address it. We dance around it, we circle it, we stand back and observe it.

"So, Meggie, tell me some more about the documentary films you made before coming home. What were the topics?"

I told him, briefly, without letting my mind dwell on flicking wet sponges or tall buildings in Los Angeles, about the homeless kids here, the orphans in India, the kids' hopes for an education in Watts, and a village in Alaska.

"Can I see them?"

"Sure." *No.*

"When?"

"Soon." *Never.*

"I'd like to see them. Are you making another film now?"

"Not an indie film. I'm filming people at our company for our website."

He wanted me to tell him about that, so I did, then I switched the subject. "Tell me what you did today."

"I thought we were talking about your films."

"We were. We're done." I could feel that black rat nibbling inside me again. I shivered.

"I'd like to hear more about them. Why you went into filmmaking, what you loved about it, what interested you, how you picked your topics . . ."

"My granddad, The Irishman, was dying." I told him the story. "I loved cameras. I saw life, and people, in a new way when I held one in my hand."

"And that was it?"

"Yes." I squirmed. "But that's about all I want to say about filmmaking." I rubbed my throat. It felt like it was filling with black feathers.

"Didn't end well?"

I laughed. It was bitter. I felt drowned by black and red. "Let's say it's not my career anymore."

We sat quietly, then he reached out his hand, picked up mine, and kissed it. *He kissed my hand.* No one had ever done that. I swear that kiss ran all the way up my arm to my heart. "If you ever want to talk about it, I want to hear about it."

"I won't want to talk about it." My tone was prickly, tight, hard.

"Okay." He nodded at me. "Maybe another time."

"No. Not another time."

I knew he wasn't happy about my response, yet again, but why lie? I did not want to talk about my film career.

We drove in silence for a while. I could tell he was comfortable with the silence, comfortable waiting for me to talk. The best way to get more information out of someone is to simply be quiet. I knew it. I would not play into it. Plus, I was trying to right my world and get rid of the biting black rat.

I did not let go of his hand, because it was warm and strong.

The Italian restaurant was candlelit, private, and fancy. I loved it. I ordered dessert first.

Blake grinned. He ordered us beer.

"I do this all the time. If I die before the meal ends, I want to make sure I've had dessert."

"I get it, Meggie. Eat away."

He had his salad. I had chocolate mousse, then my salad. He ordered a calzone, I ordered lasagna. The hot bread arrived in a basket. I actually felt myself unwinding, the tight, tight tension in my shoulders giving way.

"So, give me your life story, Blake."

"I was born in Texas." He set his beer down. "My father died when I was eight."

That was *terrible*. "How crushing. I am so sorry." I actually felt my eyes well up.

He shrugged. "Don't be. He used to beat my mother."

My eyes cleared pretty quick.

"Almost every night he hit her. By the time he died, she'd had a multitude of broken bones and bruises, and I'd had a broken arm, a broken leg, I was missing two back teeth, and my jaw had to be operated on from his abuse. I tried to protect my mother, he punched me. That was our routine. I can't tell you how many times I was thrown into walls."

"I . . ." I struggled to speak. "I . . . I can't even imagine . . . Oh, Blake—"

He shrugged again. "He was killed when he was going eighty in his sports car awaiting trial for breaking my jaw. He was drunk, hit a curve wrong and went over a cliff."

"That sounds like a good thing."

"It was." His shoulders hunched in. It was almost imperceptible, but I caught it. "My mother didn't leave him because he threatened to hunt her down and kill her, me, and her mother and sister. I heard him say that to her many times. He had guns. He was violent. He was obsessive and possessive. He would not let my mother go. He wouldn't even let her get a job. She was terrified. I remember holding her when she could not stop shaking.

"He was an abysmal excuse for a man, a father, and a husband. I remember looking at him one night, blood flowing out of my nose, thinking that I would never, ever be like him, and I'm not. A year after he died I picked up a paper route. The next year I had my own lawn-mowing business. When I was fourteen, after school and sports, I worked at a restaurant at night and on weekends. My mother worked at the restaurant, too, at night, after a full day as a secretary.

"Our lives were infinitely better after he died. We had dinner in peace. We didn't dread hearing his key in the lock. We had money, not a lot, but we had it and could control it. My mother didn't cry herself to sleep on the couch, bleeding. I wasn't scared all the time. I didn't have any more broken bones and I didn't have to watch him slug my mother."

"Blake." I didn't know what else to say. I reached, automatically, for his hand. He held on. "How did she meet your stepfather?"

He smiled and began to unhunch his shoulders. "She changed jobs when I was fourteen and worked for Shep, who was the owner of an oil company. They started dating when I was fifteen, married when I was sixteen. Shep Stevens became the only father I ever knew."

"He was a good man then?" I was so hopeful. . . .

"The best. He still is the best man I've ever known. I was able to concentrate on sports and school once Shep came into our lives, because things settled down. Neither my mother nor I felt so desperate anymore. When the roof fell in, Shep paid for it. When my mother became sick with pneumonia for two weeks, he took care of her so I didn't miss school. When there were activities going on at school, he came so it looked like I had a father like all the other kids. He talked to my teachers, to the other parents. My biological father would come to school drunk and yell. Shep was a respected man. He brought peace, kindness, and stability to our lives."

"And he was good to your mother."

"Shep was madly in love with my mother. He still is. My mother had me when she was eighteen. She never said, but my guess is that my father shoved himself on her, and she was so humiliated to be pregnant, she married him. By the time she married Shep she was only thirty-four. He was forty-four and had never been married. Underneath the hard, brusque exterior, which he had to have to develop his oil company, the man was caring and loving with my mother and me. He treated me like his son from the first day."

"I think I'm going to cry." I sniffled, grabbed a napkin, and inelegantly wiped my nose.

"Shep took me fishing a lot. Hunting, too. He asked me on one of those fishing trips if he could ask my mother to marry him. He told me he loved her, loved me, and would love it if we could become a family. I told him yes before he finished talking. It was the greatest day of my whole life. He told me later that he had wanted to marry my mother within a week of hiring her, but she'd told him she would never marry again and Shep knew she wasn't ready after what she'd been through. He told me it was important for me to know that, because he didn't want me to think, man to man—those were his words—that he hadn't treated my mother respectfully."

He shook his head, his hard face softening. "I'll never forget that. Anyhow, I blew the proposal for him, though. I was so excited when we returned from fishing I ran into the house, hugged my mom, and whispered, 'Say yes, Mom, please say yes. I'll do anything you say if you say yes.'"

"Ahhh . . . And she did."

"Yes. I then had a dad who loved my mom, loved me, wanted to go fishing and hunting and do son and father stuff. What more could I ask for?"

"Nothing." I wiped my nose again. I can be a messy sap.

"That's what I thought, too. After they were married, he moved us into his home, which was a beautiful home on a hill. He bought my mother a new car. Her car broke down continually. Shep told me that he had offered to buy my mother a car a month after he met her, but she had refused to accept a gift that was that expensive. After the wedding he drove her car off, brought home a brand-new car, and said, 'Can't say no now, Yvette.' My mother quit her waitressing job at his insistence. Shep paid her well, but she'd kept the waitressing job because she'd been broke, we'd been broke, and she saved all the money she could. She said poverty had scared her to death.

"Shep bought me a car, too, and insisted I quit my restaurant job during the week so I could concentrate on sports and school. I was allowed to work only fourteen hours on the weekend. He came to all of my games along with my mother, who had missed a lot of them because of her waitressing job. Shep had played college football, so he coached me. He helped me with my homework. He taught me how to be a man."

"And after high school?"

"I went to West Point and played quarterback. I was later in Special Forces, then retired and became involved with law enforcement."

"Your childhood had a lot to do with those choices, didn't it?"

"You bet. I had a lot of anger as a kid. I was in fights, and I did not mind swinging hard. Soon, no one would fight me. I never wanted to be helpless again. I hated that I couldn't defend my mother, that I had to watch her being hit. I know what it's like to be on the weak end of life and I know what it's like to know you can defend yourself and the people around you. I prefer to defend."

"In your work as a police chief you must run into the same situations of domestic violence that you endured as a kid."

"I do. I have a program here to deal with it. Our officers are trained. We do all we can to protect abused women and children." He told me more about the program.

"Blake Crighton, you are one stud of a man."

He grinned at me. Ah, that grin will kill me one day. So inviting and friendly and manly.

"Thank you, Meggie O'Rourke. And you are one gorgeous, smart woman."

I couldn't deal with that comment, so I played with my silverware then asked, "Where do Shep and Yvette live now?"

"They live in Maui. I visit every year. It's a hardship, of course. I have to surf, swim, snorkel, that type of torturous thing."

I laughed. "That's a splendid love story. Your mother deserves him."

"She certainly does. She's an outstanding lady who literally took the blows for me from my dad again and again."

I wondered what Yvette would be like as a mother-in-law.

I thought of my own ex-mother-in-law and swallowed hard.

Last time I'd seen her she called me "Meggie Bitch."

Later that night I scrambled out of Blake's truck, none too gracefully, when he dropped me off at Lace, Satin, and Baubles to pick up my car.

"Thanks, Blake, for dinner." I stood outside his truck, my escape route wide open.

"You're welcome. Please say yes again."

I smiled, couldn't help it. "I'll think about it."

"You'll think about it?" He laughed, low, gravelly. We were at a place where we could laugh.

"Yes, thanks again."

I am running a lingerie business. I am not so young anymore. I have been through a whole bunch of crap. I used to make documentaries. I am planning a Fashion Story. I deal with a hundred problems a day. I am capable and competent when it comes to work.

I am a mental wreck who sees and feels violence and depravity in my head, day and night. When I am left alone too long with my own thoughts they trip me into rage, blame, and shame. I am chased by relentless guilt and am trying to tear myself out of a swamp of depression. I see black rats and have clawing nightmares and bone-chilling daymares. It is only recently that I feel I have a couple of fingers on a cliff and I'm not going to fall off again.

I am not normal.

Blake is normal.

I liked him a lot, and that wouldn't do. I thought about him way too much, and that wouldn't do, either. What I wanted from him were uncomplicated naked tumbles. No commitment, no emotional entanglements. I was definitely having problems staying away from the latter.

"Bye, Blake."

I saw disappointment in his eyes. I knew he was hoping I'd lean in and kiss him. That physical attraction was crackling between us like two solar flares crashing together.

But I couldn't. Oh, I couldn't.

"Bye, Meggie."

I shut the door. I walk-jogged to my car. I felt like an idiot. I knew he would follow me home to make sure I arrived safely because he said he was going to.

I waved when I turned right and he turned left on our street.

In my tree house I flopped on my bed and looked through the skylight at the shadows of the maple tree leaves dancing beneath the whiteness of the stars.

My body arched up thinking about him. I wanted that delectable body on mine, but I did not want another man prancing through my life bringing another soul-smashing disaster. I had only recently found my soul. It was battered, bruised, and on life support.

14

⁓

My name is Roz Buterchof and I been workin' here for twenty-five years on the production end. Your grandma hired me, Meggie, and I been loyal to her ever since. You wanna talk to me about my bras on a video? My favorite bras? I work in a bra shop and now I gotta talk about them? Okay. Whatever. You the boss now, Meggie.

Bras are for the knockers. That's what my grandma Mimi told me when I was thirteen and that's what I always think. All women have different knockers. What bra was I wearin' during a momentous event in my life? A beige one. Borin' beige. Pink bow in the center. Startin' to get my own knockers, that I was.

The police came to my house when I was twelve. I was wearin' the beige bra and I remember the police because, see, they came to tell me and my brother, Jesse, you know Jesse, Meggie? He's good now. Your grandma threw him in rehab twenty years ago, now he's a carpenter. Anyhow, our parents were arrested and thrown in the slammer for stealin' a whole bunch of money from their boss. I was twelve. Jesse was ten. I think that's why Jesse started to drink when he was older, had to drown out that pain. Sometimes you gotta look behind the addictions, you know?

So our grandma Mimi came and got us. She had our dad when she was darn near forty, unheard of in those days, and her health ain't too good, but she comes and gets us and we pack up the house and leave, tails between our legs 'cause of our parents' *crimes. I have to leave my best friend, Sammy. He and I played together all the time. Didn't have a chance to say no good-bye.*

I learned about life then, yep, I did. Life can change like that, don't you know. One second you have this, the next second you don't got it. Life is like bras. Sometimes you buy a new bra and it fits perfect, sometimes you get it home and it's pretty, oh yeah, it's pretty, but it ain't comfortable. Sometimes you buy a bra for a dress for a special occasion, but the special occasion don't end up special none at all. Sometimes you wear an old bra, and you have a magical day, you weren't expectin' that at all. Sometimes the bra holds you up good, sometimes it don't. Sometimes it's too tight on the knockers, sometimes too loose.

So we move and live with my grandma, half blind and uses a cane, and I wear the beige bra and she don't never let me have nothin' but borin' beige bras, says the devil will make me do bad things with men if I have another color. Well, I get out on my own and I get bras of all colors, but it don't do me no good and she was right, it got me findin' trouble.

Then, I go back to my old town one day and I see my best friend, Sammy. He's the only guy ever got me. My first love. We been married forty years now. Forty years. I still love him. He was here yesterday. Forgot my lunch and he brings it on in, made me a club sandwich with blue cheese, knows I love that blue cheese.

The other day I felt plumb tuckered out because they cut off part of my leg 'cause of the cancer, you know, and he brings me my favorite coffee drink. "Here you are, my flower." That's what that guy calls me, "his flower." I weigh two hundred pounds, wear glasses, and the ankle that's left is huge like an elephant's, and I'm his flower.

What color bra did I wear under my weddin' dress? Red. Wore it for Sammy. You wear the color you want on your knockers. Like life, you know? You wear the colors you want. What color am I wearin' today? Purple. Here, I'll show you, Meggie. See? You're not wearin' a beige bra on your knockers, are you? Oh, I can tell by that there face that you are. Don't do that, honey. You an O'Rourke lady. Choose your color and wear it.

15

I smiled at Kalani on my computer. Beside me Lacey smiled,
too, her jaw tight.

"Hello, Meeegie. Hello, Laceeey! You belly bigger and bigger." She held her arms way out, in a circle. "You are big belly
lady, Laceeey!"

Lacey said, "Hello, Kalani. Nice to see you. You are the size
of an annoying pixie dust fairy."

"A what? You say pissy dusty Ferrari?" Kalani waved both
hands. "I like the Ferrari. I see one in magazine. Man who likes
men driving it. Ya, I think. Hair too pretty."

"Yes, a Ferrari can fly on by. Kalani," I rushed in, "can you
hold up for us the Sparkle bra that we talked about?"

"Oh, yeees. I can do. I got your e-mail! See?"

She held up the Sparkle bra.

It was a new line. Tory wanted to label it the Sparkle Seduction line. I personally was thinking of naming it Sparkle Hellfire,
to spice things up.

I groaned when I saw the bra. "She's created a boob shelf," I
whispered.

Lacey said, "Shoot me in the head."

"You like?" Kalani grinned at us.

"Uh . . ."

"See? For the boobies. For the big-boobied ladies in America!
You know, like on the Jersey show?"

Lacey dropped her head in her hands, her red curls tumbling

over. I ran a hand through my own hair. It became stuck in a ball of curls. I hadn't washed my hair in three days. I was exhausted and I could see no reason to get all cleaned up since I was dodging Blake, best as I could, until I figured out how to handle him.

"Kalani, that isn't . . . uh . . . exactly what we were looking for. We sent you the information on how to sew it, the measurements, the drawings . . ."

The bra, for some obscure, inexplicable reason, was about half a bra. It wasn't even a demi bra. It was half a bra and filled with padding. Basically, a woman's boobs would sit *on top* of the half bra. The material was a shiny green, with silver sparkles.

"No? Not right? I thought you say be . . . what is the word I think in my head now . . . be a creature . . . creature like a monster . . ." She held up her hands in claw form, like a monster. "No, you say be cree-a-tiff. You no like?"

I felt ill. "Remember the pattern we sent you?"

"Yes. I change pattern. I cree-a-tiff." Kalani tilted her head, back and forth, so happy with her work. "Tory say, get out there and live a little. Like, make some trouble. You know that Tory?"

"We remember Tory," I said. I closed my eyes for a looong second.

"Let me bang my head through the computer screen," Lacey whispered.

Kalani giggled. "This be good for you American lady. I know. I see it on TV of how the boobies are high up to the neck." She tapped her neck. "This bring boobies to neck, too. I make new design! I cree-a-tiff."

I thought of a lake as I rubbed my shoulders.

I thought of being in a canoe in the middle of the lake.

I thought of kissing Blake in a canoe in the middle of the lake and taking off his shirt . . .

"Okay, we need to start over here, Kalani."

"Start over? Over and again? Meeegie. This good bra. I like!

You American lady you like boobies up, crack showing between. See? It like black magic."

Kalani took off her shirt and took off her red bra.

"I do not want to see Kalani's boobs, especially this early in the morning," Lacey said.

"It's okay, Kalani, please stay dressed—"

"Oh, no. I show you, Meeegie and you, too, big, big Laceeey."

"I think I'll move to a shack in Montana and be a hermit," Lacey said. "Kill deer for food. Trap rabbits. Eat bugs. Less stressful."

"Lookie!" Kalani put her tiny boobs on the padding of the bra. None of her boob was covered, they were lifted up, sitting on a shelf.

"See?" She pointed at her chest. "My boobies up now like on TV. Waaay up! I got a crack between my boobies now. Hey, where Big Laceeey going?"

"Montana is peaceful. I can bring my guns, wear fur, a raccoon hat..."

I stuck my hand in my hair again and, yet again, it became caught in a tangle.

"She's going to throw her head over a toilet, Kalani."

"Why Laceeey put her head in toilet?" Kalani was baffled. "Wash hair?"

"Okay, let's you and I talk about the pattern we discussed..."

"We need to talk about the road trip, girls," Grandma said, tapping her manicured nails on the crisp, white tablecloth of Leonard's Cafe. Today she was wearing a light gray suit with a ruffled hem and gray, shiny heels. The baubles: her four strands of pearls. Her white hair was in her usual chignon.

Lacey, Tory, and I forced smiles. A road trip? All together? Who would be the most bloodied and beaten up when we returned? Tory or Lacey?

The high-end restaurant, up in a tall building downtown, was one of Grandma's favorites. The owner-chef was Leonard Tallchief. He'd grown up on a reservation. Grandma had found him leaning against our building three mornings in a row when he was seventeen, about twenty years ago. He'd taken off with friends and ended up in Portland.

She finally told him to quit being "a lazy butt and work." He had worked at Lace, Satin, and Baubles for a while but kept migrating to the staff kitchen to cook. The food was fabulous. He'd bring Grandma lunch every day. She gained ten pounds.

Eventually she put him through culinary school. He's a top-ranked chef, and reservations are required weeks in advance, unless you are Grandma. Then he makes room. He continues to send meals to her office and says that Grandma is his "angel." He's even named entrées after her—Regan Cacciatore, O'Rourke Steak—and a popular drink called ROR with Grandma's favorite whiskey.

"I'll take no excuses," Grandma said, shoulders back. "It'll be something to look forward to after the miniwar that Lacey and Tory inflict upon one another getting The Fashion Story together and it'll get Meggie living again. We'll wait until after Lacey has her daughter. A road trip will mellow all of your outrageous mouths." She picked up a silver fork and pointed it at Lacey and Tory. "We're going to have a good damn time." She looked exhausted all of a sudden. "A good damn time."

"We'll go on the road trip, Grandma," I said, taking a sip of my beer. "I'll control these two mannequin murderers and we'll have a blast."

"Yes, we will." She glared at Tory and Lacey.

"It could be a son," Lacey said.

"It's not. It's a girl," Grandma said.

"Where are we going, Grandma?" Tory asked. "Give me the setting for our post-miniwar."

"I'll let you know when you need to know, no sooner."

Our appetizer came and we thanked the waitress. She placed my slice of lemon meringue pie in front of me, which I ate before I ate the crab and tomato toasts, in case I keeled over. We would have small Waldorf salads and hot bread before our entrées.

Leonard came over and chatted, then hugged Grandma extra long. He is meticulous about his food art, especially when it comes to feeding Grandma. Her praise was high indeed, and he flushed with pride.

"One of my favorite people on the planet," she told us when he left. "By the way, I love you girls. You've been kick-ass since you were born. Strong-willed, obstinate, opinionated, liberated. Difficult and rebellious. I'm proud of you."

We basked in that love until she said, "You are all crazy, too, in your own way. Half of your brains have been misplaced, lost, they're somewhere." She made circles in the air with her fork. "Who knows where."

"I'm not proud of you, Tory," Lacey muttered. They'd had a fight about The Fashion Story before lunch. It hadn't been pretty.

"And I'm not proud of you, Lacey."

They threw each other deathly looks.

I drank my beer.

Ah, family.

So complicated.

I had a business meeting with Grandma at ten o'clock later in the week. I grimaced as she rubbed her back, "patting the fairies." That pain was plaguing here more frequently now. I knew better than to address it.

"I want Lacey and Tory to reconcile, Meggie. I want them to be friends," she said as I left her office. "You get along better with Tory than Lacey does, but you also need to work on your relationship with her."

"I do. I am. I have finally recognized that."

"Be a better sister. This is important to me." Her Irish brogue became thicker. I was surprised at how upset she was. "Your mother is, regrettably, a bizarre, elflike, quilt-making, embroidery-obsessed, outrageous sex therapist, but she wants the three of you close, as I do. Then when we're gone we know you have each other to whine to."

"Whining partners are important."

She rolled her eyes at me. "I want you to talk to Lacey and Tory about being kinder to each other. There should be love among the three of you, as there is between your mother and me, despite how far off in the next galaxy she operates." She stood up, pale around the edges, and kissed my cheek. "I'm counting on you, Meggie. Don't mess this up."

I'm counting on you, Meggie.

I would try not to mess up again.

I talked privately to both Tory and Lacey.

Lacey said, "Tory's an overgrown witch, but I'll try."

Tory said, "When Pluto is the color of my butt, that's when I'll get along with Lacey." She twisted around and pulled out her skirt. "Nope. Pluto is not the color of my butt yet."

Regan stood at my door with a ratty-looking dog beside him. The dog was brown and squat, like a hot dog with a face and floppy ears. I swear he was smiling at me. The dog, not Regan.

Regan was in tears, shoulders shaking, in his muddy football uniform.

"Aunt Meggie," Regan choked out.

"Honey, what's wrong?" Was it my sister? The baby? I clutched my throat and my stomach, as if I could protect the baby by doing that. "Is it your mom? The baby? What happened? Is she okay?"

"Mom's fine." I pulled him into my house, that blond, messy hair hanging over his green eyes, so like my mother's and Grandma's. The hot dog dog followed him.

"Are you hurt?"

"I'm not *physically* hurt. I didn't break any more bones. I didn't conk my head on my shelves or hit it on my light again. I haven't tripped over my feet and broke my toe or run into any walls, or a pole, that's good, that hurt last time—"

"What happened, then?" Fear tightened my whole body up. "Is your dad okay?"

"Dad's good. It's—" He stared at the ceiling, shaking his head, traumatized.

"What, Regan, tell me!" I grabbed his shoulders. "What about Cassidy and Hayden?"

"They're okay, but Aunt Meggie..." He moaned, gasping for breath. "My mom...my mom..."

I leaned over, hands to knees, feeling ill, frightened, stunned. What in the world? "What happened, Regan? Is it the baby?"

"She..." Sob. Sniffle.

"*What?! What happened?*" I stood up and shook his shoulders, fear burning my nerves.

"She won't let me...She is being mean! She won't let me keep Pop Pop!"

"What? What are you talking about?" I was panting, my pulse racing. "What is a Pop Pop?"

"I'm talking about my mean mom, and this is Pop Pop." He bent down and held the dog up, eye to eye with me, then set him back down. He was not a small dog. "He's a stray. I put posters up when I found him in the woods. He was so hungry, I know what that feels like. I feel my own starvation all day long because of my own problems of not being fed and watered enough. We had to take him to the vet for stitches on his neck and his paws were all bloody and he had worms, too, and she says I can't keep him!"

I sagged in relief, head down. No one was hurt. The baby was fine. It was long seconds before I could function. "This is Pop Pop?" I pointed weakly at the hot dog dog that kept grinning at me. He was a weird dog.

"Yes, this is Pop Pop. Pop Pop, say hi to Aunt Meggie."

"So your family's okay?" My heart was still on high speed.

"Everybody but Pop Pop. He's not okay at all!" Regan tried to breathe, couldn't, tried again, chest rising and falling.

I plopped onto the floor and wiped a hand across my forehead.

"He's a good dog!" Regan crouched down and scratched behind the dog's ears. The dog's smile widened. His tongue fell out.

"And he has worms?" I pictured worms in Pop Pop. Unpleasant.

"He *did* have worms. We took him to the vet. Dad and me.

Now he doesn't have any worms. He's disinfected and worm-less. But Mom says we have to find him a good home."

"Then you better keep looking for that good home."

He wiped his wet face. "I don't need to, Aunt Meggie." He set those pleading green eyes on me, then whispered, "Please? He won't be any trouble at all. He likes to cuddle. He runs quick because he likes to have adventures, but he obeys sometimes, too."

"He likes to have adventures?"

"Yes. That's why he runs, but he comes back! And see? He's smiling at you."

That was the only thing I believed. That dog did smile. The corners of his mouth were up. "No, honey, I don't want a dog. I work all the time."

"After football practice I'll come right over and walk him! I will!"

"That's not enough, honey. He needs to go outside for potty breaks . . ."

"It'll work out, I know it will! Look at Pop Pop! He wants to be here. Give him a hug."

"No, thank you."

"I will then." He hugged the dog. The dog hopped onto his lap. The dog barked at him, and Regan barked back. "Look how huggable this dog is, Aunt Meggie. He's talking to me! I'm begging you. I think he'll like Mrs. Friendly. They could be friends. And he and Jeepers can keep each other company and stop the loneliness."

"Jeepers is a hissing cat. They won't get along."

"They will, I know it! Pop Pop will smile at him."

Sometimes I can't believe what comes out of Regan's mouth. He is a dear child. Perhaps not too bright.

"Please?"

"No."

Another round of tears, shaking shoulders. "Pleeease, Aunt Meggie?"

"No."

The dog barked at Regan. Regan could hardly bark back through his overwhelming emotions as he buried his face in Pop Pop's fur.

Pop Pop slept on my bed that night, his head on the pillow next to mine.

He snores.

I would have to take him to doggy day care during the day. There was one around the corner from the company. I wondered if they would refuse to take him. That smile is almost creepy. I petted him. He woke up and licked my hand.

I thought of Mrs. Friendly, the lizard. I didn't think they'd be friends. Jeepers hissed from underneath my bed. He wasn't looking for new friends, either.

And this dog was just plain weird.

The next morning, I dropped Pop Pop off at doggy day care. On the way there in the car, he barked at me, waited, barked again. I actually found myself barking back, like we were having a conversation. "You're a bizarre dog, Pop Pop." He smiled, put his head on my lap.

Blake came over three nights later. He was holding a huge bouquet of white lilies, a bottle of wine, and a double layer box of chocolates. He smiled, soft and sexy. He was killing me.

"Hello, Meggie. I decided to invite myself over."

I opened the door. He walked on in and handed me the flowers. "Not original gifts, but I thought we could drink wine, eat chocolates, and talk."

"You're good, Blake, impressively good." He was soooo good.

"I thought those might get me in."

I laughed. "You're in."

Pop Pop grinned at him, wagged his tail, and barked. Blake petted him. He did not bark back. Jeepers hissed from upstairs. I told him to ignore the hissing, it wasn't personal. Mrs. Friendly did nothing.

I put the lilies in water. Blake opened the wine and chocolates. We sat down on my leather couch, hugged by maple trees. We chatted about our days. He asked about Lacey and her pregnancy. He asked about Tory and Scotty, my work. I heard about his nonstop meetings, a speech he'd made at lunch, a white-collar criminal who had been written about in the paper. It was so . . . normal. Reassuring. Comfortable. I tried not to get too comfortable. It was hard.

Then he said what he'd come to say: "I'd like us to date, Meggie."

"Date?"

"Yes. I want to be upfront about what I want. I like you. I respect you, and I want us to be together."

I was suddenly calm. Calm as in cold calm. The kind of calm you get when you're going to say something you don't want to say and you sense a disaster looming, but you have to say it anyhow.

"I'm going to be freakishly upfront with you, too, Blake." I could jump into those gray-blue eyes and stay there, yes, I could."

"Thank you." He nodded.

"I'm not looking to date anyone." I could tell that was not what he wanted to hear. "I'm not looking for a deep, open relationship. I'm not looking for a commitment of any type at all."

That brain of his was clicking away, rapid fire, I could tell.

"What are you looking for?"

"I'm looking for someone I like well enough."

"What exactly does 'well enough' mean?"

"It means I'm looking for someone I like but I don't love, and I'm not looking to love. Someone who doesn't need attention or fussing over or ego stroking. Someone who will not get emotionally involved with me and will not cause me any stress whatsoever. Someone who won't cling. Someone who doesn't want more than what I want."

He leaned in, elbows on his knees. I was not deceived by his casual posture. "And what is it, exactly, that you want, Meggie?"

"From you, specifically, a little laughter and sex." I wasn't even embarrassed to say it. What the heck was wrong with me? Ah yes, *that*. That was what was wrong with me. That's why I'm a cold reptile.

"No dating. No dinners, no picnics, no hiking. No prying too much into my life, especially my past. I don't want to talk about it. No talking as if we're going to have a future. I want an hour or two naked in the evenings sometimes, then home in our own beds so we can have our own space." I needed my own space. Miles of my own space so my mind could melt down and I could scream in my black feathers rat nightmares alone.

Blake's whole face and body were completely still. As usual, he waited me out, watching me, analyzing. No wonder he was such an awesome police chief. He was sort of scary and intense in a you-have-all-of-my-attention sort of way.

"What do you think?"

He didn't hesitate. "No."

"What?"

"No."

"No?"

"That's right." He leaned back on the couch. "That's not what I want."

I was surprised, but not much. "I'm offering you sex with no commitments. Laughter, no stress, no relationship. It's sort of a manlike way to go, isn't it?"

"There are men like that." He nodded. "There are women like that. But there are many of us who aren't like that. I am not like that. I don't want a relationship where I wander into a woman's bedroom, mess around for an hour, and go home."

"That doesn't appeal?"

"Not in the slightest."

"Why not?"

His jaw was set tight. "Because it's empty, Meggie, and you know it. It's lonely. It's hollow. It's nothing. It's shallow and cold and stupid. Someone always gets hurt. The kind of detached relationship you're talking about is for robots or psychopaths and young people who are naive and inexperienced enough to erroneously think it's going to be fun."

"That's too bad."

"Yes, you could say that."

I noted his controlled anger.

"It looks like what you and I want is different, Meggie."

I ran a hand through my hair. Stuck again! Why don't I learn? I needed to do something about my tangles. "How exactly do you see us?"

"I want a relationship with you. I want to see where it goes, but my ultimate goal is to be in love with a woman, one woman, for the rest of my life. I want to get married and have kids. I'm not interested in getting involved with a woman who only wants me to come over, much like a bull stud, and leave. What's in it for me?"

"The sex?" I said this hesitantly, with not much confidence. I knew why. A rat face appeared in my mind with black curls. "I can't say I'm the greatest in bed, but I can offer enthusiasm. How's that?"

He did not waver. "Not good enough. I'm sure it would be outstanding sex, but I'd roll over, or you'd roll over, and we'd be done. Nothing else. No hugging, no talking, no sleeping together, no waking up together, no nothing."

"Are you that moral?"

"Yes." He did not break our glares for looong seconds.

"How dull."

"No, how right." His expression, which had been rock hard, finally showed his confusion and his frustration. "Do you honestly want to have a man in your life who only wants to sleep with you and leave?"

"Yes." No. Yes. I had a body that thrummed for sex. Years of being deprived of it, years of unhealthiness in the bedroom, had turned it up on high speed, and the presence of the police chief here had turned it on full blast. But I could not handle more than that, that was for sure.

"Why? Honestly, Meggie, why would you want that?"

The reasons were endless. I don't want to risk being in a relationship and hurting anyone else. Ever. I would feel suffocated. I would feel like I was in emotional danger. I would worry that things would turn into a tsunami of destruction, like it had before. I don't even know how to be in a healthy relationship, how to act, or how to stay stable within it. I certainly can't trust.

But basically I hate myself, and I don't deserve a relationship, that's why I don't want a boyfriend or a husband.

"This is what I want, Blake. If you don't want the same thing, it's fine." I tried to look nonchalant, as if I was brave and confident, not quaking inside. "You're my dream man. You're smart, you're nice. I thought it would be . . ." What's the word, fun? Not fun. I don't have *fun.* "Good for both of us."

"Good for both of us?"

"Yes."

He shook his head. "My answer, Meggie, is no, and it will always be no. If you want something else from us, if you want to get to know me, then I'm up for that. If you want to be friends, see where it goes, I'm up for that, too."

"Friends."

"Yes. Friends."

"As in, maybe we can make each other friendship bracelets?" Ah, there was my sarcasm.

"Sure. I'll get you a friendship bracelet. If you want to date, please tell me, I'd love to take you out. Wining and dining you is exactly what I would like to do. You're a compelling person. You're smart as hell. You have a dry sense of humor. Currently you're closed off, and I'm okay with that. I know something happened to you and I'm not going to look around searching for what it is, because I want you to tell me when you're ready. But what I am not ready for, and will never be ready for, is cheap sex."

"It wouldn't be cheap sex." I heard the edge in my voice, the anger suddenly pouring in like hot lava. I had been here before. He was rejecting me. "It would be sex between two consenting adults who work a lot, who are both basically kind people, who will be safe with each other."

"At what point have I ever, *ever* given you the impression

that I would be the sort of man who would want to jump in and out of a woman's bed with no thought to how she felt before and after? With no commitment to her or to us?"

"You haven't. I was hoping you would say yes." My temper had triggered. He was causing me stress. "Are you done drilling me about this? You could have said no, and the conversation would have ended. Why are we going on and on about this? I heard your no. I understood it. No problem. Thought I'd ask."

"Okay, Meggie." If a gray-blue glare could kill, I would be trying to suck in air at this moment. "Good luck. I hope you don't get what you want. I hope you can't find anyone to hop in and out of your bed, because I don't think you'll be happy. I think it'll end up hurting you even though you think it won't. I think it's a bad choice and I think it's dangerous."

"Who are you to lecture me? Who are you to be telling me what to do and what's a bad choice and what will happen if I make that choice?"

"Who am I? I'm a man who wants to be with you. I like you, Meggie—"

"You hardly know me. How could you like me?"

"It's been easy to like you. I liked you the first time I met you."

I tried not to get all tangled up emotionally with that one.

"What you want is reckless and damaging and dumb—"

"Shut up, Blake." I wanted to hit him. I wouldn't, but I felt like it. "Don't you dare tell me that. I chose you, didn't I? You're the police chief, for God's sake. You're a good man. You listen. You're interesting. You're hot. You're easy to be around and you're completely emotionally and mentally stable."

I saw the confusion in his eyes at "emotionally and mentally stable." It's not something you usually list. "Frankly, chief, I think I chose well."

"You think you chose your bull stud well. Good for you. You're not interested in a normal, happy relationship? You're not interested in seeing where we could go as a couple? No, you want to work all day, then come home, get laid, and go to sleep. Alone. Nice life, Meggie. How's that's going to look for you ten years down the road?"

"Get out." I stood up. My temper was on red hot and getting hotter. "Take your self-righteous, I-am-holier-than-thou attitude and leave. I hope you find what you're looking for: Prissy Miss Perfect. Shiny smile. Hips to bear children. Mary Poppins with an umbrella she can stick up your tight ass and Pollyanna who will be so sweet she's robotic. Maybe you need a porn star in bed, too. Hope you find her."

Now we had two tempers flaring, both voices raised. "I'm not looking for Prissy Miss Perfect. I'm not looking for a Mary Poppins to stick an umbrella up my ass. I'm not looking for a robotic Pollyanna. I am certainly not looking for a porn star in bed. I am, however, looking for a real woman. A woman who can handle a relationship with a man. Obviously, that's not something you want. When you change your mind, call me." He stood up.

"I'm not going to change my mind."

"You should." He was trying hard to rein in his temper, but it wasn't working. He was one formidable man.

"Don't tell me what I should do. I don't need any man telling me what I should do or what I should think. Just go. I think I've had enough humiliation for one night."

"You feel humiliated? Because I won't sleep with you and walk away?"

"Because I asked you to sleep with me and you said no."

"So you feel rejected."

Ah, that word. "I don't want to deal with you anymore. You won't sleep with me, that's fine, chief. I'll find someone who will."

Now that shot him up. I could see it in the fire in his eyes. He was smokin'.

"That easy for you, is it, Meggie?" His words were quiet, but I was not fooled by the control. "You can go out and find some other man and that's that?"

I hesitated, then came up swinging. "Yep."

I thought he was going to yell, or toss the table. He swore, then started stalking out. I watched those broad shoulders that I so wanted to pull down on top of me. I looked at that blond hair, and thought about running my fingers through it. I thought about that tight butt and those hips. They would move exactly right, I knew it. His legs were outstanding, too. He was a huggable bear and King Kong and Mr. Protective all in one.

"If you change your mind, walk across the damn street." He slammed my door when he left.

He wanted a woman who wanted a relationship.

That would not be me.

I didn't cry.

Sometimes you are past tears about men. I am way past tears.

Pop Pop grinned. Jeepers hissed.

I thought of Aaron.

I thought of Josephine.

My fault.

Black rats were running over my body. I was trying to escape, but the rats kept leaping on me, climbing on my shoulders, biting my ears, biting my ankles.

I was back in our apartment in Los Angeles, bleak and small. Aaron walked through the door and I called to him, I screamed at him, to help me, help me.

He saw the rats jumping and lit a joint, then turned into a huge rat himself. He lumbered over to me, opened his mouth wide, and bit my head open. I could see my brains being eaten, chewed. He pushed his joint into my squished brains, then used a sponge to fill the gap.

I could feel myself dying, falling, smashing to the floor, while a massive group of black rats, tails swishing, ate the rest of my body.

When they were done, one black, broken feather floated down to my corpse.

I could hardly concentrate at work. I felt off, lost, lonely. Deeply hopeless.

I had meetings. I worked on our complicated Fashion Story. I checked on the revamping of our website, evaluated our order history, and took a serious look at how our call center was performing when people ordered from our catalog.

I was half there. I faked it, but I was half there. I liked Blake. I could trust him. I could love him if I let myself. But no falling in love. No commitment. No future.

Could I have slept with him and not become emotionally involved? I could have tried. I would have tried as hard as I could. Would it have worked?

Maybe.

Probably not.

Now it was over.

I was not going to crash into a wall again headfirst, like I had with Aaron. I couldn't do it. I was not ready for what Blake wanted.

A well of rage erupted in me. Searing hot, hurtful, all consuming. It was Blake's way or the highway, and I guess I was stuck on the highway. I picked up a stapler and threw it across my office. It banged a hole in the wall.

Abigail ran in. "Are you all right?"

I was breathing hard, trying to get control. "Yes, I'm fine. Dandy."

"Can I . . . help you?"

"No. Thank you."

She left.

I threw another stapler. It made a second hole.

"Still okay?" Abigail shouted.

"Yep."

No, I wasn't.

Pop Pop got in a fight at doggy day care. I had to leave work to get his ear sewn up at the veterinarian's. I had to plead with the irritated owner, Hildee, to let him come back. Now he's on "probation." Hildee told me, in a serious way, that I had to "talk to Pop Pop about his aggressive behavior." Pop Pop is now on dog probation. I hardly know what to say.

*   *   *

In the interest of peace, and to get out of the office, I took Lacey and Tory out to dinner at a fish house. Over buttered clams and baked salmon we hashed out the details of The Fashion Story, which Tory called "almost cataclysmic in its strangeness" and Lacey called "visionary. Let's hope we don't scare our employees so much with our vision they all quit at once."

I drank my beer to quell my nerves. Lacey poked at her salmon. Tory ordered another martini.

"Are you crying, Tory?" I asked when she sniffled after dinner.

"No. Yes. But not about The Fashion Story."

"You miss him a lot, don't you?" I said it quietly so she wouldn't screech.

"Yes, I miss Farmer Scotty."

I put my hand on her fist. Her nails were bright red. "Tory, maybe you should write him an e-mail, a nice e-mail about how you want to start over."

"No, I can't do that."

"Has he filed any divorce papers?" Lacey asked.

"No. He's probably waiting for me to do it. He's a nice, nice man, and he knows it will hurt me when the papers come, so he's waiting for me to do it." Sniffle, sniffle. "He's sweet. He's calm all the time. He always listens and hugs me. He never says anything mean back to me."

"With one hand you're pushing him away, and you wave a sledgehammer and a buzz saw to get his attention, and with the other you're pleading with him to come get you. When he comes, you push him away again," I said.

"You're like a great white shark," Lacey said. "You want more than one husband can give."

"Why can't I be with Scotty and not push him away?" Tory cried. "Why can't I be normal? Why can't I settle into my marriage and be comfortable?"

"It was your childhood," Lacey said quietly. "Your loss. Your grief, the feelings of being abandoned, moving in with us. You're afraid you'll be abandoned again. It's part of your genetics now."

"I know. Intellectually, I get it." Tory's lips tightened. "I never felt like I truly belonged anywhere after my parents died. They were there for my birthday party, and a week later, they weren't."

I tried to imagine that, I tried to imagine a *five-year-old* dealing with that.

"I know I push you two away by being a mean, blunt, fire thrower before you two can push me back and leave me all alone again." Tory bit her lip. "I'm so flippin' brain mangled."

"I'm flippin' brain mangled, too, Tory," I said. "Let me tell you about my nightmares again and how I thought I saw Aaron drinking coffee the other day at a café and I actually went into the café to check. I think I scared that poor man."

"And I feel like my brain has been divided into five parts," Lacey said. "For Matt, each of the kids, and the baby, and there's no brain left over for me to think with. I push, you push. We're still sisters, Tory. Always."

"We love you, Tory," I said. "We're a family."

"I love you, too," Lacey said. "We fight, but I always love you underneath."

"You do?" Tory asked.

"Yes," Lacey and I both said. I leaned over and hugged Tory, then Lacey hugged her.

"I worry about you two giving up on me and deserting me. I didn't like it when you were gone, Meggie," Tory said. She drank her martini. "I chronically worry about Scotty leaving me, too. During our whole marriage I would wake up in the middle of the night, scared down to my toes, and I would hug him tight, but whenever there's the slightest problem, I blow up and I tell myself I'll leave him before he leaves me, and before I know it I've slammed out of the house and end up wondering how I landed on the sidewalk with my suitcases and Jimmy Choos."

"But you understand how screwed up you are," Lacey said. "Can't you work with that?"

"Tory, try to date him." I thought the words *screwed up* were inflammatory. "Go after him."

"Too scared to do that. What if he rejects me, decides he's better off without me? Then what do I do? Build another penis?"

Tory sniffled. "Back to The Fashion Story. I can't take any more of this irritating sentimentality and cheesy emotion. It's making my liver hurt. I need to bash my punching bag."

The Fashion Story meeting continued. One question was when to tell the employees what we were planning. The conversation between Lacey and Tory was so much softer this time around.

I think it was the "I love yous."

Tory remembers both her parents, she remembers their love for her.

I wondered about my own father, Sperm Donor Number Two, that night. I knew that Lacey sometimes wondered about Sperm Donor Number One.

My mother said they were romantic quickies and she "hardly knew a smidgen of a thing" about them. Yet she'd had a goal: get pregnant.

Brianna O'Rourke is an original.

For the hundredth time, though, I thought: What right did she have to do what she did? She found two men that appeared to have everything she was looking for. She checked them out as one might check out a horse—hair, teeth, tail, brains, genitalia. She bopped into bed at a time when she knew she would get pregnant. She walked away. She didn't tell them about the babies.

What right did she have to do that to them? Most men would desperately like to know if they have children. She took that choice away from them. She took away the opportunity for Lacey and me to have fathers.

I love my mother but, like all of us, including my deeply flawed soul, she is not perfect.

Sperm Donors One and Two were out there somewhere.

Where?

Who were they?

And why did I care at this point anyhow?

* * *

She left another message on my phone. This time she swore at me and called me lots of graphic names. "You're trying to hide from this, Meggie, but it will never work. Everyone will know what kind of person you are. Are you stupid enough to think you can get away with this?"

She told me what kind of person she believed me to be in another hail of swear words. Her vocabulary was impressive.

I felt nauseated and lay down on the floor of my tree house. I watched the maple leaves fluttering until I stopped trembling. Pop Pop licked my face.

I deleted the message.

"I have an idea for you, Aunt Meggie."

"Great, Hayden. What's the idea?" He was wearing red jeans and a white T-shirt, his hair pulled back in a ponytail.

"Tassels."

"Tassels?"

"Yes, swinging tassels. Glittery, snazzy. We can attach them to the middle of the bra cup, the sides of the panties, the butt cheeks of the panties, the tops of garters, all for fun. They could be gold or silver or sparkly. You know, add some swing and pizzazz. See? I drew some pictures."

Hayden had used a black charcoal pencil to outline a woman's form and then had added the lingerie and tassels.

"We could call them Nipple Tassels, Hip Swingin' Tassels, and Tail Tassels."

"Tail?"

"Yes. Look at this drawing."

I looked. The woman had a tail tassel, starting midbottom and hanging down about a foot. It was gold. There were other tassels, about six inches long, that could be looped through a tiny plastic clasp, one for the center of each bottom cheek.

"So if they're dancing in front of their husbands or boyfriends or girlfriends, the tassels will swing, too, like twirly birds, you know? Like a pinwheel."

"I like it."

"You do, Aunt Meggie?" His face was so hopeful.

"Yes. I do. It's kinky, but a kick."

"Totally fab. And they're pretty. I like the pretty part. We can make them sparkly if we want to. Shiny. You can pick out your bra color, then your tassels. They're for romantic rendezvous, but when she's not on the romantic rendezvous anymore, she can slip the tassels off the tiny hooped claps and go to her job as a lawyer or a doctor or a painter or a mom, whatever she does."

"Duo-function."

"Yes. Then ladies don't feel like they're wasting money. We're respecting her wallet."

"We'd have a whole other market with the strippers."

He blushed. "I was thinking that. We could also sell to Vegas. . . ."

"You betcha. Vegas, here we come!"

"Woo-woo!" He put a fist in the air.

"Woo-woo!"

We had a plan for tassels.

I think there's a market for 'em.

16

Is there a phrase called "personal fraud"? That's what I think I was committed against me by Aaron.

Aaron did not tell me about his mental health history before we were married. I, as his fiancée, had a right to know. To me, that was fraud.

To me, that was very personal.

Which made it, in my mind, personal fraud.

Should I have waited longer to marry him? Absolutely. I was completely at fault there. I was swept up in love and lust, my brain nonfunctioning.

When I dated Aaron, twice during the six months we dated, he wouldn't see me. He told me he had "the bluesy blues," then sang a humorous song about it over the phone. He didn't see me for about a week after the song, then apologized, saying he didn't want his "bluesy blue" mood to bring me down. "You don't deserve that, My Meggie."

The next time he sunk into a depressive pit, he told me he had the flu and didn't want to get me sick. I had to go out of town the next day for three weeks for work, so I was not around to see that he had to be recommitted to a clinic by a friend of his. I was never told of the straitjacket, or how he pounded his head against the wall in the seclusion room.

Aaron finally told me, after attempting to jump from the building in L.A., with huge impatience, as if my questions were an affront to his sensibilities, that he had a problem with depression. "Had a problem with it comin' after me since I was a kid. My dad yelled all the time, choked my mom. He went to jail for a few years, had a drug record before that. . . . I haven't seen him for twenty years, he didn't care about me. . . . Don't ask me anything about my mom, I don't want to talk about that bitch, I hate her, she's a drunk loser, I've got some bad secrets about her, and I'm not sharing them, Meggie. Those secrets were her fault. . . .

"Yeah, I tried to kill myself twice in high school . . . once in college, with pills . . . too much alcohol . . . I had to go to the hospital . . . a clinic a few times, stayed for weeks . . . I'm not a mental whack job like the guys in there . . . I didn't belong there. . . ."

I drove him to the hospital one night in our second year of marriage when he was raving. It was the second time I'd done it. I thought he'd lost his mind. He'd taken painkillers chased with vodka.

They committed him.

I cried.

Cried for him, cried for me.

I felt selfish for crying for myself, but I couldn't help it.

I had a right to know Aaron's mental health history before I married him. What was my obligation to him as his wife? Would I have to spend the rest of my life with him in depressed chaos? Did my wedding vows extend to this? What about his lies of omission before the wedding? I was no longer in love with him. I didn't love him. Most of the time I didn't even like him, couldn't stand to be with him, but I was afraid to leave him. I knew he'd try to kill himself if I did.

I felt tremendously sorry for him, for his acute suffering.

But he was a mean terror to live with, and I went from a funky, happy, productive filmmaker to a woman who would look up at the sky and wonder if the last thread of her own sanity was slowly being pulled out of her head.

I wanted to talk to Blake.

I wanted to laugh with him.

I wanted to see him.

My wish partly came true on Saturday night. It was dark, the trees swaying in a gusty wind. I was chasing after Pop Pop, who was out on one of his "adventures" Regan had told me about. He was not obeying my commands to stop, but he was smiling back at me.

Blake drove by. He waved, but he didn't stop. I wondered if he'd been on a date.

I did not bother wiping off my tears.

Blake's rejection hurt right through to the core. The problem with people like me who are emotionally unhinged is that we think with a tsunami of bad experiences flooding our brains. We think with insecurity, and raging pain, all triggered by what has come before. We see threats to us personally lurking around corners, curves, and right angles.

I am not taking his rejection well or rationally.

Too screwed up for that.

I miss him.

"Mom's on that talk show, *Four o'Clock with Chloe and Charles.*" Lacey walked into my office, a hand on her stomach. Tory and I had actually been trying on new lingerie that we hoped would sell well. She was in purple, I was in light pink.

Lacey stopped, hands on her hips. "Both of you are so pretty you make me sick. Your stomachs are flat, you have skinny hips. Look at me." She spread her arms out. "I think I have three babies in there and one in my butt." She turned on the TV. "Let's see what outrageous things Mom has to say today."

Tory said, "What am I going to learn from the world's greatest sexpert today?" We sat on the couch together. Hanging out in lingerie is something the three of us have done since we were teenagers.

The hosts, Chloe and Charles, were like Barbie and Ken. Plastic. Overly groomed. Blinding white teeth. Cheshire cat smiles.

"Brianna," Chloe said, "people say you are the best sex educator in the country."

"Thank you, Chloe, that's lovely to hear." Our mother was dressed in a bold, clingy purple dress and red heels, her red curls pushed off her face and down her back.

"You've taught all of us a lot about . . . sex." Chloe was an uptight blonde. She did not look like she would enjoy sex.

"Sex is a natural and normal part of life. So are orgasms, which is what we're going to talk about today." Our mother grinned, tilted her head, so innocent.

The audience clapped and hooted.

Chloe visibly cringed. "We are?" She shuffled through her paperwork. No! No way! That *couldn't* be the topic. "Who told you—"

"I don't think that's on our agenda . . ." Charles said, alarmed, but smiling gamely. "I don't think we're allowed to say that O word . . ."

"Charles is a blowhard," Tory said. "Looks like he's talking with his balls in his mouth."

"Thank you for the graphic, Tory," I said.

"He does look like that," Lacey mused. "Those chipmunk cheeks . . ."

"A good question is, how do you know that a man or a woman will be your perfect orgasmic match?" my mother asked, overriding both of them. "It's quite simple: Look for qualities in their personality that would transfer well to an orgasm. Are they thoughtful? Protective? Giving and generous? Is there a desire there to please you? Do they love and care about you? Are they confident and adventurous? Passionate, humorous? Or, are they critical, selfish, narcissistic, egotistic, overly macho, rigid, boring, nonreflective? If so, you're going to be nonorgasmic. A nonmatch."

"She is so blunt," Lacey said.

"She's right though," I said.

"Scotty always did it for me," Tory said. "Always. I never missed an orgasm. He always had me go first. Ladies first."

"Not having orgasms in life will dry you up," our delicate, Southern belle/Irish elf mother said. "Not only will it dry up your vagina, it will dry up your mind, your soul, your creativity, your joy, your sense of vitality and spirit. Sex is not fun without orgasms—can we all say that aloud?"

The audience tittered as my mother turned to them.

"Don't be embarrassed! Let's be truthful, let's be honest, people. Say it with me. 'Sex is not fun without orgasms.' "

The audience dutifully said, "Sex is not fun without orgasms," then laughed. "One more time!" my mother encouraged. The audience repeated themselves, this time with more gusto. The camera panned their faces. Oh, this was fun! Brianna was fun!

"We women might say to ourselves, well, I do still enjoy sex even without the orgasm because I like the closeness. But that's bull-*beeeeeppp!*" Our mother waved a finger. "That isn't true and the woman is deceiving herself. She must tell her man what she needs in order to achieve orgasm. She has to gather her womanly courage together."

Chloe and Charles wriggled uncomfortably. The censors!

"Now, here is what not to do. One of my clients had not had an orgasm in two years and she was absolutely furious with her husband for not noticing it. He was blind to her and her successful sexual health, so one night, when he's done and rolls off, she picks up a broom and starts hitting him with it. She actually chased him around the house, screaming that she hadn't had an orgasm in two years and he hadn't noticed or cared. Don't do this. What should she have done?"

Next came a surprise.

"She should have told him to keep going until she had her orgasm," Chloe said, with a snarky snip to her voice. "What, it's only for him? Get your kicks in and go to sleep? She should have told him to man up, put some effort in, and get the job done. She's not a plastic blow-up doll. She's a woman!" As soon as the words were out, Chloe looked like she wanted to melt into the floor and disappear.

Charles said, "But he would never forget the broom incident, so that's good, right, Brianna?"

"She should have told him what to do to make her have an orgasm a long time ago," my mother said. "She should have sat him down at the kitchen table and, using a banana and a circular rind of orange peel, a cherry, and an olive, showed him. Then she should have led him to the bedroom for his first lesson. It's partly her fault for being spineless and not speaking up, demanding her orgasm, and it's partly his fault for being a selfish monkey and bad in bed."

"A selfish monkey!" Charles said, then laughed, a tiny and scratchy laugh.

"You notice when your wife has an orgasm, right, Charles?" My mother turned to him in her clingy purple dress.

Charles blushed. "Uh, oh, yeah. Yeah. I know. She makes it . . . uh . . . *clear.*"

My mother looked at him skeptically. That would be the word: skeptically.

Tory said, "He's a hopeless fool, obsessed with his pecker and his pleasure."

Lacey said, "Clueless. Totally clueless."

I said, "Arrogantly ignorant. The worst type."

"Charles, you need to take more time with your wife," my mother said. "Remember: foreplay. But you need foreplay before the foreplay. Nothing is sexier than a man vacuuming or unloading the dishwasher, unless he's doing both nude. Let me be bold and blunt. Most women will take bad sex for only a certain amount of time, then they'll turn off and tune out. You men won't be getting laid much anymore. She'll have her excuses, like a headache or fatigue, but basically, she doesn't like sex with you. You men have to pay attention to the orgasm. You do that, don't you, Charles? It's not all about you, right?"

Charles went pale, then red. "I pay attention! I do! Good attention!"

"See, an orgasm is not simply a culmination of the sex. It's the pinnacle of the relationship in bed. There can be multiple orgasms, multiple small ones, then a larger one, or a large orgasm. It will be different each time, but what there can't be is *no* orgasm."

"Charles looks like he wants to choke on his chipmunk cheeks," I said.

"Yep, he does," Tory said. "He's reviewing his last encounter and is probably realizing that he was as lame as a limp snake in bed."

"No orgasm," my mother said, "is bad." She turned to the audience. "We don't want to be bad in bed, do we?"

"No!" the audience said.

Charles swallowed hard, eyes darting. Chloe looked pissed.

"Sex is not fun without an orgasm, right, audience?"

"Right!" the audience yelled back to her. Fun fun, Brianna!

"Right!" Chloe said. She glared at the camera.

"I know we're running out of time, but if I can add that lingerie does make bedroom time special time," my mother said. "A woman is much more likely to orgasm if she feels fabulous. Take a peek at the lingerie I have on under my dress."

My mother stood up, unsnapped her purple dress, yanked it wide open, stuck out a hip and a knee, and smiled. She was in a red bustier, red lacy underwear, and a matching gauzy miniskirt. The audience went wild at this semiflashing.

Chloe's mouth dropped. Charles fidgeted.

"My mother owns a lingerie business called Lace, Satin, and Baubles. This is from the Tory's Temptations line. See how this bustier lifts the girls right up? See how there's a skirt to cover the tops of the thighs? Isn't the top of the thigh a problem place for women?"

"Yes!" the audience shouted back to her.

"Note the color. Bright red. Flirty. Naughty. And don't forget the heels. They give you a sleek and curvy line, and we feel powerful in our heels, don't we, ladies?"

"Yes!" the audience agreed, even the men.

She put her purple dress back together. "Now, the next time I'm on your show I'm going to talk about sex toys, but let me leave you with this: An orgasm a day keeps you ready for play! Can we say that, audience?"

"An orgasm a day keeps you ready for play!" We love you, fun Brianna!

"Ladies and gentlemen, our favorite sex therapist, Brianna

O'Rourke," Chloe announced, smiling and clapping. Charles was still blushing, but he appeared contemplative, baffled, confused.

The audience was on their feet.

Tory in her purple lingerie, Lacey in her maternity dress, and I in my pink lingerie sat back and cackled.

"I love you, Mother!" Lacey said, blowing a kiss to the screen.

As if on cue, our mother kissed her hand and blew a kiss to the audience, waving her hand.

She does that every time, and you know who the kiss is for? Lacey, Tory, and me.

We blew a kiss back to her.

Tory's Temptations sold thousands.

Gave us more time.

My mother called me about an hour later. I complimented her on her appearance on Chloe and Charles while I had a slice of peach cobbler. I smeared peanut butter on the top of it. Yum.

"Thank you, dear. I am e-mailing you a photo of Lacey's baby's blessing quilt. I'm having a difficult time with the colors. Can you help me with it? Are you eating vegetables?"

"Handfuls of them. Can hardly stop."

"What about exercising?"

"Every day. Sweat till I'm soaked."

"Your sisters say you're pale."

"I'm not pale."

"I can't wait to see you. Let's you and I go to the tea shop together for a visit and some clotted cream and scones."

"I love clotted cream and scones."

One would think that Lacey, Tory, and I would have grown up wild and free with a mother who was a blunt-talking sex therapist. That would not be true at all. She was kind, superstrict, involved, and conservative. "Study hard, stay in sports, focus. No drugs, no drinking, no smoking, no sex, and we'll get along fine," she said. "Break those rules and we're going to have problems."

She told us that sex for teenagers was "a ridiculously poor idea. Let me list the ways." And then she listed them: pregnancy. Disease. More diseases. She even showed us graphic photos of herpes, syphilis, and genital warts. She showed us photos of pregnant teenagers and close-ups of women giving vaginal births. She did this before we went to sleep at night many times as teenagers.

It's not something you want traipsing through your dreams.

"Hello everyone, come on over."

I stood on a chair in the middle of the production floor. I'd had everyone in the company—seamstresses, our custodian, managers, etc.—come to this meeting. It was Friday, three o'clock.

I briefly wondered if I'd brushed my hair that morning. Oh, yes, I had. Yay me. I had even put a clip on top of my head to keep my hair out of my face. I wore a pink T-shirt, jeans, and tennis shoes.

I glanced at Grandma. I could tell she hated my outfit. In fact, she stuck out a red painted fingernail at me, ran it up and down in the air, and said, "That's what you wear at home when no one can see you."

She was in a pink dress and shimmery tights. The baubles: pink topazes.

"We're going to do something different," I said.

"I like different," Edith Petrelli said. "Adds brain cells."

"Different would be titillating," Edna said.

"I'll do it," Estelle said.

I paused and smiled at the three of them. The Petrelli sisters were well into their seventies and yet they were not afraid of change, not afraid of new. Spectacular women. I coughed to clear a rush of emotion when I looked at them.

"I want you all to design lingerie that is reflective of you. A bra, panties, bustier, thongs, negligees, nightwear, anything we have."

I saw a few nods and smiles. I saw their imaginations click. We're an imaginative group.

Lacey grinned.

Tory rolled her eyes. I could hear her tapping her heels.

"It does not have to be pretty. As you know, we strive for pretty and seductive here at Lace, Satin, and Baubles, but I want you to create truth, so to speak. Raw, fanciful, funny, flamboyant, thought-provoking, artistic, graphic, emotion-laden lingerie in whatever fashion you want. We have all kinds of materials here, as you know, but I've taken the liberty of half emptying a local crafts store, and in those boxes, all lined up on the tables, you'll find more. You can, of course, use any lingerie we've already made and embellish it. For inspiration we're having strawberry shortcake. Any questions?"

"I don't think you should let Larissa do this," Beatrice said. "Who knows what she'll create when she's let loose around this place." Everyone laughed.

Larissa, who had purple stripes through her hair that day, said, "New Age wonders rock and roll," which made no sense, but that's Larissa for ya.

"Tato's probably going to make a huge bra in the shape of his Harley," Lance said.

"Humans need to find their inner Harley," Tato declared, thumping his chest with his fist. "Even in a bra."

"Does Toni have to be a part of this? This is simply feeding her odd obsession," Delia said. "We all know what she's going to do."

"Paint a picture of Robert Pattinson," several employees shouted.

Toni Latrouelle and her sisters laughed.

"Hayden's going to make something with leopard print, cheetah print, and a pink fedora," Abigail said.

Hayden nodded. "Maybe." He had a pad of paper in front of him already, and he was sketching. "But maybe I'll do something different. Something with poetic meaning."

It was a pretty funny scene. I think the group activity took some of the sizzling fear away about what might happen to the company. We all spent the rest of the afternoon making personal, highfalutin, bang-up lingerie, as I dubbed it.

At four thirty I had spaghetti, lasagna, and salad brought in.

I could not believe what our employees were creating.

I put an arm around my grandma's shoulders.

"Unbelievable," she said. "I knew they were smart, but this..."
She waved her hand. "Excellent idea, Meggie. Excellent."

"Thank you." I basked for one short second in her praise.

"Your clothes are embarrassing, though. Tennis shoes? For
work? Baggy jeans? Your hair almost long enough to wrap
around your butt? I've seen grave diggers dressed better."

I kissed her cheek. "Love you."

"You should wear the clothes I sent you, or people will think
you're a homeless person." She paused, kissed my cheek, and
whispered, "I still love you, granddaughter, despite your un-
sightly fashion style."

I didn't want to tell the employees what we were going to do
with their ideas.

That'd scare 'em to death.

Tory and I left our offices about nine that night. I was eating
beef jerky with mustard. I handed her one, and she took it.

"They all love you, Meggie. They can't stand me."

"Not true." Halfway true.

"It's because of your star sign, the Leo." She crossed her arms
over her chest. "Scotty loved you, too. He thought you were
great. He had the penis taken down, you know. I was going to
make it into a fountain."

Scotty and I had gotten along fine. He was a kind man and
madly in love with Tory. "He thinks you're great, too. I believe
he has a special affinity for Pisces."

"No, he doesn't. If he did, he'd chase me down."

"Maybe you need to chase him. Go home."

"I have chased him! I drive by our house trying to see him all
the time!"

"I believe that's called stalking." I put an arm around her,
and she bent her head.

"I hate Scotty the deserter, the abandoner!" she said. "He
should come get me!"

I hugged her close. I hoped they could work it out. It was not looking promising.

"There's a typhoon."

"A typhoon?" I used the Internet to look up the weather near our factory in Sri Lanka. "Ah, no. Those poor people."

"Yep," Lacey said. "Mother Nature has cursed us, and them. It's right over the factory."

I tried to call Kalani. I tried to Skype her. No go.

"They're not working," I said. "They're home. Good. At least they're safe, but we'll lose a day of work."

"Yep. I swear that karma is conspiring against us. The Hippie Bleeding bras, the bras Kalani designed with a shelf, the weather, the sunken ship . . ."

"Seems like it, doesn't it?"

"Speaking of conspiring against us, Larissa and Tato are coming in in five minutes," Lacey said. "They're at war, as usual."

"I know." Larissa and Tato are designers. They don't always get along. Tory was out at another meeting, so Lacey was standing in for her.

"Yes." Lacey tapped her fingers together. "One thingie you should know."

"What's that?"

"They're sleeping together."

I dropped my pen. "You're kidding."

"No. Larissa's divorce went through six months ago, and Tato and his girlfriend broke up this fall."

"So it's guerrilla warfare here between the two of them, lingerie speaking, and at home they're mating."

"You have the picture. Except they're currently in a fight. Tato gave Larissa a promise ring and she won't wear it because she says she's not ready."

"A promise ring? I didn't think people did that anymore. Ah. Well. That was nice of Tato."

"I've seen Tato cry three times in the last week. Don't tell him I told you."

I rubbed my eyes. I don't like employees dating. It gets complicated and creates a mess at the office. There's the distraction for the couple, the conflicts, and the problems that come up with other employees who think the romance is a detriment/ great source of gossip/entertaining, etc.

Like my grandma, I will fire employees who are dating someone above or below them. It's an unfair balance of power, for one, and the employee who is below the person he or she is dating could easily sue our company and say they were forced into the relationship, or they were fired because the relationship ended or, God forbid, they might have felt forced into the relationship to keep the job. I hoped it wouldn't happen, but I can't guarantee it, so no dating someone above or below you.

However. I cannot prevent everything, and neither could my grandma. Besides, no one gets in the way of two people with determined hearts, or determined libidos, that's for sure.

For example, years ago Brenner and Jocelyn dated for two years until they had a big fight and broke up. The fight was about croissants. I didn't get the details. The breakup enraged Jocelyn, and she flipped Brenner's desk over. Brenner retaliated by flipping her desk over. They met in the middle of the production floor and had a screaming match. I have no idea how they went from screaming to making out, but they did, and Brenner carried Jocelyn back to his trashed office, kicked the door shut, and nine months later they had a baby. They have been married now for twelve years and have four kids. The next set was triplets.

Both still work for us and we love them.

Zan and Latrice dated when I used to work here. Latrice broke up with Zan and started dating a banker. This pissed Zan off to no end, and we actually had to separate their offices. In a meeting one time Zan said, "We need a design that will help a woman who's flat look like she has something, even a molehill. . . . We need underwear that will help women hold in their stomachs. . . . Can we create a bra in red that women can wear when they're crazy bitches?"

I shut him down quick.

But Latrice responded by suggesting we start a line of underwear for men "who are small and piddly in that department, like a worm. Maybe we can add padding to the front of the jockey? What can we do for men who have no butt? Does anyone have a product out there that will add butt? Who wants a small-butted man? I don't."

I shut her down, too.

I told them to shut up or get out. I wasn't running a long-lost love business, and shortly after that, Zan and Latrice both left. Zan became a natural food store owner, and Latrice became a tour guide in Africa.

Larissa and Tato are not a good combination for me because of their temperaments. They are both artistically explosive.

Larissa has been with our company for twelve years. She is thirty-four years old and all her shoes are four-inch heels. I have never seen her wear the same pair twice. She has a shoe obsession, which she admits. She grew up on a farm baling hay, milking cows, and driving a tractor. She has straight blond hair with a pink streak on the right side. Or a purple streak. Or green. Depends on her mood. She has four cats.

Tato's mother is Asian, and his father is African American and an ex–pro football player. Tato's six three, played college football, and has a Harley. He also grows orchids and goes to different orchid shows around the nation. He reads books on orchids. He has photos of orchids that he's taken. The colors of the orchids are in our bras and panties and lingerie. We even had an orchid line. Poetry can bring that man to tears.

Together, those two are thunder and lightning. Thunder and Lightning were definitely unhappy. You could feel the ticked-off sizzle in our meeting.

Lacey and I had Tato and Larissa sit diagonally across from each other. I figured if Larissa leaped at Tato—yes, she's that much of a hothead—I might be able to catch her.

"I can't work with Tato when his demands are unreasonable. . . . Larissa can't commit to any design. She can't *commit* . . . Look at his idea for a spring bra, Meggie. Any woman wearing that thing is going to look like a peacock in heat . . . maybe you

should wear it, Larissa, to get some heat... shut up, Tato...
don't get personal with this... it's not personal, I simply don't
like what I'm seeing because it reminds me of an exploding acid
trip... why don't you go home and take a nap, settle your hormones down...."

Tato sniffled. Larissa's chin trembled.

"Stop." I held up a hand to Thunder and Lightning. "Stop."
They stopped. I was so, so tired. I leaned forward and said,
quietly, "Listen to me, and listen closely. Fighting will sink this
company. Your petty competition here will sink this company.
Your immaturity about each other and your relationship will
sink this company. Why? Because I need everyone giving one
hundred percent right now. Everyone. You two aren't doing that
for me. You're not doing it for the company. These doors will
shut permanently in a few months if we don't all work together.
I am not asking you two to work together peaceably, I am or-
dering you to do it." I glared at both of them. They both looked
shocked.

"I am not interested in your personal problems. You should
not be banging each other as it is, because you work together. I
am running a business that has critical problems, not a counseling service. If you want to keep fighting with each other, let me
know right now, today, and I will fire you and hand you a final
check and you will walk out that door. Say the word."

I heard Larissa suck in her breath. Tato held up both hands.

"No, no... no, we want to work here—"

"Tato and Larissa, I am not a patient person and you know
it. I have no more patience for this mess. You two get your
heads together and get your line designed and bring it to me by
Friday. I will hire someone else to do this job if you can't. We
are depending on you, as we are depending on all the employees
in this company, to help us get back on track. You are replaceable. I am replaceable. Lacey is replaceable. Everyone is except
my grandma."

Larissa was staring at her hands, shoulders shaking. Tato
rubbed his face. Couldn't have his tears showing!

"I'm sorry, Meggie, Lacey," Larissa sniffled.

"Me too," Tato said, voice pitching. "Me too."

"Good. Get back out there and work. You have until Friday to get me what I need or don't come in on Monday."

They were chastened, they were embarrassed. Thunder and Lightning left.

Lacey winked at me. "Good job."

"Thank you. They need it. They'll bond together, thinking it's them against me, then they'll get super creative, and by Friday we'll see an excellent line. They needed a referee, they needed a reason to bond together, and they have it."

"You're smart, Meggie."

"No, not that smart. But I get what motivates them."

"Which is?"

"Each other."

17

～

Hi. My name is Hayden Rockaford. My mother, Lacey O'Rourke Rockaford, is the chief financial officer at Lace, Satin, and Baubles; my aunt Meggie O'Rourke is the CEO; my aunt Tory O'Rourke is the design director; and my great-grandma, Regan O'Rourke, is the owner.

I work here part time, after school and after play rehearsal and choir. I draw designs for the company because I adore, adore, adore fashion and style and lingerie and pretty things. I have a collection of lace and piles of my fav fabrics at home.

I'm supposed to talk about myself, right, Meggie?

First I gotta take a breath since I'm being filmed. Okay. Here goes. I'm going to say something I've kept secret: In my head I'm a girl, not a boy. I call myself Holly.

Sorry. I'm nervous to talk about this. When I was younger I loved when my sister, Cassidy, and I put on makeup together and did our nails, and I loved wearing her dresses. I wanted to be a cheerleader or a princess, but mostly a mermaid. When I was five I asked my mom if she was playing a joke on me by pretending I was a boy.

It was always sad on my birthday when my presents were footballs and baseball bats when what I wanted was my own pink kitchen to cook in or a sewing machine or a ruffled dress, like Cassidy's presents.

I can hardly explain it, but when you don't feel like you're in the right body, it messes with your mind. It's like you feel insane all the time. I look down and what's between my legs shouldn't be there. I don't even like looking at it. I'm embarrassed by it. It's like it's an attachment, something that's been forced on me. I've had a lot of depression. Depression, like, I don't want to live anymore.

People think that people like me, transgender, are freaks of nature or something. They think we're losers or creepy or mentally ill. We're not. It's terrible to have to be like this, but we're not freaks. It's not our fault.

I think that when my mom was pregnant, something happened and I was supposed to be a girl but I got the plumbing for a boy instead. It's like a mistake. But I'm not a mistake. No one is a mistake.

I've felt fake my whole life. Like I'm a fake. A lie. A girl who has to pretend she's a boy so I don't get bullied, don't upset my parents, don't have to deal with everyone else. I'm tired of pretending, though.

Sorry. I don't mean to cry. But, I do sometimes, cry. Actually, I cry a lot. It was hard for me to tell my parents. I mean, they were cool about it. They cried, too. They're both struggling. It's like they're grieving or something, but I didn't die. Well, the boy me died.

I know they were shocked. They thought I was gay. I'm not really gay. I'm a girl, inside my head, so I like guys. I'm not a guy in my head, so that doesn't make me gay.

Pretty soon here, I'm going to start dressing like a girl in the dresses and skirts that I like and tell all the kids at school what's going on. I'm going to write an article for the school newspaper, because I'm the features editor. It's pretty scary, but what I'm sick of is lying. I'm sick of dressing like a boy, like a gay boy. I'm sick of not being me, a girl named Holly.

I'm a person. I'm not better than anyone, I'm not less than anyone. I should be able to be myself. I live in America, right? So I think I owe it to myself to be who I am: a girl.

I have a lot of hopes and dreams. I hope to marry a man and have kids. I know I won't get pregnant the normal way, but maybe we can adopt. I hope to be a mom. I hope to be a designer.

I do a lot of hoping.

18

I took a shower at six the next morning, dried off, and studied my hair.

I hadn't cut it in over a year. I picked up the ends. Dried and fried.

"Damn," I muttered. I pulled the whole, wet blond tail over my right shoulder and cut about six inches off. I then pulled it over my left shoulder and trimmed things up. I brushed my bangs down. They came to my chin. I cut straight across with the scissors about eyebrow level.

I put in a little cream rinse, a handful of mousse, brushed it out, then scrunched up my curls. I turned around and used a hand mirror to look in the mirror behind me. My curls were a lot tighter now without the weight. My head felt much lighter, too.

I peeked at Blake's house on my way out to work. His lights were on. I put my foot on the accelerator. I did not want to run into him.

Yes, I did.

No, I didn't.

Yes, I did.

I was so mad at him I hurt.

Later that week a chastened Tato and Larissa came into my office, where I sat with Tory. We held up their designs.

"Not bad for you two," Tory said. "Glad you're not screaming at each other anymore. You gave me a headache in my face."

"Excellent," I told them. Thunder and Lightning grinned at each other. "Original. Zippy. New. Modern. Young. Seductive."

"Good girl and confident slinky girl mixed," Tory said.

I whipped through a few more. "Ah, you put in Hayden's tassels, too."

"Yeah, we love 'em."

They hurried out. Peace had prevailed.

I winked at Tory as we reviewed their work.

Priceless. Amazing what primal bonding can do for your employees.

On my way out to my dull gray car that night, I saw a man with black curls turn the corner. I knew it wasn't Aaron. *I knew it.* I dropped my keys. I picked them up, dropped them again. I could smell smoke from one of his joints. I could feel his sharp whiskers against my face. I heard his laugh. It wasn't a humorous laugh. It was the laugh of someone who was beating someone else down into abject defeat.

That laugh trickled down my spine and wrapped around my body. It pitched up high, then low again. *Aaron.*

I ran around the corner. I ran up to the man with the black curls. I grabbed his elbow.

It wasn't Aaron. Of course it wasn't.

"I am s-s-s-o sorry," I stuttered, the smell of pot smoke, of creepy laughter, fading. "I thought you were someone else."

He grinned and gave me a peace sign. "No problem."

I leaned against a brick building and tried to breathe.

A police car drove by, and my knees became weak.

It wasn't Aaron. It wasn't Blake.

I was still alone.

I was pregnant.

Aaron and I had used condoms. One time, *one time,* it had slipped off. I dreaded having sex with him, but it made my life easier if I acquiesced. I didn't want to set him off. I wanted him stable so I could leave. If I denied him sex, he raged. Bringing a baby into the equation was not something I wanted to do. And yet.

I was ecstatic.

I was depressed.

I was grateful to be pregnant.

I felt trapped.

I couldn't wait to see the baby.

I worried she would have her father's mental health problems.

I worried that her father would make me have permanent mental health problems.

I started crying each morning in the shower. If I divorced Aaron, would he get joint custody? I couldn't trust him alone with a child, so how would this work? Would I have to stay with him to protect the child until she left for college at eighteen? Would he manipulate and criticize the child as he did me? How could I take care of one more person? Our marriage was not healthy enough for a child.

I started cleaning way too much, as if I could control my dust, I could control my life. I started having anxiety attacks. I couldn't sleep. Insomnia tracked me down night after night.

We received a grant to make another film, something we'd applied for well over a year ago, before I decided I could not work with him again. We both plunged into it even though I was three months pregnant and had morning sickness that forced me to lean my head over the toilet every morning while Aaron told me to "hurry the fuck up."

Aaron's depression lifted when he found out about the pregnancy, as if a switch flipped. He was thrilled. "This is the best time of my life, Meggie, the best time!" Before we went to bed, and when we woke up, he talked to the baby. "Good morning, baby. . . . Good night, baby. . . . You made your mother sick this morning, now quiet on down in there. . . . Are you growing, baby? We can't wait to see you. We love you. You want a brother? And a sister? Okay, I'll talk to Mommy about it."

For the baby, he made an effort to take his medication and he started talking honestly to me about the cycles of his depression.

"It feels like I'm spiraling downward, My Meggie, as if I have no control over my own self, this inescapable weight bearing down on me like a tidal wave. I have no hope, I can't sleep, I have headaches, my brain won't shut off. I can't keep up with my own thoughts. I'm all scattered, like someone has popped a balloon, the pieces flying everywhere. Then, all of the sudden, weeks later, I'll be happy, soaring like a freakin' eagle and I'm powerful again, and people need to get out of my way so I can create something brilliant.

"My stupid bitch mother had this, too. God, I hate her, but we called it the rabid dog. Her mother killed herself over the rabid dog. I wish a live rabid dog would have eaten my mother before I was eight. Then I wouldn't know the secrets about her that I know."

That chilled me to the bone and back. Would my baby have the rabid dog, too?

We laughed over my stomach, and cried.

I kept crying in the shower, too, my head against the tiles, water sluicing away the tears.

As the baby grew, a teeny tiny bump, our problems grew exponentially, too.

I went to get Pop Pop out of doggy day care. I was told his behavior was "improving."

He grinned at me, that odd thing. His tongue fell out. Maybe I wasn't *completely* alone.

That night I sat in the orange Adirondack chair and studied the stars, the maple trees swaying around me, whispering gently. Their leaves were falling off, filling my deck with orange, yellow, green, red, and brown. Pop Pop hopped up on my lap. Who knew one of my best friends would have fur?

"Glad you haven't gotten in any more fights, buddy," I told him. "Good job."

He licked my chin. His tongue fell out again.

* * *

I met him on Friday night.

It was partially Grandma's fault.

Grandma, unbelievably, wanted to dance on a bar. It was on her Bust Out and Shake It Adventure Club list.

"We're putting spice back in my life," Grandma said. "You three, too. You need it. You all work too much. Lacey's run by her hormones, Tory's stalking Scotty, and Meggie wears beige bras—a disgrace—and is living a beige life, also a disgrace. You're all joining me on the bar."

"No, I'm not," I said.

"You want a knocked-up mother to dance on a bar?" Lacey asked.

"I'll do it," Tory snorted. "Maybe I'll invite Farmer Scotty to watch. He wouldn't come. What's the point? I hate him. I sounded pathetic there, didn't I? I hate pathetic people. Pretend I didn't say that."

"Oh, blah, blah, blah. Pick me up at seven o'clock," Grandma commanded. "Don't be late. I want to be back by eleven for my cigar and whiskey."

I pleaded a headache when Lacey and Tory arrived at my tree house that night. As I had been at work since six in the morning and had, between Sunday and Friday, worked eighty hours, I was in no mood to dance on a bar. I was in no mood to leave my tree house. I wanted to eat pretzels dipped in vanilla ice cream while mentally lusting after the chief, then get some sleep before my rat nightmares ripped me apart.

"Come on, Meggie," Lacey said. She was wearing a navy blue maternity dress. "If you don't come, you'll have to deal with Grandma's fire-and-brimstone temper."

"You definitely need to get out," Tory said. She was wearing a shimmery silver sheath dress that clung here and there and shiny silver pumps. "You are the most socially dead, intense, non-smiling person I know. Work, work, work."

"Thank you, Tory."

"You're welcome. You need to change your clothes before we leave. I don't think they'll even let you in with those rags on. You look like a hillbilly. Don't worry. I brought dresses."

"I'm not going."

"Yes, you are," they both said at once.

"I have . . . I have . . . gas."

"Then fart," Tory said. "By the way, that's a lousy hair cut. One side longer than the other."

"I don't think so," Lacey said. "Her hair is so much thicker now, all those blond curls are tighter. Who did it?"

"I did."

Their mouths gaped.

"You cut your own hair?" Tory gasped, as if I'd performed an operation on my heart.

"Yes. It was in my way. I couldn't even see."

"That's why we have salons, Mrs. Einstein," Tory said.

Lacey patted my head. "Don't worry. It's only hair. It can be fixed. Don't do it again, though. Make it a one-time thing."

"Strip, Meggie." Tory reached for my T-shirt and yanked, and Lacey grabbed my pants and did the same. When I stood in front of them, in bra and underwear, they both stopped, jaws hanging open like they were trying to catch birds with their teeth.

"This is the saddest part of all," Lacey said, putting her hands to her cheeks. "We own a lingerie business and this . . . this . . . secret disgrace . . ."

"Your bra and underwear are clear signs of a broken and diseased mind," Tory said. "They'll have to do, though. I didn't bring bras and panties. Even if your dress catches on fire, don't take it off, Meggie. We can't have anyone seeing those . . . those *things*. Arms in the air, here's the first dress."

Tory had brought three dresses with heels to match. She is curvier than I am, looks far better, but she wears her dresses tight, so they fit. After trying on all three, I told them I would wear the blue dress with the square neckline.

Lacey and Tory said to each other, "No. The burgundy one."

I held onto the blue dress, with both hands, as they wrestled it off me.

Lacey said to me, face flushed, "Stop it, Meggie! We know better."

Tory said, slapping my hands, "Acknowledge you are the black plague on style and give in."

They dropped the burgundy dress over my head. It fell to midthigh and had a low neckline. "Too much boob, too much leg," I protested.

"No one asked for your opinion, Meggie," Tory said, putting two handfuls of mousse in my hair and scrunching the curls up.

"You used to dress like this all the time. Sit down." Lacey did my makeup. "Gorgeous," she breathed when she was done. "You are a naturally gorgeous woman."

"All the men are going to be looking at you and I'll never get laid and make Scotty jealous," Tory muttered. "I should have left you in that stained T-shirt, scraggly bra, beat-up underwear, and jeans."

The bar was on the top floor of a building downtown with a view of the sparkling lights of Portland. It was lit by candlelight, classy, and crowded. In the corner of the large dance floor a band banged it out. On the other side of the bar was the restaurant, expensive and gourmet, and much quieter. When Grandma, Lacey, Tory, and I walked in, all of our employees stood up and cheered for Grandma.

Grandma, in a couture turquoise wrap dress and bone-colored heels, was her usual gracious self when she found out Tory had invited Lace, Satin, and Baubles' employees. She said to everyone, "I see you all are here to observe the dance. Like hyenas. Cackling hyenas. Well, you can't chew on my corpse yet."

The hyenas raised their drinks up and cheered her.

Grandma waved her hands in a gesture of "Oh, stop it!" Then said, "I won't tolerate any silliness tonight. I'm dancing on the bar, then we're all going home."

The hyenas cheered her again. Clearly there would be silliness tonight.

"My treat," Grandma announced to everyone as she ordered a whole slew of appetizers and bought us all drinks. "For you hyenas, and because Meggie is finally dressed like a woman."

They raised their glasses to my womanhood. I rubbed my forehead. It would be a long night.

I ordered lemon cream pie, then I had wine, which made me überemotional, which is why I rarely drink it, same with hard alcohol.

Lacey put her arm around me on one side, Abigail on the other. Later I scrambled out of the booth to go to the bathroom. On my way back to the bar I met Tay.

That was his name, Tay.

He was trouble, but not because he was Tay. Friendly, open, funny, Tay.

Tay smiled and said hello, introduced himself. He was about my age, had black, short, wavy hair and a wide smile. He was cheerful. Like a black Labrador. That's how I thought of him. A cheerful black lab.

We chatted and he invited me to dinner. I declined. He grabbed a table in the bar, asked to buy me a drink, I said yes, I don't know why, then he bought crab and shrimp appetizers. When we were talking, my grandma sent over two pieces of chocolate cake. Tay seemed surprised when they arrived.

I wasn't. Chocolate cake is what my mother says women should eat before sex so they are "more moist, like melted chocolate, not dry like a desert." I have no idea how or why she believes that.

So, through the fuzz of chocolate, crab, and shrimp, and more wine, we chatted. I tried to forget about Blake. My heart ached for Blake. He was the one I wanted to be there with, not Tay, although the black Lab was darling.

Fifteen minutes later Tory and Lacey came over and introduced themselves. Lacey said, "Well, aren't you a handsome fellow," and Tory glared at me, swirled her martini with her purple-painted nails, and said, "I thought you agreed not to compete, Meggie. Hello." She nodded at Tay. "I'm her sister. She's frigid and has a bad past. She also works all the time and has a stick up her butt. Part of it is that she's a Leo. I'm a Pisces. Much better, more cerebral, seductive. When you want to move on, I'm here for you."

I rolled my eyes.

They sat down with us. Grandma sat down, too.

Tay was eager to chat.

Bark, bark.

It happened a half hour later.

I was dancing with Tay on the dance floor. I was truly shocked that I was dancing at all. I knew I could blame it on the alcohol, which had slipped through my body like liquid gold.

Lacey, Tory, and almost all of the employees were dancing, too, most of them with each other. The Petrelli sisters got down and rocked it. So did Lance and his wife, Maritza and her sisters, and the Latrouelle sisters—well, they brought down the house. Abigail proved she could, in her words, "bust a move and a roll and a cartwheel." She was a little drunk, but funny.

Grandma was in the middle. Tory had gone into the bathroom to cry, and had come out with a blotchy face. I knew she was thinking of Scotty because she'd said, "Scotty is such a jerk, and I don't want him anymore. He still hasn't called me, and I was remembering how lucky lucky lucky I am to be rid of him."

Tay was smiling at me, making me laugh, and told me I had the prettiest hair he'd ever seen. He wrapped his fingers around a curl.

I was thinking of Blake. I wanted Tay to be Blake. I squished my eyes shut and dropped my forehead to Tay's shoulder. I was almost seeing Blake in my arms. . . .

And then . . . strangely enough—*boom*—when I lifted my head, Blake came out of the mist wearing a gray suit and tie.

No, no mist, I corrected myself. He came out of the steam.

No, no steam, I corrected myself again.

I shook my head.

He came out of the fuzziness.

Not that, either.

But there he was.

I was drunk. I had to be. Maybe it was the beer after the wine, Tory's screwdriver, some sips of Grandma's frilly drink . . .

I blinked.

Blake was walking toward me on the dance floor, and he was one ticked-off dude.

I looked up at Tay. "Do you see a blond giant walking toward us, ho ho ho?"

He nodded. "Yeah, he's right there. Do you know him?"

"Hello, Meggie."

Blake stood right in front of Tay and me. I stopped dancing, so did Tay, but did not drop my arms from around his neck. This was why Tay was trouble.

"Hello, chief. Hello. Are you here to arrest me?" I blinked, swayed. Even in my semidrunken state, a state I was rather embarrassed to be in, I could still feel the zinging between Blake and me.

Zing and zing.

"No, not yet, Meggie."

"Why would you be arrested?" Tay asked. He grinned at me. "For being beautiful?"

I giggled. "I don't think so. He doesn't think I'm beautiful. I would need Kalani's black magic for that."

Tay's eyes opened wide. "Then he's blind. You are way beautiful."

"Thank you." I smiled at Tay. I wanted to smile at Blake, but he looked grim. Jaw set. Shoulders back. Tight face.

"Are you really the chief?" Tay asked, all friendly and black Lab-ish. *Bark bark!*

"Yes, I am."

Tay smiled even more broadly. Like I said, he's a friendly sort. Good looking, too. Excellent teeth, wide smile.

"Congratulations, man," Tay said, shaking his hand. "That's awesome. You know, I've seen you on TV."

Blake nodded, ever so slightly, acknowledging what he said but not allowing himself to be drawn into the conversation.

"Meggie, I'm going to drive you home."

I laughed. Giggled. Laughed. Leaned against Tay, who wrapped his arms around me again. Blake was soooo rawly handsome. I wanted to go bounce on his body badly. "No. There's a typhoon."

"Yes," Blake said with quiet, firm precision. "Let's go."

"No. I'm here with . . ." I waved my hand as a crush of dizziness inserted itself into my brain. "I'm here with my sisters and Grandma, and other people from work, and my grandma is going to dance on the bar and wiggle like a sewing machine."

Blake raised his eyebrow. "Dance on the bar?"

"Yes. She is completing her . . . what is it called . . . aha! Her Bust Out and Shake It Adventure Club list."

"What do you mean her Bust Out and Shake It Adventure Club list?"

"Her list is all the things she wants to do before she dies and goes back to Ireland."

"Is she dying?"

"No. Not at all. She's healthy as a leprechaun sliding down a rainbow can be. But she's in her eighties. Not young anymore, so she can't fly on the back of an owl." I stopped. Why was I talking about that magical story that was so grossly untrue? "At least, her body isn't young. Her mind is. Her spirit inside is flying around from Ireland and making me go with her to do all these Irish things that have to get done. She doesn't have young . . ." I could not keep track of my thoughts. "She does not have young *toes*." I blinked to clear my vision. "She does not have young intestines."

Blake looked intimidating and angry. I swayed.

"She doesn't have young toes?" Tay laughed, tightening his arms around me. "That's a great way of putting it. She's not old, but she doesn't have young toes!"

"No young toes. She's not like you, Blake." I smiled at him, though I could feel his anger coming at my drunkenness in waves. "You're handsome. She's not handsome. She's beautiful. My grandma—" I paused and took a breath, feeling emotional all of a sudden. "She's truly beautiful. I love her." I pulled out of Tay's arms and hugged Blake. I felt his arms around my back, secure and warm. "I love my grandma," I whispered in his ear. "I love my grandma."

"Aw!" Tay said behind me, "That's so nice! I love my grandma, too."

I pulled back and stared into the gray-blue fury of Blake's eyes. "Don't you love your grandma?"

"Yes, I did. But you are drunk and I want you to come with me and I will take you home."

"Oh, no. You won't take me to your home," I told him, waving a finger. "You will take me to my home. You have already told me I can't go to your home and see your bedsheets."

"That's not what I said."

"Yep." I pulled out of his arms, though he resisted and I had to push his arms away. Tay pulled me back in. He's fun. He's full of life and spirit. He is so perfect for someone else. "You don't need to drive me, I'm with..." I paused and tried to envision who I was with. "I am with a black Labrador."

"A black Lab!" Tay exclaimed, happy. "I had a black Lab named Spaghetti when I was a kid, and I loved him. I miss that dog."

"You're kind of a black Lab sort of man and this..." I pointed at Blake, whose glare could fillet a shark. "This man is more of a Doberman." The bar was spinning. Yuck.

I smiled at Tay, and he hugged me closer, then said to Blake, "Good to meet you, man," which was like saying, "Shove off, buddy, I'm with this woman," and it about set Blake on fire, he was so mad. Even through my inebriation I could see that.

"Let's go, Meggie," Blake said. "Do you even know this guy?"

"Nope. But I'm not going with you."

"It's time for you to go."

"Who are you here with, Blake?" I asked. "A golden retriever?"

"I was having dinner with the mayor and a woman from city council."

"Not with your girlfriend?" The bar spun again. Double yuck.

He was not pleased. "I don't have a girlfriend, as you know."

All three of us turned at the drumroll, and a "Ladies and Gentleman" call went out by the deejay.

"Folks, this is Regan O'Rourke. She is eighty-something years old and she wants to dance on a bar. She says it's now or never."

Gracefully, carefully, with help from Lance and Eric, Grandma climbed on top of the bar, to wild applause, in her turquoise dress and high heels. She signaled for a microphone, and obediently the deejay handed it to her.

"Greetings and good evening. I have written a list called my Bust Out and Shake It Adventure Club list. Basically I'm checking things off that I always wanted to do but didn't do in my youth. I always wanted to dance on a bar when I was younger, but I was too busy working." Her Irish brogue was lilting, lovely. "I can't even dance. Why? Same reason. When I was young and should have been dancing, I was working. So tonight's the night. I need three people up here to help me—my granddaughters, Tory, Meggie, and Lacey."

"That's your grandma?" the black Lab gushed.

"Yes, that is!" I put both hands up in the air and clapped. "The Irishman's wife!"

Tay stared at her, totally admiring. "She is absolutely awesome. Awesome!"

I was grabbed by Abigail, Tory, and Lacey. The black Lab gave me a push, laughing. I did not look at the huggable Doberman.

Grandma signaled the drummer, the drummer pounded out the beat, the band joined him, and Grandma danced, strutting, and wiggling up and down the long bar as people threw their hands in the air and clapped and hooted.

I hadn't danced in many miserable years. But I was tipsy and irrationally furious at Blake for rejecting me, so when Grandma held her arms out I climbed up and danced, along with Tory, who knew how to shake it.

I danced in my burgundy dress that dropped halfway down my thighs, with the low-cut bodice, and in high heels, which I hadn't worn in years. Tory did a shimmy thing up there—she has rhythm in her soul—and Lacey bobbed up and down, carefully, in one place, no heels, three people standing below to catch her, just in case.

Grandma's smile lit up that whole room. At the end, with a dramatic drumroll, the bass ear-splitting, applause thunderous, Grandma hugged me close. "That's my girl," she said. "You're coming back to life. Welcome aboard, and I love you."

Tory said, "There's hope yet, Meggie. You still know how to dance."

When I climbed down, the black Lab bounced up and spun me around. "I think I want to marry you!" *Bark bark!*

Over his shoulder, as I was being swung, I saw the Doberman. He may have liked the dance, I don't know, but for sure he did not like the black Lab. Too bad for him.

Unfortunately I didn't want to marry a friendly black Lab.

I didn't want to marry anyone, but if I were forced by a gun-wielding, six-legged scorpion from a sci-fi movie to marry someone, I would definitely pick the Doberman.

The Doberman turned and left.

I woke up naked on my leather couch Saturday morning with a headache the size of Arkansas.

I groaned, then dragged my sorry butt up and poured myself tomato juice. Next I dipped three marshmallows into orange juice and ate them. After that I ate peanut butter straight from the jar. Jeepers hissed at me from upstairs.

I wrapped myself in my pink, bedraggled draggy robe, then pulled on one blue wool sock and one red sock and headed out to my deck, where I sat in the blue Adirondack chair and buried my head in my hands. I was glad Blake couldn't see me from his house. Pop Pop climbed on my lap and licked my cheek as the whole night came flooding back.

After the bar-dancing debacle Tay said, "Will you come home with me later, Meggie. Please?"

He had a loose and easy smile, with dimples on the sides. He had fun and friendly eyes. He would be fun and friendly in bed.

He would allow me to escape for a while. I could forget. I could have sex. I was dying for sex. I was dying to be held. I was dying to stroke and straddle a handsome man.

But Tay wasn't the man I wanted to stroke or straddle.

I could not sleep with Tay with Blake zooming around in my head.

I also had Aaron in my head, too.

That would have made four people in one bed: Tay, Aaron, Blake, and me.

I am not kinky in bed at all, and four is way too many.

"Tay, I'm sorry . . ." I started. "No."

"How about dinner tomorrow night?" He was hopeful.

"No."

"Lunch?" Losing hope.

"No."

"Any chance for coffee?" His smile was definitely dimming.

"No, I'm sorry."

"Why?" Hope gone.

I hugged him, said I wasn't interested in dating. The black Lab was sad.

I remembered Blake's eyes boring into mine. He had not liked seeing me tipsy. He had not liked seeing me with Tay.

I felt my temper shoot on up.

Who the hell did he think he was to be mad at me?

I had asked him if he wanted to sleep with me, and he'd said no.

So what claim did he have on me if I was inebriated and clinging to a black Lab?

On my deck, my head throbbing from being drunk for the first time in forever, my body ill, I acknowledged that Blake and I had another problem. It was a clash of personalities.

Blake was used to leading. He's a leader. A natural leader.

I, however, lead, too. And I cannot, will not, follow again, as I did with Aaron. I will not be out of control of my own life or my own head or my own emotions again. I will not give up that control ever. I will never, ever *follow* again in a relationship, nor will I live reacting to disasters that mess with my mental stability.

I will never let a man run the show. I will never cater to a man again, I will never be in a relationship where I have no voice or choices, I will never be smothered, I will never be manipulated by him or be toyed with in any shape or form. I will never alter myself in any way, or let a man push my personality around to suit his needs or wants. I will never allow myself to get trapped again.

I will not allow the man to control our sex life, and what Blake was doing now, not getting involved with me sexually, that smacked of control.

Control over me.

Blake is a man who wants a serious, committed relationship. He's a man who wants the closeness and intimacy and trust that I am not giving any man again.

Therein lay our insurmountable problem.

During the third week of filming, I started having contractions.

I told Aaron. He waved his hand *in my face* and said, "You're fine. You're overreacting, emotional as usual. They're the Braxton Hicks contractions I read about in the baby book." Aaron had read three baby books. He was now an authority on my pregnancy. He told me what to eat and what not to eat, cleared food out of our pantry, and filled it with a whole bunch of stuff that looked like rabbit meal. I refused to eat it, so he called me a "neglectful mother."

"What you eat now determines the health of my baby, Meggie, so eat this. We're not leaving the table until you've eaten what I made, even if we have to sit here all night." I refused to sit there the rest of the night, so he raged, then gave me the silent treatment for a week.

He was obsessive and critical. "I'm not sure how you're going to be as a mother, Meggie, because you want to work so much and you have to have absolute control, and you're a perfectionist and way too ambitious . . . don't cry, I want to talk this out before the baby comes and I want you to be a good mother. Women like you who are career oriented often don't have a lot of maternal skills."

"Where did you read that?"

He hemmed and hawed and said, "I know it instinctively."

And I said, "I'll be a great mom. If you stop going to bed for weeks on end, if you stop throwing temper tantrums and being critical, and if you stop taking painkillers and smoking pot and instead take your medicine and see your doctors, maybe you'll be a great dad."

He flew off the handle at that, walked off our worksite, and I didn't see him for a week. Our cameraman, sound technician, and assistant were thrilled to have him gone. So was I.

When the contractions returned he said, "You can't get upset about every little thing. You're high-strung to begin with. Try to ignore your emotions, Meggie. That's what I do when I don't know what to do with you. Damn."

In the middle of the night, weeks later, I woke up with a gripping contraction, and I knew I was in trouble.

I woke Aaron. He said, "Lie down. You're fine. Don't be hysterical. At this stage of your pregnancy, you'll be even more irrational and hypersensitive. I'm having serious concerns about you being a mother."

I ignored him.

I drove to the hospital.

At least, I tried to drive to the hospital. When the pains became too sharp, my teeth clenched in agony, I pulled over and called an ambulance. The police and the paramedics arrived.

They were the kindest people. One of the police officers was a woman. She held my hand as I gave birth in the back of the ambulance. "It's too soon," I told them. "Oh, God, help me. It's too soon."

She was tiny.

She was not ready for our world.

Despite heroic efforts by the hospital staff, she was dead within two hours.

I held her in my arms at the end and watched the life drain out of her. She was a tiny soul leaving, returning to the heavens, her time another time.

Aaron was hysterical, furious, and raving. He was eventually dragged out of the hospital by security. He made vile accusations against the doctors and nurses, saying they had "murdered my child by incompetence. This is your fault. You did this! Fuck you!" He then started toppling all sorts of things in my hospital room, including my IV pole, medical equipment, and a medical cabinet.

I clutched my baby to my heart, though her heart had stopped beating—her face, her fingers, her toes, absolutely perfect, so fragile. Around me the doctors were restraining Aaron, his black curls and black feather flying, his jaw unshaven. He railed and yelled, and the most foul words came out of his mouth, along with spittle, his sweat flying.

Other doctors ran in, security ran in, a nurse jumped into the fray, and there was yelling and screaming.

The room was in chaotic disarray, like an uncontrollable human tornado had touched down. In the midst of that tornado I held my baby close and kissed her, my tears raining down on her still, pale face, my body bleeding and trembling. She had a shock of fuzzy black hair—from Aaron or from Sperm Donor Number Two? She had lips like a rosebud. She was so sweet, so loved.

I blamed myself for her death. I thought Aaron was right. I worked too hard, maybe I didn't eat right, I was stressed and anxious, I cleaned late at night, I didn't sleep enough, I became stuck on my racing and negative thoughts, and I obsessed over small things because I couldn't control the cauldron of insanity in my life: Aaron.

I cried often, which probably upset the baby. She probably thought the tears were about her. She heard her mother crying.

She had made her mother sad. I had also had small contractions and thought they were normal. I was wrong.

Yes, it was my fault. I killed my own baby. I suck. I hate myself.

I named her Josephine.

I have never felt that much pain in my life.
I thought I was being split in two with an ax.
I have never recovered from that split. I never will.
Some grief never leaves.
You deal with it as best you can.
That's what I've done. I've done the best I could.

Josephine, my beautiful baby.
Always, always in my heart.
I miss you, my sweet. Every day I miss you.
I will see you again someday. I will hug you, and kiss you. We will play and laugh and read books and bake cookies.
I am so sorry.
Mommy loves you.

19

I wasn't surprised at the photo of my mother in the Living section of our local newspaper. I had seen the show a couple of days prior.

My mother was the featured guest with Emmy Shandil, who is the host of the nationally syndicated talk show *The Emmy Show*. My mother was dressed in the pages of her book. She'd had her favorite designer make the pages into a dress. The dress dropped to midcalf. It had a low neckline with a curved bodice and a slit in front. She wore shiny red heels with it. She was a cross between a book and Dorothy of *The Wizard of Oz*.

"I love your dress, Brianna," Emmy gushed. She has exceptionally large teeth and a short brown bob. Now and then she fillets her guests if she doesn't like them.

"Ask me to tell you what I'm trying to say with my dress." My mother sat straight up in her chair, those red curls hanging down her back reminding me so much of Lacey's.

"What are you trying to say with your dress, Brianna?" Emmy dutifully asked.

"Free yourself." my mother declared, and stood. She then started pulling the pages of her book off her dress. "Free yourself from your inhibitions and fears that were drilled into you by your childhood, by your marriage, by your life."

The audience chuckled.

"Free yourself from a spouse who tells you who to be, who

smashes your sexual self, your spiritual self." There went more pages. "Don't let him suck you dry."

The women cheered. Emmy Shandil, who went through a nasty, public divorce when her husband, Brian, had an affair with a twenty-year-old actress, stood up and flung her arms straight out. "He sucked me dry, Brianna!" she announced. "I'm dry!"

The audience laughed.

"Reinvent yourself and your love life, Emmy!"

"Oh, I've already reinvented my love life, Brianna. Hellllo, Tony!"

"You decide who you want to be." My mother walked to the end of the stage to address the audience. "Stop being prey. Stop letting other people, your mother, your in-laws, your annoying neighbor, run your life." Page, page, page.

"I will not be prey again! I am not prey!" Emmy said, standing beside my mother. "He was a creep! Weak chin, floppy bottom. Pig breath. He wore my panties!"

"Daydream. What do you want for your future?" my mother asked, pages flying. "Write it down. Write down the steps to get to that goal. Follow the steps. Are you frumpy?"

A number of people in the audience shouted, "Yes!"

"Then defrump yourself." Page, page, page. "How can you be all you want to be if you're a frump? How can you be good in bed if you feel ugly?"

Page, page, page.

In the end my sixty-plus-year-old mother was standing in one of our company's leopard-print negligees and her shiny red heels, the audience totally enthralled. The lingerie had a tasteful, black gauzy skirt attached, with tiny crystals. "Join me, Emmy! Let's vow to never become frumpy!"

Emmy didn't hesitate. She's as unrestrained as my mother. She unbuttoned her own blouse and yanked it open with flair. She was wearing one of our designs, a purple lace push-up bra that my mother gave her before the show. "I will never be a frump!"

"Join me, audience!" my mother encouraged. The camera panned. My mouth dropped open. A number of women were unbuttoning their blouses and baring their bras. Three men took off their shirts.

"Say it," my mother commanded. "I won't be frumpy any longer!"

"I won't be frumpy any longer!" they boomed back.

"Take charge of your life," my mother shouted over the clapping and hooting, an arm around Emmy. "Travel. Have adventures. Be beautiful! This is your life. Don't you let it end without you in it!"

"I won't, Brianna," Emmy said, staring right into the camera. "I am beautiful! And Brian Forrester, my husband who ran off with a twenty-year-old named Tammy Underhill of Oklahoma City, you are ugly! Yes, ugly and frumpy!"

"Say it again, people!" my mother shouted. "I won't be frumpy any longer!"

"I won't be frumpy any longer!" The audience bellowed back.

Brianna O'Rourke and Emmy Shandil picked up pages of my mother's book from the floor and threw them to the audience. The camera showed the audience jumping for the pages, half dressed. Emmy grabbed my mother and they danced across the stage, Emmy in her purple bra and my mother in our leopard-print negligee and red heels.

We talked later by phone. I complimented my mother on her page-throwing performance. She said, "Thank you, dear. Did you receive your hat and scarf? Oh, I'm so glad you love it. The colors are perfect, aren't they? Are you sleeping better?"

"Straight through." No. It was worse.

"Are you being a workaholic, as usual?"

"Not at all." Fifteen hours a day.

"Are you taking time to relax and rejuvenate?"

"Every day. Yoga. Reading. Listening to music during my daily serenity walk in the woods."

"I wish you would quit lying to me, young lady."

"I know, Mom. I love you."

"Love you, too."

*   *   *

I woke up to a mouse.

No kidding, a mouse's nose was inches from mine.

I screeched, scared the mouse, and scared Regan, who let it go accidentally, and the mouse scampered across the bedspread, leaped like a kamikaze pilot off the bed, and skittered down the hallway.

"Help me, help me!" Regan yelled, running after it. "George is loose, Mom! George is loose!"

Lacey hollered from downstairs, "Then show us how fast you can move on the football field and chase that thing down, Regan. Move! Move!"

"Come here, George, come here!" Regan thundered out of the guest bedroom as Hayden came in. I was in one of Lacey's flannel nightgowns. It had yellow tulips on it. "Hey, Hayden."

"Hi, Aunt Meggie." He climbed onto the bed. He was wearing a long, blue nightshirt with a picture of Marilyn Monroe on it. "I'm glad you stayed the night after game and pizza night."

"Me too. It was fun. Thanks for inviting me."

"You're welcome. Mom seems a lot happier since you came home. Not so stressed out, less yelling."

"I'm happier now that I'm home, too." That was true. "How are you, honey?"

Those blue eyes showed how he was. He semiwhispered, "I'm scared."

"Because . . ."

"Because remember when I told you that I'm going to write an article for the school newspaper about being in the wrong body?"

"Yes." I envisioned him being jumped in the hallways.

"I wrote it."

"You did?" I envisioned him smashed into a locker.

"Yeah. Doing the video with you helped a lot. It helped me say out loud all that I think in my head. I wrote the article and I've edited it, and wrote more, and deleted some stuff, but I already talked to the newspaper teacher and she wants to print it, but she's waiting for me to be, like, totally ready."

I felt my skin tingle. As in, tingle *with fear*. A kid coming out as transgender. When I was in school, kids didn't even come out when they were gay. The rules were: Open the door to the closet, walk straight in, and lock it up with six dead bolts. Don't say a word.

Anyone who appeared gay hid it. If they didn't, they were teased, harassed, beaten up. It was awful. It was wrong. It was sick.

And now Hayden. *Transgender.* More confusion for people, more rejection, more "he is mentally ill" or "ewwww, gross, that's so weird" or "perverted and disgusting and dangerous." Gentle, kind, sweet, lovely Hayden.

I shuddered thinking about what might happen to him. "Hayden, I'm going to say it again: This could get really ugly, really fast."

"I know, but what's already ugly is not being myself. It's hard for people to understand. I get it. The only way I can explain it, Aunt Meggie, is to ask you: Do you feel like a woman?"

"Yes." A struggling woman. A messed-up woman, but yes. I felt like a woman and I like being a woman.

"If I told you that you had to be a man, cut your hair like a man, dress like a man, take on the personality of a man, and I forced you to do that for years on end, never letting you act like a woman, who you were in your heart and your head, how would that be?"

"I couldn't do it. I could not act like a man." I thought about it, knowing there was absolutely no way I could get the full picture here. "It would feel totally unnatural, fake, and like you said, I would feel like a lie."

"That's it. Now picture a whole lot of depression and loneliness, hating my own body because it's the wrong one, seeing a girl trapped in a boy body when I look in the mirror, having people treat me like a boy when I know I'm a girl, or treating me like a gay guy, and not dressing like a girl, and you'd start to get it. I mean, I'm a girl, not a boy. I know it, I've always known it, but I can't be my full self. Only a part of my full self, and that's no good. It's not good enough."

I hugged him. "Hayden, I'm here for you, and I back you up one hundred and ten per cent. Always have, always will."

Hayden left to work on a design he had for a pajama line I wanted to launch. "You'll love the frills," he said. "Totally darling."

The second he left, Cassidy skipped on in wearing a white flannel nightgown with pink ribbons and pink tulips. It covered her from neck to toe.

"Aunt Meggie, I think it's going to be wicked hard for me to get into heaven." She sat cross legged on the bed.

"I feel that way about myself, sweets. I don't let it worry me much at this point. But why do you say that?"

"Did Mom talk to you yet?" she whispered.

"No, she didn't."

"I snuck out last night after she and Dad went to sleep. I had to sneak-ola because I'm grounded." She flipped her red curls back. She looks so much like her mom. "I went to one party, came home, hugged Mom good night, then I went back out through my window to meet up with Cody."

"Did Cody spend the night again?"

She gasped. "Mom told you about that!" She threw her hands in the air, so indignant that her mother told me she was having sleepovers with her boyfriend.

"I'm afraid so."

"She shouldn't have! That's private!"

"Doesn't sound like it was that private when your mom and dad found you snuggled up with Cody under your pink bedspread like two teddy bears."

She huffed and puffed as only a teenager can do. "That night was *gross*. I can hardly get it out of my head. I feel damaged *forever*. Mom came in to check on me. Cody and I were both asleep and he was going to leave at five in the morning because he had to study for chemistry. Anyhow, she barged on in and she screamed when she saw there were two heads in my bed instead of one. We were so scared, we started screaming, too. I mean, we thought she was an ax murderer! Cody said he almost wet himself!"

More huffing and puffing from Cassidy as I tried not to laugh.

"And it got worse, if you can believe *this*, Aunt Meggie! Cody tried to get out of bed quick to save me from the ax murderer and he got all tangled up in the sheets and hit the floor on his *face*, then he stood up with his arms out, ready to karate chop the murderer."

I pictured that precious, precious scene. My sister in her nightgown, pregnant, bent over screaming, and Cody and Cassidy screaming back on full throttle, the whole room exploding as if, indeed, an ax murderer had wandered in, then Cody struggles out of bed and falls on his face and struggles up to karate chop my sister.

I laughed and laughed, my stomach starting to ache.

"Then Dad ran in because he heard everyone screaming their heads off, and I mean, like, Aunt Meggie"—her eyes widened—"I heard his feet pounding, and all of a sudden he was pushing Mom out of the way like, you know, he was going to do battle or something, and Mom turned on the light and well..." Her voice trailed off and she shrugged.

"And, well, you and Cody were there naked, not an ax murderer to be found." I wiped tears from my cheeks.

"Not naked, I'm sure, Aunt Meggie." She was indignant. "I was wearing this. This is my favorite nightgown. I like the pink tulips, and he was wearing..." Her brow wrinkled. "Okay, you're right. Cody was buck naked... standing up..." Her brow furrowed.

"Not what your parents wanted to see."

"What was even worse, Aunt Meggie, is that *Dad* was naked." Cassidy slapped both hands to her eyes. "That's why I feel that I'm damaged. I saw my daddy naked. Gross, oh so gross. That's not a sight for young eyes. It's like a scar in me now forever."

I pictured yet another precious, precious scene and tried to muffle my laughter.

"It's not that funny." Cassidy shook her head in bafflement. "They were pissed. I mean, Dad was like, *yelling* at Cody to get the hell out of the house, and I think he hurt Cody's feelings 'cause Cody started to cry and said he was sorry a million times, but Dad threw Cody out naked, then he threw his clothes out the window, and Mom was screaming at me that this was her house, I had to follow her rules, I could get pregnant if I skipped a pill, my life would be over, all this stuff . . ."

"Yes, well, you don't want to be pregnant alongside your mother." For some reason I found that hilarious, too, and it's so not funny.

"I know. That would be Disaster City! Poor Mom. Pregnant again. It's embarrassing and sickening that Mom and Dad still do it."

"Yeah, that's embarrassing. And the baby is proof of it. They can't even deny it."

Cassidy, my namesake, fingered the collar of her prim and proper nightgown. "I like to think they only did it three times, one for me, one for Hayden, one for Regan. We'll pretend this is the fourth time only. Anyhow, I was caught sneaking in and I'm grounded for a longer amount of time now. I feel like I'm always grounded."

"Does seem like you have to be home a lot."

"I don't mind being home, but I don't like being *grounded*."

"Yeah, it's tough. Brutal."

She nodded, then her face lightened. "So, Hayden and I are making holiday wreaths today. You want to make one with us? We're making them for your house to welcome you here. Also, after that, Mom and I are making pumpkin chocolate chip muffins. They are the best. Want to help? And since I can't go out tonight, we're going to make baklava together and watch Martha Stewart's cooking shows. Regan is volunteering at the animal shelter, but then he'll be home to watch Martha with us. Doesn't that sound like fun?"

"Oh, it does, Cassidy, it does." I don't like cooking or, as my mother would say, "the domestic arts."

Later, after the wreath making, Lacey and I sat down to eat pumpkin chocolate chip muffins and have coffee. Lacey muttered to me, "Cassidy can't help it that she inherited a few cells of the slut gene."

"But she cooks like a dream," I said.

"That's true. A dreamy, slutty cook."

We clinked our muffins together, as if we were saying cheers.

I bravely tried to take a bath that night.

I turned on the water. I felt my heart rate rise with the steam, my hands freezing, going numb, as visions of black swirled through my mind. I tried to stick my toes in, couldn't do it. I tried to stick a finger in, no go.

I turned off the bathwater, drained it, wrapped a towel around myself, and stumbled out to my deck, past that thing in my closet I hid from myself. I collapsed into the green Adirondack chair until I could breathe again. I stayed outside until I could no longer see the bathwater of my past. Pop Pop barked at me. I couldn't bark back.

That night I dreamed of Aaron pushing me into the tub as I struggled and kicked. He covered me with black feathers, then detergent. It was the black feathers that drowned me.

Planning a fashion show or, in our case, a Fashion Story, is like trying to hike up a mountain in impossibly high heels during a rockslide.

Especially since we were doing something special—okay, *odd*—with it.

I approved the ads for the newspaper for The Fashion Story after we'd been round and round about what the announcement should say and what photo should be displayed. We decided to use a photo of Grandma in a strawberry field. She was wearing a red, flowing, silky dress that blew in the wind, and her rubies.

The words below it: "My name is Regan O'Rourke. You're invited to the Lace, Satin, and Baubles Fashion Story. Let me tell you how I went from picking strawberries to designing brassieres."

I hoped people showed up, or all this work in finding the location, building a runway, deciding on the decor, bringing in a gargantuan amount of lighting, paying for some sort of dessert, and readying our "models" and their outfits would be for nothing.

As Grandma said to me a week before, "We're going for broke. Might as well make the whole damn thing pretty."

Broke isn't pretty. I kept hiking up the mountain with the rockslide in my heels.

"Three days before that bad typhoon, whoosh whoosh, I see it in my dream," Kalani said, wriggling her fingers at Lacey and me over Skype. "I see palm trees blowing. I see beach and pink dragon on beach and I see water like lake, with fish. I think I... what the word... Tory know this word... ah!" She pointed a finger in the air. "New American word for me: psychic! I think I psychic!"

"Good for you," I said. "Then you'll be able to tell me the future. Kalani, did you get the shipment out that we talked about?"

"Ya. Ya. I get boxes and boxes of thongs out. Those hardly no panty at all, not cover nothing on the you know"—she turned around and put her butt up so we could see it on Skype—"the boom boom."

"You're right—"

"And I check the lace, like we talk about, Meggie. Those things, mostly lace."

"Pretty, aren't they?"

"Ya. Pretty. You could wear them, Meeegie, but not you, Lacey. Not with that big boom boom." She smiled. "Look see your tummy!" Kalani helpfully pointed at Lacey's tummy as if Lacey didn't know how big it was.

"Yes, it's a healthy baby," Lacey said, under her breath she said, "You nonstop-talking skinny bird face."

"Bird face?" I whispered.

"That Tory," Kalani said. "She know fashion. I talk to her yesterday. She say I need crimson-tide lipstick. She send me some. You know Tory?"

"I think we do remember Tory," Lacey said. She wasn't in a good mood. "We're not that dumb."

"No, you not dumb, Laceeey. You no talk like that." Kalani shook her finger at Lacey. "You not dumb. You just fat. Fat lady now."

"Oh, fuck you very much," Lacey said, with a teeth-clenched smile. Her morning sickness was particularly bad today. I elbowed her. Kalani did not hear the f word.

"Yes. You welcome, fat lady. That you name now?" Kalani clapped her hands together. Whooee!

"No, that is not her name, Kalani," I snapped. That was enough. "Call her Lacey."

"Don't call me fat lady unless you want me to call you skinny crow," Lacey said, jaw tight. "I don't need to hear that."

Kalani's face fell into sadness. Cultural mishaps, that's what these are, but she heard the tone. "Ah. Ya. Okay. This bad."

I could see she was tearing up.

"Kalani." I tried to distract her. "Tell us more about being psychic."

The tears flooded her eyes. "Ya. That new American word for me. I see typhoon in my dream three days before, then it come with pink dragon." The tears rolled down her cheeks. "I go now. Bye-bye, seeesters. I love you. I love you."

She de-Skyped us.

"Shoot," I breathed. "If I were psychic I could have seen that coming."

"This fat lady real mad now," Lacey said, shoving her chair back. "Real mad. Ya."

On Tuesday night, with Pop Pop bouncing beside me, grinning, in trouble because he'd had another fight at doggy day care and was on probation *again,* I came home to a hamster home complete with colorful tubes and a hamster running on a wheel. A bag full of hamster stuff like food and shavings for the cage sat beside it.

Regan had written a note: "This is a nice girl hamster. My friend Seth is allergic to it, so his parents are making him give her up. Her name is Ham the Hamster. I think you'll like her because she's a good listener and curious. I'll come and visit. Seth wants to come, too."

I bent down and peered into the cage. Ham the Hamster was running with all her might on a wheel. I don't know why. "You're going to tire yourself out," I told her. She took no notice.

I carried her in and put her by Mrs. Friendly, the lizard. Mrs. Friendly stuck his tongue out.

Pop Pop darted in and went to play with Jeepers. Jeepers didn't want to play. I could hear him hissing.

I had a hissy cat, a weird dog on probation, a bored lizard, and a hamster that ran for no reason. I did not have a police chief. I walked outside my house, leaned over my deck, stared up at Blake's house, and hurt. That's how pathetic I am: I watch his *house*. I reminded myself of Tory.

I drank a beer on my deck, then ate a slice of chocolate cake from Cassidy, then a piece of chicken dipped in salsa and peaches mixed together.

I went to bed at two. I tried to sleep. I couldn't. First the red and black scene assailed me, then I had to curl up around my pillow and pretend I was hugging Blake.

The pillow wasn't Blake. That's why I couldn't sleep.

"Hello, Meggie."

I stopped sprinting down the street. It was dark, it was pouring down rain, and I was chasing Pop Pop. That pesky dog had squiggled around me when I'd opened the door for Jeepers to come back in. I shoved my feet into running shoes and cursed that grinning canine as he took off. I knew he was laughing at me.

It had been a rip-roaring day at work. A huge order was lost, then found; another order ended up in Seattle instead of Tampa; and Lacey had to leave work in the middle of a meeting with our accountant, who had grim news, to go to school and relieve Regan of an abandoned kitten he'd found and snuck into his coat.

"Hi, Blake." I stopped and pushed my wet hair out of my eyes. I was sweating. I had on sweatpants and a holey sweatshirt. I was panting, too. Dang. I needed to exercise more.

"Out for a run?"

Blake had clearly been out for a run. He was in an army T-shirt and shorts. He was soaked, too. "No. I'm chasing Pop Pop."

"Ah, okay. Where is he?"

"He ran . . ." I panted again, feeling like an old woman. "He ran off. He's a bad dog. He has a strange grin, he fights with other dogs, he barks at me as if we're having a conversation, and he teases Jeepers." I wiped sweat off my forehead. "I have to go and find him."

"I'll help you."

"You will?"

"Yes. Of course."

And that was that.

The glow from the street light illuminated his face. He didn't seem angry, the way he had been the last time I saw him. In fact, he seemed . . . tired.

Tired and sad.

"Are you okay, Blake?"

He didn't answer for a second. He turned his head to the right, then back at me and smiled . . . slightly. "I think I'm about to get better."

"Ah." I was still panting and I willed myself to stop. Unfortunately, looking at Blake made me pant, too. "I'm glad to hear it."

Those gray-blue eyes traveled over my face; over my hair; for a mini-millisecond dropped to my chest, which I was thrilled to see; then focused on my eyes. "Good to see you, Meggie."

"Good to see you, too."

"Okay, let's go find Pop Pop." Blake has a low voice, seductive and gravelly, and it sailed right on through my body. I loved his voice. It sounded so . . . trustworthy.

I could trust him. I wouldn't, but I could.

* * *

A half hour later Pop Pop, who had obeyed Blake's command to "come," but not mine, was snoring slightly while Blake and I were at my kitchen table eating spaghetti next to the trunk of my maple tree.

"I love spaghetti," I said. I felt . . . happy. Relieved. I was with Blake! "I could eat it every day. Sometimes I do." I did not add that whenever I have spaghetti I also eat corn flakes cereal at the same time.

"I love steak. But I have to tell you that your spaghetti is now at the top of my list."

"Thank you. I'll give credit to the jar of sauce I bought. Not surprised you love steak."

Blake leaned back and crossed his arms, smiling. He had run home to shower and was now in jeans and a blue shirt. He had a huge chest and a commanding sort of body. The man made me tingle.

I had jumped into the shower, too, and pulled on jeans and a pink blouse, then squished my curls with mousse and put on lipstick. I wished I had a delicate, lacy bra. Maybe I would bring Grandma's box home. . . .

"What is that supposed to mean?"

"It is not surprising to me that a man like you likes steak. I would not assume that you would like eating quiche or tiny pink cupcakes."

He winked. "Got me. I don't like quiche and I can't imagine eating a tiny pink cupcake."

Jeepers hissed at him.

Blake hissed back at the cat, which I found so funny, as I did the same, then he said to me, "How is Tay?"

Oh, he was smart. Get me in a squishy, happy mood, then ask a pointed question. "I would hate to be across a table from you being cross-examined."

"Did you go home with him?"

I let that question hang in the air, heavy and insulting. "I'm surprised you have to ask. Didn't you look out your window to see my car that night?"

"You didn't take your car with you. Your sister drove you to the bar. I asked her because I wanted to make sure you weren't driving home and to make sure she looked out for you. And no, I wouldn't have checked anyhow. That's too stalkerish for me. I would actually have to walk down to the bottom of my driveway and look for your car, and I wouldn't allow myself to do that." His jaw was pretty tight. "So, did you?"

I bristled. "It's not your business, is it, Blake?"

He leaned forward, elbows on the table, arms muscled out. "No, it's not, but I'm asking anyhow. Did you go home with him?"

I leaned forward, too. "I'm not telling you either way." Damn. I was going head-to-head with Blake again. I didn't want that, but neither did I want some man thinking he could pry into my personal life—yet another control issue for me.

"Why not?"

"Because you don't have the right to ask the question." My voice was trembling.

"Are you dating him?"

"Now you're switching things around. Same question."

"It's not the same question. You may or may not have gone home with him. You may or may not be dating him. I'm asking."

I wanted to tell him, no, I wasn't, but Blake's questioning was bringing up a whole lot of memories of Aaron questioning me: "Where were you, Meggie? With who? Who else was there? Who did you talk to? What did you do after that? You're hiding something from me, aren't you? You're having an affair. I know it. *I can tell.* Give me your phone. I want to check your calls again. I'm checking your e-mail, too. Don't fight me on this. What the hell is going on, Meggie? Damn it, tell me!" Then he'd often fling my phone against a wall and shatter it.

Following that, there would be the silent treatment and withholding of sex, which I didn't want to have with him anyhow, but I didn't want it held over my head like a sword ready to strike when *he* felt like having it, either.

"My life is not your business other than what I want to tell you," I said.

To my utter astonishment, Blake sat back. "Okay."

"Okay?"

"Yes, okay." He abruptly stood up and stared out the windows of my tree house into the dark while I tried to simmer down, my anger boiling, but even in my boiling anger I was saddened beyond belief. I did not want this with Blake.

He turned back toward me. "I wish that our relationship were different. You won't let me in, will you? It's almost instinctive, isn't it? Will you tell me about your marriage?"

That question pissed me off, too. "No. I already told you I don't want to talk about it. Remember?" I stood up, jerkily, and gathered up the dishes.

He grabbed the rest of the dishes as I slammed the ones I had on the counter. One slipped and shattered, and I said a bad word as I bent to pick it up.

"I'll get it, Meggie," Blake said, his voice kind as he bent down.

I bent down, too, and he grabbed both of my hands and pulled me back up. "Meggie. I'll get it. Let me do it. Go sit down."

Tears filled my eyes and I didn't want him to see them, so I stomped back out to the table, though I did not like being told what to do. I waited for a few seconds, bit down on my lip, and tried to get control before I returned to the kitchen.

I slammed a dish into the dishwasher. Blake put an arm around my waist, stood in front of me, and said, "Meggie, I told you to let me do this."

"No." I was triggering to the past. Triggering to a man who had a rat face and claws and blood, a man who was messed up and messed me up. I was triggering to a tiny baby who died in my arms.

"Yes. Go and sit down. Please."

"No. I can do my own dishes. This isn't your house, Blake. You can't tell me what to do. In fact, you can never tell me what to do."

"I'm not telling you what to do, Meggie. I'm trying to make your life easier."

"I don't want it easier! If I want to pick up my broken dish, I will! I don't need easy. I don't need you to do anything to my life. I don't need you to try to change it or me."

"I'm not trying to change you at all, honey."

Honey.

He called me honey. That was too close, too intimate.

Now I was mad and sad and the tears were coming. I blinked hard. It didn't help. They spilled over onto my cheeks. I wiped them away. "I don't need your honey-talk. I am not your honey."

Blake was watching me carefully, his eyes tired and hurt.

"I don't need you to ask questions about Tay, or Aaron, or personal questions about me or my past, and I don't need you prying."

"I'm sorry about the prying. Meggie, I like you. I want to know you better. It's that simple. When I saw you with Tay, especially when I could tell you had had too much to drink, I didn't like it. In fact, I thought about putting him in a choke hold, or punching him."

"Whom I choose to be with is not for you to dislike or like, Blake. My life is not for you to have an opinion on or for you to control." *Whew. Trigger, trigger.* "I don't need to know what you think of me."

"You're right." He held up his hands. "It's not. We're not together. We're not dating, we're not married. You don't even want to be friends. I'm sorry."

"Good. You should be." My voice cracked. "Don't ever drill me again with your questions. Don't be suspicious. Don't try to make me feel that what I'm doing is wrong. Don't try to talk to me with some disapproving, angry tone like you did at the bar. If I want to date Tay, I will. If I want to sleep with him, I will. If I want to date a whole bunch of superficial, shallow men who don't want any more of a hold on me than I want on them, I'll do it. If I want a different man on Mondays, I'll have him. If you find out about it and you don't like it, tough luck."

I brushed my hand across my eyes, feeling my heart pumping, hard and anguished. A rush of memories, all negative, some terrorizing, mind twisting, assailed me.

Blake waited me out, then he did something unexpected. He said, "Meggie," so soft, like warm satin, as the tears sprung to my eyes *again,* and pulled me close. I didn't hug him. He pulled me closer. I buried my head in my hands and my hands on his chest, his chin on top of my head, as he held me, my shoulders shaking.

It took me a long time to put my arms around his waist and lean on him.

"Josephine dying was your fault, Meggie, your fault!" Aaron yelled at me, those black curls flying as he punched a fist into the wall in that bleak Los Angeles apartment. Josephine had been dead for two weeks.

"You were a shitty mother. You never controlled that temper of yours, you were always angry at me, and that anger killed my baby. . . . You had an unhealthy body. You didn't take care of yourself. I watched you, I watched you all the time!"

I flew into a rage, even though my own guilt was shredding me. "You told me not to go to the doctors when I had contractions, Aaron, that they were normal, and I was stupid enough to believe you were right."

I had let Aaron think for me, make decisions for me, though I knew he was irrational and unreasonable, and I would never forgive myself.

Had I gone to the doctors when I started having contractions if I hadn't let Aaron's anger and condescension control me, Josephine might have lived. That I get to live with forever. "You with your mood swings, your depression, your pot and your pills, and your constant focus on you, you, you is exhausting! You know what you are, Aaron? You're a project. You're not a husband. You're a project who always has to have the attention on you, all these women that flock around you—"

"I have never touched Becky, Char, or Talia—"

"And I'm sure it's been hard for you to resist." We'd had this argument before. Aaron liked to flirt. He liked women fawning. He liked the ego stroking.

"Not hard at all. I'm married, so I've been faithful to you, Meggie, even when you ignore and neglect me."

"I have never ignored and neglected you—"

"I show you love every day. I put up with you working all the time."

"Someone has to work here, Aaron."

"Oh, there ya go." He slammed his fist into the wall again. "I knew that would come up. You think you're more successful than I am."

I didn't say anything as my frustration, my guilt, and my fury about blew my brain. Aaron had recently crashed on our latest film project and had refused to work. He stayed home and watched video games, smoked pot, swallowed his painkillers, and drank beer all day. He was barely holding on, his depression, which had come on this time like a bullet train, almost totally consuming him. I tried to get him on his meds, he refused. I tried to get him on a schedule to manage himself, he refused. I tried to get him back to his counselor and doctors, he refused.

"Do you know what, Meggie? Your films have the feel of a fast-food restaurant. In and out. Cheap. No emotions. No depth. Nothing. You worked so hard, always on your feet, always telling everyone what to do, always in charge of your fast-food films, and you forgot you had a baby in you. My baby, Meggie, mine! Mine! You wore out. You wore the baby out. She suffocated in you."

I swore at him, my voice cracking, my stomach aching, right where Josephine should have been. I bent over double, holding myself, his words *she suffocated in you* ringing in my head, killing me.

He pounded the table, both fists, the chains around his neck clanking. I used to think it was so rebellious of him, so individualistic of him, to wear the chains. Now I thought he looked like he was trying to be rebellious and individualistic. He looked stupid.

"Where are you going?" Aaron demanded, as I turned to the closet to get my suitcases.

"I'm leaving."

"You sure as hell are not."

"Yes, I am." I was done.

"You stay here and work this out. You owe me an apology for Josephine!"

"I can't stand this anymore."

"You can't stand what? The honest truth? You can't stand that Josephine is dead because of you?"

"No, I can't stand *you*." And I couldn't stand that Josephine was dead, either.

There it was. *I can't stand you.*

"You can't stand me? I can't stand you, either, Meggie." He pushed that black feather off his shoulder.

I knew he was lying and so did he. His face flushed, his shoulders slumped, he leaned against the wall, then collapsed. He started crying, in and out, gasping, broken, horrible sobs, rocking back and forth.

I dropped my purse and covered my face.

This was our cycle.

We fought, we both said knife-edged things, he fell apart like a bunch of puzzle pieces scattering across the floor, and I went to rescue him. I took back what I said, I comforted, I built him back up, soothed his ego.

He started ranting, getting hysterical, crying. "I miss Josephine. I miss her."

I ended up holding him. We went to bed and cried. We had awkward sex. At least, it was awkward for me. He liked it, shuddering and panting above me, his hot breath on my cheek, his sweaty chest on mine, then he rolled off.

He went to sleep, clinging to me like a snake that had bit me and was sucking my life into its body.

I was up all night. I cried until I was weak. I could hardly breathe. The next morning I stepped on the scale: 115 pounds. I was a bony, angular, pale, wretched woman. Grief brought me to my knees on my bathroom floor.

I missed Josephine, sweet, tiny Josephine.

Somewhere, in the midst of that churning cauldron of emotions, I recognized that I was dying. I could not live with Aaron one day longer. I would get a divorce. I was a failure. I had chosen poorly, my fault, but I had one breath left for survival, and I packed up and left.

What did Aaron do?

He tried to kill himself again.

If Aaron had bipolar depression, and no other personality disorder, and had told me before the wedding, and if he was a kind and giving person otherwise, if he went to counseling and took his meds and actively tried to stay well, to be a husband, would I have stayed with him?

Yes.

It was his razor-sharp meanness and manipulations that made me walk out that door.

People think that if you want a man who is *reliable* you sound boring, as if you're looking for a dull, dim-witted man who wears button-up shirts, has a thicker sort of glasses, a short haircut, and looks like half the other men in America. They think of someone who is not exciting, spontaneous, or romantic and passionate in bed. You can count on him to be there and he is dull. Like wood.

I find reliability unbelievably sexy.

I find reliability to be a pillar in a relationship. No pillar, no relationship.

If you cannot rely on your partner to do what he says he's going to do, if you cannot rely on him to make basic, honest decisions, if you cannot rely on him to do what's best for you two, as a couple, as a family, you can't have trust. You can't trust that person to hold up his side of the bargain of your marriage. You can't trust him to put you at the top of his list, to treasure you and your feelings, to value how you will react to and interpret his actions.

If you can't trust, you can't truly love. You are giving your heart away to someone whom you can't rely on to treat it kindly, with respect and love.

I could not rely on Aaron to be a stable, sane person.
I could not rely on him as a man.
I could not rely on my own husband to want to live.
Which is one reason that Blake is hard for me to resist.
I could rely on Blake.
That is so dangerous to my heart.

20

My name is Lacey O'Rourke Rockaford. So, what do I want to tell you about myself? I'm the daughter of the unknown Sperm Donor Number One and our mother, Brianna O'Rourke, who is a famous sex therapist. I am the sister of you, Meggie, and Tory O'Rourke and the granddaughter of Regan O'Rourke and The Irishman.

I have three kids and I'm pregnant with a fourth. Four kids. That's what I'm going to have. I'm a working mother. That means I always feel like I'm operating with half a brain, and that half is an overheated, overwhelmed mess.

What do I want to tell you about my favorite bra? My favorite bra was the one with all the hippie flowers on it that you, Tory, and I all had. Remember? You designed it when you were twelve. We had the matching underwear, too. That was when we used to braid our hair in twenty different braids. We were hippie sisters together. We were young and you laughed a lot.

So, on to you, Meggie. I want you to braid your hair all hippie like again. I want you to wrap it in a bandanna. I want you to wear red. I want you to wear yellow. I want you to wear the purple tights you used to wear and the purple leather cowboy boots and the slinky blouses that said you were confident being a woman. I want to see all the flashy jewelry again, the bangles and hoops.

I want to see you in your leather jacket in a convertible, your feet sticking out the window. I want to see you running through *the ocean waves, maybe we can skinny dip like we've done so many times, and I want to see you skiing supersonic fast, like you used to. I want to hear you laugh. That's what I want most. I want to hear you laugh again.*

Sorry for crying. Baby, I know you had a terrible thing happen to you, and I missed you so much when you were gone, but you have to climb out of that pit you're in. It's so hard to see you in it. You're my best friend, Meggie. I want you back.

I know you're only wearing white and beige bras—I can see the straps—but you should wear lacy violet like you used to, or that scarlet bra with the stringy straps, or the cheetah bras you designed with white lace. . . . Now it's only white and beige. No more white and beige, Meggie. Please.

I turned the camera off. "That wasn't what I wanted."

"It's what I want though, Meggie." Lacey stood up, brushed her tears off, and hugged me, her stomach pressing into mine, my beloved niece or nephew taking a nap inside.

21

I put my hand on the maple tree inside my tree house that night. I love trees. I love maple trees in particular because their leaves tell their story. Green, yellow, gold, orange, brown, a blend and a mix, then all the leaves drop, the branches become bare, frozen, snowy, then back to buds and green again. The leaves were gone now, winter busting on in.

I grabbed a jacket and one of my mother's hats and sat in a purple Adirondack chair with a wriggling Pop Pop on my lap. The maple tree that grew through the floor of my deck swayed above me, the branches continuing their whispered conversations.

I thought of my mother, my grandma, and The Irishman, who always made me feel so loved.

I thought of Sperm Donor One and Sperm Donor Two.

They didn't even know they had daughters.

There was the blood tie between us, but there was nothing else.

There was a gap where fathers and daughters should have stood together.

I picked a leaf off the deck. It was yellow with brown spots.

Did our fathers love trees, too?

What would Blake be like as a father?

There were a multitude of mind-numbing problems coming up with the planning of our Fashion Story. I had, however, found a location, and it was a miracle location: the building across the street. I contacted the owner, Oscar, who was about eighty and had been friends with Grandma for decades. "Go ahead and use it, sweetheart. No charge. Can't hurt it, that's for sure. I'll do it for your grandma and for all the pretty lingerie she gave my wife over the years. We sure enjoyed that lingerie. Now I have only the memory of my angel, Mabel. You tell your grandma I said greetings and good wishes."

The building had been a shoe factory, but there was nothing in there now except a cement floor, open wood rafters, and concrete walls. It wasn't that big, which was good, as then it wouldn't feel cavernous. We would decorate and transform it with soft lighting, fabric, art, candles, and a focus on the runway and the people on it.

I had other worries, though.

I was worried we wouldn't get enough people there.

I was worried about publicity. Currently I had only one reporter coming from a small newspaper. I needed more, as I needed the TV stations for free advertising.

I was worried about the runway and stage that Eric would build. I was worried about lighting, and finding an arc of something cool and catchy over the door to greet people as they walked in, something that would make a statement about our company. I was worried about the decor inside—what to hang from the ceiling, what to put on the walls. I had to get our company symbol, the strawberry, in there somehow, too. I had organizational worries and gargantuan program worries.

As Tory, Lacey, and I worked more and more on The Fashion Story, our time was crunched. I was working, often, until midnight. Tory and Lacey were, too. Grandma had stepped back in, at my request, and was doing some of my work running the company. My most pressing worry was our model issues. In fact, our models didn't even know they would be modeling. There was a chance they would fully rebel against being models.

There were a hundred other details.

We were trying something highly risky.

We would either be laughed off the runway or be considered brilliant.

I knew it would work. I knew it.

It had to.

From Boy to Girl
By Hayden Rockaford

I know this is going to shock everybody, but I am going to start dressing like a girl from now on.

No, this is not a joke, and no, I'm not a freak.

In my head, I'm a girl. When I was little I played with dolls and Barbies all the time. I used to insist on wearing dresses. Some of you probably remember me wearing dresses and bows in my hair in kindergarten. I know some of you thought I was a girl and were surprised in first grade to find out I was a boy.

I have all the—for lack of a better word that can go in a high school newspaper—*plumbing* of a boy, but I feel like a girl. I always have.

Everything about me is girl-like. I like decorating, I like designing bras and lingerie for my family's company, and I like cooking and baking. I like makeup. I like being in school plays. I like dresses. I'm a girly girl, that's the only way I can explain it. I hate football. I hate getting all dirty. I like talking to girls about the things girls talk about.

I know I was supposed to be born a girl but something got messed up. I think that somehow, when my mom was pregnant with me, something went wrong. It's not like I'm wrong, or I'm a mistake, and it's not her fault, not my fault, but something didn't connect in there right.

For me, what happened is the right plumbing didn't grow in. The plumbing was switched. That's it. I'm in the wrong body.

So, I'm still Hayden, but I'm going to be who I really am, a girl, because I hate hiding. I hate having this secret. I hate trying to pretend I'm a boy, which a lot of you probably don't think I dressed like, or acted like, anyhow.

I'm glad I've told the truth. I don't think this is going to be easy, but lying about who you are isn't easy, either, and I don't want to do it anymore. It's too tiring and, to be even more honest, depressing.

I hope you will respect my decision, and for the people who are friends with me, I hope you'll still be friends with me. I know people are going to get all weird about the bathrooms, so I'm going to use the boys' bathroom still, but it's not like it's a huge deal.

I hope I don't get beat up much.

Hayden wore eyeliner, blush, and lipstick to school on Wednesday. He wore a jean skirt and a pink shirt and black knee-high boots. He did his nails. As he told me, "Might as well go in one hundred per cent girl. You know, like diving in a lake, instead of going in toe by toe. Plus, I'm doing this in the middle of the week, so there's not many days before the weekend if I cause a riot or a demonstration or something."

Lacey lay on the couch in her office all day, stressed to the gills about how the other kids would react. She kept patting the baby and saying, "HaydenwillbefineHaydenwillbefine."

I had a hard time concentrating. I pictured Hayden, sensitive Hayden, being annihilated by teasing and harassment.

Tory said, "I'm worried about Hayden. He's a Virgo, so he has strength and courage. Today's horoscope for him says, 'Be aware of new vacation plans and say yes when you want to say no. A lover is returning to your life.' "

"I don't think he has a returning lover. Hopefully there's a vacation. I don't know what to think about the yes and the no," I said.

"I feel sick," Tory whispered. She lay down on my floor.

"Me too." I lay down beside her.

"I was so worried about Hayden, I didn't even drive by my house last night to spy on Scotty."

"Now that's something." We held hands.

"We're going skydiving tomorrow."

"Let me think about that. No," I said to Grandma. "An absolute no. Tomorrow's Saturday, and I will be here, working as your slave."

Tory said, "I am not jumping out of a plane. I sit first class. I drink champagne. I'm served by the flight attendants. I watch movies. There is no reason to leave a plane, and I won't do it."

Lacey smirked and patted her stomach. "Grandma, you are so smart. That's a great idea. I'll enjoy watching you three."

We were in the conference room, and the four of us had had another conversation about The Fashion Story (scary, unpredictable result), our sales numbers (scary, unpredictable future result), our employees (not scary; I had fired the gossipy lady), and our catalog (boring in the past. We were making it quirkier, more colorful, and artistic for the next go-round. We would use photos and videos from The Fashion Story for both the catalogue and the website.).

"We are going skydiving. I've made the appointments already." Grandma was wearing a light green dress and matching green heels, her hair up and twisted perfectly. Baubles: emeralds. She reached back and "patted the fairies," squeezing the muscles in her back.

"I don't think I want to leap from a plane, Grandma," I said. "But gee, thanks so much for the invite."

"Rebel granddaughters, difficult granddaughters, I didn't ask if you *wanted* to jump. I told you that we're jumping. Obviously there was some confusion." She stood up, ignoring our other arguments about how falling through the air had no appeal, how it might mess up our hormones and estrogen and, in Tory's case, her "horoscopic spirituality." We told her we would be happy to push her out of a plane, but not us.

"Chickens," Lacey squawked.

"Stop arguing. Stop being frightened old women. I'm finding you irritating and spineless." Grandma took a second to stare at the photo of the strawberry field on the wall, then spun on her heel and tapped on out. *Tap, tap, tap.*

Tory clutched her stomach. "Does she want all my hair to fall out in fear? Does she want my vagina to freeze up forever? Can vaginas freeze up in fear? Doesn't matter. Scotty doesn't want it. I hate him. I called him the other night and left a message on his cell and told him he was like a tick. A bad, blood-sucking tick."

"I'm not going to do it," I said. "We'll push her out and watch her go. I am landing with that plane. No jumping for me."

"You have to do it," Lacey said, flapping her arms. "Just flap your arms on the way down. Like chickens."

The drive was long and frightening because I knew where we were headed. Lacey drove Grandma's flashy red Porsche. Grandma insisted that we all wear silk scarves, which she brought us, and those bug-eye glasses, which we put on.

"Girls, we're ready for speed," she told us. "Before I die I want to go fast, super fast. Step on it, Lacey."

Lacey does not "step on it." In fact, Lacey drives slowly, like a ninety-year-old man who can't see, so Grandma's request was actually quite funny.

"I'm sure we'll get there by next Tuesday," Grandma shouted over the noise of her Porsche.

"If we go any slower, I'm going to get out and walk," Tory said, clutching her scarf.

"Slow down, Lacey," I said, adjusting my bug glasses. "If it's dark by the time we get there, we won't have to jump."

Eventually we arrived at a skydiving place for otherwise sane people who believe, for one insane moment in their lives, that it's a splendid idea to hip-hop out of a perfectly good plane. I saw people dropping down through the sky in parachutes, a few screaming, probably with unbridled fear. I put my hands over my ears and tried to shut them out.

Lacey cackled, "Have fun, ladies!" She grabbed a lawn chair, a magazine on business and economics, and sat under a tree. She looked disgustingly happy.

After a jumping lesson, and the signing of a zillion-page legal contract that basically said if we were hurt; lost an arm, leg, intestine, brain, or liver; or died, we wouldn't sue, we were boarding a tiny plane and going up, up, up into the wild blue yonder. I was strapped in front of my skydiving instructor, Jim Jim, a tall man with a wide smile who used to be in the army. I said to myself, "Don't vomit."

Tory was a puce color. She was blowing air into her cupped hands and chanting, "Be a strong Pisces, be a strong Pisces."

Grandma was laughing, those iridescent green eyes shining. "Should have done this years ago! Years ago! Look how handsome my partner is!" She pointed at the huge African American man she was strapped to named Edward. "I'm coming back for him again." Edward laughed and high-fived our grandma.

The plane made a ton of noise, and I closed my eyes.

I knew I was going to die. I knew I was going to die. I knew I was going to die.

"You ready?" Jim Jim said. He had a lot of teeth. Someone had broken his nose.

"No, no. No, I'm not. I changed my mind."

"Too late! We're jumping."

"Like hell I am."

He laughed.

He had to pry my fingers off the seat. He had to push me forward through the perfectly good plane. When we got to the open doorway, I clung to the door.

My efforts did nothing. He was muscly and ex-army. He peeled my fingers away, one at a time.

Soon I was flying through the air at a zillion miles per hour.

We spun. We zoomed. We zipped. Someone trained a video

camera on me as we fell. Later I saw that my mouth was open wide enough to catch vultures. I screamed. My cheeks flapped.

Long, frightening, and then unbelievably thrilling minutes later, I was lying on the ground, panting, watching Tory come down.

She had not stopped screaming, swearing, and chanting, "Be a strong Pisces!" She sounded like a banshee being poked by a spear. Her instructor was laughing.

Next was Grandma. Impossibly, she and Edward landed gracefully. She did not even crash to the ground.

"I did it!" Grandma shouted, arms high in the air, Edward's arm around her waist. "I did it! Now I'm a skydiver!"

We went straight to a bar in Portland called Fish and Beer.

"Girls, we have to talk about that road trip," Grandma said as we hopped up onto stools. "We'll bring Lacey's baby daughter with us. We're going to have a ladies week. We four and your mother."

"Where are we going?" Lacey asked. "And why do you keep saying it's a girl?"

"It's a secret, and I know it's a girl because she's causing you so much trouble," Grandma said. "Your hormonal mood swings are swingier when you're pregnant with girls."

I didn't doubt Grandma. She had predicted that Lacey would have a girl, then a girl, then a boy. As Hayden believed himself to be a girl she was, technically, correct.

"I don't have mood swings," Lacey said, then dabbed at her eyes. "I just feel emotional all the time. I'm up, then I'm down. I'm happy, then I feel sad, then I'm laughing and I feel like crying. But it's not mood swings."

We didn't contradict her.

I ordered lemon cake, which I ate first in case I died immediately; then baked halibut, to which I added a smidgen of ranch dressing; and one slice of pickle, cut thin.

Delicious.

We clinked glasses.

Nothing like falling through the sky to make you feel alive.

*   *   *

I leaned off my deck and peeked through the fir and maple trees to see if Blake's lights were on, as I do every night. I tried to hide behind the maple tree that grows through the center while I did it.

I don't even attempt to go to sleep anymore until I know he's there.

I feel better when he's home.

I know, that's pathetic and wimpy.

I get it.

I missed him so much I hurt.

His words rang in my head: *If you change your mind, walk across the damn street.*

I would not call. But perhaps I could think of another excuse to see him. . . .

When a doctor called and told me that Aaron had overdosed, I drove to the hospital, tears streaming down my face, sobs shaking my shoulders. When I arrived, Aaron was on a stretcher, in hospital clothes, and of course on suicide watch.

"My Meggie, honey," he rasped out. "Baby, I am so sorry. I didn't mean anything, not any of it."

I sat by his bed and held his hand. I was broken. I was savaged. I didn't want to be married to him any longer, but I didn't want him to die, either. I had been deeply in love with this man at one time.

"Aaron." My voice sounded like it was being dragged over nails. "Why?

"I can't live without you, Meggie. I can't. I love you."

"If you love me, then why did you take so many pills?"

"You left me, you left us. You deserted me. Walked out. We're married, Meggie, through the good and the bad." His voice was a cross between a whine and an accusation. "You were a great mommy to my Josephine. I know it's not your fault. Please, baby, forgive me. . . ."

I was so shut down inside, I couldn't say I forgave him.

Before he was rolled away, he brought my head down close

and the pleading, pathetic voice disappeared. He whispered to me, "I love you. I won't live without you." What happened next made me shiver from the inside out. The tears suddenly dried up in his brown eyes and his facial expression changed. Back was the anger and control. "If you leave me, you're responsible for the consequences. Do you understand that, Meggie?"

I sunk against the wall, staring at the back of his head as they wheeled him out, the black curls I had loved hanging over the stretcher. Now they seemed like black, slinky eels with crazed minds of their own. The black feather seemed to float. I noticed it was broken at the tip.

I stayed up all night long.

I felt trapped, as if I were being smashed by a rock and the rock was growing heavier each second. The cacophony from his constant harangues, his badgering, his criticisms, had disintegrated my self-esteem, even my intelligence, to dust. I had been a strong, smart woman once. I was no longer that woman.

I was so stressed I could barely eat. My hair was falling out. My hands shook. I was constantly anxious. I was grieving. My doctor ran blood tests when I fainted twice and could find nothing wrong except that I was too thin, pale, and in his words "looked mentally shaken and ill."

I thought that if I had to live with Aaron again, I would rather die.

And yet, if I didn't live with him again, he would kill himself.

I could hardly think anymore.

That's what living with someone who is mean, vindictive, controlling, an emotional roller coaster, and mentally ill does to you.

Eventually you feel like you can't think anymore.

Because you can't.

When the doctors released Aaron three weeks later, he promised things would be different. "I'm better, Meggie. I crashed because of Josephine. I've been under a lot of stress, too, then that rabid dog came and took a bite out of me."

I moved back into the apartment and he did well for about

two weeks, then he became clingy and possessive of me, even more so than before, because he knew I was pulling away from him. He could feel it. I wanted out. Out, out, out. I was waiting until he was relatively stable.

"Don't leave me, My Meggie," he told me often. "We'll work it out. I'll change. You'll change. There are some things you need to change about yourself, even the doctors told me that. You have work to do on you, too."

The doctors hadn't told him that. I had talked with his doctors extensively. They were professional, sympathetic, and understanding. They did not mind when I cried. Both of them told me I needed counseling. One said, "You're young. You have to decide what you owe yourself, too." The other said, "If you leave him, no one would blame you. If you stay, you'll need enormous support. This will never be a normal marriage, even if Aaron finally, finally agrees to stay on his medication and participate in counseling, something he hasn't done before. He also is at high risk for using painkillers, pot, and alcohol again. Can you accept that?"

When Aaron said, "I won't live without you" and "We will always be together," I knew what he was really saying to me.

He decided to stop taking his medication because it took away his "spirit, brilliance, ability to channel esoteric ideas into film, and genius" and went to bed, all day, for weeks, smoking pot and drinking. He refused counseling.

I was at one of the lowest ends of my life

The lowest was yet to come.

I worked on another film project, which took me out of town, which is the reason I chose to do it, which put me in a position to meet Henry, which led to me cheating.

I don't approve of married people cheating with others.

I don't approve of myself.

The students at Lacey's kids' high school were generally fine about Hayden's decision to be a girl once the article came out. There was the expected shock and gossip, and he did initially get hit with a lot of teasing and incredibly unkind comments, but kids are kids. The winter formal was around the corner and they didn't have a date, they had flunked a math test, they had a fallout with their girlfriend, they had their own things going on, too.

It helped that the majority of kids have known Cassidy, Hayden, and Regan for years. Their parents have known Lacey and Matt. They've known our family.

Cassidy is a popular girl. That she is a boot-kicking, now-and-then-pot-smoking rebel with a hot boyfriend is rather appealing. She's also kind to everyone and brings her treats to school all the time and hands them out in the hallway. She was homecoming queen this year.

Regan is a football star, a sophomore on the varsity team who plays the whole game. Plus, when Regan gets upset he cries, so it makes the other kids relate to him. Regan has friends in many groups at school. He's on the chess team, though he has never yet won a match. He's the secretary of the Spanish club and tries to speak to the Hispanic kids in Spanish. Lacey told me they say, "It's okay, Regan. We speak English."

He plays the clarinet in band. He doesn't understand math so he needs extra help and has friends in that small group, too.

As Lacey said, "Adults are the ones who teach kids how to be racist, how to judge harshly, and how to tell everyone else how to live. I can tell some parents are bent out of shape about Hayden, and his article, and their minds are in a twist."

One parent got all jacked up, as if he was personally affronted by Hayden being transgender. Brady Tiles waddled his beer belly over to Lacey and me at one of Regan's football games and said, "Why you letting Hayden be all fuckin' weird like this, Lacey? He don't need to start dressing like a fuckin' girl. He don't need to advertise he's gay. What's wrong with your boy?"

And my dear sister, pregnant and glowing, let him have it, both guns shooting. "Look, Brady, you've got a brain the size of a prune. Wrinkled, small, tight. You don't understand a lot of things because you don't know how to think, and your life experiences are about as broad and wide as your short dick. I don't care what you think about my family. I'm proud of Hayden. Don't tell me that my son is fuckin' weird. You know what, Brady, you're fucking weird."

"Don't you talk to me like that, Lacey—"

"Why not?" I said, taking a step to within six inches of his pig face, my anger ripping through my body. "What Lacey said is true. There were no falsehoods. You are closed-minded and judgmental. You have no class, you're not smart, you're not educated, and you're ugly. You have a narrow, dumbed-down life and you don't like thinking outside of it because it makes you feel insecure. Easier to stay dumb. You are about as valuable to humanity as a drunken mouse."

His face turned red. "Why he gotta write about it in the newspaper?"

"Because he's being honest with himself and everyone else," Lacey said.

"Because he's not pretending," I said. I wanted to slug him. "I'm not pretending, either, when I say that Hayden can dress however he damn well likes, just as you can wear T-shirts that hardly cover your beer gut. Think people like looking at you and your beaver face? They don't."

He backed away.

"Asshole," my sister called after him.

Brady turned around, red-faced.

"Keep waddling, drunken mouse," I said.

He kept walking. There were a few more derogatory comments from people who have brains the size of prunes. Three mothers called the principal. I know the names of those mothers because a high school friend, Amy, is the head secretary and she whispered them to me.

The mothers said that letting Hayden dress like a girl would "corrupt the Christian values of our school and community . . . it's allowing and accepting perversity . . . it's encouraging the other kids to dress like the opposite sex . . . it's confusing to all of the teenagers here . . . his sexual problems don't need to be flaunted . . . he has a mental illness . . . it's immoral . . . it's wrong . . . he's gay. *He's gay!*"

The mothers were at the next football game in a clump. Lacey and I approached them, smiling. Lacey was wearing a darling green maternity dress that my mother had sent her. I was wearing boots, jeans, and a blue jacket. I wasn't in a good mood.

Lacey whispered to me, "Wide-hipped, wide-bottomed, helmet-haired, Parent Teacher Committee queens who like to control the school with their iron fists and their intimidation. School is their fiefdom. They have no power anywhere else, so here they wield it with their self-righteous minds."

Lacey and I kept smiling. We like to smile before we attack.

"Hello, ladies," she said. "This is my sister, Meggie."

I said, "Hello." They returned the greeting. We all had our shiny, fake smiles on.

"Why don't you three tell me the problem you're having with my son to my face instead of going behind my back?" Lacey said.

"Well...uh..." They stuttered and fluttered. Gossipy women do not like to be confronted by their victims.

I crossed my arms in front of my chest, standing right next to Lacey. I may feel old and tired, but remember: I take no more crap. I *especially* do not take crap when it is thrown at my nephew turned niece—sweet, kind, smart Hayden.

"We feel," one mother, who had a long face like a horse, said, "that Hayden should go to a special school."

"A special school?" Lacey said, raising an eyebrow, calm and cool for the moment. "Where would that be? How special is it?"

"We think," the shortest, fattest one said, "that Hayden's going to corrupt the children here. He's a boy, but he wants to dress like a girl. That's bringing in liberal, gay influences to our school."

"And," the other mother, whose hair looked like a dead possum on top of her head, said, "we believe in healthy families with healthy family values. We don't want homosexual indoctrination here. We don't want our kids to believe the homosexual lifestyle is acceptable."

"And being transgender isn't normal or healthy or right," Horse Face said. "Not normal."

"There is no homosexual indoctrination here, you brainless idiot," Lacey said. "My son isn't trying to make anyone gay. Do you understand that that's not remotely possible? Are you that dumb?"

They huffed. "We're not dumb," Dead Possum Hair said. "But it could happen. Other kids could become gay or transgender with this out in the open."

"Ah. So my son is giving off some sort of aura, some sort of magical spell, that will make kids gay?"

Dead Possum Hair looked embarrassed.

"He can pray his way to being a heterosexual!" the shortest, fattest one declared.

"Only the people who have four working brain cells in their heads believe that lunacy," I said. "There is no legitimate medical or psychiatric group that would agree with you. You can no more pray your way to being a heterosexual than you can pray your way into becoming a dancing cat."

"I'm praying for Hayden!" Horse Face said, but her voice was weak.

"Great. While you're at it, pray that Jesus takes the brick out of your head that is posing as your brain," Lacey said. "My son has more compassion, intelligence, and courage than all of you put together. But let's talk about family values. Hayden is not bringing any liberal, gay influences into the school. He is being himself. We are all allowed to be ourselves. This is America. Even you three condescending, unfashionable ferrets are allowed to be yourselves. You have a right to annoy people. You have a right to piss people off with your sanctimonious attitudes."

"That's not nice, Lacey, and he's dressing like a girl," Dead Possum Hair said, although cowed. "He says he's a girl."

"In his head he is a girl, and he can dress however he wants. Your son, I believe, was suspended this year for cheating on the SAT test by hiring another kid to take the test for him. Cheating isn't a family value, is it? And your son"—she turned to the other mother—"got a girl pregnant last year, then ditched her. More family values! Your daughter"—she turned to the third mother—"smokes pot all the time and was arrested last weekend. Is smoking pot a value in your family?"

"This is ungodly! What about the other kids?" the shortest, fattest one said, deeply embarrassed about her pot-smoking daughter and trying to change the subject super quick. "You're trying to normalize gay and transgender people!"

"What's normal?" I asked. I could not stand these women. "Is it normal for adults to attack children like you are? Is it normal for mothers to stand around and slander a young man who finally has the courage to be who he really is? What qualifies you to judge anyone? Your own perfect children?"

"What's not normal," Lacey said, "is for you three to get so obsessed about my son. You will stop gossiping about him, and you will stop saying degrading things about him."

"We're trying to protect our school, our vulnerable children, our community!"

I stepped closer, trying not to slug them. My, it was hard. "If you three don't stop I will sic an attorney on you. I went to high school with the meanest attorney in this town, and we're still friends. I will come after you for defamation of character and harassment of a minor child. Would you like to see me in court?"

The three women looked stricken. One put a hand to her sideways bosom.

At that moment the cheers pitched super loud. I turned around. Regan had made a touchdown. That dear boy ran over to the sidelines, hugged Lacey, hugged me, then ran back out on the field.

"Look here, Horse Face, Short Fat Woman, and Dead Possum Hair," I said, my rage blowing. "I'm not screwing around here. You want a lawsuit, I'll bring one, and I will smash you. You are harassing my nephew. You are defaming him by gossiping about him to others. You are encouraging the bullying of my nephew and you are creating a hostile environment for him here

at school, and I would love, love, love"—I threw my arms out—
"to sue your bloated asses off. So, here's the choice. Shut up, or
I will see you in court. Are we clear?"

I stepped even closer and whispered, "Are we clear?"

They nodded.

Lacey and I smiled at them with our shiny, fake smiles.

"Have a good afternoon," Lacey said.

"Yes, enjoy your afternoon," I said.

Regan and Cassidy had to defend Hayden, too. They had
taken Hayden's news quite well. As Cassidy said, "We love him
no matter what. Boy or girl. We've always loved dressing up together!" Regan said, "He's kind to animals, so I know his heart
is good, and that's all I need to know about my brother turned
sister."

Hayden had to defend himself, too.

Regan, Hayden, and Cassidy found out, they told me later,
who their true friends were. Most of their friends stuck by them,
but a few didn't. As Cassidy said, "Aunt Meggie, I had a few
friends who called Hayden that fag word, or they said he creeped
them out, and I told them that I didn't want to be friends with
them anymore, but there were a bunch of kids who said nice
things to me about the article and about Hayden being a girl,
and I never, ever expected them to be nice about it. Plus, Cody
has been awesome! I can hardly wait for the hors d'oeuvres
class, can you?"

Regan said, "I didn't want to punch Pat Kolsy for telling me
that Hayden should be locked up in an insane asylum, but what
he said made me insane, plus I was sad because two of my gup-
pies died, so I took it out on his face."

Hayden cried after school a number of times about the teasing, and he cried at work, but he also said, "Aunt Meggie, the
best basketball player on the team says hi to me now, and a
bunch of kids in biology started talking to me, too. Then someone throws a milk carton at me or a pencil at my face, or trips
me, and I get upset and it makes me feel like nothing, like no
one, like I want to hide or pretend I'm a boy again. . . . "

Several teachers had a problem with it, saying the whole thing was "distracting" to other students. They voiced these "distracting" concerns in a staff meeting. Thankfully, they were the minority and were shouted down by the other teachers, who had more compassion and an intellectually based understanding of the situation.

The whole thing was wrenchingly difficult for our whole family. My mother cried over the phone and sent Hayden a pink knitted scarf. My grandma, who had been shocked over Hayden's news but was working on accepting it, said, "I'd like to knock their brains together," and Tory said, "I'm going to make sure that Hayden is the most stylish girl at his school!"

After talking with Lacey one afternoon about Hayden, I remembered one of Grandma's quotes: "Hold on to the peaceful days with both hands. Revel in them. Stop to think about all your blessings and good fortune. Listen to the birds chirp. Sing. Dance. Why? Because the shit is going to hit the fan, and you want to enjoy your life as much as possible before that fan starts whirling."

"Mother made headlines again." Lacey walked into my office without knocking.

"What did she do?" It was ten in the morning. I'd had my beer. Now I was eating carrots and graham crackers for breakfast while working at ten million miles a minute to solve company problems.

Lacey turned my computer toward her, hit the keys, and voila, the magazine article.

I read the headline. "Brianna O'Rourke describes, in detail, how women should perform fellatio on their man."

One of her quotes: "There are many ways to do this, ladies, but let me tell you what I've learned. There is a way that is sure-fire. You must start at the base, think of a stick of ice cream and your tongue as the spoon . . . with your other hand . . ."

I groaned. "I don't want any ice cream today."

Lacey moaned. "I hope Cassidy doesn't see this. No ice cream for that little devil."

"Look." The reporter had dropped in a note at the end of the article: "Brianna O'Rourke is the daughter of Regan O'Rourke, the founder of Lace, Satin, and Baubles, a lingerie company."

Our mother's quote: "Wearing a seductive, padded bra during the day keeps you ramped up for your delectable nighttime activities. I personally feel attuned to the magenta-colored bras in the Lady Slipper Orchid line. I feel my girls standing up, ready for action, and that makes me feel slinky in the sheets."

"Splendid," I said. "Splendid."

"Sure is. I'm calling sales. I bet they're swamped . . ."

The Petrellis confirmed they were.

Lacey and I high-fived each other.

"I love her."

"Me too."

22

❧

"Hi, Blake."

"Hello, Meggie." He opened the door to his house and waved an arm for me to come in.

"I don't need to come in, but thanks." I was a fool. That's why I was at Blake's house at nine o'clock on a rainy and freezing cold night. I could have called the police station and left a message or gotten his e-mail and handled it that way. I didn't because I wanted to see him and I was using this floppy excuse to be here. "I'm sorry, I've been swamped at work and I just realized my insurance company never billed me for my deductible. I called and they said you still haven't made a claim for my hitting your truck."

"That's true. I didn't." He was in a gray suit. Sooo handsome.

"But your truck is fixed."

"Yes." He smiled at me, but it was a restrained smile, watchful.

"Are you going to make a claim?"

"No."

"Why not?"

"Because I don't think it's necessary."

"Okay, whatever." I was confused. "How much do I owe you?" I took my checkbook out of my brown and saggy purse. I was wearing a brown sweater, jeans that were too big for me, and boots. The boots were saggy brown, too. My hair was back in a ponytail. It swung over my shoulder when I grabbed my checkbook.

"You don't owe me anything, Meggie." Blake leaned against the door frame and crossed his arms. I tried not to be intimidated by those muscled shoulders.

"Yes, I do. The shop fixed your car. I want to pay you for it."

"I got it, Meggie, no problem."

"Yes. It is a problem." I felt my temper rise. You owe someone, you pay up. Received that absolute lesson from my grandma and my mother.

"It's a gift," he said. "We're friends. Well, at least I'm trying to be friends. I'm hoping to buy you that friendship bracelet soon."

"You don't owe me a gift."

"I want to give you one."

"I'm going to reject the gift." I triggered back to my disastrous marriage. Aaron would give me a gift and I'd hear about it for weeks, as in, "I do a lot for you, Meggie. Remember the necklace, hello?" Or "I'm taking the necklace back. You obviously don't appreciate it, because you're not wearing it today" or "I can't please you, can I? Bought you a sapphire bracelet, still not good enough."

The gifts were often bought after he started a fight, I shut down, and he wanted me to reengage. They were always more than we could afford. He put it on our credit card and figured I would pay it off somehow. How much of a gift is that when you can't afford it and the buyer knows it? His gifts caused me enormous stress.

"How much was your car repair, Blake?"

"I can't remember."

"Look, Blake, I don't want this over my head. I don't want to know that I owe you money."

"You don't. It wasn't that expensive anyhow. They pounded out the bumper, paint, done."

"It's more than that, but fine." I wrote a check and handed it to him. He refused to take it. "I'm sorry I hit your truck."

"I'm glad you did. We began our relationship over a smashed truck."

"Our relationship." I shook my head and tried not to break down right there. There was no relationship. "Okay, well, I know you've had a long day, so have a good night."

I was still holding the check out. He didn't take it, so I stalked into his house, set the check on his kitchen counter, and turned to stalk out. I was feeling threatened by the whole situation, flashing back hard to Aaron and fighting grief over not being able to be with Blake.

"Whoa, whoa . . . Meggie, don't leave. Let's have dinner."

"Dinner? No. Thank you."

"I'm grilling hamburgers. I have salad. I was going to make corn, I think. Do I have corn?" He looked off into space. "Yes, I have corn. So, stay."

"No. That would be too much. I don't think I can resist you if I stay for dinner." I took a deep breath as I studied him. He looked tired and drawn.

"I would probably have the same problem with you."

I missed him. I thought about him all the time. I wanted to hug him.

So, remarkably, I dared myself. I walked right up to him and wrapped my arms around his neck and leaned into him. His arms went around my back, pressing me up close. I tilted my head back and his lips came straight down on mine, as if we'd done this a million times.

I felt my body roar to life, that liquid heat rushing through that is so delicious it kills every rational and working brain cell in your head. I could hardly breathe as that kiss went on and on. It was that I-Can't-Breathe-Because-This-Sex-Is-Going-To-Be-So-Awesome kind of breathlessness. I arched into him as his hands started to wander. I reached around to the front of his shirt—never breaking contact with that mouth—unbuttoned all the buttons, and ran my hands up his warm chest.

It was at that moment, my curves to his steel, that he abruptly stopped, dropped his arms, and muttered a frustrated "shit."

He ran a hand through his thick hair and turned away from me, head bent.

I struggled to breathe, my hand to my zooming, soon-to-be-crushed heart.

"I still can't do this, Meggie," he said, his voice ragged. His chest was heaving, his face flushed. Oh, how I wanted to have that heaving chest against mine.

"Blake." I wanted to cry. "Do all relationships have to be headed somewhere? We get along. We like each other. We're attracted to each other, we talk . . ."

"And you are looking for the door out, Meggie." He turned back toward me. His chest was awesome, his shirt hanging open. "You've told me that. You're looking to leave, call it quits."

He was right. I wanted that door w-i-i-i-de open so I could scamper through it at any time.

"You've admitted that you're a mess and don't want a relationship. That's not for me. Especially not with you."

"What does that mean?"

"You're different than any other woman I've ever met. You're independent and deep and sincere. You're smart and you know yourself. You're beautiful. You eat odd foods and beer in the morning. You take in animals. You jump out of planes and bungee jump because your grandma asks, and you work all the time to save her company. You stick by your sisters. I like you so much, but I'm not going to get into something with you that will end up with one of us, probably me, getting raked over the coals."

"I would not rake you over any coals."

"My answer is the same, Meggie. I need you to change yours."

"My answer is the same, too, and I don't like being pressured."

"I'm not trying to pressure you—"

"Yes, you are. Pressure may work at work, but it doesn't work with me, Blake. You're not the chief here."

"That's been made very clear to me."

"I'm not going to be shoved into something or manipulated into the kind of relationship that *you* want. I am operating on what is best for me, and a serious relationship is not what I want."

"I want you to try us." His voice was hard, persuasive. "One step at a time."

"No."

He was not happy. He did not have a temper, per se, but he could get mad. It was a controlled mad. It was not an Aaron, out-of-control type of mad. I was relieved to recognize that.

"Try to trust me. Try to see me differently than you saw your ex-husband. Try to reach. Try to see what we could have."

I shook my head and, darn it, those tears flowed out. "No, I cannot. I absolutely cannot do that, Blake. No."

"Why?" His voice was strained. "Why not? If you tell me what happened, we can work on it. Talk it out. Fix it, together."

"Ha. There is no talking it out, Blake. I'm not the slightest bit interested in that."

"So you're going to go your whole life without a relationship? You're going to let your past run your future?"

"Looks like it." I turned. "Cash the check, Blake. I don't want to owe you anything."

"No."

"Yes."

"No." His jaw was tight. He knew I couldn't make him.

I slammed the door when I left. It was churlish and immature, I knew it. As soon as I did, I regretted it. I was, however, relieved that I didn't start blubbering, that disgraceful hiccupping and gasping sort of blubbering, until I was running across the street between our houses in the rain.

I am so damaged. My mind is so screwed up. I'm exhausted from what I went through with Aaron. I'm still reacting *to* him. I'm still sickened, still scared, still depressed, and still traumatized by red and black.

I thought of my closet and what I had hidden in it. I'd rather have a monster in there.

I hate myself.
Hate, hate, hate.

He snuck up on me.

I was in a field, with my camera, and his arms wrapped around me tight. He smiled, sweet and inviting, then kissed me like he did before. He slipped off my pink blouse and pulled down my pants until we were both naked, purple and yellow tulips swaying all around us, the sun glowing like hot butterscotch.

He pulled me close, my fingers threaded with his, and we danced in the field, twirling, spinning. He told me I was his golden girl, would always be his golden girl. When I leaned against his chest, he dropped me into a dark hole in the ground. As I was falling through the black, whirling spiral, he laughed maniacally, then tossed in the feather from his hair, which turned into a rat's tail and wound tight around my neck.

He screamed at me, "I'm following you through the closet," his voice echoing as I continued to free-fall, faster and faster. I knew there were snakes at the bottom of the pit and they would bite me until I died, their venom speeding through my body.

And they did.

"I want to thank all of you for the suggestions, the thoughts, and the advice you've given me about what we should do to get Lace, Satin, and Baubles profitable again." I smiled at the employees on the production floor. Some of their ideas had been brilliant, some not so brilliant. One employee said we should all do an hour of yoga together a day. Another suggested, "Drunken Fridays," for new inspiration.

Those were in the latter category. "I appreciate the time and effort you put into it, and we're going to implement many of your ideas immediately."

Grandma was lying on a pink fainting couch. She never lays on the pink fainting couches. Lacey and Tory were standing beside me.

"Now for the fun part. I asked you to create lingerie that was all about you. Who you are. Who you've been, where you're going, who and what you love, the bad and the sad. I said you could be artistic, edgy, weird, pretty, graphic, funny, thought-provoking, anything that reflected you as a person. So let's see 'em. Who's gonna be the daredevil and go first?"

It was quiet for a few seconds.

"I will." Melissa Tonto held up her hand. She graduated from college three years ago. She'd worked here for two. Tory scared the heck out of her. Grandma told me she had an incredible portfolio of ideas when she was hired, so I wanted to see what she'd thought of.

Melissa has tattoos up and down both arms. One is of a toothy, feisty dragon. She named the dragon "Mother." They do not have a happy relationship.

She had designed several bras with a tattoo motif. Across both cups of one bra she had designed a dragon, a carbon copy of her mother dragon. Another bra had a tattoo of barbed wire. A third bra had a tattoo design of Tinker Bell sulking.

"I like it," I said. "It's new. It's young and hip."

Melissa smiled, then sagged in relief. "Tattoos say something about your life, your memories and experiences. That's why I have them. Bras should, too."

"Awesome," Lacey said. "Makes me want to get a tattoo on my chest."

Grandma said, "I think I'll get a tattoo on my butt that says, 'Sagging but smart.' "

Everyone laughed, then clapped for Melissa.

Candy, our blunt accountant with all the grim news, went next. She has rebelled against her sweet name. She is tall and wears flat and sensible shoes, long skirts, and horn-rimmed glasses. She designed an orange bustier with red flames, orange underwear with red flames, and thigh-high fishnet stockings with red flames along the top. "I have anger issues," Candy said.

"I have anger issues, too, Candy," Tory said, then muttered so only I could hear, "My anger issue is named Scotty."

"I'd wear that," Lacey said.

People clapped again. Whooee!

Our custodian/handyman/gardener/electrician Eric Luduvic had us turn off all the lights to showcase his creation. When it was pitch-dark on the production floor, we saw multicolored flashing Christmas tree lights all over the bra Eric was wearing over his naked, hairy chest.

"You see?" he shouted after the applause died down. "This is for the people out there who like surprises in the bedroom. I like surprises, myself. Hello, Santa! Give me a sec to get this bra off and the next one on. Wow. That's tight. Okay. This is the Valentine's bra. See? All pink and red flashing lights, and the cups are shaped into hearts. Halloween? Give me another sec to change... ouch, poked myself.... Behold the witch bra! See how I've arranged the lights into a witch's face?" We oohed and aahed as the green, orange, and black lights twinkled at us. That witch was evil looking.

Lance Turner made pajamas out of army material, except he'd added pink fringe on the V-neck, the wrists, and the hems. He modeled them for us. "I loved my army buddies, loved the army, don't like the dent in my head. That's why I made these pajamas. Giving these to my wife tonight," he announced. "She'll love 'em. Did I already say I loved the army?"

Edna Petrelli stood up next. "I've designed a nipple bra to feed my fantasies." Her voice crackled from age.

A nipple bra?

"When you're wearing a see-through blouse, you might not want to wear a full bra, but you don't want your nipples to show through, now, do you, dears. So this is the Nipple Bra. They're like pasties. They'll come with a bottle of flavored glue. There's strawberry, to honor Mrs. O'Rourke, and vanilla and grape, which will add sensory delight. You squeeze the glue around the nipple and aureole, then place the Nipple Bra over it. Let me show you. I made one for myself. You see?" She held her white see-through shirt tight against her chest, turning this way and that so we could all gaze upon her unbound bosom. "I didn't want to wear a bra today, but you can't see my nipples, now, can you?"

Her sisters shouted, "No! Good job, Edna!"

The employees cheered, "No nipples, no nipples!"

I stood in front of the preening Edna, whose breasts entirely showed through her shirt, but not the nipples. "You're right, I can't! Super idea!"

She smiled, angelically, arms out. "I present to you, the Nipple Bra!"

My, oh my.

Edith Petrelli patted her white hair, then stood up. "My first bra is called the Whip Brassiere. As you can see, it's made out of black leather. I like leather. I call it licorice leather because it reminds me of licorice. It'll be more expensive, honey. We have to allot for the cost of the leather and the fringe."

"The fringe?" I asked.

"Yes, dear." She fastened the Whip Brassiere over her buttoned-up pink blouse. She has a sturdy bosom. "You see how there's one inch of fringe below the cups? That'll cost more." Edith knew her cost analysis. "We have a silver zipper on the left cup"— she ran a finger across it—"and a crossbones on the right." She pointed to the right cup.

"To make this more attractive, we'll sell it with black leather panties with a handcuff imprint. I'll put them on now. This is why I wore pants today. I have to wriggle into them. Pardon me, dears, almost up, one more yank, another yank. Okay. How do you like the leather panties?" Everyone liked them! "And for my finale, I present to you"—she paused for dramatic effect—"the Licorice Whip!" Edith withdrew a whip from her bag and cracked it in the air three times.

"Impressive!" I said, as the employees hooted.

Edith cracked the whip again. "Do you see why I call this bra the Whip Brassiere?"

Oh, we did. We did.

Estelle Petrelli had made a pair of pink fuzzy pajamas with feet and a long zipper. They were cute, except for the gun. The gun pointed down at the crotch. Above the gun were the words "If there ain't no ring on my finger, ya ain't gettin' in here."

"This is for the younger women, of course," Estelle said. "We women of a mature age don't wish to marry again. We know that having a husband is like hauling around bad luggage that farts."

"You're right on that," Edna said.

"Like my fart, Scotty," Tory hissed, misty eyed. "He's bad luggage. Doesn't even appreciate me."

Estelle climbed into the fuzzy pajamas, then pulled two cap guns out of her bag and shot them into the air. We jumped, then laughed.

Lance didn't laugh.

"We can't sell guns," I whispered to Lacey.

"Not even cap guns," she agreed. We all clapped for Estelle.

We saw a white lace nightgown with tiny words printed all over it made by Larissa, who was, apparently, still dating Tato. When I looked closer I read the tiny words "Derrick Riordan is an asshole."

"Derrick is my ex-husband, a controlling and narcissistic ape, and it would be a huge favor if you could plaster his name all over this nightgown."

"You do know that we'll be sued?" I asked.

Larissa looked uncomfortable. "Maybe I'll shoot him before we get to that point. Can I borrow your gun, Estelle?"

The most poignant idea, though, came from Hayden.

He was shaking when he stood up. He was wearing a blue skirt, brown knee-high boots, and a red sweater. His hair was brushed straight down. His makeup was tastefully applied. Honestly, he was a pretty girl.

"I started thinking about life when I designed these bras. You know—" He took a trembling breath. "All the stuff we all go through. All the bad stuff, and then how we have to keep going and not let it get us down and sad and keep us sad. So I...I write poetry." He blushed. "I like to write in my poetry journals and, uh"—he pushed his hair off his forehead—"I wrote on the bras."

I saw Lacey smile. "He wrote on the bras," she whispered. "Brilliant!"

"Let's see 'em, Hayden. Hold 'em up," I said.

Hayden turned around and grabbed the first bra out of his backpack. "I used our plain pink or white bras, to give you the idea . . ."

One bra after another came out.

"I did the matching panties, too."

Even Tory stood up straighter.

"And I wrote on them. This one says, 'Sexy is Being Proud of Yourself.' And 'Being Fabulous Is My Birthright.' " He held up a pink bra. "This one says 'Power' because women need to feel that, too. The underwear says 'Power is Powerful,' see?"

We saw.

There were more inspirational sayings, for example, "I Like Being Me" and "My Future Is Full of Light." The bras and panties were particularly lacy.

When Hayden was done, there was silence on the floor.

I thought about the designs. It could be a whole new line. A line for women who wanted that strength, that self-encouragement, right under their satiny dresses and business suits.

Lance started clapping first. He stood up. "Awesome. I'd buy those for my wife. In pink or red or blue. Not white."

The Petrelli sisters followed. "We're fabulous!" Estelle shouted. "We could wear that."

Abigail Chen said, "I'll take the Power bra. Power my boobs up! I need it!"

Soon they were all standing and clapping, even Tory.

"Yeah, we can tear that one up," she said.

"Tearing it up" to her means that it will be a success. "Women'll go for it. They're great gift items, too. Mother to daughter, friend to friend. Inspirational, encouraging, all that crap. We should have star sign bras, too. Taurus. Capricorn. Scorpio." She cupped her hands around her mouth. "Not bad, Hayden."

Lacey flopped onto the pink fainting couch next to Grandma. I blinked rapidly. After all that Hayden has gone through, the emotional turmoil I can't even comprehend, because he was, in his words, "born in the wrong body," after the teasing at school, the strength it took to write the article about being a girl, now here he was getting a standing ovation.

Grandma stood up, too, and walked over to me, those heels tapping. "He's a fantastic girl."

Hayden burst into tears and waved his hands in front of his face.

He really is a she.

To celebrate, I ordered in pizza and strawberry pie.

"So, Meggie," Lance shouted across the room, getting everyone's attention, "what are you going to do with our designs?"

I smiled into the sudden silence and said, "You're going to wear them to the fashion show."

"What?" . . . "You're not serious!" . . . "Is this a joke?"

I waited for that moment of shocked chaos to subside.

Grandma's face was peaceful. She was on board with me.

When I had told Tory what I wanted to do, she said, "At least you're an insane person with good teeth."

Lacey said, "I'll be enormously pregnant. I am not wearing a thong on a runway."

"We could have a normal fashion show with models parading up and down the runway," I told them. "But that's been done before a zillion times. We've done it, too."

I did not say that there was no way in this galaxy that we could afford the models, stylists, and all the other fashion paraphernalia that went along with a high-end fashion show.

"I wanted something new. Something that showed the heart of this company—you all—people who care and have lives and challenges and joys. I wanted us to come across as a woman's power type of business. A business that creates a product that helps women be better. Stronger. More daring. Gorgeous. A business with employees who have soul, for customers who have soul.

"At the fashion show—which we'll call The Fashion Story because we're going to be telling stories, the story of Grandma, the story of us—you'll model what you made. For some of you, the employees who have been here the longest, you're going to stand onstage a little longer while the video that I took of you runs."

I heard the whispering, the nervous chuckles, the uncertainty. "What do you think?"

There was another stricken silence, a few pale faces. I knew what they were thinking. They were too old, too fat, too many stretch marks, etc., to be on a runway.

Finally, Lance stood and said, "Hey, if I can dodge gunfire in Afghanistan, I can wear these pajamas with the pink fluffy stuff down a runway."

And Abigail said, "I escaped out of Vietnam. If I can do that, I can do this, no problem. I'm in."

Tato, who designed a nightgown with a motorcycle on it and a Hell's Angel biker dude, said, "I'll do it, Meggie, but I'm drivin' my Harley down the runway."

"The Nipple Bra and I will be there!" Edna Petrelli shouted. She pulled her shirt tight against her nipples to re-model her creation. Edith cracked her whip. Estelle shot off her cap guns again.

Tory tapped her heels. Lacey grinned, hand to stomach.

"Yes or no?" I asked our employees.

It came back, pretty loud. "Yes!" They clapped for themselves. "Yes!"

I glanced at Grandma. She had a victorious look on her face.

I helped her stand on a chair next to me. She tried to speak, couldn't, overcome by emotion. She tried to speak again, couldn't. She put an elegant hand to her mouth. We waited.

"I am damn proud of you all." She blinked rapidly, those green eyes shining. "Thank you. Thank you all. You've made my life beautiful."

The clapping had my grandma's tears flowing.

She waved her hands, then yelled, "Stop it! Stop this cheap, unnecessary sentimentality immediately. It's making me nauseated."

They clapped louder.

She rolled her eyes. "This is irritating! You're irritating me!"

23

Woman magazine
Interview of Brianna O'Rourke,
by Gabrielle Madeiro

You have helped women all over the nation, even the world, get in touch with their sexuality. You write books, a popular column, and you're a coveted guest on talk shows. Do you ever get tired of talking about sex?

Yes. Sometimes I never want to say "sex" or "sex toys" again in my life. But it's not a twenty-four/seven occupation. I have a life. I have a mother, three daughters, and grandchildren. They are my priority. I also bake and I love to embroider. I sew and knit.

You knit?

Yes, I love knitting. Don't you?

Uh, no. Do people come up to you in public and ask you about sex?

Yes, all the time. Happens in airports, restaurants, and cafés. For example, last night I was at a dinner and a man asked me what a clitoris was. He asked what he was supposed to do with it. I used two slices of lime, an olive, and half a cherry to explain it to him. I told him exactly what to do. He was so grateful he hugged me. I wrote instructions on the napkin. He took the napkin and ate the olive. I ate the cherry.

I also use bananas a lot—less intimidating. Apples come in handy, too, as do lemon quarters and chocolate fudge sickles.

Why do you think so many women reportedly lose interest in sex?

Many reasons. Oftentimes women are simply not attracted to their partners anymore. Their partners are boring in bed or self-centered, inane, ridiculous, abusive, or gross. It's not what men want to hear. They want to blame their wives and girlfriends, but it's the truth. Sometimes women are flat-out exhausted. There can be medical issues, like thyroid problems or depression. There can be hormone issues, too. Who likes blowing up in bed with night sweats? Working too hard will kill a sex drive, too, as can motherhood and its demands. There may be abuse in a woman's background that needs to be addressed immediately.

Sometimes women don't feel sexy anymore, too fat or frumpy, or they're self-conscious performing. Let me tell you, ladies, dim the lights, light candles, put on a negligee, and your partner will be so glad he's getting some, there should be no complaints. If there is, dump him and get a new partner.

You absolutely must get to the bottom of why you're not interested in sex. There's a reason, find it, attack it, get back in bed.

But does our society put too much emphasis on sex? Isn't it okay to lose interest in sex?

If you want to feel like you have a dried-up raisin living in the heart of your vagina, yes, it's fine. If you want to lose that feeling of youth and vitality, sure, give it up. If you want to go to bed every night and simply sleep and give up your sexuality, go ahead. If you want to miss out on the rush of an orgasm, the intimacy with your lover, being in a close relationship, sure. Embrace the raisin.

You do sex counseling for couples. How does that work?

It words darn well, honey. First off, I listen to the husband and wife individually, then I work with them together. One of my clients, the wife, said that she doesn't like sex because her husband treats her vagina like he's holding a cattle prod and the cattle prod has to keep poking the vagina. It drove her bananas. He thought he was turning her on. I was blunt and told him to knock it off. I had another husband complain because his wife made this singsong sound when they were having sex, like a tortured whale. I told her to make the sounds. It was awful. I told her to knock it off.

Those are easy fixes. Sex counseling can be painful because much of how a relationship is working or is completely dysfunctional comes out in a couple's sex life. We get down to what's going wrong between the two of them. Could be an affair, an addiction, the couple is not in love, or one person is gay or frigid or bored to death or a jerk. Their sexual patterns could be at odds—one person wants it more than the other. It could be money issues, work issues, penis issues, vaginal dryness issues. We dig in and go.

Next I work with them about what they like during sex, and what they don't. We talk boldly and honestly. When they leave, they're usually pretty steamed up. My office overlooks the parking lot, and often they're having sex in their car.

What should couples always do to have a happy sex life?

Have sex.

That simple?

Yes. Have it regularly. Have a Sex Night each week. Sex can be serious, passionate, fun, even funny. Try new things, new positions, new places. Try not to get arrested. That's embarrassing.

Any other advice?

You must get to know your clitoris. You must figure out your orgasmic rhythm. You must figure out what you like and don't like. You must ask your partner to do what you want to have done. Also make a brutal assessment of yourself. Are you good in bed? Truly? Are you open to trying new things? Adventurous? Exciting? Are you doing what you can to keep your partner in love with you? Are you a supportive, friendly, loving spouse or partner?

Anything else?

As my mother always says, "Live your life with love. When you die, that's what you're leaving behind."

24

That night, I pulled on two jackets and the knitted hat and scarf my mother sent me. The hat and scarf were pink, but there were three flowers in purple, yellow, and orange on each one. I loved them.

I sat on my deck, in the yellow Adirondack chair, right under the maple tree, and ate an artichoke with mayonnaise and hot garlic butter. I thought about Sperm Donors One and Two. Their relationships with my mother were decades ago and, according to her, one night stands.

But when my mother become famous years ago, did they recognize her on TV? Did they remember that one night?

Did they ever wonder if she became pregnant?

I tipped my head back and studied the branches above my head. The maple trees are one reason I love this tree house. Maybe I would buy it.

But could I handle living across the street from Blake? What if he got married, had children?

No, I couldn't stay here.

Absolutely not.

I already missed the tree house.

And I had never stopped missing Blake.

He would be a great dad. I wondered if Sperm Donors One and Two were great dads.

* * *

"It's only one more cat, Aunt Meggie. One more!"

Regan stood at my front door. He was wearing his basketball jersey—football had ended—and he was wet because he'd walked to my house in the rain. He had a gold cat the size of a small hippo in his arms.

"It's a tiny cat. See?"

"But you already brought me Jeepers."

"I know, I know. How is Jeepers?"

"He's still hissing. Come on in."

Regan took off his high-tops, one foot after the other. He towered over me.

"Jeepers is a good cat, right? Patient and sincere? He needs a friend." He slung the new cat over his shoulder like a sack of potatoes, then bent to pet Pop Pop. Pop Pop licked his hand and smiled extra wide. He barked. Regan barked back. This did not seem to bother the hippo cat.

"Jeepers does not strike me as the kind of cat who wants friends."

"He does! I'm sure of it." Regan nodded eagerly. "This one is a stray." He held the cat up so we were eye to eye. "I've had posters up for two weeks. No one claimed her. She came to our back door and kept eating our cat food. Her name is Breadsticks because I like breadsticks."

Now that made sense.

Two weeks ago, Regan made three touchdowns. After the second touchdown, and after getting tackled by a couple of joyful teammates, he leaped up, ran about three feet, and caught a frog. He ran the frog back to Matt, Lacey, Grandma, and me in the bleachers.

"Mom, please! I think this frog has been separated from his family!" he whined, helmet still on.

"Put the frog back, Regan, and get back out on the field," Matt ordered.

"Dad, come on! Hermie needs a frog friend!"

"No, he doesn't," Lacey said. "He already has three frog friends."

Regan's helmeted head fell, and his shoulders slumped. His friends patted him on the back, sympathetic to the lost frog dilemma.

The coach yelled, "Rockaford, Peterson, Lumchuko, get your butts back over here right now!"

Regan started crying.

"Oh, for God's sakes!" Lacey said. "Give me the frog." She tossed her Coke through the slats of the bleachers, grabbed the frog, and dropped him into the empty cup. "Now go, you three! Go!"

A smile lit Regan's face, and he sprinted back out with his buddies.

"He's not my brightest child," she muttered.

"It's an obsession," Grandma drawled. She'd come to the game in a blue lacy dress and blue heels with a black toe. Baubles: sapphires. "He is peculiar. He must marry some sort of horsey woman or a woman who collects cats who will understand."

"He loves animals. What's wrong with that?" Lacey peered at the frog in her cup with disapproval. He hopped, and her head sprung back up.

"He has to be a veterinarian," I said. "Has to be."

"This is his second year in Introduction to Algebra and he barely has a C," Lacey said. "He's not going to be a veterinarian."

"I think he's going to live in a home in the middle of nowhere in Wyoming," Grandma said. "And he'll have fifty pets, and people in town will say he's that funny animal recluse man."

"Thanks, Grandma, you're ever so kind," Lacey said, totally exasperated. "Did I need to hear that?"

"Your son is an animal collector. Like some people collect . . . spoons or thimbles. Odd, but endearing. Bizarre, but somehow likable."

"You smoke cigars and sling back Irish whiskey," Lacey said. "You have the warmth of a corpse sometimes. You're so tough, I check to make sure you're not made out of leather. You have more shoes than I do body cells, and he's odd?"

Grandma shrugged her shoulders, fiddled with her sapphire necklace. "I adore him. I adore odd. He told me he wants me to create a line of animal underwear."

The frog jumped out of the cup. I had to chase it down across the bleachers.

Regan sat down at my kitchen table and slung the hippo-sized cat onto his lap. I brought him some apple pie that Cassidy made me and two glasses of milk. He inhaled it. I cut him another slice. The cat sat quietly on his lap while Pop Pop bobbed about like a drunken sailor.

"Thanks, Aunt Meggie. I was starving. I could barely stand. Feels like I haven't eaten all day."

"But you did eat, right?"

"Hardly at all. Four eggs and toast and bacon and cereal for breakfast, then two sandwiches and three apples for lunch, then two slices of pizza and three bananas for snack. I was starving."

He looked plaintively at me with those innocent green eyes. He had no idea how he sounded. "Glad you're fed. That cat is not a small cat."

"No, it's a tiny cat. Feel her. Doesn't weigh anything. Hardly a pound. Look at her, Aunt Meggie!" He held the cat up with one hand. The cat bent into an upside-down U shape. "Breadsticks won't bother you, and she wants a home and family."

"Why don't you keep her then?"

His face crumpled. "Because you know we already have a bunch of cats and Mom says I can't have any more or she'll be called that weird cat lady, or something like that. I don't think she's weird. Cats have good spirits. Please, Aunt Meggie? I'll come and visit her. Can I visit Jeepers right now? And I want to say hi to Mrs. Friendly and Ham the Hamster and play with Pop Pop now that I'm fed and watered."

I didn't laugh out loud when he said "fed and watered" because he said it in all seriousness. Poor guy. "Let's bring this cat upstairs to see Jeepers. Jeepers likes to be alone, so I'm not sure how they'll get along."

We introduced Breadsticks and Jeepers.

Immediately they rolled into a cat fight—hissing, clawing,

screeching, fur flying. We had to leap in and separate them, which was a struggle because twice they wriggled out of our hands. Pop Pop watched, tongue out, darting back and forth, panting and grinning, like he was some bookie who would win a bunch of money depending on the outcome of the fight.

"Aunt Meggie, this isn't a problem after all," Regan said after he tossed Breadsticks the hippo cat back over his shoulder. Jeepers scurried under my bed, still hissing. "I've solved this problem with my brain. You keep Jeepers upstairs and Bread-sticks downstairs. That's a good idea, right?"

"Ah, perfect. So give them a list of rules and read it to them? One stays up, one stays down?"

He looked confused, baffled. "Uh . . . well . . . if that'll work, that'd be good. I don't know if Breadsticks speaks English. . . . Okay, I gotta go. I have math homework and Dad has to help me, because I don't get this math at all. This is my second year in Introduction to Algebra—I told you that, right—and it's . . ." He looked pained. "It's so hard. It's like trying to read space alien language. I love you, Aunt Meggie." He gave me a big hug. "Good-bye Jeepers." He bent down to smile at the hissing, trembling Jeepers under the bed.

He climbed down the ladder with Breadsticks still slung over his shoulder, then bent to say good-bye to Mrs. Friendly and Ham the Hamster. "Good-bye, Pop Pop."

Pop Pop barked, and Regan barked back.

Regan set Breadsticks down and she darted under the couch, meowing. I hugged Regan before he left. "Uh, can I take a small piece of apple pie with me for a snack on the way home? I need more feeding."

Pop Pop barked after he left, then looked at me and barked again. He always wanted an answer. I barked back.

Ham the Hamster rode on her hamster wheel. Who knew where she was trying to go.

Mrs. Friendly stuck out his tongue. Breadsticks meowed pa-thetically.

My tree house had become a zoo.

* * *

At eleven o'clock that night, through hail and rain, I had to take Jeepers and Breadsticks to the pet hospital. Breadsticks had not obeyed the new rule about staying downstairs. Obviously she didn't understand English. The cats got in another fight and both needed stitches. Pop Pop, the dog bookie, seemed to enjoy the action.

On my way home at one in the morning, I saw Blake on his deck on the phone. I am sure he saw me, as he turned when I turned into my driveway.

He still had not cashed my check for his truck.

I felt like I owed him, which I truly didn't like. It made me nervous and off balance.

But I had to smile, a tiny smile.

It was so . . . chivalrous.

I hate to sound like a swooning maiden, but chivalry was so romantic. It wasn't the gift of the money, it was the gift of the generosity behind it.

My defenses were coming down, I could feel 'em.

Two months after Aaron came home from another stay at yet another clinic, I cheated on him.

I cheated on him for four weeks.

I was in Boise finishing up filming a documentary about a young man with cerebral palsy and how he had raised $100,000 for the Red Cross.

I met a man there named Henry Russell. Henry owned sixteen tire shops across the western states. I met him in a Mexican restaurant the first night. He was tall, broad, friendly. He was not married. I never would have done what I did if he were married, and yes, I do know how shallow and hypocritical that statement sounds.

I told Henry I was married the first night. By the third night I was crying over an ice-cream sundae that he insisted I eat. I told him about Aaron's mental illness, how I hadn't known before I was married that he suffered from it, how he'd been committed multiple times, how he'd tried to kill himself. I did not speak about Josephine, that pain too private and raw.

I met him every night for dinner, sometimes a movie, a dessert. He always insisted on paying, which I found so romantic. He was gentle and kind and completely, utterly, mentally stable. He was fun and made me laugh.

He was, essentially, great.

I had never been treated with such respect, such warmth, by any man I'd dated. I was beyond desperate for love, attention, affection, and a friend, and the time with Henry saved me.

Being with Henry made me realize that I wasn't the problem; it was Aaron. Intellectually I knew it, but emotionally I was too exhausted and battered to internalize it. Henry made me believe that I was worth something, that I was a person worth laughing and talking with, and holding hands with at the movies. He made me see that I did deserve more in a marriage.

I slept with him starting the fourth night. I went to bed with a mentally stable man who hugged me all night, then I woke up to a mentally stable man who brought me coffee in the morning. He had a modern log cabin for a home, and he made things easy. He wanted to continue seeing me. I told him I couldn't. He cried. So did I.

He wanted to get Aaron stable and healthy, and then he wanted me to leave him. I had blown through all of the money I'd saved for years on Aaron's care and supporting his films that had never made money. I was almost totally broke. Henry offered to pay for long-term treatment for Aaron. I could not accept that gift.

I had given Henry my phone number. As Aaron regularly went through my phone when I was home, and I couldn't have Henry calling me, I bought a new phone and pitched the other one.

That was the end of Henry.

I cried all the way home on the plane, a blubbery mess.

I cried because I felt terrible for hurting Henry. I had loved being with him. I cried because I had known from the start, had told Henry from the start, that I was going home to a husband, that I could not leave Aaron. Still, who was I to play with someone else's emotions, even if Henry was a grown man and knew

what the end result would be? I had hurt him. He hadn't deserved it, and it made me feel worse.

I wondered deeply about myself as a person. How could I
cheat on my husband and not feel guilty? What was wrong with
me? Did I have no moral code? No ethics, no conscience? Was I
a horrible person?

I finally came down to two questions that summed up how I
felt.

Should I feel guilty for cheating on my marital vows because
it cheapened what and who I had vowed to be in front of God
and family and friends?

Yes.

Should I feel guilty for cheating on Aaron?

No.

Aaron had broken our vows on our wedding day. He had
promised to love, honor, and cherish me, and he had not done
that. He had lied by omission about his mental health issues and
previous suicide attempts, which I had a right to know about
before we were married. His rages, his mind control, his cold-
ness, the continual silent treatment and the withholding of sex,
put me in a tornado of sickness with him. I was trapped in our
marriage because of his mental illness, his suicide attempts, and
his threats of doing it again.

Would I cheat again? Never. I won't marry again, for one. But
if I were in a relationship that was so bad I was tempted to
cheat, I would break it off. That I know for sure.

I don't condone cheating at all. I don't condone it for myself.
I believe I've mentioned that I hate myself.

But here is what I've learned, through my own experience: If
you are mean, nasty, oppressive, or abusive with your spouse,
he or she may well cheat. If you stop speaking to your spouse or
withhold sex, repeatedly, for weeks or months on end, they may
well cheat.

So who cheated who first?

Now whose fault is that?

*   *   *

I Skyped with Kalani after my morning beer, fog clouding my window.

"Bad day, bad day, Meeegie." She shook her head sorrowfully. "Bad."

"Why?"

"Lots of the sewing machines broke. Ya. Broke."

"Did you get someone in there to fix them?"

"Ya, I did." Her face darkened. "It a man."

"Was that a problem?" I asked, but I knew. Kalani is not a fan of men.

"Ya. He tell me how much money to fix machine and I say okay, you get butt in there and you fix."

"And the problem was?"

"When he done, he make double the price. He try to cheat Kalani." She put her balled fists up. "No one cheat Kalani. I get cheated by mean husband who bit ear off. See my ear? See my nose? Wrong place, nose. Scar on chin. Knife. I no cheated by men again."

"And what did you do?"

"I tell him, no I pay price I say I pay no more. And he yell and say, then I take machines with me and I say, no, you no take machines. Here the money I say I pay. You go. Go now." Her voice pitched.

"And what did he do?" Now I was getting nervous.

"He turn and he take out pipe and he start hitting machine to break and I had to get shovel and hit head."

"You hit him with your shovel?"

"Yes. In head. He knock down on floor. Me and ladies, we drag him outside. He no bother me again."

I was alarmed. Very, very alarmed.

"Kalani, you need to make sure the doors are locked. Don't leave the building without other women around you. No one is to leave alone. Do you understand?"

"Ya. I understand. But I Kalani and I strong." She brushed the tears off her cheeks. "Why men mean?"

"I don't know. It's a mystery. We need black magic for them."

"Black magic. Ya."

We stared at each other for a while until she pulled herself together.

"I'm sorry this happened to you." I was saddened, and scared, for Kalani.

"Ya, I know you sorry. We seeesters, so you sorry. I sorry, too." She put her tiny fists in the air. "But machine fix and no man cheat Kalani!"

The fog hadn't moved.

That night the cheating repairman snuck back to the factory and tried to burn it down. A worker from another factory nearby saw him skirting through the shadows pouring lighter fluid around the entire building. He was stopped and the police arrested him. I would not want to be in one of their jails.

"Are you okay, Kalani?"

She nodded. "Ya. I okay. In my factory, almost all women. So, no problems. All good. I wish whole country, all the business, run by women. Better that way. More peaceful."

"I hear ya, Kalani."

"Ya, I hear you, Meeegie. Hey! I show you new neg-la-jays!" She grinned. "You see? Tiny. No cover butt at all. Only lace. Don't know why you Jersey American lady like, but we make anyhow! I love you, seeester."

"Love you, too, Kalani."

A few days later, as if cursed across the ocean, three sewing machines quit and for some inexplicable reason the heat wouldn't work. The rain poured down and a corner of the roof started to leak, so we had to get a roofer up there. When he was up there it started to hail, so he came in.

Our bank loan application that would have floated us another few months was denied again. The banker was apologetic. We'd worked with him for years. "I can't, Meggie. I've seen the numbers. Your debt load is too high. I can't. Good luck."

Pop Pop threw up, and the doggy day care called and told me

I had to come get him. He was now in my office, grinning. Two nights ago the cats got in another fight. Back to the vet I went at midnight for more stitches.

I was working twelve- to fourteen-hour days. I was constantly rushing, on my phone, on conference calls, meeting with the design staff, the production staff, sales, managers, etc.

The good news was that I was loving what I was seeing. Our lingerie was stunning and seductive. We would be incorporating many of the ideas, in one form or another, from our employees' lingerie. We were using "baubles" more, in honor of Grandma. Sequins. Beading. Some embroidery. Sparkly stuff. We were implementing Hayden's tassels. We were also in a heightened state of work frenzy because of The Fashion Story, and people's part in that, and I was loving how that was pulling together.

My mind was in a tizzy, almost burning up the wires in my own head. When my brain wasn't crackling from stress, I daydreamed about Blake. Blake laughing, Blake hugging me, Blake naked.

By coincidence, when I took a rare run to a coffee shop so I could clear my head after a particularly rambunctious meeting, I saw him.

He was with other officers, across the street, yellow crime tape stretched across a storefront. I later learned that a jealous husband had shot his estranged wife. He had broken the restraining order she had against him.

Blake was taller than the other officers, commanding, clearly in charge.

At one point, as if he could sense me, he looked across the street and we locked gazes. I wanted to walk over and hug him.

Within seconds, one of his officers came up to talk to him and he reentered the shop. I went back to Lace, Satin, and Baubles and lay flat on the floor with Pop Pop. I was reeling with both lonely loss and unbridled lust. Loss and lust together. Never good.

Pop Pop climbed on my lap while I sat on my leather couch late that night. It was getting colder and colder, the temperature dropping. I had seen a few snowflakes, and the streets had been slick in the mornings.

Breadsticks crawled up on my lap, too. Both Pop Pop and Breadsticks were now sleeping with me. Jeepers hid under the bed, hissing. Ham the Hamster kept running, and Mrs. Friendly stuck out his tongue. I hoped he was enjoying the white moonlight in my rafters, but he never said.

Pop Pop started snoring. Breadsticks meowed.

The joy of animals, I have learned, cannot be underrated.

I noticed that Pop Pop never tried to water the tree in my tree house. For that, I was thankful.

Blake's lights weren't on that night until eleven o'clock.

When I knew he was home, I went to bed with my zoo.

I was drowning in a river of blood. Aaron picked me up out of the river with his rat claws. Higher and higher he flew with me, cackling, then he dropped me back in the river, where the red swallowed me up. At the bottom of the red there was a closet. I didn't want to open the door. It opened up anyhow, and behind the sponges and detergent, I saw what I didn't want to see.

I curled into a ball, hands over head, and drowned.

25

You ready, Meggie? Here I go. I'm not so good in the speak-ing department, but I'll be doing my best.

My name is Delia Latrouelle. I work here in PR and market-ing. My sisters, Gloria, Sharon, Toni, and Beatrice, work here, too. We all love it. We call ourselves the Bra Sisters.

What's my favorite bra story? Oh, I know. Easy pie, easy pie.

It was the bra I was wearing when Danny came into our lives. You know I had . . . oh, bless me, I'm so sorry. I always cry when I say it. I had . . . darn it all, give me a minute to blow my ol' nose. . . . Charles always says I sound like a foghorn having a fit when I blow my nose when I'm crying. That man!

My favorite bra was the tangerine-colored one we created in the Lady Lacey line, with the lace band and crisscross straps. I was wearing it when we received the call and . . . by golly . . . shoot! Looks like I'm crying again. My emotions overrule my good sense all the time.

I was wearing the tangerine bra when the foster care people called and told us they had a child for us. None of the mothers were choosing Charles and me to be the adoptive parents of their babies because we were too old. But we wanted a child so much, and after four miscarriages . . . You know we lost the fourth one in the sixth month. Six months. Arms empty again. No baby. All those tiny gravestones. My husband, my sisters, and I, we all cried for those four angels. . . . The Lord giveth and the Lord taketh away.

Now, here I go again, scootin' through the story. So Davinia at the foster care agency gives us a ring. We had told her we were looking for a baby or toddler to adopt, and she said, "Delia, Charles, we have a fourteen-year-old boy. He needs a home for a while."

Charles says, "Bring him over. We'll take care of him until you find another placement."

And I say, like my momma always said, "Home is where the heart is and we've got two hearts to welcome him."

Danny comes over that night with the caseworker. He's fourteen but he's six feet tall and skinny. Way too skinny, and he seems scared to death. His shoulders slumped like someone was pushing him down, and he couldn't look on up. I gave him a big ol' hug.

You know, first he hesitated, but then he hugged me back, and Charles hugged him—Charles's six four, so that's a matchup.

Danny wiped his eyes, and we brought him in and he ate a whole pizza, and he was quiet and polite, but he kept petting the dogs and the dogs loved him, so we knew he had a good soul. We put him in a bedroom upstairs, and he lay on the floor as if he didn't think he was worth more, and we told him to get himself on up and sleep on the bed, and he finally did. The dogs slept on the bed, too.

I gave him a hug and a kiss good night, Charles gave him a hug, we said a prayer together, and that was it. It was like we were meant to be, the three of us. Three peas in a pod, it was. We loved Danny.

So Charles and I take a day off and we take Danny shopping. That poor boy has nothing. His clothes don't fit at all. You know how hard it is to be a teenager? Try it when your pants are six inches too short, your shirts don't go to your wrists, and your shoes hurt your feet like the dickens.

We get him jeans, cords, sweatshirts, shirts, shoes, and every time we buy him something he thanks us and wipes tears off with his sleeve again. We get him a backpack and we get his hair cut and sign him up for school and football. All is going good, as good as a sunrise on a warm July day.

On the third night he tells us he has a younger brother and a sister, and he's sick, he's so worried about them and he starts to cry. His shoulders are shaking, and I think, "We can't take on two more kids," and Charles says to me that night, "We can take on two more kids," and I think about it and I say, "You're right as rain on a cornfield, we can." That night I was wearing the tangerine bra again.

The placement for the brother and sister fell through because one of the foster dads committed a felony, and after school one day Charles and I drive to Danny's school and wait outside, and pretty soon he comes out and Ian and Ria, that's his brother and sister, bless them, they see Danny and they go running for him, and I have never seen three kids so happy. They're laughing and crying and hugging, like Jesus wrapped a rainbow around the three of them.

Charles puts his arm around me and he says, "Delia Bear"— that's what he calls me, Delia Bear—"God has blessed us with a family."

And I put my arm around him, and I can't believe it. And I say, "You're right. We've got ourselves a family."

He kisses me and then our kids come back . . . see, I'm crying again, Meggie, I called them "our kids," from that first day. Our kids. We all hug together, and Danny, he says, "Thank you," says it a hundred times.

I was wearing my tangerine bra then, too.

It's my best gifts bra, that's what I call it, because that's what I was wearing on the best days of my life. We lost four babies but now we have three children. Gracious me, life is full of tears and full of joys, isn't it, Meggie? Yes, it is.

Tears and joy, God bless my family, God bless your family, too, my friend.

26

~

Aaron was hospitalized again and again over the next few years.

I wanted to leave him, but I didn't know when I could. If I could.

It sounds so harsh. Your spouse is hospitalized because he won't treat his bipolar depression and all you can think about is leaving. But my mind had crumbled under his onslaught.

My health was in shambles. I could not gain weight, the scale still tipping at 115 pounds. I had more trouble swallowing. I had to force myself to eat three meals a day and not get up until the food was gone. I had hives. I had a persistent stomachache and, often, splitting headaches. I had insomnia. My hair had thinned.

I cleaned obsessively. We were broke, my savings run through. I made some money off my films, but this is not a business where a lot of money is made. What I made paid for our living expenses. I sold off what I could, including my nice car, so I could pay off Aaron's medical debts. I bought myself a clunker. Aaron refused to sign off on his titles so I couldn't sell his Corvette or his motorcycle.

Worst of all, I remember sitting on a rock at Trillium Lake on Mount Hood after Aaron had been arrested for speeding and arguing with a police officer. He was back in the clinic. I was thinking that I would rather jump in the lake and drown than live with him anymore. I threw that thought off, but a week later, as I drove over a bridge in Portland, I wondered how hard I would have to hit the rails to go over. My hands actually moved about a quarter of an inch on the steering wheel. If I moved it a few more inches I could die, be away from Aaron, and be with Josephine. Two minutes later I pulled over into a parking lot, my sobbing uncontrollable, my head on the wheel.

I wanted to leave Aaron, but I was afraid he would kill himself.

And yet . . . is that a solid enough excuse to stay in a marriage that is killing *you?*

Cassidy and I went to dessert class because she had not had anything to drink, including screwdrivers, her favorite, or pot, which she smoked to "loosen me up."

We learned how to make lemon mousse cake, orange petit tarts, Baked Alaska, strawberry cheesecake, and a chocolate mint mousse over the course of the weekly classes.

Cassidy loved it. The teacher loved Cassidy. She asked the right questions and was absolutely enamored with the whole process. She chatted with the other class participants. She was a bright light, friendly, a happy cook.

"That was the best night, Aunt Meggie," she gushed as we ate spaghetti and garlic bread together in a restaurant nearby after the first class. "I can't wait until the next class. I'm also going to qualify for hors d'oeuvres class with you."

"Excellent. No drinking, no pot?"

"Nope. I don't even think of pot as an herb anymore."

"You're so darn smart, I'm surprised your brain isn't on fire. How's Calculus?"

"It's rockin'! I have an A. I'm taking AP Calculus next year."

"Good for you."

"Yep." She grinned. "We have to get the recipe for this spaghetti sauce. It's delicious. I'll go ask the chef."

She skipped off. I stared out the window. It was starting to snow. I used to love the snow because then I could go to Mount Hood and fly down it on skis . . .

Cassidy had the recipe in hand when she returned.

"I'm going to make this for Mom on Saturday night. She loves my Italian food. I'll make her garlic bread, too, and I'll make her the lemon mousse cake that we made tonight. She's gonna love it."

Cassidy is a dear, thoughtful, brilliant, and extremely naughty hellion girl who loves her momma.

I woke up to icy, snowy roads.

I pulled on boots and walked to work. I do not drive in the ice or snow because I'm afraid I'll kill someone. On my way to work I saw several cars spin out and a number in the ditch.

I called Lacey and told her to stay home. I did not need that hugely pregnant sister of mine outside.

"I'm coming. You know we have work to do for The Fashion Story—"

"We'll e-mail, call, and Skype. It's not for almost three weeks. I'll send smoke signals. Stay home."

"I'll wait till the roads clear some and then I'll be in."

"Please, pregnant lady, you're making me nervous. Don't."

"I'll see you at work," she said.

"No, you won't. Stay home."

"Good-bye. I love you."

"Love you, too. Put your feet up."

We had our employees-turned-models practice strutting up and down the runway in the factory across the street later that afternoon. About half had made it into work. Eric Luduvic had built our long, wood runway and painted it pink. Some of the models understood the walk, and others didn't.

"Beatrice looks like she's trying to grip a squirrel between her knees," Tory stage whispered. "I like that Dee'andre designed hummingbird wings, but it looks like she's going to fly off into the great blue yonder. Carly's scared to death, isn't she? She'll need to be slightly inebriated. I'll give her a gin and tonic before The Fashion Story. . . ."

Lacey called out to the employees, "Less hip, Edith, remember to crack the whip. . . . More swing, Melissa, leave your arm bare so we can see that dragon tattoo of your mother. . . . Shoulders back, Candy. You're going to have to work that bustier. Work it, girlfriend!"

"This is going to be the weirdest Fashion Story ever," Tory muttered, opening those gold eyes wide. "No one does it like this."

I removed the pen I was clenching between my teeth. "We do, Tory. Lace, Satin, and Baubles does it differently."

"We're a lingerie company and we're not using real models? Have you lost your mind? Is it floating around in your butt?"

"No, I have my mind. And we're working on how to dress the employees."

Our employees were not all thin and tight. They were normal women who believed that eating was healthy. They were all wearing their own designs, but we'd added lacy skirts with slits, skin-colored sparkly tights, gauzy veils, creatively tied sashes, silky sarongs, etc., to hide those parts of the body that women like to hide while still showcasing the lingerie.

Hayden would be modeling his creations with tassels. He had already chosen to wear a silver sequined skirt and a bra with silver tassels. I was nervous for him, but he was insistent. "I'm gonna be brave. Plus, I'm proud of the tassels. You like them, too, right, Aunt Meggie?"

I sure did. They were getting several pages in our catalog.

I looked up at the rafters of the factory. The lights would be up shortly. It would allow us to change colors—pink, purple, yellow, orange, a blend, etc. I had found a production company that was loaning us pink, yes *pink,* velvet curtains that we would use at the end of the runway for our employees to line up behind before they hit the runway themselves.

I had spotlights rented, chairs rented, tables with white tablecloths rented. Eric would be our sound technician, and Tory was choosing the music. Lacey would be in charge of running the videos I'd taken of a bunch of our long-term employees as they headed out for their spin on the runway.

"We're going to go down in history as having the Most Bizarre Fashion Show for Shrink Head Numbskull Crazy Hormonal Women Ever," Tory said.

"Thank you, Tory," I drawled.

"It's a Fashion *Story*," Lacey said, hand on her stomach, her red curls in a ponytail. "It's the history of Lace, Satin, and Baubles, Grandma, our family, and our employees."

"It's the story of Grandma, who became the story of us," I said.

Tory rolled her eyes. "Us. Puss. Cuss. Cussy. Pussy." She exhaled loudly and tapped a red designer heel. "We're opening ourselves up like a surgeon doing a heart transplant. Only the surgeon is going to use a table saw on the ribs and he's going to operate with a knife and fork and he's going to forget to sew the guy up again."

"Lovely image," Lacey said.

Tory put two fingers to her temples. "Insane people don't know they're insane."

Lacey's coffee brown eyes flashed. "All you do is complain, Tory. All you do is discourage. This whole time. Negative, negative, negative. You didn't have a better idea. You still don't." She suddenly bent over and grabbed her stomach.

"What is it! Oh, no!" Tory bent down. "Are you okay, honey?"

Lacey nodded.

"Breathe in, baby," Tory said. "Breathe in."

Lacey put one hand on Tory's shoulder, one on mine. She closed her eyes.

"It's okay, I'm good." Lacey breathed in.

"We told you not to come in," Tory admonished. "I yelled at you. You never listen to me. Now you're here, making me all scared and nervous and sweaty. My horoscope told me to be brave today, but I'm not brave right now. You go home—"

"It's only Braxton Hicks," Lacey said. "Whew. I'm good."

She pulled us in for a hug. The three of us.

Tory said, "Let's not get all sentimental. It's embarrassing," and hugged us tighter.

I remembered my Braxton Hicks contractions.

I squeezed my eyes shut tight. I still missed Josephine, sweet Josephine. I always would. You take some losses with you forever and accept they're never leaving. Sweet Josephine was one of them.

I had my out.

Aaron had an affair.

It was with a young woman who was "working with him." I found out when I came home early and found a naked girl named Arianna straddling my husband's face. She was about twenty-five, with black hair, and a tattoo of a Japanese cherry tree up the left side of her torso.

I didn't blame her, I wasn't even angry. In fact, I was relieved. I felt lighter, as if I were being carried off by white feathered wings, maybe the wings of a stork or an angel.

I stood in the doorway of our bedroom and watched for a second. With all the groaning and thrusting, they didn't even hear me come in.

Aaron was lying on our bed, his head on a pillow, the tattooed girl over his mouth, holding onto the top of our headboard. Her head was back, and she was rocking back and forth, Aaron's hands on her butt.

For a second I studied the butt.

I used to have a nice butt like that. Full and plump. My butt was too thin now. I could hardly sit in a chair for long without my bones hurting. My pants were loose, but I didn't buy new clothes because I didn't care enough to do so. I didn't exercise anymore because between work and being home with Aaron, who had entered another raving, yet possessive stage, I didn't have time.

Beneath her my husband was doing his work. He's good at that when he wants to be. He was completely naked, that penis I didn't need to see again straight up.

I wasn't angry at her, I wasn't angry at him.

I felt like I could breathe normally for the first time in a long, long time.

I watched as he made groaning sounds and said, "Oh, baby. Baby, baby." It was like watching a film. A bad film. I do not watch porn, but this looked pretty close.

I laughed.

Laughed out loud.

The tattooed girl jumped and whipped her vagina off my husband's face. She made a screeching sound.

Aaron sat straight up, the tattooed girl's leg hitting him in the face.

"Oh, my God!" he yelled. *"Oh, my God!"*

I laughed again. My heart felt so free. This was perfect.

I could leave.

I could go.

I could start over. I wasn't trapped because I felt guilty leaving a husband who suffered from depression, an illness in his head, I was leaving because of an affair. It was an acceptable excuse—in my mind—to take off.

"Oh, baby," Aaron said to me, already crying and pushing his black curls off his face. He hurried toward me, his dick still straight out as the naked woman shrunk back against the corner of the bed.

"Oh, baby," I mocked him. "Oh, baby."

I turned and went to the closet and dragged out a huge suitcase.

"What—what are you doing?" Aaron said. "Oh, baby. What are you doing?"

"I'm leaving you." I turned and smiled at him, I couldn't help it. Maybe I was semihysterical. I had spent so much time fixing and helping and comforting him, and he had been a lousy, soul destroying husband. I had not deserved that. I deserved better.

As I surveyed my closet, then my dresser drawers while Aaron had a meltdown next to me, I realized that I didn't have a lot of clothes to pack. I used to have pretty clothes, so many pretty clothes, but in the last years of darkness I had stopped buying them. I decided I wanted none of my clothes. I wanted nothing that I'd had with him.

I packed frames of my family as he whimpered and argued.

He grabbed my elbow to stop me, and I wrenched it away. He tried to wrap me in his arms, and I kicked him. He tried to hold my arms down. I stomped on his foot, then picked up a beer bottle, smashed the bottle, and held the jagged edges straight out at him. "Back off, or I'll use it," I said. He was shocked. I shocked myself.

I calmly turned and packed the treasured things that were mine before I met him—my favorite books and journals and gifts from my family. He trailed me around, naked, his dick now down and shrunken. He had been so proud of his dick, talking about how big it was, how talented he was in bed.

"I'm sorry, oh, my God, I'm sorry, Meggie. You made me do this. You travel a lot, you don't call me enough, you don't pay me enough attention, I don't feel loved..." Then, when I laughed, a bit maniacally, he said, "You have to take some responsibility for this."

I laughed again and ignored him.

When he could tell he wasn't getting anywhere with that, he tried a new tact. I was used to that. One argument doesn't work, switch to another one. He'd twist what he was saying, twist what I was saying. He'd attack, lie, minimalize, blame me, backpedal, apologize profusely, compliment me, cajole, plead, confuse, attack again. Round and round.

"I won't do it again," he whined. "I promise. I'll be faithful to you. This is the worst mistake of my life. It only happened once. I love you!"

I carried two suitcases out to my junky car. Luckily, all my film equipment was still in my trunk. Aaron fought me all the way, a pair of jeans now on. I put a suitcase in my car, he took one out. I put it back in, wrenching it from his hands, and he took it out, crying, almost shrieking. Again and again he blocked me from leaving until I punched him in the face. *I was leaving. I would not let him stop me.*

For a moment he was shocked, then he hit me with a closed fist and I went flying into the car and onto the ground.

It hurt like heck, but it solidified what I'd done.

"Shit! I'm sorry, Meggie!" He tried to help me up, fumbling

when I pushed his hands away. "I can't believe I hit you. Don't leave me, don't leave me. Please, I am begging you!"

He stood in my way, my head reeling, and I shoved him. Two of my neighbors sprinted up. They had never liked Aaron, because he is a prick. They held him back while I packed my suitcases and got in the car.

"Thank you, Tyrone and Johnny." I blew them a kiss.

"Keep in touch!" they said, waving cheerily as Aaron swore and struggled between them.

I drove off. In the rearview window I saw Tyrone and Johnny let Aaron go. The tattoo girl hung out on our porch, smoking a cigarette in one of Aaron's T-shirts. I felt sorry for her. She reminded me of a young me.

Aaron swore up a storm. He tried to hit Tyrone, that black feather with the broken tip flying through the air. Tyrone decked him. Aaron's feet flipped into the air and he slammed into the ground. He scrambled up, swung, and Johnny decked him, his feet flying up again.

I had wanted out.

My face was throbbing, on fire, but I was out. I was gone. Good-bye, Aaron!

I had finished what I needed to do with my most recent film, so I drove home to Oregon after leaving Aaron. He called, texted, e-mailed me. I blocked my e-mail. Finally I took his call. "You can marry the girl who was on top of your face. I'm out."

"Why can't you forgive me? Why can't you work this out? Why can't you give me a second chance?"

"Because I don't want to, Aaron. I've given you a hundred second chances. I don't want to be married to you. I don't want to talk to you. I don't want you to contact me at all again, ever."

"What the—"

I hung up. I blocked his phone number.

He flew to Oregon. When he arrived, I left and went to the beach for three days and ran through the waves. My mother called the police and they hauled him off.

When he flew up again two weeks later, I went to the mountains and hiked through a meadow filled with wildflowers. My mother again had to call the police.

He resorted to writing letters. I burned them without opening them.

I hired Cherie Poitras, a tough-talking, gun-slinging divorce attorney, and she got the paperwork rolling. I knew that Aaron would be served soon.

I went to Alaska to start the process of making a film about Native Alaskans and their lives in a tiny, remote village, covered in snow, prowling with polar bears, and sunk in poverty.

My mother called me two weeks after I arrived. Aaron's doctor had called her, at Aaron's request.

Aaron had been arrested for getting in a bar fight, then passed out in the police car from too many painkillers. He was recommitted when he wouldn't stop raving about "My Meggie, My Meggie."

Aaron lay on top of me. I tried to push him off, but it was futile. His black curls covered my face, the cold chains around his neck settling between my breasts. He giggled, then took the black feather out of his hair and stroked my naked body, from forehead to toes, up and down again and again, slowly, seductively, waiting for me to be seduced.

When I would not kiss him back, when I would not French kiss him, his dark eyes grew furious. He forced my mouth open with one hand and with the other he rammed the chains down my throat. I gagged and struggled, but he held me tight until I had swallowed all of them. When the chains were gone, he took the black feather and held it over my head. It turned into a wriggling rat. He dropped the rat into my mouth.

I swallowed the rat, too.

He locked me in my closet where that thing was hidden.

I heard him giggling again.

Tory and I walked out of the factory, back to our building, with our arms around Lacey. The snowflakes were thicker, the streets glazed with layers of ice and snow, inches of it. It was the most snow I'd ever seen in Oregon.

"Be careful, Lacey," Tory snapped. "Don't walk so fast. You have to slow down. It's icy out here. Don't be your usual clumsy self."

"I'm not clumsy!"

"You are. Aw, crap." Tory lost her footing and generously let go of Lacey so as not to bring her down. Tory landed on her rear. Lacey and I bent to help her. She refused Lacey's help, saying, "Hello? Use your brain. You're pregnant, remember?" but took my hand. My cell phone rang when Tory was back on her feet.

"It's Leonard Tallchief," I told Lacey and Tory. "We're going to discuss the desserts for The Fashion Story. You two go on. I'll be right there. Hi, Leonard." I braced myself. The man is a maniac about making perfect desserts, and the fact that Grandma wanted him for The Fashion Story, well, he was in a jazzed-up tizzy.

Arm in arm Tory and Lacey walked gingerly across the street, fighting about who was more clumsy.

Portland shuts down when there's snow and ice on the streets, so there was hardly any traffic. We use it as an excuse to stay home and throw snowballs or catch up on stupid reality TV shows.

But not everyone was home. I saw the white truck turn the corner. He wasn't going fast.

The driver slowed when he saw Lacey and Tory.

"Meggie," Leonard said. "I'm going to bake three exquisite sample cakes. I want you and Tory and Lacey to come to the restaurant and taste them. Then you choose which type is most scrumptious. I'm going to have different icings, too. Again, which is tastiest? What combination? Finally, we have to look at the aesthetics. What should the cake look like? Six tiered? Shaped like a strawberry? A strawberry field, perhaps, to honor your grandma's hard work? A bra? A thong?"

The truck tried to stop, but his brakes didn't work on the ice and he started to skid.

Everything slowed, so slow, slow motion.

"Oh, my God!" I shouted.

"I know!" Leonard wailed back. "I'm so nervous. Anxious. I want this to be perfect, it's for your grandma, my angel—"

I dropped the phone and my bag. "Go!" I screamed, trying to run toward Lacey and Tory, my feet slipping. "Go Lacey, run! Run, Tory! Run!"

Time slowed, a second became a minute.

They turned around to stare at me, and I screamed. "The truck, the truck!" I pointed at the truck, now skidding down the street sideways. I slipped and fell, my feet going out from underneath me. I landed on my back.

I scrambled up on my knees, then tried to run again. I had to reach them, had to get Lacey and the baby—

I saw it coming. I saw the trajectory. I saw the inevitability of it all, one slow moment after another.

Tory and Lacey tried to run as the truck careened across the snow and ice, the back end now forward. Lacey fell first, then Tory, right in the truck's path. Tory tried to stand and yanked at Lacey as I tried to run toward both of them. I slipped again, landed on my stomach, gave up, and crawled.

The driver honked his horn. His tires spun. The ice crackled.

I saw each detail. I had time to see it, as time was no longer normal.

I screamed.

It was too late.

I was too late.

Too slow. I was too slow.

I screamed again, raw and primal, my scream bouncing off the buildings and the snowflakes, high-pitched, desperate.

In a tiny, beige hotel room with a creaky bed in Alaska, in the midst of a roaring blizzard that whitened the view outside my window, I hung up the phone. My mother had told me about Aaron, the painkillers, the bar, the My Meggie part, and being recommitted.

As I listened to the wind howl, I thought about how I'd loved

Aaron so much at one time. Loved his smile, his passion, his wit, his brilliance. There was no question that he was one of the most compelling people I'd ever met. He was almost like magic, the way he could attract people to him. And, stuck so often in his own emotional muck, he had a keen, finely honed insight into other people, other problems, other lives, that was attractive.

I lay down on the bed. In the weeks since I'd left Aaron, I'd gained ten pounds and felt so much better. I could swallow normally. My hair was no longer falling out. My cheeks actually had some pink in them, and it wasn't all because of the fierce Alaskan wind.

I thought of the films we'd made together.

I thought of how he'd gotten into my head, then spun me around, flinging me this way and that. I'd allowed him to get inside my brain, my voice, myself. I let myself be trapped.

I knew Aaron.

He would expect me to fly down like a winged angel to his rescue.

I studied the blizzard swirling outside my window. I listened to the howling wind.

I felt sick at the thought of being with Aaron again, weak. Anxious and panicked.

I couldn't do it. I could not survive any more time with him.

I picked up a camera with trembling hands and wrote down who I needed to talk to tomorrow, what questions I needed to ask. I felt happy thinking about my new documentary and what truths it would tell. I felt myself coming back to me. The other day in the village I'd even bought a bracelet with a J on it for Josephine and two pairs of earrings.

I decided not to fail myself. I stayed in Alaska.

I screamed, the sound piercing, from the depths of my soul.

I saw Tory shove Lacey in front of her as the truck spun three hundred and sixty degrees, out of control.

The truck hit Tory on her side, threw her up in the air, and deposited her on a parked car, as if she were no more than a black-haired doll. I could not see Lacey at all. I didn't know where she was. The truck continued sliding until it smashed into the next car. I crawled across the street on all fours, screaming Lacey's and Tory's names.

I saw people rushing toward us as fast as they could on ice, two falling. The door to Lace, Satin, and Baubles burst open as our employees stumbled out. I reached Lacey first. She was clutching her stomach, gasping for breath.

"Lacey." My voice cracked as I wrapped my arms around her. "Honey . . . Lacey."

"Get an ambulance," she whispered, her face pale, pasty. "Get an ambulance, now. Please. Hurry, Meggie, tell them to hurry."

I didn't need to call. People already had their cell phones out. Lance Turner wrapped his arms around Lacey, too. The Petrelli sisters slipped before reaching us on their knees. They all took off their sweaters and covered Lacey.

"Hang on, honey. Hang on. We're getting help." I put my shaking hand over Lacey's on her stomach, my forehead against hers, my arm around her back. "Breathe in, breathe out. Relax. Relax for the baby. . . ."

Our tears ran together.

"Where's Tory?" she gasped. "Where is she?"

"She's . . ."

Lacey's face paled further. "Is she all right?" She burst into tears. "Is she all right?"

"Hold on, Lacey, I'm sure she's fine." Oh, I didn't think that at all. I had a vision of Tory flying through the air. I was panicked, frantic. I was with Lacey, but I wanted to be with Tory, too. Both of them. Oh, no. Oh, no. Oh God, no.

Lacey recognized what I wasn't saying in the midst of this tragic chaos. "Go see her. Go, go!"

"No, I won't." My voice was raw. "I won't leave you."

"Meggie, help her. You must. Go!"

She doubled up, gripping her stomach, and let loose a ragged cry. I curled myself around her, devastated, Lance on the other side.

*   *   *

Aaron called me from the clinic. I didn't have that number, so I hadn't blocked it.

He was well versed in how to get to me, on how to get me rescuing him again, coddling, praising, encouraging.

I refused to engage in it.

"How are you, My Meggie?"

"I'm fine."

"You heard that I had to go back in the hospital?"

He knew I'd heard. It was his opening to get me to say what he wanted to hear.

"I heard."

"Too many painkillers to kill the pain that you caused me, My Meggie."

"You caused it yourself. I believe you had your face in another woman's vagina."

"One mistake."

"No, there have been hundreds of mistakes. I have to go, Aaron."

"What do you mean you have to go?" I heard the snap in his voice. "Are you with someone else?"

"That's none of your business."

He threw a fit. Swearing. Stomping like a bull with an arrow stuck in its hide.

"Aaron," I interrupted, knowing that being this adamant about how I felt was best when he was already in a secure setting with a gaggle of psychologists, psychiatrists, and counselors. "Don't call me again."

I hung up. Blocked the number.

He tried to call using different lines. I blocked them all.

I went back to work when the blizzard died down and the howling stopped.

I bought two new sweaters. One red, one green, and two scarves.

I looked at myself in the mirror that night. Not so skinny. A red sweater. A fuzzy orange and red scarf. Huge silver hoop earrings.

I smiled.

Free. I was free.

Josephine's mother was free.

The sirens screamed from two directions.

"Baby's coming," Lacey whispered, gritting her teeth in pain. "Contractions. It's too early, too early! It's coming!"

"Hang in there, Lacey, the doctors will help. They'll help—"

She shook her head, tears racing from her eyes into her red curls. "Meggie, go and check on Tory. It's worse for me," she panted, and I knew she was in labor. "Not knowing . . . she was hit, check on her, help Tory—"

Lance's arms were securely around Lacey. "I have her, Meggie," he said. "Trust me." The Petrellis were there, too. "We have her, dear." They reached for Lacey as I left. Abigail and Maritza met me, and we slid-tripped over to Tory.

Tory was unconscious on the back of the car, sprawled across a broken windshield. Larissa, Tato, Delia, Lele, and Tinsu were with her, hands holding her still.

She was bleeding profusely from her head. I put my hand carefully right over that bleeding wound. Her arm was set at a wrong angle. No one had dared move her.

"Tory." I laid my face right next to hers, cheek to cheek, her blood hot, streaming, horrible, seeping through my fingers. Too much blood, oh, too much. "I love you, Tory. Hang on, honey. Hang on."

She was so pale, absolutely still.

She looked dead.

I could feel her breath on my cheek, but dear God, she looked dead.

No, please, no, Tory. I need you, I love you.

Sister, I love you.

Six months later I flew from Anchorage to Los Angeles the day before Aaron and I were to meet to sign the divorce papers. Cherie Poitras, my attorney, would fly down to join me. It was all simple, as Aaron and I didn't have anything in terms of assets. We had blown through all of the money I'd brought into the marriage on his medical care, his films, and his credit card that he continually racked up. It was a formality to break up the marriage.

Aaron asked me to meet him at the apartment. He called me from a friend's phone so I didn't recognize the number and answered it. "I found some things of yours that your mother and grandma gave you."

"What?"

"Come and get them." He hung up.

I shouldn't have gone, but I wanted whatever it was. I felt like I was contaminating my mother and grandma to leave anything of theirs with him.

After being in Alaska, I felt like a new person. It was like I'd shed a nightmare, a rat's claws, and a dark, suffocating cape that wrapped tight around my body and squeezed.

Until...

The paramedics carefully put Lacey in one ambulance, Tory in the other. I went with Tory, holding her hand, pleading with her to wake up, while the paramedics went to work. I heard words like "head injury ... low blood pressure ... okay, she's crashing ... move people, move now," and I watched them do CPR.

I watched, shocked and panicked, as they pumped air into my still and silent sister. When we arrived at the hospital, she was whisked away by a group of doctors and nurses shouting orders and information, and I sank against the wall, ill with worry, stopped by a kind but forceful nurse from following Tory.

Seconds later, the ambulance with Lacey came screaming in. Neither had been able to drive fast in the ice. I rushed to it, and held Lacey's hand. She was on her side, clutching her stomach, crying. Lance had gone with her.

I held her hand as long as they let me, then let go.

"The baby's coming," she panted. "It's coming. It's too soon. Call Matt. Call Mom. Call Grandma."

I had said the same words about Josephine.

It's too soon.

Oh, baby, I thought, *please live. Please, baby, live.* We love you, baby. Stay with us.

I collapsed against the hallway yet again for a minute, then stood up, my legs weak. I made those tragic calls to Matt, my mother, and my grandma, who had been at home resting.

They are exactly the sort of calls that no husband, no mother, no grandma ever wants to get.

I called Scotty, too.

I knew that Scotty still loved Tory. She was impossible to live with and exhausting, but the love was still there. It was confirmed by his reaction. A stricken *"What?"* and a "Where are you?" and an "I'm coming." He hung up.

I saw him minutes later as he sprinted through the emergency room doors, like a cannonball that had been shot off. That tall, lanky, kind man was crying, and he didn't bother to hide it. Yes, the love was still there, going strong.

When I arrived at my cavelike ex-apartment in Los Angeles, I saw Tyrone and Johnny from next door and chatted with them for a minute.

"Aaron's still a prick," Tyrone told me pleasantly.

"He was livid when you left. Trashed the place," Johnny said, his voice singsongy. "Outta control."

"He accused me of having an affair with you," Tyrone said.

I rolled my eyes. "Nah. You're way too good-looking for me." I smiled. I was proud of myself. I'd made a flirty comment.

"No, sugar," he drawled, winking. "You're way too pretty for me."

"Why are you back?" Johnny said. "Want more of the torture chamber? You think we didn't know what you were going through over there?"

"We couldn't understand why you didn't take off sooner than you did," Tyrone said, shaking his head. "Bad, bad move, girl."

"We told you to get your butt outta there," Johnny said.

"I know." They had. "Aaron isn't well." It was a long story. It was a hard story. I didn't even want to think about it. "He said he had some things of my mother's and grandma's, so I came by to get them. We have an appointment tomorrow with the attorneys to sign the divorce papers."

"Atta girl, Meggie." They high-fived me.

We chatted more, and I caught up on their lives. I'd met their mothers so I inquired about them, plus Tyrone's brother and Johnny's sister. They asked about Alaska and my future plans.

A few minutes later I knocked on Aaron's apartment door. He didn't answer, so I opened the door, walked in, tried to shut down hard on all the tarlike, clingy memories, and called his name.

The bathroom door was open and I saw his black boot sticking out of the tub. I thought that was strange.

Aaron was wearing his black rat T shirt, black jeans, his chains around his neck, and a silver hoop in his left ear. His black feather floated in the water.

The water was red.

Someone started screaming from the depths of a tortured, ruined soul.

Tick . . . tock.

The waiting room at the hospital was soon jammed with people we knew.

"Waiting room" is incorrectly named. It should be named "The Room From Hell." Waiting to see how a loved one is after a bloody accident. Waiting to see how a loved one is after a heart attack, liver failure, surgery, stroke, or a new cancer diagnosis. That is hell.

Time does not move in The Room From Hell. It's as if someone has a tiny, shriveled finger on the hands of the clock and won't remove it. Your life stops. Every other worry in your life becomes irrelevant. You understand how insignificant those other problems are. You beg for problems that are small instead of that one, and while you're begging, you believe the fear inside you will rise up like a vengeful phantom and choke the life out of you.

Time stopped when Lacey and Tory were behind those closed doors. Time stopped in The Room From Hell.

Tick . . . tock.

My grandma, in a lavender-colored suit with four-inch matching heels and her amethyst baubles, sat controlled and quiet. Jaw tight.

My mother had been, fortunately, on a plane from San Francisco to Portland. She came straight from the airport. She had on her glasses, beige slacks, and a white blouse, buttoned almost to her throat. In her last talk show interview she had been wearing a cat suit. She was trying to encourage people to wear costumes in the bedroom.

They were holding hands. Both had been crying, but they had done it privately, walking out to the fountain in the atrium. "No need to blather in public," my grandma told me.

We were brought food, coffee, and water from friends, employees, neighbors. We couldn't eat or drink. People patted us, hugged us, murmured inane things that meant absolutely nothing. Matt was with Lacey.

I sat down next to my mother, and she reached over and hugged me. "I love you, Meggie."

"I love you, too."

We waited, clawed with insidious panic and grief.

The hands of the clock didn't move.

My hands shook.

My mother held a handkerchief to her face, gasping for breath.

My grandma's shoulders slumped.

The hands of the clock didn't move.

My mother bent over. I knew she was close to fainting.

My grandma put her shoulders back up, rubbing the pain out with both hands, "patting the fairies" from the whippings. Her mask slipped, and her eyes filled.

My whole body shook.

A doctor walked by and greeted my grandma. She uncrossed her legs, grabbed his elbow, and steered him away down a hall. I had no idea how he knew her. It hardly registered.

The hands of the clock didn't move.

I wanted to call Blake.

I wanted him here with me.

I wanted to hug him and sit in his lap.

I wanted to cry on his shoulder.

I wouldn't call, though.

No, he was not in my life, so I couldn't.

He was in my head, though, always in my head.

And my heart.

We waited, for news of the unconscious and bleeding Tory, for news of the laboring Lacey, for news of the curled-up baby who shouldn't be here yet, there in The Room From Hell.

Tick . . . tock.

27

Aaron had made a movie before he died. He was the star of it.

It was on his dresser. I found it after the police, paramedics, the coroner, and detectives came to the apartment; after they'd lifted his soaking, bloating body out of the tub; after the water and blood mixture had sunk into the floor and the carpet.

The envelope with the DVD said, "To My Meggie. Watch this." It was titled, "Why?"

I knew what it was.

It was another instrument meant to mangle me.

Aaron had gotten into the bathtub clothed in black.

He had turned on the water.

He had slit his wrists.

I'm sure he watched the blood draining out of his body with some sick, vengeful, perverse pleasure. . . . But now and then I wonder if at some point, in that blood-soaked tub, he tried to live, tried to fight, changed his mind, reached for the edge, but it was too late . . . too late.

The doctor told me he was loaded with enough scotch and painkillers alone to kill him.

He was loaded with misery and manipulation and desperation and illness, too.

My grief for Aaron, my shock, my horror, knocked me to my knees.

I am still trying to stand.

*   *   *

Tick ... tock.

"Okay," Lacey's doctor said to us in a private room off The Room From Hell. She pushed a strand of brown hair off her face. "Unfortunately, Lacey's in labor. We've done all we can, tried different medications, but we have not been able to slow it down."

My mother covered her mouth, both hands, her face crumbling.

My grandma swayed.

My whole body clenched tight in rejection of her words. "It's six weeks too early. Six weeks." As if that could reverse anything.

"We know." The doctor nodded. "We've given Lacey shots that will help the baby's lungs."

"What about Lacey?" I asked.

"Lacey's okay," the doctor said. "She has bruising up and down her right side. She broke her right wrist in several places, and she hit her head. We think she has a minor concussion, but we will not be running a scan, even later, because we don't think it's that severe."

Tory's doctor walked in. Her face was grim, too.

"Tory's still unconscious. Bad head injury from hitting the windshield. Left shoulder broken. Left collarbone broken. Both will heal, of course. Severe bruising on her legs and hips. We're waiting for her to wake up."

They talked more. I could hardly hear a thing.

When you hear incredibly bad medical news, it's hard to hear past those first few sentences.

We settled back into The Room From Hell, where a tiny, shriveled finger made time stand still. I clutched my mother's freezing cold hand. She closed her eyes. I could see her lips moving as she prayed, her flats crossed at the ankles.

Grandma sat rigid. She did not look well at all. She looked ill, weak. I sympathized. I had seen a mirror. I looked like I'd been run through a meat grinder.

"Lacey's baby girl will be fine," Grandma said, that brogue defiant. "She'll be fine. She has O'Rourke blood in her."

We waited more.

The hands on the clock were stuck.

I was sure of it.

Tick . . . tock.

The police sat me down to ask questions about Aaron, to make sure I hadn't killed him myself. My whole body was jerking. I couldn't control it. *Jerk, jerk, jerk.*

They asked me three times if I wanted an attorney, and I said no, no, and no. I told them that I'd flown in from Anchorage that day, and I showed them my airline ticket and rental car stub, which had the time I'd picked the car up stamped on it.

Johnny and Tyrone confirmed that we'd chatted outside, and they'd heard me a minute later screaming, as Tyrone said, "Like she'd seen Jack the Ripper with his knife pointed at her."

Johnny and Tyrone burst into the apartment and called an ambulance right before I passed out. I woke up to the paramedics peering down at my face, running an IV into a vein.

Jerk, jerk, jerk.

The police didn't suspect me. The proof was irrefutable. The medical examiner's office confirmed it. Aaron had been dead for at least three hours by the time I had arrived. I was in the air when he'd taken his last breath.

I refused medical care. When I could stand without jerking, I drove to tell Aaron's mother.

Rochelle opened the door to her decrepit home, the home that Aaron had come from—endured—and immediately began a tirade. "What are you doing here, Meggie? Come to gloat? You won, you won, you Barbie doll bitch. Aaron told me this morning on the phone that you're divorcing him. You're taking him for all he has tomorrow, aren't you? Taking every cent he earned, you Tinker Bell, tiny-titted psycho who rides his coattails. . . ."

She had a scotch in her hand. I could smell it seeping from her pores. I was surprised that Aaron had even called her. No, I took it back. Based on what he'd done, I wasn't surprised at all. It was his last contact with his mother. His good-bye call.

I asked if I could come inside.

"No, you cannot. I won't have the likes of you inside my home ever. Never!" Two of her neighbors came over to see what all the yelling was about. They looked at me pretty sympathetically.

"Rochelle," I started.

"What?" She swayed.

"Rochelle, I think we should go inside . . ."

"You and your rocks for brains will never darken my home like a bad smell. You've brought enough pain to my life, you stole my son from me—"

"Rochelle, I'm sorry to tell you, but Aaron is—"

"He's what? What lies about things that never happened do you want to spread about my son now?"

"Aaron's dead." I said it softly, as kindly, as I could. The neighbors took a few steps closer to Rochelle as she paled.

"That's a lie!" She poked a finger up into the air three times. "I talked to him this morning for the first time in a long, long, and long time. He was mad at me, *at me,* for things that didn't happen a long, long, and long time ago. Said I betrayed him. Said I didn't save him. Save him! None of it happened, and I didn't do anything about what he told me because I didn't know. He was lying as a child. His imagination made him say those things! Nothing was wrong. You made him like this. You turned him on me—"

When she took a breath, I told her what happened—that I'd flown in and found him in the bathtub, that the paramedics had come, that he was at the morgue. I spared her the details.

"Morgue! Morgue! That's a place for dead people! Aaron's not dead!" She threw her scotch glass. It shattered about a foot from my feet. "I didn't kill him! I didn't let him get hurt by Dirk. I didn't give him up to him a long, long and long time ago. I didn't look away. He's not dead!"

She toppled to the ground.

Another ambulance was called.

"You're here." I walked straight into Blake's arms in The Room From Hell and held him, my head on his chest.

"Yes. I heard about the accident, then heard the names of the people, and came up. I'm sorry, Meggie. I am so, so sorry."

"Thanks for coming," I said, then cried all over his uniform. "I'll make you spaghetti again soon."

"I look forward to it." He smiled and kissed my temple, then my forehead. "I'm glad to be here with you, Meggie."

Blake stayed. When I was in and out of Lacey's room, and later Tory's room, he worked on his computer, made calls. A few of his officers were in and out, coming in small groups or individuals.

All through the afternoon, into the night, he never left me.

"She hasn't woken up yet," Tory's doctor told us an hour later.

"What does that mean?" I said. "Why?"

My mother collapsed in a chair, panting, hands cupped to her mouth. I knew she was having an anxiety attack. I put my hand on her shoulder.

"It means that we would have thought she would be awake by now. We're checking a few things. . . ."

"What do you think is the problem?" I asked, leaning against Blake.

"Harsh knock on the head . . ." She went off into complicated medicalese. Basically: We don't know. We're alarmed.

"But she'll be okay?" my mother asked, wobbling as she stood. Blake grabbed her. "She'll be all right?"

The doctor's face was serious, drawn. "We are doing all we can, Mrs. O'Rourke. All we can."

All we can.

Everyone hates hearing those words out of a doctor's mouth. All we can. That means you're close to hopeless.

"You certainly are not doing all you can, young woman," my

grandma said, her voice pitching up and down. "You can't help her when you're jabbering away here."

I apologized to the doctor for my grandma, then Blake and I caught my mother as she fell straight back in a dead faint. Two nurses ran out to help, along with the doctor. My grandma wobbled, collapsed. Blake caught her, too.

Tory had not woken up yet. She had a head injury. She had broken bones and bruising because she'd pushed Lacey out of the way of an out-of-control truck. Lacey was giving birth six weeks early to a baby who wasn't ready. She had bruising and broken bones. She probably had a concussion, too.

I let the tears flow while holding my mother. My grandma, from her own place lying on the floor in Blake's arms, said to my mother in a snippy voice that overrode her panic, "Wake up, Brianna. For God's sakes, buck up. I can't take any more. Are you trying to give me a heart attack?"

Two hours later I hardly noticed when another doctor said to my grandma, who was now sitting in a chair next to my mother, "Oh, hello, Mrs. O'Rourke. What are you doing here today?"

Aaron's funeral was immediate.

We had a graveside service. Lacey and Matt flew down, as did Tory and Scotty, my grandma, and my mother. There were a number of friends there, too, from our work in the indie film business, neighbors, close friends of mine from the University of Oregon and high school, and friends from the company. Rochelle was there, of course. Tyrone and Johnny were there. The naked girl who was sitting on Aaron's face did not appear.

The minister spoke. He had never met Aaron, so he said inane things about him.

Aaron's best friend, Mikey, spoke. Mikey was stoned and said he hoped Aaron "rocked on" and "kept kickin' it," and "your films were awesome when you were working with Meggie."

A friend from rehab said, "Man, when you were high, you were high and you could do anything. This is not gnarly." I expected that friend to relapse any day.

When it was my turn I gave an overview of his life. I said he was born to a loving mother—not because it was truthful, but because I felt sorry for Rochelle who was half-drunk and stumbling about, muttering.

I talked about how we worked together as filmmakers. I talked about some of the adventures we'd had, the people we'd met, the states and countries we'd been in, how Aaron could get anyone to talk to him, and how he worked to make the highest quality film he could make. I said that we should not remember Aaron for how he died but for how he changed all of our lives.

I had to stop in the middle of a sentence because Rochelle screeched, "I can't take it anymore, you bony bitch!" She stalked right up to me, pear body swaying, arms waving. "Shut up! I was a good mother, and you did this to him, Meggie! You killed him!" Rochelle's face was squished up tight. "You're a disease, Meggie. You're a black widow drunken spider and you poisoned my son!" I could smell the alcohol emanating from her body.

I didn't hate her, I pitied her. She was an alcoholic, critical and cruel. Her son had wanted nothing to do with her, and I understood why, but she didn't deserve this. Her grief had snapped her mind.

I did, however, put my arm up to defend myself when she swung at me, standing near the grave. When she swung her other arm, I ducked, and that did it. She tottered on her heels— one brown, one black, too drunk to know—then fell straight in and halfway landed on Aaron's lowered coffin.

I will never forget that *thunk,* never forget the sound of her body hitting the coffin, then her head. Unbelievably, Rochelle was able to struggle up onto the top of the coffin, where she laid, splayed out, hugging it. She cried from the deepest, most wounded part of her soul.

"I won't forgive you for this, Meggie bitch," she hissed at me, minutes later, refusing to get off of the coffin. "You killed my son. This will haunt you for the rest of your stupid life."

My family crowded around me, arms around my waist. I bent my head and lost it. I cried for a week, straight through. Guilt seared my entire body, as if someone had stuck a hot poker down my throat and burned my insides. I felt a sense of despair so strong, I thought it would stop my heart. I fell into a deep, clutching depression, much like Rochelle had fallen on top of the coffin.

Rochelle's words echoed in my head again and again. *"I won't forgive you for this, Meggie bitch. You killed my son. This will haunt you for the rest of your stupid life."*

She was right. I am haunted. I expect the haunting to last my whole life.

I felt responsible for killing Rochelle's son.

I certainly hadn't done enough to save him.

Isn't that the same thing?

"The baby's in NICU and she's struggling," the doctor told us in The Room From Hell.

My mother whimpered, wrapping her arms around herself.

"My granddaughter will be fine," my grandma said, tilting her chin up. "She's an O'Rourke woman. She won't give up. We never give up. Never."

I vaguely realized that, yet again, my grandma had accurately predicted the sex of Lacey's baby.

"How is Lacey?" I whispered. I leaned on Blake. He put an arm around me but watched my mother, whose head was wobbling from stress.

"Lacey's recovering. We're going to set her wrist later," the doctor said. "It was an incredibly bad jolt, and if Tory hadn't pushed her out of the way, we would have been in a whole different position now. A baby could not have withstood that crash. It would have been catastrophic, probably fatal."

"Can we see Lacey?"

"Yes, soon. A nurse will come and get you when she's ready."

We waited again, that shriveled finger on the clock. *Tick ... tock ... tick ... tock ...*

A nurse came to get us. "Lacey wants to see all of you. She told me to tell you to come up."

Blake stayed in The Room from Hell. "I'll wait for you here, honey," he said, hugging me, then kissing my temple. "Watch your mother and grandma. They may faint again."

My grandma in her amethysts, my mother in her prim white blouse, I in my usual frumpy clothes, and Lacey in her hospital-issued gown had a long, tearful hug.

My mother said, her voice wavering, "I love you, Lacey. All will be well. I have already sewn the baby's blessings quilt." She pushed her glasses up her nose. "And booties."

I said, "Lacey—" and I could say no more, the vision of Tory and Lacey slipping on the ice, holding onto each other, their expressions of total panic as the truck bore down on them . . . Tory pushing Lacey out of the way . . . Tory hit by the truck and flying through the air onto the car . . . the crash she made as she hit the windshield, then the banging of the truck as it smashed another car . . . Lacey gripping her stomach as she lay on the ground in the snowy street, gasping . . . Tory not moving, splattered on the car like a broken doll, blood dripping . . . it was playing again and again in my head.

Grandma said, "You're a tough old bird and your baby is a tough old bird. You'll both be fine. Now get your own toughness on and quit crying, Lacey."

Her words didn't have as much power as usual, as Grandma was crying her eyes out as she bent over Lacey, brushing her red curls gently back with an unsteady hand.

Matt hugged all of us. He was a wreck, but strong. He was The Man.

We continued to wait, ill with worry, to hear about Tory. Scotty was with her. The doctor had said that Tory was lucky to have such a "devoted, loving husband. He's extremely upset. We may have to give him something to calm him down."

When Tory's doctor walked in an hour later, we all braced ourselves, holding hands tight.

"She's not doing well, but she's fighting," she said. More medicalese. Basically: They couldn't get Tory to respond.

Matt climbed into bed with Lacey and held her.

"Fight, Tory, fight," my mother pleaded.

"You're a ball breaker, Tory," Grandma insisted, her voice cracking. "Break some balls and wake up. Don't be a wimp. O'Rourke women are not wimps. You can't let a tiny thing like a battered head get you down. Damn." Her voice floated to a whisper, and she put her hands together in prayer. "Oh, my dear God, help us . . . Our Father, who art in heaven . . ."

After Aaron's funeral, I wandered.

I brought the "Why?" DVD with me to punish myself and to remind me what I had done to another person, though I could not bring myself to watch it. I brought my cameras, too. I went to Montana and ended up working on a ranch. I met the owners, Tom and Avery, a husband and wife in their seventies, when they bought me a meal at a diner. They told me later I looked like I was going to self-destruct.

In Montana I met a gal named Caroline who was leaving for Mexico in a month to build churches. I went with her for four months and built churches in poverty-stricken areas.

In Mexico I met a man named Olaf, from Russia, who was going back to Russia to work in an orphanage. I went with him and worked in a heartbreaking orphanage for five months. We were good friends, that's all.

In Russia I met a woman named Tanya who was going to the Ukraine to work in a place where girls forced into prostitution could be safe. I went with her and stayed another four painful months.

In a barn in Montana I saw Aaron. In a packed pickup truck in Mexico, I saw Aaron. I saw him in Russia in an outdoor café and in the Ukraine in the middle of a city square. It was like his soul was caught on the branch of a tree and the branch was following me.

I chased the visions down, like a scrambled-brain fool. When it wasn't Aaron, I felt my mind slip and slide one more inch.

I forced myself to concentrate on helping others, seeing beyond my searing pain to theirs.

Helping others saved me.

I filmed this, and I filmed that, my camera offering me solace.

One day, perhaps I'll make a film out of it.

I'll call it "Wandering to Save My Mind: If You Could See What I See."

When I went back downstairs to The Room From Hell, I walked straight into Blake's arms and held him.

He didn't say anything, and I didn't either. There was too much, there was not enough.

He felt like home.

To say that a family member or friend committing suicide is devastating is not even in the realm of truly describing the mind-shattering loss.

It is always heartbreaking to lose someone you love. But if it's an accident or disease, you can assume that the person did not want to die. They did not choose to leave you.

With suicide, the person has a choice. Their choice is to die. Their choice is to leave you and everyone around them.

People kill themselves for all sorts of reasons. Mental illness that's not treated, or mental illness that has been treated but the person still feel hopeless. Drug or alcohol use that has scrambled their brains. Depression that won't quit. Bipolar that creates such enormous swings it's like flying out of a slingshot in an arc and crashing into a wall. Grief for someone else. Failure. Fear. Financial collapse. Divorce. A bad breakup. A belief that everyone will be better off without them. A combination.

Sometimes it's one colossally bad time in life that makes someone kill himself. A day later, even an hour later, and he'd have made a different choice, but it's already done.

What is left for the survivors is a mental car wreck that doesn't heal. We're left hanging over a churning, dangerous pit, our emotions flowing out volcanically, only a finger hooked on the ledge to keep us from falling in. Suicidal thoughts can trip through our own heads from the grief, guilt, fury, shame, and the *what else should I have done* and *what signs did I miss* and *how could I have prevented this* and *was this my fault* types of questions.

I'm a bad mother/father/brother/sister/spouse/friend.
I am bad.

Living through a suicide is agony. It's a plague. It isolates you and leaves you almost paralyzed as to what to do next, how to do it, and who you are. It's hard to think. It's hard to plan. Your brain doesn't work anymore. You think you're going to lose it.

People treat you differently after a suicide than if a loved one died of a heart attack. It's like there's a question to their sympathy, a morbid curiosity, perhaps some blame.

Your entire life is changed. Your trajectory is changed. You are changed. Permanently.

Anger swirls around me as easily as wind swirls around everyone else. I am furious that Aaron killed himself, but I don't think I'll ever stop blaming myself. Was it my fault? No. Intellectually I know this.

Aaron was suicidal as a teen. He was mentally ill. He suffered from bipolar depression, anxiety, probably a personality disorder. He took painkillers and drank too much. His father was jailed when he was a small child, and his mother was a nasty alcoholic who had boyfriends in and out. I know all that logically.

But I left him. I left him knowing that he might kill himself. When he was committed the last time I refused to go home to take care of him because taking care of him had dissolved my own sanity.

How could he do what he did? Did he want to punish me that bad? Did I deserve it?

I don't think I will ever get over this.

Ever.

"You can go and see the baby," the doctor said to me the next day, smiling.

I was allowed into the Neonatal Intensive Care Unit for a few minutes to be with Lacey and her new daughter. The baby was unbelievably tiny. *Way too early,* I thought, not even bothering to wipe my tears away. Way too early.

But the baby was alive, and doing much, much better. She had stepped away, by the width of an angel's white feather, from death.

I thought of Josephine, tiny and fragile, too.

Lacey held my hand. "I'm thinking about Josephine, too."

I put my other hand to my throbbing heart. "And I am thinking of your baby. When she's kicking a soccer ball, or twirling a baton, or tackling Regan, we'll remember this."

We put our foreheads together. Exhausted, hurting from labor, still bleeding, broken bones, bruising up her side, a mild concussion, panicked about her baby and Tory, and Lacey was thinking of Josephine and me.

"You are my best friend, Lacey," I whispered.

"And you are mine."

"And Tory is going to be our best friend, too."

"Absolutely. She's in the club."

She should have been in the club a long time ago, we both knew that.

Our tears mixed as we worried ourselves sick over our tiny baby who seemed to take only the minutest of breaths, and our high-heel-stomping, wickedly opinionated, lingerie-busting club member, Tory.

Grandma, Mom, and I were in The Room From Hell—*tick* . . . *tock*—when Tory's doctor came to see us.

"Good news!" she said, smiling. I tried not to see the blood on her scrubs. "She's awake and telling us she wants a martini!"

"Let me explain this scenario to you, Meggie. I'll do it slowly so you'll understand," Tory said to me from her hospital bed three days later. "Pushing Lacey out of the way of that truck, taking the hit, is the best thing that ever happened to me. The best *freakin'* thing."

"What do you mean this is the best thing that's happened to you? You've had a bad head injury. You gushed blood like a fountain. You were conked out." I was baffled. "You broke your shoulder and collarbone. You have purple and blue-green bruises all over."

She sniffled. Sniffled again. "First off, it's the best thing because Lacey and the baby both survived. I pushed her out of the way, I took the hit and I was the one who was dumped on top of a car instead of her. I'm a certified heroine. You know, like a superhero, only I'm a superhero in high heels and couture. Saving them, that's the best, even though Lacey's butt is big again, and I'm going to tell her that. It took a lot of strength to push that big butt out of the way. I'm telling her that, too. But"—Tory wiped her cheeks, the bravado dimming a bit—"I feel like . . ." She blew her nose, totally honked it. "I feel like now I belong."

Now I belong.

"Oh, Tory." I wanted to cry. I felt so guilty, so *bad.* "You've always belonged. We've always been family—"

"But I wasn't born into the family. I walked in when I was five, more fluent in Spanish than English. You two had the biological sister bond. I was the adopted one, the outsider.

"And Mom doted on me more probably because she felt sorry for me and could see that I didn't fit in with you two, and that made you jealous." She waved a hand. "But now neither one of you will forget what I did. I feel like I showed you, both of you, how much I love you even though you are an uptight, workaholic perfectionist who isn't that much fun anymore and you dress like a hag, and Lacey is like a fire hydrant, always on high and spitting." She sniffled. Two tears snuck out, which she wiped away impatiently saying, "Oh, pish on these tears. What am I, a baby?"

"Tory, you were heroic. Absolutely heroic. If you had not pushed Lacey, you both would have been hit. She was on your right side, and she would have taken the first hit, and pregnant, oh . . ." I groaned even thinking about it, shaky hand to forehead.

"Don't you see, though? Hello, are you thinking?" She tapped my head. "This is now all about me. Me, me, me, Tory, me. I wanted to be close to Lacey and to you. And because of this, I'll be included now and I'll be included in Lacey's family, too. This—" She ran her hand from head to foot—the casts, the bandages on her head, where they'd shaved her hair away, the bruising. "It's all worth it. The baby's alive, Lacey's alive, and I can start over with her and with you."

I bent my head and cried, the ugly cry, with snot and a red, blotchy face. Tory's so difficult, harshly blunt, like a sledgehammer, rude like an avenging vampire, yet all this time she only wanted in with Lacey and me.

She brought up a bruised hand and stroked my hair. "Your hair is a wreck, Meggie. Honestly. It's a disgrace. It's dry, it's scraggly, the ends are awful. I can hardly touch this mop. I can't believe you cut it yourself. You are no hairstylist." She kept stroking my hair, so gently. "You and I are going shopping together and we're getting your hair and your nails done. What, you don't know what a lipstick is?"

"It's not flattering, is it?" I choked out.

"When I'm outta here, we're going to add color to your life again. You're going to funk out like you used to. Agreed? You're so beautiful underneath the frump."

There had been too much red and black. Too much pain. Too much being in the pain, and I couldn't tolerate myself any longer. "You're right, Tory. I think I need to get myself some color and funk."

She raised a scraped-up, bruised fist in the air and shook it. "Victory. You need a makeover like gorillas need bananas. Let's get drunk, too. They won't bring me a martini here and it's *pissing me off*. Can you bring me one?"

I stood up to leave when Scotty—lanky, tall, and smiling, holding at least three bouquets of flowers—ambled back in. Earlier, the nurses had had to give him a couple of pills to calm him down.

Tory flung the one arm out that wasn't broken, her face lighting up like nothing I'd ever seen before. "Baby!"

He hugged me, then enfolded Tory ever so gently in his arms.

I heard what Tory said loud and clear: "Take off your clothes quick, get your monster out of your pants, and get in bed with me. I need to get laid."

Before I shut the door she yelled, "Get me that martini, Meggie!"

I know why I decided it was time to watch the movie that Aaron made me. It was because of a particularly gruesome nightmare that left me in a pool of sweat at one o'clock in the morning, five nights after the accident.

This time Aaron was chasing me as I ran through the slums of India, the dilapidated homes of a small village in Alaska, and across the freeways of Los Angeles. When he caught me, inside our apartment, he had a DVD on top of his head in a Baggie. His hands turned into rat claws and he scraped my skin, making deep gouges. He shoved the DVD into one of the bloody gouges on my neck.

He bent down to kiss me, again and again, soft and sweet, then he stuck his tongue in my mouth. His tongue went down my throat, down my neck, into my body, suffocating me.

I fell down through a whirling spiral. On the sides of the spiral were pills, pot, alcohol, and someone yelling. When I was at the bottom of the spiral, Aaron came to me again, looking perfectly normal and sober, and handed me the DVD. "Watch it," he said, in a friendly tone. He kissed me again, as if he loved me, as he had kissed me during the times when he was sober and sane, and hugged me close. "Watch it, My Meggie." He flew back up the spiral on black, broken wings, black feathers falling all around.

At the end of the dream I was standing with my feet in the ocean, the waves breaking, a sunset full of luminescent color and puffy clouds ahead of me. Up in the clouds was a closet door. The door was open, the golden sun behind it.

I woke up, gasping, my sheets tangled around my naked body and my neck. I brushed sweaty hair off my face.

I left all the lights off as I shakily climbed down the ladder; opened the closet; pushed aside the sponges, detergent, and Baggies; and pulled out the DVD. With my whole body sweating as if I'd sprung a hundred tiny leaks, I inserted the disc into the DVD player and sat back on my couch, suddenly freezing.

Aaron opened with a smile and a greeting. I could tell he was sober.

"Hi, My Meggie." He waved. "I miss you. I wish you hadn't left me, but I get it. I understand why you did. I don't blame you at all, love. But after you left me, it was like, I can't live." Those black curls and his feather brushed his shoulders, those dark eyes steady on the camera, on me.

"I tried to live, but I couldn't. I'm in too much pain. I'm always in too much pain. I've been in pain since I was a kid and my dad went to jail and my mom, my drunk mom, had all those boyfriends, in and out, boyfriends. I didn't tell you, but one of those boyfriends . . ." His voice trailed off and he shook his head in disgusted disbelief. "Let's say that men should not be doing that stuff with boys, and it went on for two years. It happened after my eighth birthday. It hurt, can't tell you how much it hurt." The calm left, to be replaced by that raging anger I was so familiar with. "He'd hold me facedown on my mom's bed when she was at work, arms above my head. I told my mom. She didn't believe me. She never believed me. Said I was a liar."

He gritted his teeth, trying to get control, then teared up and ran his arm across his eyes. "Yep. She didn't believe me, so it kept going on and on. It only stopped because he was arrested for kidnapping some other kid." His face scrunched up and he exhaled, jagged and harsh. "So, lotta pain, Meggie, lotta pain. I started drugs early, started drinking early. Not good choices, but I was trying to get him out of my head. I was trying to kill him out of my head. I was trying not to kill my mom for what she did. Actually, for what she *didn't* do.

"You said that I should have told you before we were married that I had all these problems. The depression and the nerves and the times when I was younger and tried to kill myself. You're right, I should have." The calm was back, the anger gone. "I didn't tell you about it because I didn't think you'd marry me if I did. I know, that was wrong, but see, My Meggie, I was totally in love with you. I was in love with your brain, lady, and your heart, and your soul, and how you thought, and I was in love with how you loved me. I didn't want you to know. It was selfish. All about Aaron. Always about Aaron.

"I know I wasn't a good husband. You think I don't know that? I do. I said so many mean things to you. I ruined many years of your life. I'm a nightmare. I know I am, and so often I could feel myself slipping, hitting the downward spiral, my brain on fire, my thoughts so fast I couldn't even hold onto them, like they're on a train and I'm not, and you paid for my being on that train.

"It might seem like I was always angry with you, but honey, I wasn't." He smiled, a gentle smile. "You didn't cook chicken that well, though. Remember when you served that one chicken dish with rice and you forgot to turn the oven on? Remember the spaghetti that you left to boil until the water dried up and the pan was burning? That was so funny."

I smiled back. Couldn't believe it.

"But you were good, Meggie. Except . . . you were not good at documentary filmmaking." I stopped smiling and felt the fire in my belly flare up. Aaron had done everything he could to criticize and demean my work.

"No, you weren't a good filmmaker." He pointed at the camera. "You were an excellent filmmaker. Beyond excellent. Better than me. We both know it. You were innately talented. You were perceptive and introspective. You knew what had to be pulled out of the film, what you had to make people see, and feel. Your success made me feel . . . less than a man, though. It wasn't your fault. I'm not saying that. It was mine. I'm being honest. Don't have anything to lose here. You were the best."

He ran both hands through his black curls. They were longer than I'd seen them before. He was an awesome-looking man. Women had always loved him. I had, too.

"I'm sorry, My Meggie. That's what I really want to say. I'm sorry for ruining your life when you were with me. I changed you. I saw it. You were different at the end than you were when we first married. I'm sorry for what I'm going to do, but I wanted you to know that it's not your fault at all. It's not my fault, either. Well, I take it back. Some of it is. I'm a shit, I know that. And if it makes you feel any better, I hate myself for how I was to you. I hate myself for what I'm going to do and how you'll feel."

I put my hands to my head. I had said the same words so many times. *I hate myself.* I hated who I had become when I was married to Aaron. I hated that I was staying in the marriage, that I felt trapped, that I couldn't think rationally. I hated myself for hating being married. I hated that I left him, hated that he killed himself.

And all along, he'd hated himself, too.

"Living with this bipolar crap, you know, sometimes I feel like I can do anything, that I'm powerful and brilliant, better than the planet, and other times I feel like I can't even lift my head off the table. It's been going on forever and I know it will never change. I always feel like I'm being swung back and forth." He fiddled with one of the chains around his neck. "I love the highs, but the lows, my lady, I want to put a bullet in my head. I can't even explain how it feels, except to say it's the rabid dog, hunting me down.

"I don't want to live anymore. I can't do it. I love you, Meggie, I always have. I want you to have a spectacular life. You deserve it. You were good to me and you stayed a lot longer than anyone else would have. This isn't about you, or anything you did or didn't do. It's about me. Don't blame yourself. Bye, baby."

He used the camera to scan the bathroom, the filling tub, the razors he later used, the alcohol, and the pills.

"I'm sorry, My Meggie."

He smiled slightly at the camera, resigned, defeated, hopeless. He winked at me, then pushed the camera closer and closer to his face until the only thing I could see was his eye, his right eye, huge, unblinking, staring back at me.

"I love you, babe. Tell my mother she should have believed me."

The screen went black.

I ran outside to my deck, the rainbow of Adirondack chairs behind me, almost mocking me with their cheery colors, leaned over the rail, and retched into the dark night.

28

Tory, Lacey, my grandma, my mother, and I stood over the baby in her incubator.

It had been a hellacious week and yet it had ended sweetly. The baby was doing far better than the doctors thought she would, her lungs pumping. Tory was rebounding, although she was a difficult patient with her demands for "private time" with Scotty and martinis.

Lacey's wrist had set well. Her bruises were purple, blue, and green, but she was healing.

"Look at that hair," I marveled. The baby had a shock of black hair. Not brown like Matt's hair, but black.

"Not surprising, the way genetics work," my grandma drawled. "The generations are different, and sometimes a DNA mystery from the past pulls on through."

I saw my mother elbow her.

"What do you mean?" Lacey asked.

"You never know what color hair a child will have," my mother singsonged. "That's all she means."

"Sometimes you can look back to the grandparents," Grandma said, crossing her arms. "That's where you'll find surprises."

Yes. Surprises. From Sperm Donor Number One, Lacey's father.

"She's a beautiful baby," my mother cut in, moving off the

possible topic of Sperm Donor Number One, her least favorite topic, equal to the topic of Sperm Donor Number Two.

"We decided on a name," Lacey stated, calm and joyful in a beige dress that she called her "skinny pregnant dress."

"What is it?" I asked.

Tory said, "Why don't you call her Martini? I like martinis. Or Rebel Child? Or, Impatience. You know, instead of naming the baby Patience, like in the old days, name her Impatience, because she came so soon. Her nose is scrunched. Call her Scrunched Nose."

"Aren't you clever?" Lacey said.

"Name her Satin," Grandma quipped, her blue sapphires glowing on her neck. "You're Lace, she's Satin. You can call her Satin Buttons."

"Name her for someone you truly love," my mother said, knitting a tiny pink baby sweater, glasses on, her red curls back in a tight bun.

"Good idea, Mom." Lacey patted the baby's tummy, then looked up at Tory. "Because Tory, you saved my life, and hers, Matt and I decided that her first name is going to be . . ." She grinned. "Victoria."

Perfect. The perfect name. Emotion welled in me like a wave. This was incredible. Tory's mouth dropped open, and she whispered, all choked up, *"What?"*

"Her name is Victoria," Lacey said, her voice quavering. "For you."

Tory's face crumbled, she sniffled, she bit her lip, she moaned, then the waterworks started.

"Tory's not speaking," I said, linking an arm around her bent shoulders.

"Enjoy the moment. It'll pass way too soon," Grandma said.

"I'll stitch the name Victoria on her blessings quilt immediately," my mother said, adjusting her glasses because her tears were making them slip.

"Are you friggin' kidding me?" Tory asked, her voice wobbling over every word. "Victoria?"

"Not kidding, Tory," Lacey said. "This one's named after you."

My heart actually skipped a beat, those hot tears streamin' on out. Ah, Tory. Always felt like she didn't belong, and she always had. And now, a baby named for her.

Tory made a gasping sound. She turned away, she turned back, then she did it again, her hands to her heart. "I can't believe this!"

"Your namesake, Tory," my mother said, completely undone, dabbing her face with a homemade lace handkerchief. "Your sister's child, named after you. It's a glorious day in this family."

"It's a miracle!" Tory cried, hands fluttering up in the air, completely overcome. "A damn miracle."

"You're the miracle," Lacey said, hardly able to talk through her deep, endless gratefulness. "You saw the truck coming and I fell. You pulled me back up and then pushed me out of the way and took the hit. . . . You took the hit. . . . Oh my gosh, Tory. I know I already told you thank you, but thank you a zillion times, sister, a zillion times. Without you, we would not have baby Victoria. I know it, and the doctors know it, too."

"You were heroic, honey," my mother said.

"Superhero," I told her. "The bravest thing I've ever seen in my life."

"Oh, stop it! Stop it!" Tory said, waving her trembling hands. "No more!"

My grandma put an arm around her. "Tory O'Rourke, you have been a gift to us your whole life."

My mother stood, her legs not so strong. "Always, Tory. My daughter from the first day."

"Yes, always, sister," I said.

"This is getting ridiculous," Tory said. "So cheesy. It was incredibly hard for me to push Lacey, what with all the weight she gained in her butt."

We all laughed, in the middle of our tears, in the presence of baby Victoria.

Tory leaned over the baby, and one of her tears fell on her cheek. "Hell's bells. I have a baby."

The five of us hugged over the baby. She looked so angelic.

"She's named after a rebel," Lacey sighed. "When she's a teenager, she will drive me to absolute distraction, I'm sure of it. My hair will be white, my face a mess of sags and bags from her wildness . . ."

"And I'll sit back and laugh," Tory said. "I'll say, you go, Victoria! I'll take her shopping for fashion-forward clothes and high heels, because if you're going to be bad, you better look good doing it." She reached down and held Victoria's teeny hand in her own. "She is so precious . . . so precious . . . oh, my baby is so precious."

"She'll understand fashion, thank heavens," Grandma said, as if that was the penultimate gift. "It'll be in her DNA. Look at Tory."

Tory leaned over and kissed Lacey's cheek, then whispered, "Thank you, Lacey. I mean it from the bottom of my Jimmy Choos. *Thank you.*"

"No, thank you, Tory. I love you. And Mom, and Grandma and Meggie." She looked up at me. Oh, what a neat sister I had. "I love you, too."

"I love all of you crazy people." Tory blew her nose. "And I need that martini badly. Come on, Meggie, let's go slam a few."

The next day, sitting next to Lacey at the hospital, both of us watching our beloved Victoria, Lacey received a call.

"Yes, this is Mrs. Rockaford." Lacey sucked in her breath, her eyes flying open wide. "What? How is he? What happened? When? Where?"

"What? What is it?" I fluttered my hands to get her attention. *"What is it?"*

"We'll be right down." She hung up and stood, her expression despairing. "Hayden was beaten up at school."

"Sit down." I pushed her back down. "You stay, I'm going to the school. Call them and tell them I'm coming."

"No," she cried, her chin trembling, getting up again. "I'm going to Hayden. Matt's two hours away in Eugene for work—"

"You are not going. You have to stay here, with Victoria. She can't be alone without her mother. Don't do this, Lacey, let me handle it."

Lacey collapsed back into her seat. "Call me right away and bring Hayden home!" She broke into sobs, but I didn't stay to comfort her. Our beloved Hayden was beaten up, so I would go to Hayden.

"What happened?" We sat in front of the principal in a semicircle. Next to me was Hayden with an ice pack on his eye, dressed in a beige, ruffled skirt and green sweater. He grinned at me.

Regan was sitting next to him, with an ice pack on his cheek. He had been crying, his face all blotchy and red. I assumed it was because he was in the principal's office. He did not like getting into trouble. It made him feel, as he put it, "worried. Like a lost cat."

"How's B-B-Breadsticks doing?" he stuttered.

Next to Regan was Cassidy with an ice pack on her chin. Her skirt was too short and her top was too low. She smiled at me and whispered, "I am so excited for hors d'oeuvres class, aren't you, Aunt Meggie?"

Cody, the tall and naughty boyfriend who spent the night in Cassidy's bed, was holding Cassidy's hand. He didn't have an ice pack, but his knuckles were all scraped up. "Hello, Miss O'Rourke." He stood and shook my hand. "Nice to see you again. I'm excited for hors d'oeuvres class, too. The pastries that Cassidy made me from dessert class were delicious." He shook his head in awe. "She's a world-class cook! World class! My mouth got all watered up looking at them. Don't you just love Cassidy? I do."

The principal, a man in his sixties with a bulging stomach, ill-fitting suit, and wire glasses, peered at me as we shook hands. "I understand that you are Meggie O'Rourke."

"Yes, I am. I'm Hayden's, Regan's, and Cassidy's aunt. Their mother is at the hospital with her baby who's in the neonatal unit."

He humphed at me. I wanted to groan. Uptight. Proper. Conservative. So much better if we'd had someone else. . . .

"Can you tell me what happened, Mr. Harrison?" If he thought I was going to be intimidated by his glare and severe demeanor, he had another thing coming. I had faced off with far worse than him.

"Hayden has been coming to school dressed as a girl."

"Yes, he has. He's transgender. He's a girl." I should have said "she's a girl." "What's the problem?"

Out of the corner of my eye, I saw Hayden smile.

"The problem is that the other kids here were not prepared for his . . . coming out."

"So what? Hayden is not here on this planet to live his life according to what other people think he should and should not be or whether they're ready for him to change. It's not relevant."

"But he had to be aware of what the reaction would be from the other students."

"Of course. He's not an idiot." I heard Regan crying and muttering something about "poor, innocent frogs." Cody the boyfriend reached out his long arm behind Cassidy and patted him on the back.

"Hayden is a young man wishing to be a young woman." Mr. Harrison studied Hayden, as if he found him derelict in some way, something to study with dispassion, scientifically. I saw Hayden's chin tip up.

"No, Hayden is a young woman. He was born with a boy's body. I asked you what happened." I sat up straighter. I am a screwed-up person, wracked by guilt and remorse. I've been chased by Aaron, black feathers, and rats for a long time, but I am hard into my No Crap Zone—especially when it comes to the kids.

"What happened, as I understand it"—the principal tapped his pen—"is that a group of boys—"

"Five boys," Hayden said. "And one girl."

"Yes, and one girl"—the principal agreed—"cornered Hayden."

"Then what happened?" I turned to Hayden.

"One of the boys swung at me. I swung back and clocked him in the face. The second kid socked me in the stomach, and I went down, then came back up and hit him. But there were five of them, and I couldn't get 'em all, and it's hard to have good balance in heels you know, Aunt Meggie."

"Sure is. What happened after that?"

"Well, Regan was late for class and came sprinting by—"

Regan moaned, distraught. "I thought it was third period, my Spanish class, but it wasn't, it was *fourth* period and I was supposed to be in Introduction to Algebra. Remember I told you I had to take that over again, Aunt Meggie?"

I nodded.

"I was confused about where I was supposed to be because I was so upset . . ." He groaned. "So upset . . ."

Cassidy hugged Regan.

Cody said, "Be strong, buddy."

"What were you upset about?" I asked.

Regan ran his hands over his hot, wet face. As usual his blond hair was a mess. "I was upset . . ."

Hayden ruffled his hair.

"What?" I said. "What else happened today?"

"I was in biology class." Regan snuffled, then inhaled, exhaled, trying to calm himself down. "And it was . . . oh, my gosh, it was terrible, Aunt Meggie! I had to leave and go throw up."

"Regan, why?"

"I had to throw up once and I felt like I was going to throw up again, so I had to keep leaning over the toilet, and it was so gross, all coming out—"

"Got it, Regan. But what was so bad?"

"It was"—he gasped, shaking his head back and forth as if to erase the tragic memory—"it was *frog dissection day!*"

Aha. I leaned back. I understood.

"And all those frogs...those *dead* frogs. All I could think about was Hermie, Princess Bob, Russell Max, King X, and Sergeant Elizabeth, and how much I love them. How I can talk to them and hug them, and there were these dead frogs! They should have been in ponds, Aunt Meggie! Outside hopping, not inside"—his voice pitched, semihysterically—"where kids *cut them up!*"

Cody had had it with the sobbing Regan. He stood up and kneeled in front of him and hugged that huge kid. Cassidy patted his back, and Hayden patted his head.

I swung my gaze back to the principal. He shifted, pulled at his tie. "It's been part of the curriculum for decades...."

When Regan finally settled down and could breathe again, I said, "So you saw Hayden getting beaten up?"

"Yeah, I did," Regan said. "And I still felt sick because I'd thrown up, I told you that part, right, Aunt Meggie?"

I assured him he did.

"I mean, I had to bend over the toilet, and I'd had two peanut butter and jellies, a piece of chicken, two apples, Cassidy's cookies, three milks and—"

"Honey, I understand. So you saw Hayden getting hit..."

"Yeah, and I was so mad when I saw that. It wasn't only the frogs that made me mad. I mean, if Hayden wants to dress like a girl, why not? I'm getting used to it. It's still Hayden, right? So I jumped in and started hitting those little fuckers for hitting my brother, who is now my sister."

I raised my eyebrows. Regan never, ever swears.

He howled, destroyed once again. "I'm sorry I used those words, Aunt Meggie. Oh no! Now I feel bad about that, too! Dead frogs, hitting, swearing and I'm in the principal's office. It's a bad day, a *bad day!*" He flung his head back and stared up at the ceiling as if asking God to take him now. "I started swinging, then Cody and Cassidy came, too—"

"You were out of class, also?" I asked.

Cassidy grinned at me. "We'd been making out behind the bleachers and lost track of time." She held Cody's hand.

"Yeah, I mean, Cassidy's my woman, and ever since her dad ran naked into her bedroom, I mean, that freaked me out, *freaked me out,* and I can't come over now, so I haven't been able to spend as much time with her, and I love her so much—"

Hayden dropped his ice pack to his lap. "Regan and I are fighting back. Regan's fists are so fast, it's like a blur, then all of the sudden Cassidy is in there pummeling. I mean, she screams at them and she jumps on Ricki St John's back—he's always beating kids up—and Ricki swings at her over his shoulder . . ."

"Uh, excuse me, Hayden," Cody interrupted. "I don't wanna interrupt you, but I don't want Miss O'Rourke to get the wrong impression here." He turned toward me. "I didn't want Cassidy in that fight at all, Miss O'Rourke, but all of the sudden, she was in it before I could protect her, and I was hitting Stepho Zacks, boom boom, like that"—he showed us the boom boom with his fists—"and I didn't see Ricki take that swing at Cassidy or I woulda been right there, I mean, right there, protecting my woman, okay, Miss O'Rourke?"

I nodded. Knight in shining armor.

"But as soon as I see Ricki take that swing and Cassidy went down, man"—Cody actually flushed and boom boomed both his fists together again—"I . . . man, I was so mad, I think I had steam on my head, and I said two words to myself: 'Destroy that jerk.'"

"He was awesome, Aunt Meggie!" Hayden bobbed in his seat. "He swung at Ricki, and Ricki went straight down, got back up, and Cody swung at him again, and Ricki didn't get back up. Then Cody hit Stepho again, and Stepho ended up on his back with this frickin' stunned look on his face, like he couldn't believe it."

"Yeah, but Hayden, he had Mick down, man," Cody said, giving praise where praise was due. "He took care of Mick."

"In my heels, too!" Hayden said. "Regan wiped out Bryan and Ramon, all this blood flyin' from their noses, and Cassidy, she shoved Yolanda up against the wall so hard her head thunked because, you know, Regan and Cody couldn't hit a girl, but Cassidy could."

"So it was a family fight?" I asked.

"Yep," Cody said, grinning. He fist-bumped Hayden, Regan, and Cassidy. "Family fight."

"Family fight!" Cassidy threw her arms up into the air and cheered, "We won!"

I looked at the principal. He looked tired.

"There was a lot of blood," Regan said. "No blood on the frogs."

"Yeah, blood on the enemy," Hayden agreed. He crossed his legs. I liked his heels.

"It was a battle, Aunt Meggie," Cassidy said. She hooted again like she was at a football game. "I wish you were there."

"The only bad part was the frogs," Regan said, tearing up again, that big, blond head swinging back and forth. "Those poor frogs. I don't think I'll ever get over their deaths."

"So what we have here," I said, "is five boys and a girl attacking my kids. My kids defended each other. How long will the other kids be suspended for?"

The principal shifted his oversized bottom on his seat. "The other students will be suspended for ten days. Their parents have already been called."

I was surprised. Surprised that he'd been fair. I hadn't pegged him that way initially. Bad me. "Good. Thank you. And now my kids can all go back to class?"

The principal nodded, then turned to Hayden. "I'm going to do all I can to protect you, Hayden. I've got zero tolerance for what happened here, and these kids getting suspended will send the student body a message." He sighed. "I don't understand it, but I'm trying. What I do understand, kid, is that you're a good person, and at my school you're going to learn and be safe like every other person here. I'll take care of this."

Hayden nodded. "Thanks. I appreciate that. Thanks."

Regan said, "If I have to hit people to protect Hayden, my brother now my sister, I will, but I'm not going back to biology till the frog killing is over." He was overcome again. "Even though they're dead, they had feelings and they were alive!"

"I'm family," Cassidy said, standing up and wiggling her hips in her too-short skirt. "I'm a Rockaford, and I enjoyed the fight."

"I'm family," Cody said. "I protect my bros and sistas." He picked Hayden up and hugged him in his skirt. "And I protect my sista who used to be my bro."

"You did, you did, Cody!" Cassidy gushed. "It was so romantic how you jumped in there and started bashing their heads together, dropping those kids to the floor. I'm going to bake you your favorite cherry pie tonight."

"And I'm going to start a petition that there be no more frog dissection!" Regan declared. "It makes me sick! As in throw-up sick!"

"Ah, Cass. I love your cherry pie." Cody leaned over and kissed her. She put her hands behind his head and pulled him closer. He wrapped his arms tightly around her, lifted her up, her ankles in the air ... and then Cassidy had the audacity to moan.

I stood up lickety-split and tried to pull them apart. "Okay, you two, break it up, break it up, come on! *Cassidy!*"

The principal put a hand to his forehead. I think he's ready to retire.

As I drove away from the high school, after Hayden, Regan, Cassidy, and Cody had all hugged me, and Cassidy made me promise to come over soon and work on a seven-layer chocolate cake with her, and Regan asked me to write him a note to keep him out of biology, and Hayden said, "Can we talk about the pink negligees with the tassels? I think they should be gold tipped. It'll be a smash," I thought about my role as an aunt.

I had visited over the years, but I'd been gone a lot out of their lives.

They needed me. They did not need me to be another mother. They had a fantastic mother. They needed an aunt.

That fact, right there, lifted my heart into a happier place.

I was needed.

I would not be gone again from their lives. I owed it to them to be present.

She called the next day and left a message. She told me she hated me. She blamed me for Aaron's death. "It was your fault, Meggie. All your fault. Why did you kill him?"

I did not feel as nauseated this time as I deleted the message.

29

My name is Edna Petrelli. Our family is from Sicily. Yes, our grandfather was in the mob, and so was our father, until he was shot like a pigeon on Madison Avenue. He was an attorney for the big guns. We hid that from people for a long time when my mother moved us out to Oregon from Jersey when we were young. She was so ashamed, but why hide it now? He was a mobster, scars all over his face, a bullet stuck in his shoulder, but he was good to us. A loving father.

I'm Edith Petrelli, and Edna's right. Daddy was in the mob, but he could bake bread like no one's business. I remember how he rolled it out, those huge hands kneading it with precision . . . he was missing the ring finger on his right hand . . .

I'm Estelle. Daddy often had men over—tough, tough men. I could see their guns, and they would casually talk about hits on one person or another, money laundering, a snitch, the unions, a lot of times dipping Daddy's bread in soup or olive oil and spices. I heard them talking about rolling a body into the river twice. They didn't think we were listening, but we were. We have big ears, all of us.

Daddy loved Momma. Her daddy was in the mob, too. They fought it out sometimes, they did, enough to raise the roof and bring it down on top of us . . .

. . . but they made up well, too. Daddy would pick Momma up, throw her over his shoulder, head to the bedroom, and we

*wouldn't see them for a couple of hours, but when we did they
would be smiling.*

It was a love match, with some fireworks thrown in.

*I have worked for Lace, Satin, and Baubles, along with my
sisters, for, let's see, how many years? I think it's forty now, isn't
it, girls? I invented a nipple bra recently. Funny, too, because
Daddy had a friend in the mob called Nipples. Wonder if that
played into my thinking?*

*I designed the black leather licorice bra with the fringe, zipper,
crossbones, and whip. We're all wearing a prototype of the leather
bra today. Okay, girls, lift your blouses, one, two, three. See there,
Meggie? I wonder if my love of leather has to do with Daddy. He
used to wear a lot of black leather, too. Had a crossbones tattoo.*

*I think Daddy and all those guns may have influenced my
own design with the pink fuzzy pajamas with the gun pointed at
the crotch. . . .*

*We loved Daddy and Granddaddy. They played checkers
with us.*

*Oh, and Daddy's five brothers were also in the mob. One
went to jail. One was shot by the FBI. One disappeared. One
became a U.S. senator, and one owned—*

Shhh. You're not supposed to say the name of the company.

*That's right. Almost forgot. It's a huge company. You know
it, Meggie.*

*But Daddy, the uncles, and Granddaddy, they were so good
to us. Family dinner every Sunday night.*

Daddy loved us, we knew that.

He did. You could taste the love in the bread he made.

*I want to tell my sisters on this film thing you're doing, Meg-
gie, that I love them and I can't imagine my life without them.
That's the most important thing here, I think. Love.*

Yes, it's love.

Love you, sisters.

Love you, too.

We're the Petrelli sisters.

Always have been, always will be.

Petrelli. From Sicily.

30

It was a scary thing for me to do. On Thursday night, about eight o'clock, I walked across the street, through the snow-flakes, and up the small hill to Blake's house. The lights in his great room were on, his truck in the driveway.

I climbed the steps of his white deck, then scuttled back down like a chicken.

I crossed my arms over my chest and tried to gather up some courage. I had run three different meetings today at work. I looked at a financial ledger and saw problems instantly. We had shipping issues, and I handled 'em.

And there I was, trembling, in front of Blake's house under a swaying, gnarled oak tree. It's like there are two Meggies: The confident one who runs a company and doesn't blink, and the one that is immobilized by insecurity in her personal life.

I headed up the stairs, then scuttled back down, yet again.

I would go and talk to him.

I wouldn't.

I would.

I put my hands to my hair.

I tried climbing the stairs one more time. I made it halfway. With my courage in shambles, I twirled back around to scuttle off for good.

"Are you coming in or not?"

Blake's voice cut through the blackness of the night and my

humiliation like a chain saw cuts through a loaf of bread—maybe Petrelli mob bread.

"I don't know." He was in jeans and a white T-shirt. He was tough and handsome and cowboy-ish. I couldn't believe I'd even dared to come over.

But I was desperate. I liked Blake with every ounce of my scared, stick-figure body.

"Hmm," he said. "Well, why don't you come inside until you decide?"

"You watched me going up and down your steps, didn't you?"

"I've had a lot of training about things that go bump in the night, so to speak," he drawled. "I always check out noises."

"Dang." Humiliating.

"Yep. Dang. Sit down with me, Meggie. You can eat dessert first. I bought pecan pie."

Argh. "Okay. I'll try to talk to you."

I could see his smile. "Trying is all I've ever asked of you."

"It's going to be hard."

"I like challenges."

"Not this one, you won't."

"I think I will." He cocked his head. "In fact, I already do."

"I am not happy without you, Blake."

He closed his eyes and bent his blond head, his hands clasped between his knees as we sat together on his leather couch, a fire flickering in the fireplace.

"Blake, I have never met a man like you. I wish I had met you years before."

I studied his face. So dear to me. So strong, hard, fierce looking. I could see how he would scare people. But then I stared into those gray-blue eyes, as they gentled for me, warmed for me. Respectful but sexy. Wanting but not pushing.

"My marriage toyed with my mind and then exploded it, and I've been trying to get myself back together." I wrung my hands.

I had told him, choking on one truckload of emotion after

another, about Aaron, my mind-twisting marriage, the black and red of his suicide, my year of wandering, the nightmares, the daymares, the rats, the broken black feathers, the blood, and the screaming in my head. I told him about sweet Josephine.

"I have major trust issues, damage issues, trigger issues, anger issues, but I'm trying to work on them. You have been paying for all of those issues, even though you are nothing like my late husband. Nothing. I don't think I could find two more different men."

"That's true," Blake said, lacing our fingers together. "I am nothing like him. You haven't been able to see around him to me. I understand. What you went through is tragic. Impossible. I am so sorry, Meggie. I will always be sorry for that pain in your life."

"I don't want you to feel sorry for me. It is what it is." Yes, it was. Sometimes that's the healing point, right there: acceptance. It happened, now let's move forward. "I think I'm getting healthier in my head. I wouldn't even describe myself as a basket case lunatic anymore, and I don't think I hate myself as much as I used to."

"You were never a basket case lunatic. You're an amazingly strong, moral, caring woman, Meggie. You stayed to save Aaron, you never stayed for you. Don't hate yourself, please, Meggie."

"Blake, I would like to start over with you. I understand if you don't want to start over with me. I get it. You might even be dating someone else." If I met her I'd want to pull her hair out.

"I am not dating anyone else. I haven't even thought about it. I've been waiting for you. Hoping for you. How could you think I would be dating anyone else, Meggie?" He lifted my hand and kissed it.

I shivered, and smiled. How romantic can this guy get? "How could I think that? Because you are smokin' hot and thoughtful and kind and smart and I am crazy about you. I'm sure thousands of other women are, too."

"I don't want thousands of others, Meggie. I have only ever

wanted you. I have always made that clear. But I didn't want you on the terms that you wanted for our relationship. I try not to sabotage myself."

Okay. I could do this. I could handle it. I could, could, could. "Then let's do us your way."

"My way?"

"Yes." I wanted to leap on his lap and hug him, though I was still scared about the leap. "Your way."

"As in, we're going to date, and be together, not just jump in and out of bed, and you'll be open to falling in love with me if I'm extra nice and don't burn the steaks?"

"Yes." In love? *In love?* Ah, that sounded nice.

"What about your aversion to a committed relationship?"

The thought of a commitment still scared the bejeezus out of me, but when I smiled at Blake, friendly Blake, I said, "I'm gonna try. Give it my best shot, rah rah rah. I'll be brave and invite you to take a few rendezvous with me."

"Trying is good." He smiled back, slow and sure. "And I'll take the rendezvous."

His arms wrapped around me, his warm lips meeting mine as if we'd rolled down this road of passion many times before. I cupped his face in my hands and we had a long and rockin' kiss. I pulled him down on top of me on his leather couch, the snowflakes falling, the fire crackling.

Architecturally speaking, there was no better backdrop for our lingerie than the shoe factory across the street. The juxtaposition of lace, satin, and lingerie against the rougher edges of the building, the concrete, brick, exposed rafters, and the cavernous ceilings was bang-up perfect.

At the entrance, our handyman extraordinaire, Eric Luduvic, had created a twelve-foot-long sparkly bra made out of pink lights. Across the cups it said "Lace, Satin, and Baubles" in red. It was catchy, it was fun, and, as Lacey said, "*tit*-illating."

Swaths of pink satin, white lace, and white lights hung from the factory ceiling. We also hung strawberries. Yes, enormous wood strawberries, painted red, rimmed with silver glitter and red lights, also by Eric.

At Hayden's suggestion, we brought in trees and wrapped white lights around them, too. We had circular tables covered in white tablecloths, and in the center of each one we'd placed a two-foot-tall black-and-white photo of Grandma when she was sixteen and in the strawberry fields, looking tired and dirty but proud and strong, her hair windblown. The farmer's wife took the shot.

Along the sides of the factory, we had current photos of Grandma, juxtaposed next to the weathered boarding house and tiny room she lived in while sewing nightgowns after picking strawberries all day. We had photos of the first small building she'd bought for the company, then the second factory, and finally the enormous pink and white building we now own.

The pink runway was lined with two-foot-tall glass candleholders with three pink tea lights floating in each one, also Hayden's idea. White chairs lined the runway four rows deep.

The music was loud and upbeat, thanks to Tory. We had decided to play music that made people want to dance. We were expecting hundreds of people. We'd given free tickets to the employees' friends and family to pack the house, and I'd worked the phones and finally convinced a bunch of media people to be there. When I was stonewalled, I had my mother call. They said yes to her. Funny what a Southern belle/Irish elf sex therapist can do when she calls her contacts.

And the cakes, made by Leonard Tallchief?

Exquisite. Leonard said he was "up all night, worrying endlessly, for weeks, the anxiety tripping my anxiety! Which cakes would be most delectable? I changed my mind, changed it again, my brain numb and hyperventilating. Only the best for your grandma, the best for Regan O'Rourke, my angel. After a companywide tasting and meeting and vote, group meditation, and a call to my uncle, our tribe's chief, who is also a phenomenal chef, I decided..."

He had made five huge cakes that can only be described as

spectacular culinary art. One was a lacey red bra with huge cups, another was a pink negligee, the third cake was a white lace thong with purple bows, the fourth was a red and black bustier, and the fifth was orange and yellow flowered panties. We put bowls of strawberries between them.

Delicious.

In the back, behind the stage, where our "models" were getting ready, I should have been shaking.

I wasn't shaking.

I was more focused than I think I've ever been.

"Here we go," Lacey said.

"This works and we relaunch this company," Tory said. "It fails and we start laying off people and hope we don't have to sell Grandma along with the rest of the inventory."

"Thank you for boiling it down to such grim news," Lacey said.

"You're welcome," Tory said. "I don't think anyone is going to want to buy Grandma, though. Rather cranky old lady."

Backstage we had organized chaos. More chaos than organized, but our lineup of "models" was ready. Because they were in lingerie, and some, okay almost all of them, didn't feel confident strutting around in their designs almost naked, we'd added lacy skirts, gauzy veils, creatively tied sashes, silky sarongs, fanciful hats, capes, butterfly wings, and one space alien outfit that opened to a striped nightshirt. The New York shows have fantabulous, out-of-this-world clothing, why couldn't we?

"Hello, Grandma," I said.

My grandma studied me, head to foot, noting my silky purple dress and high heels. "You don't look like the cat dragged you in after rolling you down a hill."

"Thank you." I leaned in and kissed her cheek. She pulled me close and whispered, "You look like a model, Meggie. Gorgeous. Most important, I see the light on in you again. Don't ever let it extinguish again. Stay strong."

She was resplendent in a floor-length blue velvet dress with a long train and her four strands of pearls. Her hair was up in her usual chignon, but she'd added two sparkling clips. My mother stood beside her in a black dress and fishnet tights, her red curls falling down her back.

"Hello, honey." My mother kissed me, Lacey, and Tory, taking care not to bump their casts. "I am so proud of all of you. My lovely daughters! We're all together, as a family. My heart is joyous."

I was, once again, glad to be home. Win or lose tonight, the company saved or the company burned, I was grateful to be here with family. And I was grateful that Blake was in the audience. My Blake. Sweet Blake.

Minutes later Eric flickered the lights, turned off the dancing music, and invited our guests to take their seats lining the pink runway and floating candles. Behind the pink curtains we waited until everyone was settled and quiet, then we dimmed the lights, one spotlight on the front of the stage.

"That's you, Grandma," I said.

Grandma smiled at all of our employees backstage, most of whom were scared to death about their impending journeys down the catwalk. She said, "Thank you," then paused and put two fingers to her lips, blinking rapidly. "Thank you. You are my life." She blew them a kiss, which was completely uncharacteristic of our butt-kickin' grandma.

She disappeared behind the pink curtains and I heard wild applause as she took the stage. Our employees applauded, too. I grabbed Tory's hand. She squeezed back. "Here we go," she said. "Let's start dancing with the devil."

"Welcome to the Lace, Satin, and Baubles Fashion Story," my grandma boomed. "Welcome! Thank you for coming."

Everyone clapped again and hooted. When they settled down, Grandma said, "We were going to have a fashion show, a typical fashion show, with tall, thin, unsmiling models who look famished. We were going to have them model our lingerie, our bras, our pajamas. But we've done that. We've all done that in this business. Repetitive. Boring. I hate boredom."

They laughed.

"What we decided to do is show you who we are. To show

you who is behind Lace, Satin, and Baubles. Who's running the company, who does what, who designs our products, who works in sales, what family members work here together. We wanted you to know us. We wanted you to know why this business is my legacy. That's why we are not calling this a fashion show. It's the Lace, Satin and Baubles Fashion Story.

"Our employees designed their own lingerie. We asked them to create lingerie that reflected them and their lives. Some of it we'll change, alter, and sell to you. Some of it is simply for fun. Tonight we have rebellious, thought-provoking, artistic, funny, and out-of-this-world lingerie. Our employees have been unbelievably brave." She paused. "They are the ones who are going to model the lingerie for you."

Whooee! The audience liked that.

"Sit back, relax, enjoy, and let's embrace the night together!"

The audience cheered into the dark, there was a drumroll, and Maritza, her hand clinging to mine in that last second, stepped from behind the curtain and strutted down the pink runway to some toe-tapping music, the spotlight following her. She was in black lingerie; a gauzy, flowy, see-through black skirt; and four-foot-tall gold and silver butterfly wings.

The audience clapped and hooted. They loved those wings!

After Maritza owned that runway, hips swinging, she stopped and posed on the stage. The lights went off, as did the music.

A huge video screen above the stage showed Maritza talking about her escape from Mexico in an enclosed semitruck with her sisters and her late mother. No one moved when she talked about being raped, how she was allowed to stay in America, and how my grandma hired her and her sisters. When it was over, the spotlight again shone on Maritza and her butterfly wings.

Her standing ovation lasted three minutes. She cried. She waved. We cried backstage.

Grandma introduced Lance Turner next, who walked up and down the runway, shoulders back, wearing the army pajamas with the fuzzy pink trim and his army boots. His video about his service in Afghanistan was next and how he felt about the dead mother in her white bra, blood staining it as her children crawled over her body. Standing ovation, too. He had to come out to take another bow.

Following Lance was Melissa and her tattoo bra. Melissa somehow knew how to strut. She rocked that runway. On her video she talked honestly, and with wry humor, about her relationship struggles with her mother and the dragon tattoo she named Mother. She was followed by Candy in her flaming bustier, her anger issues and her funny tale of trying to find a date via the Internet.

Tato rode down the runway on his growling Harley to raucous cheering, wearing his nightgown, a biker dude, a black bandanna over his head, and dark glasses.

We sent the Latrouelle sisters out together. They wore matching nightgowns, and in their video they talked about the women in their family, their history, their ancestors. We showed Delia's video, too, as she talked about her adopted children. I heard people sniffling over that one.

The Petrelli sisters strode down that runway, as if they'd done it a hundred times. Edna wore her nipple bra *over* a pink, shiny dress. She used her pointer fingers to bring people's attention to it. Edith wore the Whip Brassiere in black leather and black leather pants. She cracked a whip in the air. Oh, how the audience adored the whipping. Estelle wore her fuzzy, pink pajamas with the gun pointed at the crotch. At one point she stood in the middle of the runway and shot off two cap guns—three times. The crowd loved that, too, leaping to their feet.

Their video about the mob, their nine-fingered father with a bullet in his shoulder, and his loving bread, made everyone laugh.

Hayden told me he was going to "faint like a dead bat," but he made it down the runway in a silvery skirt and silver bra with swinging tassels. His video about being transgender initially brought dead silence, and I cringed. Lacey sucked in her breath.

Turns out it took a second for people to absorb it—that was a *boy* who strutted down the runway? Again, thundering applause.

Our other employees—some with videos, some not, as that would take too long—followed.

Lacey wore a gold bra and gold skirt, gold boots, and a red cape. In her video she talked about the accident and how Tory saved her life and her baby's life. She held up baby Victoria, with Hayden, Regan, Cassidy, and Matt behind her. When the video was over, she had Tory come out. Tory had not known she was going to be asked out onstage with Lacey.

Lacey flipped the red cape over to show a superhero logo and put the red cape around Tory's shoulders. "You're my superhero, Tory," she cried as they had a long, emotional hug. My mother was in even worse emotional shape than me at that hug, her handkerchief soaked.

Tory walked barefoot onstage later in an innocent, pink lace nightgown holding her purple dinosaur and yellow lion. She stood quietly as her video ran where she talked about her shock and grief over losing her parents.

"The night after my parents died in the car wreck I was wearing a pink nightgown like this. I was five. My parents were gone. My whole life was gone. I didn't even understand what death meant then. What heaven was. How could my parents not be coming back? But then Brianna O'Rourke came and hugged me, and I was invited to join the O'Rourke family. I became a granddaughter, daughter, and Lacey and Meggie's sister. From utter ruin to a new family, and I love them."

The video ended, and Tory took the pink nightgown off over her head, swung it around, and stood in front of Scotty in a black and red ribboned bustier, garters, fishnets, and high red heels. She leaned over and did a shimmy right in his face. We all laughed. The penis caper story was well known. "My name is Tory Martinez Stefanos O'Rourke," she shouted into a microphone, "and I love my husband, Scotty."

I wore a boring beige sheath dress. I walked up and down the runway barefoot. In my video I said that my husband had killed himself. I then talked about my year of wandering. I talked about the ranch in Montana, building churches in Mexico, the safe house for prostitutes in the Ukraine, and the orphanage in Russia. I talked about trying to bring color back into my life, and how that had been a struggle until I came home. When it was over I pulled apart the beige dress, which had been attached with Velcro. Underneath I was wearing a red lace negligee with a red lace skirt that fell to my knees, and red heels.

I deliberately turned toward Blake when I opened the dress like a flasher and smiled at him. He smiled back, and I saw the surprise, then the passion, and over it all, the love and friendship.

Grandma's video was last, with her seated in her light pink office in her red suit and four strands of pearls. She had told my mother, Lacey, and Tory about her story two days before so, as Grandma said, "They wouldn't get their panties in a twist on the night of The Fashion Story."

Their panties got in a twist, anyhow. So did their minds. That kind of story twists you all up inside.

"My name is Regan O'Rourke. I am the founder and owner of Lace, Satin, and Baubles." Up on the big-screen TV, Grandma told how she'd worked in the strawberry fields at sixteen, had one room in a boarding house, sewed nightgowns at night, fought poverty for years, and worked constantly to build the company. "Our company symbol is the strawberry so no one ever forgets where I came from.

"But the story before the story of Lace, Satin, and Baubles has been a secret. The only one I ever told was my late husband, Cecil O'Rourke, The Irishman. I told my daughter, and my granddaughters, and anyone else who dared ask, that I slid off the curve of a rainbow with a dancing leprechaun and flew to America on the back of an owl from Ireland." She rolled her eyes impatiently. "I have decided, however, that I want to leave a truthful legacy. I want you to know that my early challenges were a part of my life, but I didn't let them take *over* my life. I didn't let them tell me who I had to be.

"My story starts in County Cork, Ireland. My parents' names were Teagan and Lochlan MacNamara. I had a sister named Keela. We were poor. My father had been hurt in an accident and was in a wheelchair. Few people living here know poor the way that we knew poor. We had one meal a day for weeks at a time, and we ate an endless amount of potatoes. My sister and I often did not have shoes that fit. There were bugs and lice. We froze in the winter. My mother had two miscarriages, probably because her health was so deteriorated, and she lost a baby when he was seven weeks old."

Her brogue soft but sure, Grandma talked about how she went down the road one day to help a neighbor with her vegetable garden with the promise that the neighbor would give them vegetables to eat. "That's when our house burned down. My mother, my father, my sister, gone. Burned to death. How? We had a fire going, and my guess is that sparks flew and my mother and sister could not get my father in his wheelchair out in time and refused to leave until it was too late."

Grandma paused, closed her eyes, bent her head. We waited for her, stricken, in that dark, silent factory, our eyes glued to the video.

We waited.

Waited more until her head came up once again.

"I was fifteen years old and I had nothing." Her voice cracked. "My grief overwhelmed me. I wanted to die and be with my family. Several people in my village made gravestones for my parents and sister, and we buried them in a corner of the local graveyard. I spent hours there, sometimes all day. The woman who had the vegetable garden took me in. I later learned why she spent so much time in that garden." Grandma's face hardened. "She was trying to avoid her husband, who liked to beat her.

"I became his new toy to rape and beat. When I fought off being raped, he beat me with his fists, and when he couldn't break me, he whipped me. Not with a belt, but with a whip. One night he whipped me so hard, my wounds became infected.

I was ill for three weeks. His wife tended to me. I thought I was dying. I saw my parents, I saw Keela, as if they were waiting for me, waiting to take me to heaven.

"When I could finally stand, I knew that I could no longer stay in their home, so I hitched a ride in the back of a truck filled with chickens and went to the docks on the ocean. I didn't want to do what I did next, but I didn't see a way out. I had no money. I had no food. I became . . ."

She paused, she struggled, sitting there in her red suit and ropes of pearls.

We waited in the dark, a heavy hush making that room absolutely silent.

Waited more.

"I became a prostitute."

It was as if everyone inhaled at one time.

"Would you like to judge me on that? My parents and sister were dead. I had no job, no education, no skills except for sewing, which my mother had taught my sister and me to do. Her greatest hope in life was that one day we would become seamstresses. I had already been raped multiple times by a brutal man, and I thought I was nothing. You cannot imagine the degradation of being a prostitute, the danger, the disgust, the cloying and nauseating scents, the often vicious men. I hurt all the time, physically and mentally. Prostitution almost decimated me. One man, after another, after another. Rough, fat, skinny, angry. I saved every penny, only paying the doctor when I needed medication and care for the things that come with being a hopeless prostitute.

"My goal? Get out of Ireland."

She continued to tell the story of that cataclysmic year, how she was hired as a maid on a ship going to America through a "client."

"I took the job, and left Ireland. We were hit by two storms. We almost died. At that point, the boat listing and pitching, I was so miserable and alone, I thought that death would be better for me. We landed in New York, and I was ill and half-starved. The captain told me I had to pretend I was well or the officials would send me back to Ireland. I smiled. I pinched my cheeks for color. I chatted. I passed. I was in. I was an American.

"I used the money I had to take a train to Oregon. Why Oregon? Because I met a woman on the boat who said you could hide from your past and be a new person out west. Hiding appealed to me. On the boat over, I decided that I could no longer be a prostitute. I would rather die. On a farm near the river I got a job picking strawberries for the summer."

She talked about being broke, not having enough money for food or shoes, and certainly no money for anything pretty or frilly. "I was in survival mode. I ate strawberries morning, noon, and night. When I could, I snuck corn, tomatoes, lettuce, and carrots out of another farmer's fields."

After getting fabrics, lace and satin from the farmer's wife, my grandma talked about how she made herself a silky pink slip and what it did for her all day long under her one, drab blue dress. "I felt pretty for the first time in my life because I was wearing silk. I felt like I could do something different, be someone different. I could look people in the eye because I didn't feel so destitute and desperate. Maybe if I wore nice clothes, no one would know that I had been whipped and raped. No one would know that I had been a prostitute. I needed to hide, and silk and satin helped me do that.

"When I was nineteen I met The Irishman. His name was Cecil O'Rourke, and he had arrived from Ireland a few months before me. He, too, was an orphan. I would not become his girlfriend at first, because I did not feel worthy. I was dirty. I was used." She put her hands together, her pearl and diamond rings flashing. "But I made the mistake of giving in to my passion for him one night. I, the young woman who had sold herself to many men for food, pulled away, then ran away from him as fast as I could. Cecil followed me, and I told him everything, his arms wrapped around me. He told me..." She stopped, the memory still overwhelming her, her voice cracking. "He told me the past was past, that our love would be the future."

I heard many sighs from women in the audience.

"Cecil was broke, like me, but he was smart, and he worked hard. He built a construction company. I built a lingerie business, and in between we loved each other madly." She smiled, soft and almost sweet.

"I used the color pink in Lace, Satin, and Baubles because it was my mother's favorite color. The lights in our factory are shaped like tulips because my father brought my mother tulips before his accident. I put in fainting couches because I felt faint so often from hunger when I was younger. The fainting couches remind me to be thankful that I have enough to eat. I use chandeliers because we didn't have electricity in Ireland, and the chandeliers remind me that I'm not in poverty living with lice and bugs.

"To me, Lace, Satin, and Baubles is not just another company. It's my legacy. It's me. It's in honor of my parents, my sister, The Irishman, my family. I gave myself, all of myself, to get here, and I want to leave something of value for others. Providing jobs is of value. It means that people can buy a home, they can pay for their children's educations. That's my legacy. We've given money away to charities and for scholarships. That's my legacy. This company has provided for my own family, the people I adore and love the most, the people whom the Irishman adored and love. That's our legacy.

"My name is Regan O'Rourke. I was a desperately poor, hungry girl in Ireland. My family burned to death in a fire. I was whipped and raped by an evil and violent man. I became a prostitute. And then I came here, to America, and I overcame my past." She lifted her chin. "I became the owner of Lace, Satin, and Baubles. I am grateful. And, by damn, I'm proud of myself."

The video went off. The room was completely black, utterly silent, except for the flickering of candlelight.

The sound of Grandma's heels tapping on the runway—*from the other end*—echoed through the factory. Everyone's heads spun around, the standing ovation thunderous as Grandma proudly walked the entire runway in her full-length, blue velvet dress with a flowing train. When she arrived at the front of the stage, one lone spotlight on her, she stood, regal, proud, chin tilted up, a slight smile on her face. She was magnificent.

Lacey, Tory, my mother, and I stood behind her, trying hard not to bust out in tears.

Grandma indicated that people were to sit down. When it was quiet again, she took off her pearl earrings and handed them to Lacey. Tory received her pearl bracelets. My mother received two strands of her pearl necklaces, and I received the other two. Eric stood to the side with a video camera, so Grandma was also on the huge screen above the audience.

I unzipped the back of her blue velvet dress while Grandma faced the audience. I unhooked her black bra, then turned her toward us, her back to the audience. She held my gaze. I waited. She closed her green eyes for one second, then nodded. Gently, my mother and I pulled her blue velvet dress to her waist.

She stood half-naked onstage, the video camera projecting her head and back onto the screen.

I heard the gasps. I heard the horrified exclamations, the choked, "Oh, my God!"

The whip marks were still visible, still raised, crisscrossing her spine, her shoulder blades, and her slim waist, decades later, from Ireland to America, down the curve of a rainbow, on the back of an owl.

I looked at my mother, who had given up all pretenses of keeping it together, her tears a river of pain. Tory and Lacey clutched each other, Grandma's scars a scar for all of us.

After a minute, I refastened her bra and zipped her up. Lacey handed her her earrings, which she reattached. Tory fastened her bracelets around her wrist, and my mother and I put her pearl necklaces back on.

I handed Grandma a microphone, then we all stood back, out of the spotlight.

"Lace, Satin, and Baubles is not only about lingerie and negligees," Grandma said. "It's about women. It's about how we want to live our lives. It's about what we think about ourselves and *how* we think. It's about valuing ourselves enough to wear something stunning, something lacy, not to show it to someone else but because we know that we deserve it. We know that we can get out into a world that is sometimes cold, and sometimes dangerous, and be someone in it. We can become who we dreamed of becoming, we can leave a bad past behind, and we can look beautiful doing it."

She stopped when the clapping became too loud, and waited for silence again.

"I am not defined by my body or what has happened to it. I am not defined by beatings or an arching whip or a dangerous man, or by the wreckage of prostitution. I am not defined by my age. I am not defined by what others think of me. I am defined by myself. I will define myself to me. I will live, I will laugh, I will love. I will not be silenced. I will not be invisible. I will be me until the very end. And I will look beautiful."

The clapping and cheering started again, people on their feet, arms in the air.

"I dared," she said, those green eyes glittering. "I dared to found a company that would leave a legacy. I dared to live the way I damn well wanted to live."

The clapping almost overrode my grandma's message, so she raised her voice, her words echoing across that factory, over the satin, over the lace, over the baubles, and back to Ireland.

"I dare you to live the life you want to live and to leave your nightmares behind you. I dare you to dance, I dare you to sparkle, I dare you to wear gold tassels. *I dare you,*" she shouted above the cacophony. "*I dare you*"—she pointed at the audience—"*to be you.*"

The lights snapped off, the factory in total darkness, the cheering absolutely deafening.

When the lights came back on, all of us, including Lacey's whole family, Blake, Scotty, my mother, and all of the employees in their lingerie, were on that runway, Grandma in the center of it.

As it should be.

The next morning, newspapers from all over the nation were talking about our Fashion Story. They talked about our life stories. They ran photos of the embellished lingerie that our employees had designed. They could not get enough of Grandma's life story. The whole Fashion Story was on YouTube, this time uploaded by Eric.

Our website crashed twice. We hauled it back up.

We were inundated with orders.

Lace, Satin, and Baubles had made it.

Lacey and Tory have many talents.

One of them is shopping. They came by my tree house to get me three days after The Fashion Story.

Lacey said to Tory, "Get a trash bag."

Tory grabbed a bag.

"Hey!" I protested.

They ignored me. Everything in my closet was thrown out. The only things I managed to snag back were two green and yellow college sweatshirts and an orange and black high school sweatshirt. All my clothes fit into one large, black trash bag.

Tory and Lacey stood and studied me, their eyes sad, that one saggy bag between them.

"What?" I asked, defensive.

"A closet is a reflection of how a woman feels about herself," Lacey said.

"Your closet says that you feel nothing about yourself. You feel that you are dog poop. You want to be invisible. That's what your closet shows," Tory said. "And it makes me mad!"

"Why on earth would my closet make you mad, Tory? It's not like you have to dress from it."

She shuddered. "Don't even say that. The thought makes me feel like Humpty Dumpty. I'm mad because you should not feel like this about yourself, Meggie. Like an empty closet."

"No." Lacey shook her head. "You're better than this, Meggie. You need to sparkle again. Shine. Give yourself some lovin'. Like Grandma said at The Fashion Story."

"Ya ain't no trash lady, but this—" Tory waved her hand. "It's inexcusable. I'm taking this to Goodwill. I don't want the ex–Frumpster Dumpster Queen to have any chance to put these rags back on. No, bag lady"—she put up a hand to ward me off—"stay away or you'll find out how much of a weapon my cast is."

My grandma said she was tired and didn't want to shop no matter how much we pleaded, and she made me promise I would start wearing the clothes she bought me so I wouldn't look like a lost, possum-hunting hillbilly. We met my mother at the mall. I thought my debit card was going to burst into flames.

Afterward we went to a late lunch of sushi, then headed to a spa. My hair was highlighted and trimmed to the middle of my back. My eyebrows were waxed. My facial smoothed things out. My massage took out the kinks. My fingernails and toenails were pampered with pink flowers.

Lacey clapped, then raised both hands in the air, and yelled, "Meggie's back!"

Tory said, "You are more delicious than a martini, and that's saying a lot." She kissed my cheek.

My mother, dressed in her beige slacks and comfortable shoes, wagged a finger at me and said, "You and the chief could so easily play 'Chief Captures the Thief.' It's a titillating bedroom game . . ."

It was vain.

It was silly.

It was like being in high school and getting all dressed up, hoping that the boy you like sees you. You deliberately go to wherever he is and prance around.

I wanted to prance.

I crossed the street and knocked on Blake's door. It was late, but he'd told me to come by any time for dinner after the shopping spree.

I smiled. I almost *giggled*.

I was wearing tight jeans, four-inch cheetah print heels, a purple, low-cut shirt with a cross-bodice, our best purple push-up bra, a turquoise-silver necklace and matching earrings, and beaded bracelets.

My curls were soft and tight, sort of that uncontrolled look that I'd had before, that I still felt belonged to me. I had on lipstick, liner, and mascara, so I didn't look pale sick, like I had hepatitis or the plague. My dark brown, coffee-colored eyes looked happy.

Blake was speechless.

I smiled into those gray-blues, shut the door, walked into his arms, and pulled his head down to mine. He responded with fire and passion. How I love that man's fire and passion.

"How hungry are you, Meggie?"

"Not hungry at all."

"Good."

He carried me to his bedroom in his arms, and it was two hours before we ate. He was absolutely stellar in bed. This did not surprise me. He also liked my push-up bra. I liked him liking my push-up bra. It had been designed by Tory. She privately called it her "Slut Line." It's actually called Satiny Seductions.

He liked my lacy purple panties, too. Those were also part of the "Slut Line."

They came off quickly.

And later, "Meggie, I love you no matter how you look."

"I love you, too, Blake. Kiss me again, would you?"

He would.

31

Ireland is a country that sings to your heart. County Cork, where Grandma, my mother, Tory, Lacey, the baby Victoria, and I were staying, is Irish magic. The beauty wraps itself around you like a hug. My mother kept telling me to look for leprechauns.

It's a country of different shades of emerald green stretching to the ocean. It's a country of Blarney Castle, glowing rainbows, soaring cliffs, craggy beaches, fog-touched mountains, and rivers that wander. It's a country of colorful homes filled with the memories of generations of people long gone lining up on the water, church steeples that touch the sky, and villages that look like they were drawn from a picture book.

And, as Tory would say, the pubs aren't bad at all. Grandma liked the cigars, loved the whiskey. She took a lot of naps after the whiskey.

On Friday, we set out for our destination. After getting directions, we drove down a long road that seemed to meander here and there, sheep on one side, then a meadow, then a white stone house, next a bay with sailboats, followed by stones in a circle.

We finally arrived at a small, well-tended cemetery.

For the first time in her life, Grandma put her hands out to my mother and me, and we helped her, her gait unsteady, tears streaming, as we headed to a corner of the graveyard. At one point she stopped and "patted the fairies" on her back, her face pale.

Her composure deserted her as she stood over the graves of her mother, her father, and her sister: Teagan, Lochlan, and Keela MacNamara. She dropped to her knees and touched the gravestones, her tears watering each gray slab, her body seeming to crumble before my eyes as she leaned over to kiss each one, her fingers caressing the names that had weathered with time.

"I'm coming home soon," she whispered hoarsely to them, her Irish brogue thicker than I'd ever heard it. "I'm coming home."

The evening we returned home from Ireland, we dropped Grandma off at her house. We walked in with her, unpacked her suitcases. My mother insisted on staying, but Grandma refused her company. "I saw the rainbow, the leprechaun, and the owl. Now I need to be alone, Brianna."

Tory argued and said she would stay, but Grandma said, "I've had enough of our family's company. Go get a martini."

Lacey said she would stay but wouldn't bother her at all. Grandma said, "With Victoria screaming, no, thank you."

I said I wanted to stay. "I'll be quiet, Grandma. No talking."

"No, you won't, you chatterbox. My ears need a rest."

She reached out her arms and hugged each one of us, then opened up the traveling jewelry box she'd brought with her.

The longest strand of pearls she gave to my mother, who held her mother close, their cheeks together.

She gave Lacey, Tory, and me the other strands, all equal in length, placing them gently over our heads.

"I love you," she told us. "Thank you for being a part of the Bust Out and Shake It Adventure Club, and thank you for going to Ireland with me."

We hugged her, told her we loved her.

Grandma died that night.

She was with Teagan, Lochlan, and Keela MacNamara and Cecil O'Rourke, The Irishman, once again.

Regan O'Rourke was home.

* * *

My grief for my grandma swept me off my feet, held me aloft in shock, then dropped me down to earth where the pain spread like I'd been hit by lightning.

She had had a heart attack. She had been diagnosed with lung cancer.

"You knew that Grandma was sick?" I asked my mother in disbelief at my grandma's kitchen table the next afternoon, after the mortuary had taken her away. Lacey and Tory were there, too, also looking as if they'd been hit by lightning.

She nodded, lifting her glasses up and wiping her face with a white lace handkerchief she'd sewn herself. She had gone by Grandma's to check on her and found her in her chair, a glass of whiskey spilled on the floor, her cigar in the ashtray.

"She told me about a month before the Ireland trip. She asked me not to tell anyone. She's known for about a year."

Known for about a year. That's why she was so insistent that I come home. . . .

"But"—Lacey shifted baby Victoria to her other shoulder, then borrowed my mother's hankie to wipe her own tears— "why didn't she want us to know?"

"Because she didn't want the fuss, honey. She didn't want the panic and stress. She didn't want people to treat her any differently than they were."

"But why didn't she agree to treatment?" I asked. I could not stop my tears. I took the hankie from Lacey.

"It was hopeless. When they found it, it was too far along. She didn't want to go through chemo and radiation. Besides, even the doctors said it would extend her life for weeks only, if at all."

"So she said to hell with that," Tory said. She was pale and leaning heavily on the table.

"It wasn't going to cure her, so, as she said, 'Why inflict torture on myself?' She chose to live the end of her life the way she chose to live her whole life. On her own terms," my mother said. "She accepted medication from the doctors that made her life easier, took away some of the pain, but she didn't try to cure herself. She didn't want to spend the last months in the hospital.

She hated hospitals, she hated going to the doctors, she hated needles. She was adamant."

I sat back in my chair, stunned, sunlight glittering off the chandelier. Lacey lifted up her shirt and nursed Victoria, wiping her tears off Victoria's face as they fell.

"Your grandma did what she wanted to do, girls. She spent time with you all finishing up her Bust Out and Shake It Adventure Club list and making memories she knew you wouldn't forget. She wanted you all to laugh and have adventures together, to heal the rifts. She wanted you, Meggie, to be happy again, to live again. She spent time at the business, her legacy. She took mornings off so she could rest and read and, as she said, 'Be quiet and shut my mouth for once in my life.' "

"Mom, you should have told us," Lacey said.

My mother shook her head. "I couldn't. I swore I wouldn't. She deserved her privacy. She deserved to die the way she wanted to die. It was not for me to override my own mother. She was not senile. She had no signs of dementia. She made a rational and reasonable choice. Who was I to force her to undergo treatment? Who was I to tell you all about her health? This wasn't about us, it was about her and her having control and enjoying every minute that she had left. How she handled her death and illness was not my decision."

I would miss my grandma forever, I knew I would. Her illness explained why she only worked part time for the first time in her life. It explained why the doctors at the hospital knew her name when we were there after the accident. Most of all, it explained her eagerness to restore my relationship, and Lacey's relationship, with Tory. She believed in family and love above all else.

"She wrote two letters. This first one is for us," my mother said, taking the hankie back from Tory as she pulled the letter from the envelope. Although my sisters and my mother and I inherited the bulk of her estate, the letter gave us specific directions on how much money to give to a list of people, including funds to pay off Lance Turner's home, continued support for Mrs. Wolff who had Alzheimer's, and to the local community college for scholarships. It also told us how she was to be buried and what her memorial service should entail.

"She has got to be kidding," Lacey said, about the memorial service.

"Rockin' it till the end," Tory said.

"She rocked," I said.

At her request, we had Grandma's memorial service at Leonard Tallchief's restaurant, which was shut down for us. Family, friends, neighbors, and employees were invited.

I read Grandma's second letter out loud to the entire group after hors d'oeuvres were served.

"I wanted to invite you to one last formal dinner with me." I choked up. "Everyone here was invited because I love and care about you. I want you to remember, as you go through the rest of your life, that I thought you were damn special. Damn special." I laughed, couldn't help it. "This will be a seven-course dinner that Leonard and I planned down to the finest detail."

I looked up at poor Leonard. He was a wreck and wiping his eyes with his white apron.

"You will enjoy the meal," I read. "If you must stand up and talk about me, you can only say something funny. That's it. Only laughing at my service, no tears. I'll miss you, you'll miss me, blah blah blah. Buck up. No whining. My death is a part of my life. Don't ruin this last day for me by getting all gushy. It's embarrassing. You especially, Brianna. I love you, daughter, but you are overly sensitive and prone to uncontrolled emotions."

We all laughed.

"I have a special treat for you," I continued, hearing my grandma's voice in my head. "I've hired a band, and I want you to dance. Dance for yourselves, for me, for us. Dance because life is a precious gift and you have to accept the good with the bad. My death might be considered bad, but what's good about my life is that I was privileged to have you in it with me. Now, don't be all reserved, boring, and stick-in-the-mud-ish. Have fun tonight. For me, make a promise that you'll have fun. This is my last gift to you. I love you."

When I was done, people were not obeying Grandma. They cried, some louder than others. I heard muffled sobs, hand over mouth. I saw shaking shoulders. Even the men were blowing their noses, wiping tears away. I hugged Hayden, Lacey hugged Regan, my mother hugged Cassidy.

Then Tory stomped up to the front of the room in her stilettos and purple dress. "What is wrong with you people? Look at you! Crying like babies! Blubbering about. Blah, blah, blah. Do what Grandma told you to do, buck up!" She waved at someone at the back of the room.

A band entered—long hair, bass guitars, a drum set already up. "Everyone," Tory said, her voice snappish but insistent, "we're gonna do what Grandma told us to do. We're gonna party. Now get off your butts and dance."

The band strummed the guitars. The drums rolled. They jammed.

Dancing. Now?

Why not?

I grabbed the police chief, Lacey grabbed Matt, Tory grabbed Farmer Scotty, the kids grabbed my mother, and we headed to the center of the dance floor. Soon we were joined by the rest of the gang.

We danced. For Grandma. For her and her legacy to us.

Because life, as she said, is a precious gift.

"I'll miss hearing her heels tapping down the hallways at work," Tory said to Lacey and me at three in the morning, after the party. "It was like listening to a human battle-ax coming your way, but I'd do anything to hear it again."

The three of us had gone back to Lace, Satin, and Baubles. We sat in Grandma's office, at her long antique table, under the chandelier she bought for sparkling light to get rid of the darkness of poverty, and pink, because her poor, exhausted mother loved that color.

"I'll miss the way she ran the company," Lacey said. "Part military commander, part fashion maven."

"I'll miss her cozy warmth and affection," I said, and we laughed.

"The only thing on her Bust Out and Shake It Adventure Club list she didn't get was Tony Robbins," Lacey said.

"That's a shame," I said. "She was so close."

"Tony missed out," Tory drawled. "He, Grandma, and I could have had a threesome."

"I can't believe she's gone," Lacey said. "I can't believe it."

No, it is hard to believe in death.

But it forces you to believe in it eventually.

And yet. My grandma had lived. She had truly lived. Hers was a life of poverty and brutality, loss and grief, hard work and determination, character and courage. She had hit the absolute bottom of despair and degradation, yet she had lived with love and hope and compassion for others. She had built something. She had triumphed.

Yes, she had lived.

I put my hand out. Tory put her hand on mine, Lacey's on top of Tory's.

We cried *together*.

As Grandma had always wished it to be.

Part of me thought I was aching for more punishment by flying down to Aaron's grave a week after the private burial for my grandma, but the other part of me knew I had to do it, and the time was right.

I would be gone for one night only. I left on Saturday morning. I told Blake where I was going. He wanted to go with me. I declined. He was hurt that I was excluding him and hurt that I didn't want him there for moral support.

"Blake, I have to go alone. I have to."

I had shown him the DVD, although I didn't watch it with him. I thought he needed to know what I had dealt with in my marriage. Maybe it would help him understand my garbled-up mind.

He walked over to my tree house after he watched it. I sat in a yellow Adirondack chair, and he sat in a green one. Pop Pop jumped up on his lap, Breadsticks curled up on mine.

I could tell he was deeply moved. "Aaron was mentally ill. Don't let him hurt you anymore, Meggie." He gently suggested a counselor. It had been suggested to me many times. I'd always said no. This time I said yes.

On the airplane to Los Angeles I was sitting by a two-year-old and her flustered mother, who was holding a crying baby. I put my arms out for the baby, and turned it toward the window, where the sun was streaming in. The baby went to sleep. The mother thanked me profusely, then proceeded to down two small bottles of scotch. She told her daughter it was "adult water."

Aaron's grave was in the back of a graveyard under a jacaranda tree, the purple and blue blossoms lush and scented, hanging right over his gravestone.

I sat down and talked to him, the sun warming my shoulders. I talked about how much I'd loved him, how the romance had swept me up. I told him what I admired about him, his intellect, his ability to make films that touched people's hearts, his compelling personality, how romantic he could be, and how I admired his fight against his bipolar. He could have given up years ago, but he didn't. He tried.

I told him I forgave him.

I told him I was still angry and would never forget what he'd done.

I told him I wasn't as angry as I was before.

I told him he didn't have the right to do what he did to me.

I told him I was sorry that he had so many mental health issues but I was more sorry that he refused to deal with them.

I told him I was sorry that I shut down on him and on his problems, that I had been overwhelmed, sucked dry, almost paralyzed in my inability to address him and his issues anymore.

I told him I was moving on with my life.

I told him I hoped he was at peace.

I told him I didn't think I would ever have total peace.

I told him I forgave him for cheating.

I told him I had cheated, too, and I forgave myself.

I told him the DVD had followed me around the world before landing in my closet behind detergent, sponges, and Baggies, that it was excruciating to watch.

I told him the DVD had helped me to internalize that it wasn't me who had caused his problems, nor was it my responsibility at all that he had killed himself. I thanked him for it.

I laid down beside him. I stared at the branches of the jacaranda tree, the delicateness of the purple-blue flowers. I stared at the white, puffy clouds that morphed into one animal or another if I let my mind go blank. I cried.

I was there for two hours.

Before I left I broke the DVD into four pieces and stuck them into the earth. I couldn't have it haunting me anymore.

When I was done, my cell phone rang. For the first time in a long time, I answered her call. "Hello, Rochelle."

"Finally, you answer your damn phone!" She went off on a raving tangent, and I knew she was drunk. "I'm having you arrested, Meggie. The police are coming with the FBI and drug enforcement, and I've talked to my attorneys and they're going to file criminal and bad charges against you and make you pay me for what you did to Aaron. I blame you. You were a stupid wife, always leaving Aaron to work, leaving him when he needed you. This was your fault, all your fault, what he did—"

"Rochelle, I am very sorry that you lost your son." I would not be mean to this woman—she had lost too much—but she had been a pathetic, bottom-rung mother, one who refused to protect her own child from a pedophile, despite Aaron's pleas for help. "He had an extremely difficult childhood."

"Difficult childhood? I loved him." She went off on another tangent, nonsensical but threatening. "I was a good mother!" she repeated, with a moan. "A very good mother!"

I wanted to reach through the phone and strangle her. I wanted to shake her. I wanted to stomp on her. I thought of Aaron when he was an innocent eight-year-old and that hideous thing that had happened to him, how he'd told his mother, and how she'd chosen a pedophile over her own son. My hands shook with fury as I stared at his gravestone. "Don't call me again, ever, Rochelle. Don't contact me."

"I can call you whenever I want, or telephone you or cell phone call you! I'm going to make your life hell, you Meggie bitch, like you've made my life hell in a bowl with the devil. I don't have my son anymore because of you. He's lost somewhere—"

I hung up.

For long moments I couldn't move. I felt a violent rage toward Rochelle. What a hideous mother she had been. Her behavior had been criminal. I hadn't stopped her calls in the past because part of me thought I deserved it. No more. Never again.

I traced Aaron's name on his gravestone underneath the jacaranda tree one more time. I blew him a kiss. "Good-bye, Aaron. I am truly sorry for what happened to you. I am sorry."

Rochelle called again.

I blocked her number.

If she called again, I would tell Blake and get a restraining order against her.

I was done.

I love my tree house. I love how small it is, how cozy, how safe. It represents what I've wanted for years.

I love the psychedelic rainbow swirling kitchen tiles. I love being wrapped in a hug by the maple trees with their everchanging leaves, being near to the clouds and the sunshine, the snowflakes and raindrops. I love walking up the stairs to my deck where the Adirondacks in purple, blue, green, yellow, orange, and red are waiting for me.

I can even sit in the red Adirondack now. It doesn't bother me at all.

And I love Blake and my collection of animals, too.

"Meeegie! How you doin'?" Kalani waved at me with both hands through Skype. "We so busy now! Ya. We busy since that Fashion Story thingie. I hire more women, no men. They play with their balls, like Tory say. You know Tory? Hey! Thank you putting my story in Fashion Story thingie, about that bad husband and he bite part my ear off, how I have job and house now, no bad men, I the boss. But first I tell you how I am because you say, 'How are you, Kalani?' "

I groaned quietly, so quiet, keeping my teeth out and smiling for her. "Tell me how you are."

"I do badly."

"Why are you doing badly?" Oh no. "What's wrong?"

"I tell you, I cry over your grandma, ya, I cry like this. See my tears? I miss that old, old lady. I always miss her. She tough. She don't ask me how I am much, but we still talk. I work for her. She my boss. She save Kalani. I tell you already, I tell you again, sorry about that, Meeegie. She good woman, like you. You good, too."

"Thank you. She really cared about you, Kalani."

"Ya, I know. I try no talk to her about my gas and my curses, not like that kind of friendship, you know, you and me and Tory and Laceeey, we have that seeester friendship. Laceeey not so fat now with that baby out, but I cry for her, too, when there bad accident, and I cry for Tory, too. All night. I cry so hard for all you and for the teeny, tiny Laceeey baby. I cry for her, so happy baby happy now. Ya. I happy about that."

"Me too, Kalani."

"Ah, when Laceeey back? I send present, too, for new good baby. So sweet and good. She probably be like her momma. Not like Tory. Tory not good girl. Tory tell me good girls boring, they don't get no have fun. I like the fun. Black magic. You want to see new bras now, Meeegie? Here, I ready. I done saying how I am. I show you."

"Okay, Kalani."

She showed me the bras and thongs and panties and lingerie. She put on a number of the bras over her own chest. "I like this one. Ya. I like tassels on this purple and gold bra. Women freedom! And this? What you say? Bustier. Black with red flames, for the angry lady. Good. I like tattoo bra, too. Rough ladies wear tattoos. I like nipple cover. I try on for you. See my nipple?

I try scented glue in vanilla! Yummy nipple bra now. And whip! That's liberty. Black leather bra with zipper and skeleton. Ya. I like power when I wear the leather."

It all looked good. I sighed with relief. Finally, no disasters.

"I'm delighted with the work, Kalani. Deee-light-ed."

"Oh ya. Me too. We make best bras whole world, right, Meeegie? All these little pieces in bras, so many things must go right, all the parts, sewing, wire, colors, material, lace, the cups be perfect. So hard. But for your grandma we still make all this lingerie pretty. Honor Grandma. Honor ancestors. They still with us. In our hearts. Right? It, what you say, the other day? New American word for me: legacy. It your grandma legacy."

"Yes it is. It's Grandma's legacy."

"Okay, bye-bye. Love you, seeester Meeegie."

"I love you, too, Kalani."

Tory and I had Cassidy, Hayden, and Regan for the day. We took them to a pancake restaurant, then to the movies, then home to my tree house for tacos. First, however, we had Baked Alaska, which we'd learned how to make in dessert class, and Cassidy set it on fire, as we'd been taught. We all cheered. It was getting to be a regular occurrence—the five of us out doing something fun.

Regan played with all of the animals. Pop Pop grinned. He was on probation at doggie day care yet again. Jeepers hissed and hid. It took Regan fifteen minutes to get Jeepers out from under my bed upstairs so he could cuddle him like a baby. Regan also held the lizard, Mrs. Friendly, who was not affectionate; Ham the Hamster, who ran away under my couch; and Breadsticks, who was afraid of Jeepers.

"I want to talk to you about one more cat, Aunt Meggie. She has a good heart like Pop Pop, and the curiosity of Mrs. Friendly, and the brain of Ham the Hamster . . . and Aunt Tory, I think I have the perfect dog for you. It's a small Great Dane named Spider . . ."

Hayden said that school was better. He was teased some, but not near as much, and tried to ignore it. He'd lost a couple of friends but gained more than that. Hayden was wearing a white dress and sandals and gold hoop earrings, his hair in a ponytail. He had the lead in the school play. He would play the part of Juliet in *Romeo and Juliet*. Tory worked on his acting with him. She's impressively dramatic.

Lacey and Matt were talking about what his future would look like in terms of an operation, hormones he could take, etc. It's complicated, it's not easy, nothing was easy, but there was no question that Hayden was more comfortable, happier now in many ways. As he said, or as I should say *she* said, "I have to be on the outside what I am on the inside."

Cassidy received another 4.00. As she also takes AP classes, Calculus, etc., she is hoping to be valedictorian her senior year. "Cody and I are going to take a year off after high school and travel. Mom says no, I say yes, and I'll be eighteen. We want to make love in ten different countries. That's our goal."

What to say to that one? Tory said, "I think Scotty and I should have that same goal."

That night I sat in the yellow Adirondack, Tory purple, Cassidy red, Hayden green, and Regan blue. Pop Pop sat in my lap. Breadsticks sat with Tory. The cats had had a small fight, but we separated them before stitches were needed.

"We have the best aunts in the world," Cassidy said, so pleased. Regan and Hayden agreed. I saw Tory hide her delighted smile in Breadsticks's fur.

The maple trees were budding. Soon we would have green leaves hugging us again.

"Can we talk about the sperm donors?" I asked my mother. Lacey, Tory, baby Victoria, and I were at her Snow White house, drinking coffee and eating banana, zucchini, and orange bread and chocolate muffins. My mother had been up all night again, grieving for her mother, so instead of wasting time in bed, she'd baked.

"We don't need to talk about them," she said. She waved her hand as in, "They are nothing." "The chocolate muffins have a silky svelteness to them this time, I think. I added two types of chocolate chips: semisweet and baking chocolate, light crust of sugar on top."

"We need to talk about this," Lacey said, nursing Victoria. "Please, Mom. You've always said you had one-night stands, two of them, to have Meggie and me, and you only knew our father's first names, but that doesn't make sense. You're too smart, Mom."

My mother picked up a china platter. "Please taste this banana bread. It's scrumptious. I added orange peel and an extra dash of salt."

"You know more, Mom," I said, dipping my banana bread in my tea.

"I'll have banana bread," Tory said. "My horoscope says I should pay attention to what I'm putting into my body so I can settle my inner serenity."

My mother took a sip of coffee. Today she was wearing black slacks, flats, and a light green crew neck sweater. Her hair was in a prim ball, glasses on. The other night she'd done an interview where she encouraged everyone to buy one sex toy this year. "Just try it!"

"They were your sperm donors, girls. That's it. They are not your fathers. It's always been us, not them."

"But it's not that simple, Mom. We accepted your story that you didn't know more about these men, but you do," I said. "Why keep the secret anymore? We have a right to know."

"Why can't we have a pleasant morning drinking coffee with cream and eating my breads?"

"They are good," Tory said. "I'm exhausted anyhow. Scotty and I did it three times last night."

"Good for you, dear." My mother patted Tory's hands. "Sex is good for the complexion, and yours looks wonderful. I must say"—she peered over her glasses at Lacey and me—"both of you look particularly pink and healthy, too. I'm pleased."

"Mom, please," I said.

"With the zucchini bread I used a Mexican vanilla for that extra punch."

"Mooomm," Lacey said.

She sighed. "What do you want to know?"

"I want to know the nationality of Sperm Donor Number Two, my father." I put my coffee cup down. "What do you know about my biological dad?"

"I know that his grandparents were African American."

"What?" My father's grandparents were African American?

"His grandparents were African American, but they told me there was white in both their backgrounds because of slave owners attacking the women, those poor women." My mother paused, collected herself. "Their son married a white woman with Norwegian blood, so your father was half black, half Norwegian. His skin wasn't dark, actually. This makes you one quarter African American, one quarter Norwegian, and half Irish. I think that's why your eyes are so dark, dark brown, Meggie. They are so like his grandmother's. Lucy was a warm, wise woman. We baked together twice. She's who I learned how to make fried catfish and hush puppies from. I learned how to make Norwegian meatballs from his mother with allspice and red wine."

"Mom!" Lacey cried, shocked.

"I think there's been a lie told here," Tory said, shaking her head. "The truth now emerges like a bomb. It's like reading your horoscope and knowing you're going to clash with a Virgo or a Sagittarius that day."

I could hardly breathe. "You told us it was a one-night stand! But you knew his family. You baked with his grandma and his mother! Why didn't you tell me this before?"

She waved her hand again. "Does it matter?"

"Of course it does, Mom. You must be joking."

"Your father was a handsome, handsome man. My goodness, he made my knees weak." She patted her heart.

"That's what Scotty does for me," Tory said. "Makes my knees weak. Makes other parts weak, too. And excited."

"Did he know you were pregnant?" I asked.

"No, dear. I didn't want a husband, and he would have wanted to get married. He was old-fashioned and conservative, a true gentleman."

"And you never told him about me?"

"No, he doesn't know."

"That wasn't fair to him, Mom, or to me." I felt my anger growing, step by step, like it was leaping up a ladder.

She looked unsteady, then regretful. "No, it wasn't."

"What's his name?"

She paused. "Jefferson. Tobias Jefferson, from New Orleans."

"Why didn't you tell me this? You've always told me you only knew the first name of my father, but you knew his last name. You could have told me."

"I could have, but then I would have had to deal with him, and I didn't need that. I wanted to live here, he lived there. I was a young woman on an extended vacation, and I certainly didn't want to get married."

"I like being married to Scotty," Tory said. "And I've promised not to leave again with my Jimmy Choos."

I sat back in my chair, stunned. This was a completely different story.

"What about Sperm Donor Number One?" Lacey asked. "Tell me about my father."

My mother held up the platter of zucchini bread. "With a dash of extra cinnamon and walnuts, not too many."

I rolled my eyes. Lacey clenched her teeth. Mother got the hint.

"He was Mexican American, Lacey. I met your dad in Texas, at a bar. His family owned an enormous cattle ranch. That's their business. They went way back in American history. His Mexican ancestors were living in America before America was America. He was dark, brooding, lots of black hair, so tall. You look Irish, Lacey, like my side, except for your eyes. Your eyes are his eyes. The shape, the dark brown color. It's like looking into his eyes again. So interesting that both of you girls have such dark eyes. Coffee eyes." She sighed. "That man made me quiver.

"And the way he sat on a horse, ummm...He *rode* that horse." Her eyes became dreamy. "In that cowboy hat, those jeans, that swagger, the way he handled me. Never met a man with so much machismo. We dated for a few weeks—"

"A few weeks!" Tory, Lacey, and I exclaimed.

"Yes. I went out to his family's ranch. They even took me on a cattle ride. His parents were intellectuals. Father had been to Harvard, mother to Wellesley. I learned how to make flautas and Mexican chocolate mousse with a sprinkle of cayenne pepper from his mother."

I slapped my forehead.

Lacey said, "How could you lie to us all these years?"

Tory said, "The story is now upside down completely. What we thought we knew, nope, nada. Not true. Lacey is half Mexican, like me, and Meggie is one quarter African-American, one quarter Norwegian, and half Irish."

"What is my father's name?" Lacey asked.

"Your father's name is Manuel Del Torrosso."

I rolled that name around in my mouth.

I rolled the name of my father, Tobias Jefferson, around in there, too.

We glared at her.

"Don't you think our fathers had a right to know?" I said, "They were kind, weren't they? Not abusive?"

"Both delightful. Whip smart. Articulate. Sophisticated, but warm and friendly, too. I choose my men carefully, and they were perfect. Look at you two! You're proof I know how to pick them. Who wants a slice of my orange bread with yogurt and raisins?"

"And all you wanted was sperm," I said.

She threw up her hands. "Yes. What you need to know is that you're my daughters, your grandma's granddaughters, and you're American. Americans are a blend and a mix from all over the world, and there are a lot of surprises in our genetics that we don't know about."

"But there shouldn't be these secrets," Lacey said, "from us or them."

"How are you better off knowing this information than you were before you walked in the door?" she asked.

"I'm better off because," I said, "I've always wondered who he is, who his parents are, if he has siblings, if I have half siblings."

"I wanted to know where the other half of me came from," Lacey said. "And you hid it by deliberate omission."

Tory said, "The halves of me came from Greece and Mexico. At least I've always known where my passion comes from, my ability to do the tango, my love of wearing only a sombrero for Scotty, tacos, sunny weather, Greek history, and island hopping. . . ."

The conversation went round and round.

Lacey and I were furious.

Our mother tried to hug us when we left.

We did not hug her back.

She was very upset. "How about another cup of coffee with cream?"

"Think we'll ever go search for our fathers?" Lacey asked me later that night as we swung on her porch swing, Matt, Hayden, Regan, and Cassidy laughing inside.

"Yes," I said. I held Victoria. "No. Maybe. Never. Tomorrow. I don't know. They don't know about us, so this will be a total shock. It's like dropping an oversize stork into the middle of their family room carrying a grown woman."

"I'd like to meet my father," Lacey said.

"Part of me wants to meet your dad and my dad. But does our want, our need, to meet them override what's best for them? And what is best for them? They don't know they have daughters. Will they grieve for all the time they didn't have with us? Will they sue Mom? What if they want to be really involved in our lives, more than we want? What if we want more time than they want to give? What if we don't like them? What if they don't like us? What if they don't want us in their lives at all? What about their wives? How fair is this to them? We probably have half siblings. What about them? Some might want to meet us, some might be virulently opposed. Do we have the right to cause friction and stress in their families?"

"Would it be simpler and better to let everything lie as is?"

"I don't know."

What to do?

Lacey and I let the conversation float in and out over the next few weeks. We did not feel compelled to come up with a quick answer. I am a decisive person, but one thing I've learned is that impulsivity can land me in a bad place. We did not have to rush to see our fathers.

We could, however, start some private research on our own. . . .

Lacey made the call to a former high school classmate, Dan Kawa, who was now an investigator. He was a hunkin' machine when we were in high school. Lots of fights. Defensive line on the football team. I mean, he was *the* defensive line on the foot-ball team. He was huge.

He's still a huge, hunkin' machine, but now he's married and has six kids.

"I'll look into it, Lace Lace," he told her, using his own nick-name for her. "Tell Tory Tory and Meg Meg I said howdy-do. And I know I told you this at the funeral, but I'm sorry about your grandma. She was one special lady."

Blake and I went skiing on Mount Hood, the mountain that invited me each day from my windows at work to ski on it.

It was the first time in many years.

I had to buy new skis, boots, poles and a helmet, as I'd left my gear in the L.A. apartment.

We took one warm-up run, then we went to the top and skied the black diamonds. We kissed on the chairlift. We kissed at the top of the run. We stopped and kissed midrun.

I refound my love of skiing fast, and hard.

It was like I'd never left.

Only this time, I had someone to ride the chairlift with, and he was huggable and lovable.

Dan Kawa called us back within the week.

Our fathers were both alive.

They were both in long-term marriages. Lacey's father had

four children, and my father had five, not counting us, of course. Lacey's father still owned the cattle ranch; it was successful, one of the biggest in the country. My father had a doctorate and was a business professor at an elite private college.

Lacey, Tory, and I talked. We talked endlessly to our mother, too.

She had decided that Lacey and I would have Sperm Donor One and Sperm Donor Two instead of fathers. She had shut down on all our questions by pretending she knew nothing about them. She had lied. We understood she didn't want a husband, but shutting us out completely from that information, especially as adults? Denying all of us—including the fathers—an opportunity to have a relationship? That's a hard one to work through.

What did we decide to do about the dads?

Nothing.

Yet.

But at least we knew.

And we knew we still loved our mother from Oregon to Louisiana to Texas and back.

My nightmares were receding, especially since Blake held me close at night.

My daymares were receding, too.

I could take baths now, if Blake was in there with me.

I did not have anything against the color red anymore.

I was not seeing Aaron around corners.

Regan had gotten himself a pet rat named Charlie.

I even held Charlie. He is a good rat and does not bring on any flashbacks.

"I can get you a rat for a pet, too, Aunt Meggie," Regan told me, so eager to help the rat population. "I know of one who is curious and understanding."

I thanked him for his offer, and declined.

"Why Mom?" I asked. "Why have you never married?"

"Dears, marriage is for other people." She bent to pour tea

for Tory, Lacey, and me in her Snow White house. Lacey's kids were upstairs watching a movie, Victoria asleep in her car seat. We were over for the afternoon because mom wanted to bake and ice cookies in the shapes of flowers with the whole family. And, most important, she was trying to mend our relationship.

"What's the real reason, Mom?"

"Marriage is stifling."

"The truth, Mom," Tory said. "Don't gargle it all up like a female gargoyle."

"Sleeping with the same man would never satisfy me."

"Nice try," Lacey said. "What is it, Mom?"

"The truth is, dears . . ." she said, then hesitated, setting the silver teapot down.

"Yes?" I said.

"What is it, Mom?" Lacey said.

"Yank it out of yourself," Tory said. "Spit it out."

"The truth is . . ." She patted her hair, back in a bun, then pushed her glasses up her nose.

"Come on, mother who wears cat suits and negligees on TV and makes a dress out of the pages of her book, why have you never wanted to get married?" I said.

She nibbled on a tulip flower cookie, then she let off the bomb.

The sucker punch.

"I have never married . . ."

"Because . . ." I prodded.

"It's a challenge to say," she said.

"You can handle it," Tory said. "We know what you say on TV, can't be harder than that."

"The true reason is that . . ." She set down the tulip cookie. "I don't like sex."

"You what?" I asked, stunned, even though I'd heard her.

"How . . . what?" Tory said, her purple nails flying through the air. "What did she say?"

Lacey dropped her rose-shaped cookie. "You . . . for how long . . . have you always . . . but then you . . ."

"I don't like sex, darlings, at least not that much. If I had to choose between my knitting and needlepoint and sex, my baking and sewing and sex, time with my girlfriends and sex, the knitting, needlepoint, baking, sewing, and friends would come first every time. And I can't imagine having a man around all the time. That would make me feel smothered and faint, dizzy with claustrophobia."

"Is this a joke?" Tory asked. "You're a sex therapist—"

"You tell people how to have better sex lives. You show them," Lacey said. "Using bananas and limes and cherries—"

"And you don't like sex?" I finished for her.

Our mother gave each of us another flower cookie to ice. These were daffodils. "No joke, dears. When you all were younger, I had to support myself. I was a single mother. I could not work for General Grandma without handing over my sanity to her on a platter.

"I took my degrees and I ran with them. I was a therapist to couples, and sex always came up. It was a popular, steamy topic, and I grabbed it and ran like the wind. I wrote my columns with humor and enough detail to titillate. I wrote blunt books, often using my imagination, and voila!" She spread her hands out. "A career that kept me home when the three of you were young so I could be a full-time mother and bake cookies and sew my quilts, and it paid bunches of money." The Southern belle/Irish elf smiled, sweet and innocent. "I think it all worked out superbly well. Better than I could have hoped. More tea, girls?"

32

I've thought a lot about what I owe others versus what I owe myself.

I believe that I owe it to my grandma to keep her legacy alive. Lace, Satin, and Baubles is her legacy.

I like working here, especially since we're back into profitability. I do different things every day. There are many moving parts—design, production, manufacturing, sales, advertising, accounting, people, on and on. It's a challenge, no question. We're able to donate to the community college scholarship fund, which supports one of Grandma's rules for living: Keep a hand out to help someone up, but don't give them two hands or you'll enable them to be a weak and spineless jellyfish.

I particularly like being near to my mother—even though I am still mad at her—Lacey and Tory, Matt and Scotty, the kids, and the other people that I have known and loved for years who work here.

I loved making films. That was my passion. My experience with Aaron dimmed that passion. It took the soul out of it for me. I don't know if my love of filming, of cameras, of storytelling, will ever come back like it used to be.

And I'm okay with that.

My life changed. It is what it is. As Grandma would say, "Blah, blah, blah, don't whine."

I will work one day to put together a film on my year of wandering. I'll show the ranch in Montana, the church building we did in Mexico, the orphanage in Russia, the prostitute safe house in the Ukraine. I hope to hold the cameras in my hands again and think, *If you could see what I see*. I think I'll find it healing.

But, for now, I'm going to work at my grandma's legacy, be with Blake, and enjoy my life.

Yes, that's what I'm going to do.

I'm going to enjoy my life and be grateful for it.

I bought a blue sports car. It goes fast.

Based on the Bust Up and Shake It Adventure Club, I think Grandma would like that.

There is something magical about Maui. I had never been. In fact, I had not been on a vacation in years. I do not call my Year of Wandering a vacation, as I worked and volunteered the whole time and tried to muffle the screaming in my head.

I hardly knew what to do on a vacation, and it took several days for me to calm down and not work. Same with Blake. But the sun shone down, the waves splashed, the fantasy-like fish and enormous turtles swam only feet away from our snorkels, and the sunset view from Blake's parents' home took our breath away.

The most magical gifts, however, were Blake's parents.

Shep and Yvette were kind and welcoming. Their home was single story, filled with light and air and a garden overflowing with pink lokelani; kukui blossoms; red ohia; bougainvilleas; birds of paradise; and banana, koa, and palm trees.

They had a guest house in which we stayed. Our bedroom had a view of Lanai across the ocean. There was a bathtub built for two. We took baths at night together, and I filled the tub with bubbles named Tropical Flowers, Hawaiian Heaven, and Waves of Paradise.

We went to a luau with Shep and Yvette and ate Huli Huli chicken, kalua pua'a, taro rolls, watermelon, pineapple, and mangoes. We took a boat trip to Molokini to snorkel, but mostly we hung out at the beaches together or at their home.

Yvette told me as we walked along the beach one morning, "I

am so happy, Meggie, that Blake has met you. It is a gift to my heart to see you hugging him, holding his hand, and the way he looks at you. . . . I've wanted to see him with someone like you. Exactly like you, Meggie. And I can't wait to meet your mother. Can she come over with you next time? I have a few questions to ask her, her *specifically,* if you know what I mean. Also, I'm looking for lingerie that hides the not-so-young spots but enhances my bust. What would you recommend? Shep likes to see lace in bed. Blake, I'm sure, is the same way. Voracious, aren't they, dear? It never ends. I'm so glad you'll be officially joining our family soon." She put both hands up in the air. "Hallelujah!"

"Uh . . . officially?"

Her hand flew to her mouth. "Please. Why can I not control my words? I'm old. I should be able to do this by now. . . ."

My heart felt like it was going to fly straight out of my body. I couldn't help but remember Blake's story, and how he had given away the secret that Shep was going to ask Yvette to marry him, too. I laughed. She put an arm around my shoulders. "I do so hope you'll say yes."

Later that afternoon, on the patio, palm trees swaying, the sun golden butterscotch, the clouds tumbling across an azure blue, Blake handed me two boxes. Inside one box were two gold bracelets, entwined, and encrusted with tiny sapphires, emeralds, and rubies.

"Friendship bracelets, honey," he told me, slipping them on my wrists.

"I love them," I whispered, and kissed him. "I love you, too. You're my best friend, Blake."

"And you're mine, honey. Love you, too." He handed me the other box. A ring box.

It was a beautiful diamond solitaire, with two bands filled with diamonds on either side. He picked me up and put me on his lap.

"How about it, Meggie O'Rourke? Would you like to be my Mrs.?"

I kissed him, held him close, laughed.

"Is that a yes or a no?" he asked.

"It's a yes," I said through my tears. "It's a definite yes."

My name is Blake Crighton.

Put the camera down and take your bra off, Meggie.

That's all I want to say, honey.

Oh, and I love you.

I'll always love you, babe.

Now take your bra off.

Ah, purple today.

Nice.

Very nice.

IF YOU COULD SEE WHAT I SEE

Cathy Lamb

ABOUT THIS GUIDE

The suggested questions are included
to enhance your group's reading of
Cathy Lamb's *If You Could See What I See.*

DISCUSSION QUESTIONS

1. If you were going on a trip, would you take Regan, Brianna, Meggie, Lacey, or Tory with you? Why? Where would you go? What would you do? What advice would they give you about your life?

2. Describe Meggie. What are her strengths and weaknesses? Was she fair to the police chief, Blake Crighton? What did her clothes say about her? Would you want to be friends with her?

3. Aaron Torelli did not admit to Meggie that he had severe mental health issues before he married her. Should he have? What was Meggie's obligation to him after she found out? What should she have done differently in her marriage? What would you have done? Would you have left sooner than she did? Would you have left at all?

4. Was Meggie justified in leaving Aaron after he had an affair, despite his severe mental health issues? Was Meggie justified in having an affair with Henry while still married to Aaron?

5. How did you like the structure of the book? Did the flashbacks to Meggie's marriage enhance the story? What are the overarching themes? What did the tree house symbolize? What did Mount Hood and Lace, Satin, and Baubles symbolize?

6. Is Lacey a good mother? Can you relate to her struggles as a working mother to three unique teenagers? Did you like Tory? Was her anger merited? Did Scotty deserve the wood carving in his front yard?

7. Hayden Rockaford said, "I know I was supposed to be born a girl but something got messed up. I think that somehow, when my mom was pregnant with me, something went wrong. It's not like I'm wrong, or I'm a mistake, and it's not her fault, not my fault, but something didn't connect in there right. For me, what happened is the right plumbing didn't grow in. The plumbing was switched. That's it. I'm in the wrong body." What did you think of this character and his struggles? How was it handled by the author?

8. "Kalani Noe applied for a job at the factory as a seamstress. Her husband did not want her to have a job. A job meant independence. A job meant money. Both threats to him. Her lip was split in half. One eye was swollen shut, and there was a bruise down her left cheek. During the interview, she kept dabbing at her ear, which her husband had partially *bitten* off." Why did the author put Kalani in the story? Contrast Kalani's life with the O'Rourke sisters' lives. What does her future look like?

9. Which scene did you enjoy the most? Which scenes made you laugh? Were there any scenes that made you cry or were especially touching? Were there any scenes that reminded you of your own life or struggles?

10. Of all the bra videos that Meggie took, which voice was the most memorable, the most poignant to you, and why? Did the bra videos enrich the story?

11. Regan O'Rourke said, "I am not defined by my body or what has happened to it. I am not defined by beatings or an arching whip or a dangerous man, or by the wreckage of prostitution. I am not defined by my age. I am not defined by what others think of me. I am defined by myself. I will define myself to me. I will live, I will laugh. I will love. I will not be silenced. I will not be invisible. I

will be me until the very end. And I will look beautiful. . . .
I dared to live the way I damn well wanted to live." Are
you like Regan?

12. Brianna O'Rourke says that women lose interest in sex
because "oftentimes women are simply not attracted to
their partners anymore. Their partners are boring in bed
or self-centered, inane, ridiculous, abusive, or gross. It's
not what men want to hear. They want to blame their
wives and girlfriends, but it's the truth. Sometimes
women are flat-out exhausted. There can be medical issues, like thyroid problems or depression. There can be
hormone issues, too. Who likes blowing up in bed with
night sweats? Working too hard will kill a sex drive, too,
as can motherhood and its demands." Is she right? How
does Brianna's own admission to not liking sex impact
her ability to be an effective sex therapist, or does it?

13. Brianna was not honest with Lacey and Meggie about
Sperm Donor Number One and Two. What does that
say about Brianna? How will this impact their relationship in the future? What should Lacey and Meggie do?
Contact the fathers or leave things alone? What would
you do? If the story continued, where do you think the
author would take that plotline?

14. Discuss Meggie's character arc. What were the most sig-
nificant events in the book that caused her to change by
the end?

15. If you were in The Fashion Story, what lingerie would
you design for yourself? What would your videotape say
about you?

16. Grandma Regan and the O'Rourke sisters had many adventures with the Bust Out and Shake It Adventure Club
list. What's on your list?